The Love Queen
of the Amazon

Also by Cecile Pineda

Face
Frieze

The Love Queen of the Amazon

A NOVEL

Cecile Pineda

LITTLE, BROWN AND COMPANY

BOSTON   TORONTO   LONDON

First Edition

The characters and events in this book are fictitious.
Any similarity to real persons, living or dead,
is coincidental and not intended by the author.

"Working Women" by Gina Valdés excerpted from *Comiendo Lumbre*,
Maize Press, 1986. Used with permission of the author.

Library of Congress Cataloging-in-Publication Data

Pineda, Cecile.
    The love queen of the Amazon: a novel / Cecile Pineda. — 1st ed.
        p.   cm.
    ISBN 0-316-70812-7
    I. Title.
    PS3566.I5214L68   1992
    813'.54 — dc20   91-25500

10 9 8 7 6 5 4 3 2 1

MV-NY

*Published simultaneously in Canada
by Little, Brown & Company (Canada) Limited*

Printed in the United States of America

For Tom, Marvin,
and
Arturs Patagonia, of course

Working Women

Mi amigo, un cholo transplantado,
anda todo alocado con su Monte Carlo
amarillo con swivel bucket seats,
sun roof y quadrophonic sounds.
Me lleva low riding por El Cajón
a mirujear a las rucas on display
this working night, una con sus
tight red pants boogying on the curb,
fast gone, una gordita con su little
skirt hasta el ombligo y su fake fur,
otras dos waiting sentadas for a trick,
y el chota con sus two fast guns
acercándoseles a otras dos, y ahí into
Winchell's Donuts entra el pimp con
sus red pants, white shirt y su
cocked felt hat, y yo no sé que ando
aquí cruising so low, mirujeando
this working women's scene, thinking
of what rucas and rucos do to pay
their rent and eat, I, a poet hustling
hot verbs, a teacher selling brainwaves
in the S.D. red light school district,
feeling only un poco mejor than these
rucas of the night, a little luckier,
just as worn, my ass grinded daily
in this big cathouse U S A, que a
todos nos USA, una puta más in this
prostitution ring led by a heartless
cowboy pimp.

                                        — Gina Valdés
                                        from Comiendo Lumbre, 1986

The Love Queen
of the Amazon

I

Many years later, when there was little doubt left, people still marveled how Ana Magdalena as a young girl at least had possessed all the qualities you would expect in a young girl of good but impoverished family. "Who could have imagined," they said, "that one day she would become known as a succubus?" And they remembered that she came at once when summoned, she spoke only when addressed (and then only just above a whisper). Her braids hung in two straight undeviating lines; she curtsied gracefully without a touch of flamboyance, and cast down her eyes with befitting and appealing modesty.

Her mother, Andreina, a thin, depressive woman who suffered always from the cold, was inordinately proud of her. To any who would listen, and the many who would have preferred to do otherwise, she was always quick to extol the virtues of her daughter. True, she had no other standards of comparison: all her other children had died mysteriously in infancy.

Ana Magdalena's father, Hercules Figueroa da Cunha, came from a well-heeled family known for its prowess in the field, although later his wife used to muse out loud, why anyone armed to the teeth with such an illustrious pedigree would want to comport himself like some kind of low-life drifter. Their opulent nuptials fueled the town gossips for a number of seasons. Already early in their union Hercules came and went exactly as he pleased, in keeping with the local custom. It was said that on those rare occasions when he returned home to Andreina it was to give her yet another painful pregnancy or to change his shirt. Once when she was pregnant with Ana Magdalena she caught sight of him riding by in a stylish Victoria, whores to either side of him, turned out in colors of unspeakable vulgarity — reds, purples, heaven knows what — having fun. She came close to miscarrying.

Her physician, who in the course of a long career had perfected a mortician's smile through teeth yellow as piano keys, recognized in Andreina the signs of an incipient and fatal melancholia. Alarmed, he prescribed hot baths. But because bathtubs were still a rarity in Malyerba, Andreina was obliged to order a galvanized metal tub of gigantic proportions, which had to be transported by mule back from Lima and over the Andes at great cost, and almost insurmountable personal hardship for the muleteer, an Andean Indian of resilient strength and Inca descent. Because the passes were still snowed in much of that spring, the tub could be delivered only in the ninth month of Andreina's pregnancy. Every afternoon, following the siesta, she would have her servant heat water to scalding temperatures. This she would mix with cold water from the well until it was exactly the temperature and consistency of her own blood, and, sighing with resignation, she would remove her shift and lower her swollen body until she was entirely immersed in water up to her chin.

On the particular afternoon of Ana Magdalena's birth, Andreina experienced the severe lassitude that comes of unrelieved depression. She sank gratefully into the warm and dreamy water of the bath, and almost instantly, feeling the great weight and mass of her body eased by the water's buoyancy, allowed herself the folly of falling fast asleep.

When she opened her eyes, however, she realized almost at once that she was no longer alone. Swimming vigorously in water tinged a delirious aquamarine by her ruptured amniotic fluids was a sturdy female infant whose back was entirely covered with downy black hair. Although at first she found her daughter's hairiness somewhat disconcerting, it never came to her attention that the condition, admittedly rare in newborns, augured a future that, whatever can be said of it, was going to be singularly free of virginal modesty or unnecessary chastity. She christened her daughter not ten days later with the name Ana (after her maternal grandmother) and Magdalena, the name of a deceased maiden aunt.

Embittered by her husband's neglect, Andreina had become so

chronically neurotic that by the time her daughter was six years of age, she had abjured smiling altogether and her face had assumed the sour, pinched expression that prompted the people of Malyerba to shun her in the streets.

"*Mira la salmuera.* Look, here comes The Pickle," they would say as they crossed quickly to the other side.

But to a child, even one whose birth was as mythic as Ana Magdalena's, a mother is a mother. And by extension it must follow that all mothers have forsaken smiling, all mothers must be hopelessly pinched and neurotic. Gossip had it that at a tender age, Ana Magdalena must have read her mother's heart. And it was perhaps for this reason that she came at once when summoned, lowered her eyes with appealing modesty, and spoke only when addressed.

And, too, there were other influences, influences that must be mentioned here. Because at an early age, Ana Magdalena's education was entrusted to the nuns who kept a local learning institution, a convent for young ladies. It was there Ana Magdalena learned the feminine arts: music, dancing, embroidery, watercolor, sewing, lace making, washing, sweeping, and keeping accounts — in sum, all the qualities that make a woman a woman. And not a man. Ana Magdalena did not exactly take to these arts as a fish does to water, but perhaps the metaphor is not altogether misplaced, because if she paled in the face of the household arts, Ana Magdalena displayed not the slightest fear of water.

Once a week the sisters took their charges to the river to bathe, there being no plumbing facilities in the convent at that time. One must remember that where the convent was situated was then at the outskirts of Malyerba, where the river meandered just beyond the town's outer limits. Bathing was an event heralded by preparation bordering on the ritualistic. Early the preceding week, the younger girls crowded into the convent kitchen to make soap from lye and suet under the watchful eyes of the kitchen sisters. Garbed in white pinafores designed to preserve the spotlessness of their pastel clothing and to emblemize the spotlessness of their thoughts as well, the young initiates allowed themselves to be shown by the kitchen sisters how to stoke the wood-burning stoves: first with newspapers, which they were not allowed to read, then kindling, and finally with great logs of wood, a process guaranteeing that with the application of a single match, the strategic blaze would leap to life. Then the great, gaping vats of suet were placed on the open flames to melt, and the youngest girls had to perch on lovely pinewood stools to stir them with enormous wooden paddles.

It was a grueling apprenticeship, and the young participants fulfilled their part of the bargain with exemplary dedication. But it must be said here that, although lengthy and exacting, it was an apprenticeship appallingly ill suited to a class of young ladies whose mission in life was prescribed from the first. They would aspire to marry well, to enter the somber mansions of their class, and to allow themselves to be washed, perfumed, and dressed by the dark-skinned and silent servants who would bring them tea in the endless afternoons, dress their hair, and throw out their slops.

It must be pointed out that this very unsuitability was not their fault. And perhaps not even the fault of the reverend mother and her devoted little band of sisters. Perhaps, at best, it can be assigned to a failure of the religious imagination, the question being: How better to prepare for a life of indolence, boredom, and indifference?

Somewhere there must have lurked the assumption that things like the making of soap instilled character. There was, for one thing, a rigidly established sequence involved, and, at last, when the molten mess was poured into the cooling trays, there were all the dos and don'ts that guarantee the formation of a perfect cake of brown, foul-smelling saponifacient, abrasive, and sufficiently unpleasant-to-the-touch to discourage the remotest hint of sensuality.

Nor was that all. On Wednesdays, the girls were marched to the riverbank, their soiled linen piled high in baskets, each one of them armed with a cake of the evil-smelling soap, there to squat over the river stones, rubbing and beating their laundry the prescribed number of strokes. And as they rubbed and beat and wrung, nothing stopped them from watching the river traffic. It was there Ana Magdalena first laid eyes on the young dockhand who was later to lend a hand shaping her destiny. Sergio Ballado had shining brown skin, and as he worked stripped to the waist, the writhing of his muscles began to trouble her.

"My God," she whispered to Aurora Constancia, the young lady who squatted next to her, "just look at him!"

"Don't get overwrought," replied her friend. "That's Sergio

Ballado. Everyone knows about him. Remember: you didn't see him first."

"That doesn't mean a thing."

"Anyway, he's bad news."

"How come?"

Aurora Constancia leaned close enough to whisper something in her ear.

"Oh, my God!"

Whether it was shock or some other more complex emotion need not concern us here, but Aurora Constancia could see she had made a deep impression on her friend.

"No talking, now," admonished the good sister as she passed them. "Keep your mind on your work and don't forget to count your strokes."

On Sundays the girls were lined up in the convent courtyard, and once they had been counted by the porter sister to make sure each one was present, the great carriage doors swung open. They marched out in double file, wound along the alleyways and streets, crossed the boulevards at a furious clip to arrive at church just as the procession of priests and acolytes and altar boys made its way to the altar to celebrate High Mass.

The good sisters had arranged this down-to-the-wire entrance with some premeditation, because in order to take their seats, the girls had to pass the rows of already-seated boys from the local Jesuit academy, and it was thought that rushing them down the aisle just in time to reach their pews would discourage any kind of contact — although on one particular occasion, despite such extreme vigilance, there took place a hurried exchange of hymnals between Aurora Constancia and one of the more enterprising Jesuit boys.

"What's going on?" Ana Magdalena whispered to her walking partner.

"Oh, nothing," replied Aurora Constancia nonchalantly. "I'll tell you later if you promise not to spill the beans."

Silently and piously both girls took their seats.

The morning of the bath — always a Saturday, regardless of the temperature or inclemency of the weather — the girls returned after breakfast to their dormitories to dress. Dressing for the bath may seem a contradiction. But in that golden age of progress it was nothing of the sort. Stockings, corsets, petticoats, and ruffled pastel dresses were cast off with abandon.

A flock of thin white arms threaded themselves into the great and massive tents of the bathing tunics, as their young and virginal charges prepared for the bath under the sisters' watchful supervision. Then, armed with the very same towels that earlier in the week the young ladies themselves had beaten into immaculate submission, they lined up, cakes of foul-smelling brown soap in hand. The procession wended its way through the courtyard, out the gate, and along the rows of fruit trees in the orchard, until it reached the wall. There, before she could unlock the gate, the porter sister counted her charges to make sure all were present and accounted for.

No sooner had the wooden door squealed open on its rusty pins than a remarkable and astonishing transformation took place: pandemonium, which had been carefully held in check all week, broke out. Laughing and screaming, the girls poured through the gate and raced each other down the slope to collapse in a breathless heap on the sandy riverbank. Indeed, their abandon was of chronic concern to the mother superior and her entire staff. Such deportment, the reverend mother would repeatedly remind them, resembled nothing more than the stampede of biblical pigs, squealing and snorting, that followed the Divine Lord's each and every casting out of devils.

But once the gate was open, repeated evidence seemed to indicate there was no longer any way of civilizing them. Once in the water, they seemed to quiet down, particularly if the river was glacial, which it not infrequently was, being fed from its source in the very high Andes. But once they became accustomed to its bite, the girls frolicked as before, splashing one another with huge fans of icy water, shrieking and howling with terror and delight.

The chaperon nun had to beat strenuously on a frying pan to bring the proceedings to some kind of order. When decorum was restored at last each girl found a shallow place in the stream where she could squat and reach under the massive folds of her bathing smock to soap the dark and exquisite repositories of her female sex.

It was from their vantage point concealed in the bushes on the opposite shore that the town boys from the Jesuit Academy would wait for just this silent moment to contemplate in solemn and collective lubricity the fate of the happily straying fish who might, with better luck than theirs, be able to eye his piscine fill.

One has only to imagine the spectacle for a moment — a flock of white-clad innocents hard at work, rubbing their fragile and concealed flesh with cakes of soap more abrasive than sandpaper, the theater of spectators giggling and sniggering in the bushes, and the lone force for order sitting far up on the river bank, blinkered in her wimple, armed with nothing more threatening than her frying pan — to marvel that utter chaos took as long as it did to break out.

One must not for a moment imagine that — in this respect at least — young ladies are more backward than their male counterparts. In the endless stretch of hours after their meager evening collation and before the curfew bell, what more fervid subject for furtive conversation than courtship and marriage, whispered in corners, in corridors, in the shelter of their curtained dormitory beds. In proliferating variety, heated discussions raged defining the subtle and various conditions of virginity, true virginity as opposed to false virginity, measures to restore virginity should it haplessly be lost.

"Poor little innocents." Aurora Constancia took on a condescending tone. "What do you poor things know about it? Virginity comes in many shapes and sizes, everyone knows that. Everyone knows the one about the pregnant lady pretending she swallowed an olive pit, but with real virginity you know the signs. It has to be as bouncy as a trampoline."

"The bed . . . ?"

"The *bed?!* That's a good one!"

"It has to be so resilient you can spin a gold piece on it."

One of the girls began to cry. "*Dios mio,* what'll I tell my mother? I don't have anything like that."

"How do you know?" Ana Magdalena challenged her.

"I just know," she wailed.

"Don't cry, *pobrecita!* You can always have it fixed. Did you hear the one about the Paris cocotte who was so old and tired, she had to have an operation?" All eyes turned to Aurora Constancia. "They had to take her eardrum and graft it —"

"— to her . . . ?" By now the girls were squealing with delight.

Aurora Constancia nodded. "Everything was perfect, but she became so hard of hearing, she took to reading lips."

Bathing in the river, the older girls at least knew from the start that they were being watched. And they knew very well that, basking in the protection of the frying pan sister's gaze, tantalizing as they might wish to be, they were assured of nothing more forward than those heated schoolboy glances. They were aware of just how provocative is the soaping of a nubile, pear-shaped breast, and how, once wetted, the clumsy bathing smock could be carelessly arranged to show a lovely nipple to titillating advantage. And, even as they splashed water and laughed at one another, in the toss of their dark manes, in the rosy flush of their bright faces, in the luster of their beautiful white teeth, they were already hard at work ruthlessly scoring the points that later would assure them entry into those gleaming white mansions that, unbeknownst to such unsuspecting innocents, were to become their mausoleums.

It was on one such occasion that Ana Magdalena first set herself apart. Spring had been prematurely at work, warming the chilled earth, teasing open the reluctant young buds of forsythia and mountain laurel; stimulated by this already lush abundance, small birds set about preparing their nests in a Babel of warbling.

These were not the only signs of stimulation, as we shall see. On the appointed Saturday, equipped with soap and towel, the little procession of smock-clad future womanhood proceeded quietly through the orchard. Everywhere, fruit blossoms had erupted with breath-stopping violence, forced by the unseasonably balmy temperatures. Bees hummed, droned, and buzzed in a drunken frenzy, hauling their fat and furry bodies over petal's edge into the receiving hearts of blossoms, and in the bushes on the riverbank, the entire Jesuit school waited in spring-heightened eagerness.

The porteress nun fumbled with the keys (a lapse untypical of her). Then, having forgotten the count, she turned back to her pressing crush of smock-clad charges to count them once again, but already they had broken ranks, and it was only by dint of repeated pounding by the frying pan sister that a semblance of order was reestablished. Laboriously the porteress re-counted, adding up the numbers under her breath with fierce and uncompromising sibilance. And then, at last, the enormous key was reinserted in the shaft, and the door squealed open on its rusting pins. Pandemonium fell shouting and tumbling down the riverbank. Sixty-three young female savages headed whooping for the water. It was a savagery born of being constantly reprimanded for the least infraction: at five A.M. Mass; at their sparse breakfast of stale rolls and tea; at their drawing and painting lessons; over their embroidery frames; under the stiff and punishing baton of the music master (a man who would finally reach the peak of his ambition as an army executioner in suppression of the miners' strike); under the mincing and emaciated effeminacy of the dancing master; over the great wooden paddles of the kitchen sisters; by the stentorian and raucous pounding of the frying pan sister; in short, by all the stringent oppressions scheduled in a day that began with Matins and moved in stately and unyielding procession through all the canonical hours, ending with Compline.

All sixty-three hit the water with the grace and fragility of a herd of water buffalo. In the ensuing chaos it was not at first apparent that one of the sixty-three had in mind a purpose far removed from the ritual rubbing of abrasive soap on tender maiden flesh. Screaming and shouting punctuated great sprays of water as the girls tried to submerge and drown one another. The frying pan sister, out of her depth, altogether, was powerless to restore the least semblance of civilized decorum. She smacked and rang and pounded in red-faced abandon, to no avail. Exhausted at last, she loosened her wimple and surrendered to the spring. Assured that no one saw her, she lay winded and perspiring on the riverbank, and soon fell fast asleep.

Far from subsiding, the water games grew in frenzy and momentum. The river rang with shouts. It was under the cover of such unseemly distractions that Aurora Constancia quietly separated herself from the group and began wading gingerly toward the opposite bank and the bushes.

Among the Jesuit boys, suppressed giggles reached fever pitch. A violent discussion broke out as to whether or not to send out a "rescue" party. It was because of their ferocious altercation that they failed to see what happened next: Aurora Constancia's delicate white foot missed its purchase, tumbling its owner into the fast and dangerous current of the river. Like anyone about to drown, she surrendered all decorum instantly. Her arms flailing, trying to remain above water, screaming for help, she began to churn about in circles, because the flailing of her right arm far overbalanced the more restrained and ladylike floundering of her left. "Help!" she cried again and again as she took in mouthfuls of icy water.

It was then that Ana Magdalena, who had been quietly washing herself somewhat apart from all the activity, caught sight of a sodden smock, churning round and round in the river, presumably with her friend in tow. She did not think nor hesitate; she struck out into the rapid current of the river. The initial shock of finding herself swimming in the subarctic waters of the river nearly caused her to founder, but almost at once her surprise gave way to a surge of rising ecstasy. Kicking and stroking, she reached the gasping Aurora Constancia. Grasping her under the chin like a sack of drowning kittens, she hauled her spluttering and struggling toward the shore. By then, all the fun had stopped. Sixty-one girls looked on in horrified fascination. Not at the drowning girl, who lay at last, choking and gasping, on the riverbank, but at the one who, singlehandedly, had brought her in — because Ana Magdalena was naked.

Shouts gave way to a great collective gasp. The frying pan sister woke in time to feel a bottle fly start from her nose. She sat up in alarm. What her eyes told her, her mind could not believe. "Cover yourself," she screamed, "cover yourself at once!" And she leaped to her feet and raced down the riverbank. Her skirts actually rose an inch above her knees. The girls marveled at the flash of her severe black stockings. "Cover yourself at once," she huffed. But there was no need to urge Ana Magdalena. She was already swathed like a mummy in her oversized bath towel. Her teeth were chattering, her skin nearly blue. The good sister was therefore able to turn her attention to the gasping, choking Aurora Constancia. "Don't stand there like a gaggle of geese. Help me hold her upside down."

At once a crush of the older girls grasped Aurora Constancia by the ankles. They groaned and heaved. The frying pan sister squatted close to Aurora Constancia's face. Rivulets of river water eased out of the victim's nose, and when her mouth fell open, a small fingerling dropped out and thrashed about on the puddled ground. At once, color began to return to her cheeks.

"Lay her down gently," commanded the frying pan sister.

Nothing happened.

"Lay her *down!*

Still nothing happened. When the good sister looked up to see what was amiss, she saw that the unfortunate position in which Aurora Constancia found herself had caused her smock to slide down about her chin — revealing the waterlogged contours of a black lace undergarment of astonishing design, engineered to reduce an already wasp waist to near extinction, and aggressively to display even the most indifferent of breasts.

"Cover her at once," the frying pan sister shrieked.

But alas, the harm had been done. Sixty-two young ladies, all of them vigorously straining to see, had had revealed to them in all its questionable splendor the tricky intricacies of Aurora Constancia's undergarment, its now-sodden red velvet ribbons cunningly threaded at hip and bosom. The lives of Aurora Constancia and, for that matter, Ana Magdalena Arzate de Figueroa would never be the same.

"Back at once to the orchard," shrilled the good sister, and for reasons known to none but herself, she began thumping on the frying pan till the inhabitants at the edge of Malyerba poured out of their houses convinced someone had sounded the tocsin.

All sixty-three girls obediently formed ranks. And, but for the racket and Ana Magdalena's provisional towel, no one viewing the procession could have sensed anything amiss. But the Jesuit boys knew. That morning, on the pretext of embarking on a birdwatching expedition, they had clustered like foreign agents in the bushes. Armed with binoculars, they had waited in breathless anticipation for the glorious moment when Aurora Constancia, for the briefest instant, would raise her troubling smock to reveal the confirming realities of what had been until then (at least for most of them) only the subject of their adolescent fancy.

That the event had been prearranged became glaringly apparent when the nuns, gathering evidence preparatory to Aurora Constancia's summary dismissal from grace — and from the convent — confiscated all her effects except the shirt on her back, in order to submit them to careful examination.

To forestall any possible further moral contamination in any of their charges, the good sisters sequestered both Aurora Constancia and Ana Magdalena in separate cells. Hoping to ensure a return of their detainees' senses, they prescribed a three-day menu of bread and water, and a similar diet of reading, which included the lives of the martyrs and saints, and "The Meditations and Homilies on the

Four Nails," a step-by-step replay of the agony and crucifixion of Our Lord Jesus Christ. But happily, the young ladies had sufficient resources in the persons of friends who were willing to slip them the latest bodice-ripping romances through the barred windows of their cells. Meanwhile, one by one, the sisters examined the guimpes, petticoats, bustles, garters, stockings, shoes, sachets, lace-edged nighties, and bloomers belonging to Aurora Constancia. Concealed in her lowest bureau drawer they discovered a hollowed-out hymnal, and in a corner where they least expected, hidden between her holy pictures, they discovered letters from one of the more precocious students of the Jesuit Academy, one of them encouraging her to model, albeit in the river, the latest trend in ladies' lingerie. There was no longer any doubt. Word spread like wildfire that Aurora Constancia was about to be dismissed. The whole school waited in anticipation, but there was no sign of her.

On the morning of her release from solitary confinement, Ana Magdalena was feeling slightly out of sorts. For this reason when the schoolrooms emptied and the entire school repaired to the refectory for the midday meal, Ana Magdalena was not among them. She lay in her little dormitory cubicle with the curtains drawn. To her great surprise, no sooner had the hallways emptied than she heard the sound of hurried footsteps. Aurora Constancia in the company of a chaperon sister entered the room.

"You have fifteen minutes to pack," the sister reminded her.

Ana Magdalena leapt off her bed. Try as she might, the chaperon sister could not prevent the friends' distressed embrace.

"What happened?" Ana Magdalena wanted to know.

"Nothing. I got expelled."

"What for?"

" 'Unbecoming moral influence.' Something like that. I didn't really catch it."

"How awful! What are you going to do?"

"Ten minutes left to pack," interrupted the chaperon sister.

"Pack, I suppose. Sister Watchdog isn't leaving me much choice."

The two friends set about emptying Aurora Constancia's bureau drawers.

"Hell and damnation!" whispered Aurora Constancia, "they must have found it."

"Found what?"

"The hymnal, dummy."

"What hymnal?"

"The dummy hymnal with the merry widow in it."

"It was in *there?*"

"Oh God! They must have found his letter, too!"

"You mean he helped you plan it?"

"That's the idea."

"No wonder they're giving you the sack —"

"It's not the tragedy you're making out. Who needs this musty old nunnery anyway? I'm going to have fun."

"At home?"

"Sure. My family is probably going to marry me off."

"*Marry* you? To whom?"

"How do I know?"

"Oh, God, that's *terrible.*"

"What's so terrible about it?"

"Marry someone you don't even know? How do you know you're even going to *like* him?"

Aurora Constancia took her friend's hands in hers. They sat on the edge of her dormitory bed. "Cheer up, darling, it's not the tragedy you think. Just because you marry someone doesn't mean you have to like him, silly. You don't even have to know him! All you have to do is go through the motions. After you're married, that's when the fun begins. You have money to spend, a carriage. You can go out, visit friends, see the opera, take lovers. Once you're married, you can do anything you want!"

"Yes, but what'll *I* do after you're gone? This place is going to be a dungeon." Ana Magdalena began to cry.

"Cheer up! They may expel you, too."

"Time's up," barked the chaperon sister. "Hurry or we'll miss the train." And she hustled Aurora Constancia down the corridor toward the street, where the carriage was waiting to take her to the depot.

"Write," called a tear-streaked Ana Magdalena.

"Oh, I will. I will. I promise."

Relieved of the troubling responsibility of harboring a hellion in their midst, the sisters now turned their attention to Ana Magdalena.

Search her affairs as they might, they found nothing of the slightest interest. Her underwear was mended, of a plainness verging on the monastic: cotton drawers, and stockings. Unadorned chemises and petticoats; shoes with no evidence whatsoever of frivolity; and two dresses of a severity bordering on the oppressive. Having served her requisite three days of bread and water, she was summoned to appear in the library.

"And in the river, what became of your smock, dear child?" asked the mother superior sweetly.

"I don't know, Reverend Mother."

"It didn't vanish by magic."

"No, Your Reverence, I took it off."

The gasp of the assembled sisters was unequivocally damning.

"Were you aware of the gravity of your actions?"

"With the smock on, I could never have managed to reach her."

"Nonetheless, you might at least have tried."

"There was no *time* to try, Reverend Mother; she was drowning."

"Through her own fault," the mother superior was quick to point out.

"Reverend Mother, will I be allowed to stay?"

"That is what we are about to deliberate, my child." And the porteress sister showed her outside.

Sitting on the visitors' bench, Ana Magdalena gave way to a momentary surge of panic. She remembered when she was six years old. Andreina had wanted to take her to see a traveling carnival.

"We'll only circle the tent a little," Andreina had coaxed. "We don't have to go inside if you don't want."

But Andreina had not kept her promise and once again, the presence of those dark rooms leapt out at her. There were dead things in them, skeletons of small, defenseless animals, the vertebrae of snakes strung on animated wires, fusty dead herbs and flowers, votive candles, and a row of women dressed in angel costumes, their eyes sewn up with darning needles. It was a house of horrors from which her mother had had to carry her, nearly lifeless and paralyzed with fright, and from which it had taken her three weeks to recover; weeks in which she refused to sleep without bright lights washing out the shadows, even the ones that lurked reluctantly in corners, and then only if Andreina agreed to sit soundlessly next to her as she

16

closed her eyes and in a prayer whose fervency bordered on the incantatory, commended her soul, the soul of Hortensia, her doll, and the soul of all three of her imaginary playmates, including Armando, her toothless crocodile, to God the Mother, God the Father, and God the Baby Jesus.

Now, she barely managed to regain her grip. She tried to review her situation calmly. On the one hand, her life in the young ladies' seminary was not an unmixed delight; but on the other, she did not want to be a disappointment to her mother. From what she could tell, the community's attitude seemed to be uncompromisingly severe.

Without any question Ana Magdalena had appeared on the river-bank, for a brief moment at least, as naked as the day she was born. And what she had concealed under her straight and disciplined braids and the genteel poverty of her clothes, the force of the river current had exposed: She was young, she was beautiful. Her body had begun that process of generous endowment which was to culminate many years later in a singular fame that made her celebrated from the Andes all the way to the mouth of the Amazon — because aside from her physical attributes, Ana Magdalena knew how to swim.

The good sisters remained *in camera* deliberating for the better part of a week, while the kitchen sisters, exempt from the weightier concerns of the community, racked their brains to know how to marshal the girls. There is a limit to how much soap can be made, how many towels can be assaulted on the stones of the riverbed before they are shredded to ribbons, how much soup can be concocted from bones the town butcher would otherwise discard. In desperation, they called in the music master, the drawing master, and the dancing master, who busied and badgered the girls from morning to night. It was because of this unprecedented crisis that Ana Magdalena was allowed to remain with the other girls to learn from the emaciated and mincing dancing master the shocking new steps that made good society act like pimps and whores, and perfectly good whores act like society.

While the girls learned to tango, the ethical discussion raged. Indeed the good nuns had time for almost nothing else. They sat in the chapel with the reverend mother presiding. Among the first

17

called to give testimony was the frying pan sister herself, who in religious life was known as Sister Annunciata.

"The defendant was naked! When I looked up —"

"Just a moment, sister. You say, "When I looked up. Was your nose in your missal?"

In her heart of hearts, Sister Annunciata knew she had been asleep. She had loosened her wimple. She had allowed the soft spring breezes to lull her, to whisper their startling promises in her unbridled ears.

"No, Reverend Mother."

"What then, my daughter?"

The congregation was waiting. The moment of truth had arrived. She would have to admit that she had slept, that she had in a moment of dizzying sweetness relaxed her vigilance, allowed her frying pan to slide into the dewy and receiving grass. She had not counted on the effect of immediate recognition her silent hesitation was to occasion. It occurred to all of them (but not to her) that she had simply had to answer a call of nature, and was occupied wiping herself with a leaf.

"And when you were done," offered the reverend mother kindly, "what did you see?"

"When I looked up again —"

The terrifying moment had passed.

"— I made my way as quickly as our habit would allow to the site of the disaster."

"What did you do?"

"I urged the young lady in question to cover herself."

"And did she do so?"

"At once. With her bathing towel. I then turned my attention to the other young lady, who lay on the riverbank wetter and more bedraggled than a toad."

"Were you of the belief that the victim had drowned?"

"Mercy, God save us, no, Reverend Mother. I told them to help me lift her upside down by the ankles."

"A curious measure, surely —"

"But no, Reverend Mother, because I read somewhere on the matter of drowning that if you dangle the victim like an angler's trophy, it forces the water to come out of the lungs."

"And did it so?"

"Praise God, Reverend Mother, I am relieved to say. The entire river seemed to take leave of her mouth, and at once the young lady began to take on a more healthful complexion. But in the excitement I noticed her smock had become bunched up at the chin, revealing a most unfortunate attire."

"And what was your reaction?"

"I maintained the strictest decorum, Reverend Mother, and made every effort to cover the proceedings with some semblance of decency. But with all due respect, I hope you will excuse me from further testimony. I am not in my normal state of mind. Besides, the matter before us now is the second young lady, who was without any garment at all."

And Sister Annunciata slumped down exhausted, overcome by the weight of her own testimony.

"Thank you, sister. And now," said the reverend mother, "we must decide what to do. If we have summarily dismissed the young lady who modeled the garment in question, what even sterner measures ought we to bring to bear on someone who modeled nothing but skin?"

Sister Immaculata stood up. "On the one hand, it must be said the young lady in question freely admitted to the deliberate shedding of her smock —"

"Yes, sister," interrupted the reverend mother. "We heard her reply there was no time to wait and see. Presumably, the first young lady had already taken in several gulps of river. Is it true, as she claims, that a bathing smock could impede a swimmer's progress?"

There was a perplexed silence. None of the good sisters knew how to swim. It was consensually determined, therefore, that the question at issue was whether or not to give Ana Magdalena the benefit of the doubt. Some argued that throughout her time in the convent, their young charge had proved irreproachably truthful. Others impugned her judgment on the grounds of her youth. Put to the vote at last, the assembly found her to be trustworthy.

"But what about her nakedness?" insisted Sister Simplicitas.

A groan escaped all those assembled. Hadn't they already spent nearly a week debating the issues? Wasn't adjournment the only possible course?

"I move to expel her at once for letting the other girls see, thereby providing a fresh occasion of sin," said Sister Purissima.

And, eager to be dismissed, the assembly voted for immediate expulsion, but with mitigating circumstances.

It was for this reason that when the convent gate swung shut behind her, Ana Magdalena was wearing a hastily improvised medal for heroism; in addition to the reticule she carried crammed to bursting with her meager belongings, she also clutched a diploma, although it was hardly even spring.

In those days, progress had yet to visit Malyerba. Potholes had not yet been invented. Ruts, on the other hand, were still in plentiful supply. Rains could reduce the roadbeds to sorry stretches of mud. But with spring, footmen began to dust and polish the carriages that the great houses still chose to affect, as the good families once again took to the road. The prestige of each house could be gauged by the volume of dust raised by a vehicle, and none could surpass in grandeur the passage of the vehicle of the house of Orgaz, the most illustrious — and dusty — family of all.

Besides the carriages of the great, there were few other even remotely imposing vehicles to be seen in the streets. Now and again, a carter offered a shabby wagon for hire, but as a general rule, the wheel has always exhibited a certain bashfulness making its appearance in the New World, its relative merits being still in dispute. The most common vehicle of transport is still Man, Man in the general sense; because although women are also known to carry, it is "Man" — in all his glory — that resides in common use. And that particular spring morning, as Ana Magdalena began her long trek home, Man could be observed dogtrotting through the streets of Malyerba, carrying seventy-five-pound loads of firewood on his back, one-hundred-pound bales of straw, eighty-pound loads of terracotta water jugs, and ninety-pound loads of papayas and avocados, all neatly bundled in nets woven of hemp. It was entirely too early for any of the great families to be about, although here and there a footman had been sent out on the double to fetch a morning paper or to haul a sack of newly roasted coffee from the mill. Serving girls already crowded the vegetable stalls in the market, baskets in hand, laying in supplies for lunch. Of course the common people were about, but they are always about in any case, and deserve no great attention here.

It was into these streets that Ana Magdalena found herself untimely thrust. Her situation, as she was well aware, was not unclouded. There was the matter of her mother's shock and disappointment when she discovered her daughter freshly cast out from her young ladies' institution. But even more critical — and here Ana Magdalena's assessment already showed her uncanny analytical ability — there was the matter of the neighbors. If Ana Magdalena already showed a marked indifference to outside opinion, she knew her mother held equally strong opposing views. Andreina's home was situated in what still was Malyerba's most prestigious district, where only servants ever went about on foot. No unaccompanied young woman of good standing ever allowed her foot to touch a roadbed. Such presumption was tantamount to an immediate and catastrophic loss of virginity. Ana Magdalena pondered how best to arrive at her mother's house in a manner befitting the social position of the Figueroas, a position her mother had made heroic efforts to maintain. Almost at once she hit upon what that manner might be. She paused in the roadway just long enough to plait a handy set of braids, which disguised not only her appearance but her race and caste as well. From her reticule she extracted a pinafore and tied it tightly about her waist. It was therefore in the guise of a servant that she knocked at her mother's kitchen door. Because that worthy lady was given to frequenting the kitchen as little as possible, and then only to give orders, it did not surprise Ana Magdalena that Andreina was a long time answering. After a while, she knocked again. Still there was no answer. Although Ana Magdalena had not been home in some time, she knew it was not her mother's habit to go out in the mornings. Andreina liked to sleep till noon. Ana Magdalena thought it best therefore to sit on the back steps. She knew sooner or later the servant would return from her trip to the morning market. She was not long waiting. She heard Berta's bare feet brush against the flagstones of the alley. When the Indian girl saw her, she immediately dropped her shopping basket and ran to embrace her young mistress.

"*Niña,*" she murmured, "*niña,* what brings you home?"

"*Dios!* Berta, don't tell my mother. I got expelled!"

"Expelled? By the sisters?"

"Yes! They sent us home."

"Us, who?"

"Me and Aurora Constancia!"

"For good?" Berta was getting excited.

"For swimming!"

Berta broke into laughter. She clapped her hands. "But that's wonderful! Oh, that's just wonderful! Wait and see! The señora, your mother, will be *delighted!* I can't wait till she finds out. Come on! Come on inside!"

"Oh, God, Berta, *please* don't tell her."

"Of course we won't *tell* her. What an idea! We don't *have* to tell her. She'll be delighted anyway."

Berta picked up her basket and unlocked the door. They passed through the kitchen and through the courtyard until they came to the doorway of the vast and airless parlor with its tufted Victorian sofas and black lacquer Regency sideboards, all inlaid with mother-of-pearl.

There sat Andreina surrounded by enormous piles of linen. It lay every which way, on the sofas, on the piano, piled in corners, some stacked nearly to the ceiling. There were sheets, pillowcases, chemises, tablecloths, napkins, towels, serviettes.

Ana Magdalena was aghast. "What — ?"

"Shhh," whispered Berta, pressing a finger to her lips. "She hates to be disturbed when she's monogramming."

"Monogramming?"

Andreina was bent over a piece of linen that she had fastened to an embroidery frame. She must have become aware that someone stood in the parlor doorway. "Berta, please get me some tea," she ordered without looking up.

"Yes, señora." Berta left Ana Magdalena standing on the threshold.

After some time, still without taking her eyes off her embroidery frame, Andreina asked, "Why are you still standing there? Didn't I just send you for tea?"

Ana Magdalena entered the parlor as silently as her buttonhook shoes would allow. She crossed to where Andreina sat working. Andreina did not look up.

"Put it on the table here." Then, thinking better of it, "There isn't any room! Put it next to me, here on the floor."

Ana Magdalena stood without moving.

"Don't just stand there, ninny," Andreina wailed, "you know how I hate it when you spook me. Put it down."

"Mother —"

Andreina was thunderstruck. She let her embroidery slide to the floor. "Oh, my child, my darling!" And abashed at having mistaken her only daughter for a servant, she threw herself sobbing into Ana Magdalena's arms. Her joy seemed to be so great, she barely heard when Ana Magdalena told her of the near-drowning and her heroism, she hardly noticed when Ana Magdalena presented her with her diploma, let alone that it was postdated.

"Don't trouble yourself, my darling," she said, waving a careless hand, "we'll have it framed as soon as there is any money. You're just in time to help me monogram."

Andreina had taken to embroidering initials on the trousseau linens of young ladies, but only young ladies of the finest families. In those days, it was the custom at baptism to assign to female children as many names as possible, in the hope that each of the corresponding saints would see to it their virtue did not go unprotected. It was not unheard of for a monogram to include up to ten initials: eight for a young lady's given names, one for the illustrious name of her family of origin, and one for what, it was hoped, would be the even more illustrious name of the groom. None of this fevered attention to pedigree made Andreina's occupational choice any easier.

It has been said earlier that Ana Magdalena showed little enthusiasm for the household arts, but what has not been explicitly said is that of all these arts, needlework of any kind — in particular embroidery — was pure unadulterated anguish, nothing less. Now, late into the night, she sat with Andreina under the oil lamp, straining to see. Repeatedly her needle found its mark not in the painstakingly outlined rebus of the bride-to-be's initials, but in the rosy cushion of her own fingertips.

"Aiee!" she would exclaim with a sharp intake of breath, as the

24

hapless finger found its way to her full and blushing lips, there to be sucked of its offending bloodburst.

Andreina, who was already of a nervous disposition, would fret and fume. "You're going to ruin the linen. Remember, bloodstains have no antidote. We can't afford replacements. Keep your needle low, out of the way of your adorable fingers, child." And on and on she would go about why she had been born into the world to suffer one misfortune after another, how she had lost or misplaced so many children, how she came to be married to such a spendthrift good-for-nothing who never gave her any money and how her own family had disowned her for marrying such a scoundrel just when she needed help the most.

Ana Magdalena bore these jeremiads of her mother's in silence. She renewed her efforts, only to redouble her pinpricks. Patiently, she rethreaded her needle when time after time the thread pulled out because she had cut it too short, but no matter how hard she tried, her efforts produced a monogram so bunched up it looked like the hallmark of a leaf curl. Clearly, she was not the best recruit for Andreina's enterprise.

There were, of course, further complications. In order to market her work, Andreina had had to resort to a subterfuge. Her customers were all from the best houses, the very people she least wanted to know that she, Andreina, had fallen on times hard enough to require her to stoop to any kind of labor, even this, the most genteel. And so she pretended that it was Berta, her Indian servant, whose skill at embroidery had been acquired from the good missionary sisters, who was embroidering the monograms in her spare time. Didn't a house as imposing as hers require the work of a full-time servant at least, they wanted to know? Oh, yes, indeed it did, she assured them, but Berta did it only at night, and she worked very fast.

The Mendosa and Garcia and Martinez ladies were only too happy to accept her explanation because they themselves had a surprise in store for her. When Andreina presented the finished work, they took her into their sumptuous parlors.

"*Voy a ver, voy a ver,*" they would say, "let's see, let's see," and one by one the great ladies would raise a critical lorgnette to each monogram, looking for any possible flaws. "Well, what can you expect from an Indian?" they would say. "We can't pay for this anything close to what we initially discussed. Anyway, we didn't sign a contract, did we?" And without batting an eyelash, they would press a mere twenty-five escudos into Andreina's hand. "Here. To help your poor dear little Indian. It's too generous, really." Caught in her own trap, there was nothing Andreina could do or say. She knew that a monogram was, in some ways at least, as chancy as a lottery ticket; like the numbers, initials were not interchangeable.

Many times as she bent over her embroidery frame, Ana Magdalena thought of Aurora Constancia. She pictured her at home, caught up in La Paz's breathless social whirl, polishing her manners and her repartee, dazzling every handsome admirer with her charm. She wondered why she never wrote. But when at last a communication arrived postmarked La Paz, in her excitement she nearly destroyed the contents as she tore the envelope apart. It was an elaborately engraved wedding invitation. Ana Magdalena's presence was requested at the ceremony. A hastily scrawled note further suggested that she must not even think of refusing Aurora's invitation for the "entire preceding week — there'll be preparations, showers, stag parties and balls. Come quick!" Aurora Constancia had scrawled in her schoolgirl hand. She had dotted all her *i*'s with cunning little globes. From that moment, Ana Magdalena neglected her monogramming. Her eyes took on a dreamy look and her embroidery frame slipped periodically from her hand and slid to the parlor floor.

La Paz, she would whisper to herself like a prayer. She imagined endless evenings of candlelight, pink satin ball gowns whispering their silken promises in the corridors, secret messages delivered at midnight by liveried footmen, love notes, invitations to an endless round of balls, glittering soirées where the napery was shining white, and the finest porcelain platters rested on genuine gold salvers, and crystal goblets were filled with wine the necromantic red of rubies. And through it all, she, Ana Magdalena, would preside, her luxuriant hair coiled in dark and abundant waves about her alabaster shoulders, her décolleté relentlessly provocative, her lovely jeweled hand raised to drink a toast, her waistline encircled in the fever of the dance, and, as she spun, her stockinged leg flashing up above her thigh. The tango! She could hardly wait.

"Mother, I've nothing to wear but these *brown* things." She wrinkled her nose in disgust.

"Darling child," her mother reminded her, "let's not get ahead of ourselves. There are some things we have to discuss."

They were bent over their embroidery frames. Ana Magdalena's heart pounded with misgivings.

"How can you travel without a chaperon, dear child? Just think, I can't take a minute away from my monograms and I can't spare Berta for a second. I don't see how I can allow it — unless other girls are going, too."

"From the convent?" Ana Magdalena could just imagine asking the reverend mother, "Are any of the girls going to attend Aurora's wedding?" They would be standing on the thick plush rug of the convent parlor, where it always smelled of wax.

"Aurora Constancia, my child, is doing the work of the devil. We have cast her out for moral unresolve, turpitude of the nth degree. It's a wonder the devil hasn't yet collected his due. And you *dream* of traveling to La Paz? Perdition! Perdition awaits you there, ravening for your glorious, pure, virginal soul."

"Ugh!" said Ana Magdalena aloud.

"Did you say something, dear child?"

"I said I would find out tomorrow."

Ana Magdalena rehearsed her performance several times under Berta's tutelage, so that before Andreina her delivery was flawless. She was so excited she could barely contain herself. All the girls in Aurora's class had received invitations! Patricia was going, and Claudia, and Maria de Lourdes, and possibly, besides these, four others would be allowed to go as well. Of course, she had had to recruit Berta, who claimed she was only chaperoning Ana Magdalena through the streets on her way to and from the convent, whereas in fact they had both been employed going to the railroad station to buy Ana Magdalena her round-trip ticket with money Berta had had to lend her young mistress from her meager savings. But Berta could be counted on to keep any kind of secret.

Even Andreina succumbed to a stunning attack of generosity. All her fine dresses came out of storage. She laid them out on the vast canopied bed.

"But first," she said, "you're a young lady now. You have no business wearing sensible cotton homespun anymore. Take those bloomers off at once. What horrid things. I'll tell Berta to burn them at once. Only silk should be worn close to the skin." She unveiled a store of carefully folded lace-edged silk chemises, and provocative silk drawers that hung down to midthigh.

Ana Magdalena slipped into the step-ins. They fitted her perfectly.

"My, my, you're quite the young lady. Look how they're made for you. Now try the chemise."

One by one they tried the dresses, luxurious peignoirs, middy blouses, tennis dresses, and pleated skirts, until a week's wardrobe had been assembled. There was even a vamp dress whose deliberately bedraggled hem made it admirably suited for dancing the tango. Andreina actually took the time away from her monogramming to make the small alterations necessary — a tuck here, a hem there.

The only obstacle was the inability of the household to produce an appropriate traveling bag. The storage room was crammed to bursting with relics of their decayed affluence: minuscule reticules, antique suitcases with frozen locks or sprung hinges. But to transport a wardrobe of such elegance, they could find nothing suitable.

"Why don't you settle for a market hamper?" said the helpful Berta.

"You mean the kind of basket *indios* use?" Andreina wrinkled her nose.

"No. A hamper," specified Berta, lending what she had in mind a certain minimal air of distinction. And because there was a dearth of money at the time, Andreina accepted the solution as a sensible one.

On the appointed morning, ticket in hand, Ana Magdalena was ready to leave for the station far earlier than necessary. Berta prepared to accompany her. To Ana Magdalena's stupefaction, however, the door to Andreina's bedroom opened. Quickly, Ana Magdalena concealed her ticket in the hollow of her sleeve. Her mother, who was wont to sleep till noon, stood there fully dressed.

"I'll just have a little sip of coffee, and then we'll see you off," she promised her daughter. Behind her back, Berta and Ana Magdalena exchanged troubled looks. Berta cast about for some solution. "Señora's very thoughtful," said she. "If I don't need to go, I can set about my morning chores."

"What do you mean, 'don't need to go'? Who'll carry the hamper? You don't expect me to, I hope. And you know I can't walk back alone."

They waited in silence. Andreina sipped her coffee. At last she was ready.

On the way to the station, Andreina was full of maternal advice. Ana Magdalena, however, was more than usually silent. She was puzzling what to do. She didn't want Andreina to find out she was traveling alone. Simply boarding the train, as she had originally intended, was out of the question. By the time they reached the station, they could hear the engine whistle. A great plume of steam shot up in the far distance, and hovered against the backdrop of the distant cordillera. The train rumbled and hissed and snorted into the station. Before Andreina could make her way to the ticket window, Ana Magdalena stopped her.

"No, Mother. You buy the ticket on the train."

Andreina did not appear to be convinced. Suddenly, Ana Magdalena detached herself from her companions and began to run along the entire length of the platform, seeming to search for someone or something from wagon to wagon.

In the very far distance she momentarily disappeared. When she reemerged she was waving, running back toward where Berta and Andreina stood waiting with the hamper. When she came abreast of them she was entirely out of breath. "I can't find them anywhere," she pretended dismay, "but Maria de Lourdes' mother is in the first carriage. She says I can ride with her."

They began to walk the vast length of the platform at the fastest clip the heavy hamper would allow. The train's departure was imminent. The boarding whistle sounded.

"Run, run," urged Ana Magdalena, "there's still far to go!" But she knew that Andreina had forgotten how to run. At best she could take only little hobbled hopping steps.

"Wait! Wait! You're going to need some money!"

Ana Magdalena stopped just long enough to accept her mother's carefully rolled-up wad of bills.

"Faster! Faster! It's starting to move!" urged Ana Magdalena.

And indeed, the wheels began a very slow grinding.

"Berta," panted Ana Magdalena, vaulting onto the metal boarding stair. "Toss me the hamper." Berta began to run alongside her, raising the basket as she ran. Ana Magdalena reached for it. Her hand fastened firmly on the handle. With a great heave, Berta lifted it toward the corrugated-steel boarding platform of the now rapidly moving train.

The last glimpse Andreina had of her daughter, Ana Magdalena was waving and blowing kisses, standing on the open platform of the carriage next to her vast hamper. Andreina wondered how she would manage to haul it clear to the very front wagon to join Maria de Lourdes' mother. And she wondered even more when she discovered later that the first carriage is usually the mail car.

Long before Ana Magdalena attained the summit of her not inconsiderable career, she was to place this first trip of hers to La Paz in some kind of perspective. She was to decide that it was to be the very last big disappointment of her life. Because from the moment Aurora Constancia's maid and her footman met Ana Magdalena at the railroad station until the time she boarded the train exactly one week later for her return to Peru and her mother's house — with the exception of the magnificent wine-red silk velvet dress which she wore to Aurora Constancia's high nuptial mass — of the entire sumptuous wardrobe, Ana Magdalena was to wear only one nightgown and the pleated skirt and matching middy blouse. Most outings were out of the question, there being almost never an available chaperon to accompany the young ladies to the brilliant soirées, dance parties, or balls; and no festivities were conducted in the house itself because everyone seemed to be caught up in the frenzy of last-minute wedding preparations. Even the tennis courts were off limits, and the girls were forced to miss a Charlie Chaplin movie because at the last minute the overworked duenna slipped accidentally and sprained her coccyx.

The eve of the wedding day, Aurora Constancia's family tried to arrange a small informal reception where intimate friends could meet the groom.

"I can't wait to see what he looks like," Ana Magdalena told Aurora Constancia.

"Oh, he's got all the parts," Aurora replied nonchalantly.

"Then you must know him really well."

"Sure! We held hands at the cinema."

"That's *all?*"

"Don't be funny. My parents want a proper match for me."

But the reception was conducted more in the style of a wake: the guests were present, but the groom was not. He was said to be attending a prenuptial stag celebration.

"Oh, you know Alejandro," enthused his mother (who *was* there), "he just loves his schoolboy pranks!" She threw her well-coiffed head back and issued one of her stunning pearly laughs from between heavily rouged lips.

Ana Magdalena kept trying to have a private word with her friend behind a convenient potted palm, but Aurora Constancia was busy being charming to her guests. From time to time she threw Ana Magdalena a pained look of discouragement.

When the last guest had departed, Aurora Constancia was permitted to retire to the bedroom she shared with her friend.

"Where *was* he?"

"Who?"

"Your groom."

"Darling," said Aurora Constancia, taking her friend's hands in hers, "you're such a funny little sentimentalist! That's just not how it's done."

"Then how *is* it done? I want to know."

"Listen. Right now, Alejandro is probably on his way to some cathouse or other with several of his sporting friends. They've stuffed themselves with an enormous dinner, and over every course they've exchanged remarks of the rudest sort, the kind men really enjoy, having to do with that funny thing they have, where it's taken them, and where they intend to drag it, not just now but in the future."

"That's *terrible!*"

"But it's discreet. They will respect my family, they will respect our name, and I will not be so much as even alluded to, neither by my fingernail nor a hair of my head. None of this will have to do with me, or any other decent woman. And they don't even mention the *other* kind by name."

"Isn't that thoughtful. . . ."

"Anytime they want to refer directly to a woman like *that,* they just allude to a body part."

"Then you don't know him very well —"

"But don't you see, darling, he doesn't know much about me, either! And that's the wonderful part of the bargain. Because" — she lowered her voice to way below even a whisper — "he's not exactly getting fresh goods, either."

Ana Magdalena gasped. "You mean you did it?"

"What do you suppose? Don't you think I had fun with my Jesuit boy?"

Ana Magdalena saw her friend in a new and even more admiring light. "Oh God!" She let herself sink onto the soft mattress. "Oh, God!"

"Didn't you?"

"Not ever," she said with a voice full of wonder and regret. "Not yet. What was it like?"

"Oh, it was okay. . . ."

"*Okay?* Did he —"

"He put his finger —"

"His *finger* —"

"You know. So later it wouldn't hurt, dummy!" And they both laughed uproariously.

"You see, darling, the best part of it is you don't have to like someone just because he happens to be your husband — all you have to do is marry him. Once you're married, you don't need any miserable *dueñas* anymore. They just take it for granted that you're not fresh goods. So you get to go around anywhere you like. You have money and a carriage, you *can even go on foot!* And you can take any lover that catches your eye, provided you have a way of catching his. And *they* just love it. Because while they're busy seducing you, they just know *their* wife is safe at home in bed!"

"Holy Mother!" Both girls began to giggle wickedly.

"Oh, God, I wish — if only we could have danced the tango. Even once."

"But we can."

"We can?"

"Of course."

"You've *got* to see this dress. My mother lent it to me."

"Let's see."

Ana Magdalena took the vamp dress from the hamper. It was

diaphanous silk, and its tatters whirled tantalizingly when she spun.

"Holy Mother," breathed Aurora Constancia, "that's awfully provocative. Wait!" And she rummaged in her wardrobe until she extracted a swishy black taffeta number, tighter than glue through the torso, flaring out just below the thighs. "Hook me up, darling, will you? Now, watch this," she said. She went through a fiery and complicated sequence of steps.

"Oooh, I *love* it!" Ana Magdalena joined her. The two locked arms and began to dance. "Ta rump, ta rump, ta *rump,* pump pump," they sang. "Ta rump, ta rump, ta *rump* pump pump, ta *rump* pump pump de dump!"

At last they fell on the bed, breathless with exhaustion, laughing in each other's arms.

"Oh God," whispered Ana Magdalena, "that was heaven!"

"Ummm," said Aurora Constancia, gently stroking her friend's flushed cheeks. She began to brush Ana Magdalena's lips with the faintest of kisses. "I just *love* kissing, don't you?" she whispered.

Ana Magdalena thought of Sergio Ballado. "Umm," she murmured, transported. And she let her lovely pink tongue escape between her rosy lips.

As she rode the train home from La Paz, Ana Magdalena had ample time to reflect. She watched the splendor of the passing countryside through a fog of reminiscence and regret. Reminiscence of the enchanting night in Aurora Constancia's bed, the whispered conversation, the excitement of their kisses, and then the lovely feeling as the warmth rose up in her, and she wanted, wanted more than anything . . . and when Aurora Constancia . . . and how good it felt . . . and how she would never forget it; and how, smack in the middle of the ceremony, when Alejandro was about to place the gold ring on Aurora Constancia's finger, her friend had turned and deliberately sought her out, and fixed her with a look, a look so wonderful, so piercing, that it said everything.

And regret, because she would probably never see her friend again. La Paz was so far away, and the train ticket was more expensive than she had ever imagined, even second class. But she felt a kind of puzzlement, too, a troubling kind of confusion. Why was it that Aurora Constancia knew so much, laughed so much, had so many secrets, but her life in La Paz was a humdrum round of disappointments? All week they had been trapped in the big house with nothing to do, and nowhere to go, and on the night of the reception, the night Alejandro was supposed to be introduced to all her friends, he never showed up because he evidently had more interesting things to do. And even on the wedding night ... Ana Magdalena had to stay over, because the train didn't run till the next day. She excused herself early to brush her teeth, put on her nightgown, and slip into bed. She lay in the dark, unable to sleep, her eyes open wide, staring at the ceiling, letting her mind wander, imagining Aurora in the arms of Alejandro, wondering ... wishing ... She must have fallen asleep because all of a sudden there was someone shaking her gently by the elbow, and when she opened her eyes, there was Aurora, eyes shining in the dark.

"Shhh." She put her finger to her lips. "Don't say anything."

Ana Magdalena couldn't imagine what she was doing in her own room on her wedding night. "What —"

"Shhh." Aurora Constancia covered her mouth with the most delicious of kisses. She shut her eyes. She didn't want to talk anymore; she forgot all her questions. She let herself float on the delicious bed of night.

When she woke up, Aurora Constancia already had her eyes wide open. She lay with her magnificent dark hair spread like a halo on the pillow.

"I'll never forget you," she whispered to Ana Magdalena. "You'll be my special friend."

"For life." Ana Magdalena nodded. Then she remembered. "What happened?"

"He went out." Aurora shrugged. "I don't know where."

Ana Magdalena returned from her visit to La Paz a changed woman. But she found Andreina in worse straits than ever. There was no money left even for oil, their credit with the oil merchant having long ago been exhausted, because Andreina had taken to embroidering only at night.

"Why can't you embroider in the daylight?" urged Ana Magdalena.

"But I don't want them to see me."

"Who?"

"The clientele."

"So what if they see you."

Andreina gasped.

"Say you're working for pleasure," Ana Magdalena went on.

"What! And risk losing half my customers? There *is* no work for pleasure, my girl! You call this monogramming pleasure? It's shit!"

"Then let's be done with it now and for good," Ana Magdalena replied without batting an eyelash.

"Sure, and how do you expect to feed your greedy little maw?"

"We could find something to do with a lower overhead."

Andreina had never heard of overhead. Ana Magdalena explained it to her. Her mother was impressed. "Dear child, what a quaint idea. Why didn't we think of it before?"

Ana Magdalena and her mother set about listing the various kinds of services whose performance they might be able to attribute to the industry of their remarkable Indian servant, Berta.

"Berta, what kind of work would you do if you had to take in work?"

"Don't I have enough work already?"

"Yes, but *theoretically,* what kinds of things would you choose?"

"You ladies know very well. I would do exactly what I do already. Fifteen hours a day. And sometimes even more."

"Yes, but just imagine if you could."

"Señora knows I don't have time to imagine anything."

Seeing that Berta was not willing to lend herself to their scheme, they imagined what Berta would imagine if she had had the time. There was taking in wash (not sufficiently genteel); cooking takeout casseroles (too-high overhead); baking bread (too hard work for too little gain); knitting (Ana Magdalena shuddered); making sachets and pomanders (Ana Magdalena wrinkled her nose); and making soap.

So it was that by default they settled on making soap. They would have to use their very last escudos to order suet from the butcher and lye in vats from the dry-goods man. The household was already possessed of the vast cauldrons necessary, and there were innumerable bake trays that could be pressed into immediate service.

"All we need now is firewood. Go at once to the market," Andreina ordered Berta, "and see to it we get a week's supply. Get them to give us credit."

"But señora —"

"No buts. Go at once! Do I have to belt your feckless hide?"

Berta wrapped her shawl tightly about her shoulders against the morning chill before setting out on what she knew must be a futile errand. She already knew that what little credit, what scant goodwill there was for the Figueroas, had long ago run out.

She was gone little over an hour. When she returned without her load, Andreina was beside herself.

"I've a good mind to kick you out."

"Please, señora —"

"All I do is feed you!"

"But señora —"

"You never do a lick of work."

But Berta was accustomed to her mistress's tirades and she knew she had an ally in Ana Magdalena. She knew that sooner or later she could count on her to interrupt the scene.

"Mother, don't waste time getting so upset. Just fire her," chimed in Ana Magdalena right on cue.

"*What?*"

"I thought we needed to trim our expenses."

"Don't tell me what to do."

"But everyone knows. You don't think for a minute no one realizes who's been doing the monograms, do you? Don't you think everyone can see you squirming? Why keep up the pretense?"

"But the Figueroas would never *think* of being without their servants," Andreina protested.

"Servant," corrected Ana Magdalena, "and now maybe it's time to let her go."

This was the moment Berta habitually fell to her knees, burlesquing sobs as if her heart would break. "Señora, *please!* Please let me stay. I have nowhere else to go. They canceled my village. The Brol plantation ran over it!"

Andreina felt abashed. She shot a guilty glance at Ana Magdalena.

"Señora knows I know how to cut wood. Just give me an ax — or a machete," pleaded Berta through her sobs.

Ana Magdalena gave her mother an approving nod.

Andreina broke down. "Very well. But just remember, we can't afford to pay you extra."

"Señora hasn't paid me anything at all in over fifteen months."

"First have breakfast before you leave," suggested Ana Magdalena.

It was the first time since the start of her employ that Berta had ever eaten breakfast. She was nineteen, and the kindness was not lost on her. When she returned at sundown, she carried seventy-five pounds of firewood strapped to her back.

"Now," she said, triumphantly dropping her load, "stoke the stoves! Nothing can stop us!"

Andreina had to admit to Ana Magdalena that she found Berta's enthusiasm catching.

Because they had never approached the suet butcher and the dry-goods man for credit, they found to their great relief that their initial capital outlay could be deferred. They sent Berta to pick up the merchandise, concerning themselves, as was only proper, with the organization of the project. Ana Magdalena even unearthed an old decommissioned oar which was to serve Berta as a stirring paddle. The Figueroa saponifying enterprise was underway.

The gentlewomen had not foreseen what a stir the smell of melting suet would create in the refined nostrils of their neighborhood. One by one the householders sent their servants to inquire what might be the source of the curious aroma. Were the Figueroas making sausage? Their persistent inquiries threw Andreina into a perilously evil humor.

"They're all such pathetic snobs," she railed at Ana Magdalena. "I have a devilish headache already and the morning's only just begun." And she took to her vast canopied bed.

For this reason when the first inquiries were discreetly made as to the availability of her daughter, it was Ana Magdalena herself, and not Andreina as would have been more proper, who answered the pull of the bell rope.

Already, just after sunrise, the day was unusually promising for the making of soap, and by ten a vast number of bake trays lay cooling in the courtyard, their gray and viscous substance slowly hardening under the merciless summer sun. The clangor of the bell resounded in the patio, and Ana Magdalena, sleeves rolled up, in her saponifying pinafore, her magnificent dark hair spread about her shoulders, went to answer. She pulled the porter's door open and stood on the threshold of the carriage entrance. Doña Eduviges, solemnly clad all in black lace as for a funeral, stood in the doorway.

"Well, my dear, and aren't you going to ask me in? Where's your mistress?" And she handed Ana Magdalena her beautifully engraved card. Amid the whorls and curlicues, Ana Magdalena deciphered the name with some difficulty.

"Of course!" she said, recognizing at last the identity of her caller. "Please have the kindness to step inside." And she led Doña Eduviges into the musty parlor. "Have a seat," she said. She pulled open the heavy velvet drapes to allow the sunlight in, releasing a cloud of dust into the air. "I'll go at once to call my mother."

Doña Eduviges had ample time to contemplate the motes of dust as they slowly returned to settle on the surfaces of the ponderous velvet-upholstered furniture and the rosewood grand piano, which had long fallen into disuse, and to reflect at the same time that the girl she had mistaken for a serving wench was in reality the prize she had come to seek.

In future years, Andreina would perversely remember the arrival of Doña Eduviges, not as the answer to all their woes, but as a towering inconvenience. Mummified in her flannel nightgown, cold compresses glued to her temples, she responded with less than enthusiasm to Ana Magdalena's tapping at her door.

"What the devil do you want, for the love of God?" she finally bellowed from beneath the bedclothes, where she lay in a sulk.

"Mother. It's Doña Eduviges. She's come to call."

"The *matchmaker?*" And recognizing the name of the person whose presence more than any other struck fear and trembling into the hearts of respectable families with eligible daughters, Andreina sat bolt upright in bed, her migraine miraculously cured.

"Open the door, idiot!" she shrilled. "Don't stand there gawking. Get me my stays." Andreina struggled out of her night clothes and into her most respectable peignoir.

"Quick, my hair!" She made Ana Magdalena comb it out and pin it up and arrange a row of fetching little spit curls ringing her forehead and temples to disguise her wrinkles. After daubing the last bit of powder on her patrician nose, she swept into the parlor every bit the grande dame, although much of her elegance was improvised with the help of safety pins.

"Doña Eduviges, what an unmixed delight," she purred. "And what brings you here this morning, may I ask?"

Doña Eduviges failed to be taken in by such a fabricated display of innocence. She had a way of pausing for effect, of charging the silence around her with distress and uncertainty, just enough to throw everyone off guard. She removed her tiny gold-rimmed eyeglasses and made a great show of polishing them, though they already gleamed with the deadly luster of lead crystal. She brought her fine pointed tongue to the tip of her nose. She was about to speak.

"Nothing, my dear Andreina. It just seemed a morning entirely too splendid not to be given over to a little social visit."

She was much too much the mistress of her trade to come directly to the point. Under the guise of apparently innocuous social chatter, she went about the business of gauging a family's true material position with the thoroughness of a barracuda. One by one, she went through the leading economic indicators. Had the year been a good one, dear Andreina? Was dear Ana Magdalena already home on holiday? Was it true she had been awarded her diploma somewhat ahead of time? Had the rumor been well founded that she had saved a young lady of dubious virtue from drowning? And so on. At last, she was able to come to the matter at hand. How fortunate for Señora Arzate de Figueroa that the scion of a most illustrious family, a world-renowned fabulist who, rumor had it, was soon to be nominated for an internationally prestigious literary prize; an extraordinary man of letters, the first from the New World to achieve an international reputation on a par with that of the many very superior writers of Europe; a man so illustrious, in short, that she must keep his name confidential until the negotiations were virtually complete (although in due time, she was willing to arrange a meeting) — how fortunate for the poor Figueroas that such a man had expressed more than a passing interest in Andreina's only daughter.

Andreina was on the verge of bursting her stays. Never in her wildest imaginings had she projected the possibility of such a manifestly brilliant match, even for her only jewel of a daughter.

"Well." She shrugged with an elaborate show of indifference. "It will have to depend on Ana Magdalena entirely, I have so little to say in the matter. Marriage has never entered her head, as far as I know."

"The gentleman would require no dowry. In fact, in light of your daughter's bravery he's willing to settle a small sum on the family by way of a reward."

Although she refrained from mentioning it to Andreina, she had informed her client of the family's penury, an especially persuasive selling point, given his middle age and his tendency to corpulence.

"Especially in his works of fiction, my client is much taken with heroism," she went on, "even in members of the female sex. Although between us, I believe he looks for endurance more than actual bravery in a wife. . . ."

"What kind of endurance, may I ask?"

"My client has the sad misfortune of being a widower three times over."

"Then he's not exactly fresh!"

"My client is a man in the full glory of his prime," Doña Eduviges asserted with a rapier dart of her tongue. "He is a man whom better-situated women would give their very reputations to attract. It is a very great honor that he has delegated me to negotiate for the hand of your daughter. But hadn't we perhaps better call the young lady herself to place the matter squarely before her attention?"

Andreina stood up to ring the servants' bell. Berta came running, wiping her suet-greased hands on her apron.

"Bring Ana Magdalena here this instant."

"But she's stirring the soap," blurted Berta.

"Tell her to get out of the kitchen at once. And bring us some tea while you're at it."

Andreina grinned sheepishly. "The things they teach them in the convent!" And she threw up her hands in mock dismay.

When she entered at last, Ana Magdalena found the geometrical center of the moth-eaten parlor rug to go down in a deep and becoming curtsy.

"Oh, no need to put on the dog with me, my dear. Get up at once. Your mother and I have a fabulous proposition to discuss with you. How would you like to marry the foremost writer of his generation, the man who —"

"Marry?" She appealed to Andreina. "You want me to marry? I can hardly think of a single reason why I should. Can you?"

"Just listen, my darling, to what Doña Eduviges has to say."

Later, when they were alone, Andreina wasted no time pointing out the distinct advantage of the match. "What other suitor would require no dowry?" she wanted to know.

"That's because he's probably mortician's bait." Ana Magdalena broke into tears. "I don't want to marry some moribund old tyrant. I want the Ballado boy, someone with round strong arms, small, hard, perky little hips, and a stomach sleek and furrowed like an animal's. I want a man who won't look like a calamity dancing the tango."

"The tango is a dance for riffraff, my dear, and the poor Ballados are one step up from scum. Besides, there's something Doña Eduviges didn't tell you." She lowered her voice for effect. "He's willing to settle a small sum on the family." Andreina saw no compelling reason to let Ana Magdalena know that the settlement was to be awarded explicitly for her daughter's bravery, nor did she think it relevant to mention that it amounted to the considerable sum of fifty thousand escudos.

Ana Magdalena eyed her mother in a completely new and comprehending light. "You mean ... ?"

"Our troubles are over," breathed Andreina.

And it was a good thing, too. Because when it was finally ready, Berta took the soap to market, and no one bought a single cake.

Andreina never stopped marveling at how she preserved her calm in the face of Ana Magdalena's startling revelations. Somewhere — goodness knew how — her daughter must have learned about things like overhead. Somehow she had picked up the intricacies of the tango, that infernal dance that His Excellency the archbishop of Lima and the Vatican itself had strictly condemned as the dance of Satan.

It seemed to her she actually saw her daughter's lips curl in a hellish smile, revealing white and perfect and predatory teeth between lips that glowed a diabolical shade of scarlet; and in the toss of her daughter's willful head, Andreina actually believed she saw the perverse and dyed ringlets of a flapper's bob.

But it was the mention of the Ballados that most put the fear of scandal into Andreina's heart. How could it possibly have happened that her daughter, carefully sheltered from the slightest exposure to any questionable influences, supervised day and night by the unflagging vigilance of the convent sisters, could have come into even the slightest contact with *anyone* of the Ballado clan, let alone the sole surviving son?

There was no way she could have known of the weekly laundering expeditions organized by the good sisters themselves, who delivered their charges to the riverbank, there to slap their linens on the river stones and watch the river traffic as they slapped.

There was no way she could have followed Ana Magdalena's eyes as she first observed Sergio Ballado cast off in his peeling boat; or listened with Ana Magdalena's ears, as week after week she learned to distinguish the sound of Sergio Ballado's outboard long before his skiff hove into view; or felt Ana Magdalena's heat as the blood suffused her cheeks with a rosy, incandescent glow, a glow that was not lost on Sergio Ballado.

But there was one thing that stood out very clearly: Ana Magdalena must marry, and she must marry quickly to avert any further contamination. And, now that opportunity had miraculously offered itself, she would marry well.

III

Within a week Doña Eduviges reappeared, this time accompanied by an advocate, a scrawny little man who sat tentatively on the edge of his chair affecting the fashion of a bygone age, a faded black suit that hovered high above his neck and shoulders as though, like a beetle, he wore a gigantic carapace. Ana Magdalena was allowed to observe the proceedings from the opposite side of the parlor but to say nothing. With great solemnity, they unfurled the marriage contract on the dusty surface of the rosewood piano, there being no table large enough.

Doña Eduviges, with the help of her tiny gold-rimmed glasses, began to review the parchment clause by clause.

"Just a moment," interrupted the advocate in a voice as grating as a cicada's, "where is the subject father of the subject bride-to-be?"

Andreina opened her mouth, but before she could respond, the cicada cut her short.

"The father of the subject bride must give his consent unless there are seriously mitigating circumstances, in which case his approval may be waived. Otherwise, I regret to say, the contract is null and void."

Andreina took a deep breath, but before she could formulate a word, Ana Magdalena spoke up.

"Your excellency," she addressed the cicada, "what exactly do you think a father is —"

"My dear young lady, that is a matter of conjecture. This is not the time or the occasion to delve into questionable matters —"

"— because if it happens to be someone —"

"Quiet!" barked Andreina. "You have gone quite far enough.

I'm sure Doña Eduviges can supply the proper 'mitigating circumstances' to explain why Hercules Figueroa da Cunha had to be absent today."

"Because he's a rakehell and a ne'er-do-well," averred Doña Eduviges matter-of-factly, "and the bride *and* the contract are better off without him. And now can we proceed?" Doña Eduviges licked the tip of her unsuspecting nose with a rapier thrust of her tongue. She began to read.

"The bride is to make herself available at the pleasure of her husband to listen at any hour to the reading of his manuscripts.

"The bride is to keep a strict accounting of all household expenses. Any sums that are not accounted for must be replenished from her own pocket.

"The bride is to present medical proof of her virginity.

"The bride is to prepare a trousseau consisting of —" Here she listed over one hundred and four items of essential linen.

"The bride is to allow her husband periodic conjugal rights.

"The bride is to provide entertainment for her husband's friends and colleagues on immediate demand, with displays of food and drink appropriate to his prestige and position.

"The bride is to be permitted two days a month of celibacy for the exercise of her monthly periods.

"Any and all household servants are to be hired at the sole and singular pleasure of the groom, although they will be placed under the constant and vigilant supervision of the bride.

"The bride is to live at all times in apartments prepared for her and at her sole disposition, but in the domicile of her husband.

"In consideration of each and every of the above terms, the bride is to be found acceptable without any exchange of sums normally associated with a dowry."

Doña Eduviges came to the end of the recitation. The advocate handed Andreina the pen.

"Wait."

Aghast, all three turned to stare at Ana Magdalena.

"I don't agree to any of this."

"But you really have nothing to say in the matter," observed Andreina pointedly.

"I have everything to say."

The advocate shifted uncomfortably in his oversize suit. Never in his more than fifty years of adjudicating marital contracts and disputes had he ever observed behavior remotely resembling this upstart display. A sickly smile played about his ashen lips.

"But, my *dear* young lady, it's the standard contract. It isn't customary —"

"It's my virginity you're disposing of so 'customarily,' and I'll present whatever proof of it I please. And to whom I please."

Doña Eduviges interjected, "It's a *superb* contract, my dear. Your mother and I have spent a great deal of time going over it already."

Andreina appealed to her daughter. "It seems a shame to argue over a single and after all rather insignificant point —"

"The point is far from insignificant, Mother."

"Yes, yes, of course, but Doña Eduviges must know. Isn't there a way you could ... isn't there some way ... a more ... *fluid* ... wording could be found?"

Doña Eduviges sucked moodily on her pen. "Very well," she muttered between clenched teeth, "the bride is to provide evidence of her own choosing in proof of her clear and unimpeded virginity."

"Oh, yes, that's much, much better!" sighed Andreina. She eyed Ana Magdalena with a steely look.

"He's probably too busy to notice the change in wording, anyway," remarked Doña Eduviges as she passed the pen to Andreina.

"And now the time has come," announced Doña Eduviges, rolling up the contract on the rosewood piano, "to reveal to you ladies the identity of my client. However, he appears to have made a most unusual request. He requires that both the young lady and her mother be ready at half past eight this evening to accept the convenience of his carriage and the service of his footman to be conducted as his personal guests. He would like to keep his identity a surprise until he introduces himself to you this evening in the ambience of his private literary salon."

Andreina clapped her hands. "Oh my, oh my, oh my, his very own private literary salon! What a singular delight!" She moistened her lips in happy anticipation, but when she turned toward her daughter, she met Ana Magdalena's glassy stare.

"Come, come," Andreina said. "Anyone can cultivate a love of literature. And it's never too late to start."

When Ana Magdalena picked over her meager lunch of dandelion greens, Andreina hardly gave it a thought. It was only after the siesta, when she woke with a headache in her canopied bed with the painted cherubs all around, unable for a moment to recognize exactly where she was, or who she was, or what time of the day or night it might be, that Andreina succumbed to a vague feeling of unease.

Rising, she went directly to Ana Magdalena's room.

"Child," she called softly, "are you awake?"

There was no response. She knocked softly.

"Child? Child, are you up?"

She did not let the silence alarm her. She simply tried turning the knob. To her relief, it gave easily, but instantly the door caught on some obstacle. It refused to budge no matter how vigorously she shook it. "Ana Magdalena!" Andreina tried to shout. No sound came. Something was choking her. Her heart drummed like the hooves of an escaped stallion. She ran down the corridor to the kitchen door. She flung it open. She ran to the bedroom side of the house. She caught sight of the open casement. As she came abreast, she already knew what she would see. She read the signs: the footprint in the earth, the chair placed against the sill, and in the dark recesses of the room, the chair rail braced against the door. She stood there silently, contemplating the window of her calamity. Her darling daughter, the precious jewel she had guarded from all and every danger, had fled.

She found herself vaguely drifting from room to room and through the patio as if she were looking for something. She investigated the dusty storerooms behind the kitchen. The house seemed to breathe with a foreboding silence as if she were caught in the invisible jaws of a vast and cosmic animal, unable to move or run.

"Ana Magdalena." Her sobs echoed in the empty rooms. But there was no response. She went outside to the shed that stood behind the house, where Berta, her servant, had strung her humble hammock. Moving with the trancelike gait of a somnambulist, she reentered the house and, passing through the corridor past the parlor, opened the porter's door. She stood just beyond the threshold imagining she would see Ana Magdalena approaching along the street outside. But it was still the hour of the siesta, and the street was hot, dusty, and deserted. As if in a dream, she reentered and shut the door. And it was as if, in that moment, she closed the door on her life, on the years she had patiently waited for her no-good husband to return from the last of his Lotharian trysts, on the years she had sat at the window, waiting for her daughter's stint in the convent to come to an end. She turned to face the invading monster of her loneliness. She found herself at last in the room with the canopied bed and the rosy polychrome cherubs trumpeting above the headboard in silent and ironic virtuosity, and she threw herself sobbing on the hard and loveless mattress of her bed.

It was there Berta found her when, at a quarter to six, she had finished heating the bathwater.

"Señora, Señora, get up at once. There's not a moment to lose. There's just time to get dressed. Don't you have to be ready at a quarter past eight?"

"Berta, Berta," she sobbed all over again, "it's the young mistress!"

"The young mistress? What happened?"

"She's gone!"

Anyone less bent on the joys of literary anticipation could have foreseen very plainly that matters would have to take a complicated turn, but the sudden invitation to such an august gathering had thrown Andreina into a giddy panic. Her only thought was what to wear to make the most irreproachable and at the same time stunning entrance of the evening. The floor of her room was strewn with shawls and high-heeled shoes and beaded evening bags and feather boas, heirlooms from her dear departed mother and sisters, all waiting in mothballs to emerge for just such an occasion, and the sight of all this bygone splendor set her to sobbing once again.

"Señora, señora, it's terrible!" Berta began to wring her hands. "We must do something!"

"Berta, there's nothing to be done. Dear God, my sweet little girl has disappeared."

"She must have gone *somewhere.* . . ."

"Yes, but *where?*" Suddenly the flow of Andreina's tears came to a halt.

Berta stood poised on the tips of her toes, ready to spring into action. "Señora has thought of something, hasn't she?"

And indeed, Andreina *had* thought of something. She had thought of Sergio Ballado, and the thought set her to weeping uncontrollably.

Ana Magdalena had never liked dandelion salad. She found it too tough and too bitter for her delicate and discriminating palate. It was not meant for human consumption, particularly not for humans who were troubled. Even in normal times, she believed dandelions were for cattle to graze on, to bring up repeatedly from one stomach or other. She picked over leaf after leaf. Over and over Aurora Constancia's advice haunted her: *You don't have to like him just because you're married to him. Just go through the motions. After you're married, things get more interesting. You have money to spend, a carriage. . . .* And all the time she could see the muscles of Sergio Ballado writhing under his glistening, sunburned skin. She remembered the sound of her own voice. It was a new sound, one with which she had only now become acquainted. *It's my virginity, and I'll present proof of it as I please. And to whom I please.*

By the time Ana Magdalena rose from the table, her dandelions had hardly been touched, but a new and shining resolve had come to visit her restive heart. She retired to her room for the siesta and carefully shut the door. Bracing a chair against the knob, she set about shedding her clothes. Off came the pinafore and the oppressively plain brown frock, off came the cotton chemise, down came the slip and the drawers with their demure lace cuffs. Ana Magdalena stood coolly surveying herself before the massive antique mirror of the armoire. She placed her hands beneath the small white doves of her breasts. She raised them ever so slightly toward the glass. At once, her nipples sprang to life. They stood proud, like fat, rosy little beaks eagerly testing the air. She passed her hands over the rounding contours of her belly. She raised her arms to exult in the dense tufts of thick black hair that marked her body's secret hollows. Slowly she turned her back, craning her neck to survey the high and blushing rotundities of her cheeks, and to admire the two provocative dimples that nestled at the base of her spine.

Ana Magdalena had never really examined herself naked. It was a new sensation, one that required no effort to get used to, but it left her breathless and slightly dizzy. Yet she knew there was little time just now for any dreamy self-indulgence. She flung open the armoire and retrieved a silk chemise, which she quickly threw over her head. She found a matching pair of lacy silk drawers of a semitransparency that betrayed the contours of her loveliness to shadowy advantage. Over these she raised the wine-dark silk velvet dress, the one she had worn to Aurora Constancia's wedding. It was a dress cut on the bias so cunningly that it molded itself to every sinew, every curve. She closed the armoire once again. She turned slowly to gauge the effect. She was not displeased. In a small beaded purse, she stuffed only the barest essentials: a handkerchief and a mirror. She picked up a pair of high-heeled slippers. She was ready. Carefully she opened the window casement. She stood on a chair to ease herself over the sill and quietly let herself down into the flower bed below. She brushed the dirt from her bare feet, and slipped into the shoes.

The way to the river, even in this modern day, is a long one, although now, of course, the roads are paved. But in those days, the ruts and cobbles were ill-suited to a fine pair of silken lady's slippers. By the time Ana Magdalena reached the river's edge she was carrying the heels of both shoes in her hand (they would not fit into her tiny beaded purse). She was dying of thirst, but she dared not cup her hands at the water's edge (the water was still fresh in those days, and you could see the river bottom) because she knew that water leaves indelible marks on silk velvet, and she wanted to look her best.

Every step of the way, she had imagined the scene as she thought it would take place. She would arrive flushed and breathless on the half-rotted dock where Sergio Ballado berthed his little boat. And luck would be with her. He would just be putting in. She would hail him.

"Sergio, Sergio!" The wind would carry her call to him like a flight of evening doves. He would wave his recognition, his great joy at seeing her. She would leap onto the tiny dock and, picking her way carefully so as to avoid catching her heels, she would nevertheless manage to run toward him breathlessly, her long dark ringlets flying in the wind. She would come abreast of him. . . .

Here the scene repeatedly had a way of breaking down, because in reality, although Ana Magdalena and Sergio Ballado had exchanged what could be described as heated looks, they had as yet exchanged no words.

Ana Magdalena would walk back slowly along the pier and start again. She would hoist herself sedately onto the dock, taking care not to snag her velvet frock on the nails of the pilings. She would move in a stately but compelling fashion toward the slip where Ballado berthed his boat. He was busying himself at first, appearing not to notice either her or her remarkable getup, but as she walked the interminable stretch of the pier, his attention would be caught by her undulating gait and by the great coils of her black luxuriant hair tousled by the wind, and as she came nearer, the clinging innuendo of the wine-red velvet dress would rivet his poor doomed attention. He would know at once the purpose of this visit. He would place his capable, rough, seafaring hands on the slight, ridged bones of her hips.

"Come below," he would whisper hoarsely.

"I have come to talk. . . ."

"Come below," he would insist in his urgent baritone as he lifted the hatch.

But here the scene would take a most uncomfortable turn. Just as he was taking away her purse to lay it on the bulkhead, she would find herself blurting out, "Marry me. You *must* marry me straightaway."

His left eyebrow would arch clear to his hairline.

"My dear, for what we are about to do, we need neither priest nor prayers."

"They're going to marry me, don't you see," she would plead piteously, "they're going to marry me to some fat old man, someone I don't even know, someone who . . ."

But obstinately bent on his purpose, Sergio Ballado would remove the soft silken slippers. . . .

And here the scene broke down altogether, because Ana Magdalena's foot caught on a stone, and this was the place where the first of the fragile heels broke off its slipper.

She began again. She found a ladder to step onto the dock. She approached the berth at a businesslike clip, limping, however, in one heel-less shoe. Sergio Ballado was at work on his boat. . . .

"Sergio Ballado?" she would intone with the unblushing assurance of knowing what she was about to do.

"That's me," he would reply.

(*Idiot,* she would think, *of course, I know it's you* — but instead she would smile in a mysterious but engaging way.)

"May I sit down?"

"Of course." He would dust off an oilskin cushion before placing it on the prow. He would extend a square, capable brown hand to her. She would jump down into the skiff and allow herself to be conducted to the seat he had prepared for her.

"My name is Ana Magdalena Arzate de Figueroa. I have come to you for help."

And she would outline the nature of the unfortunate circumstances in which she found herself. She would describe what little she knew of the groom. "He's going to *read* to me!" she would blurt. "I despise reading. And I *loathe* reading out loud. Holy Mother, what am I going to do?"

And she would appeal to him silently, with enormous, limpid eyes, waiting for him to have the next word.

"I could ferry you downriver — perhaps as far as Belém."

(*No, no, imbecile,* she would think, *I don't want to hire you.*) But keeping her silence, she would bow her head.

At last, he would ask, "Did you have something else in mind?"

And she would lift her great liquid eyes to his. "Marry me." Her chin would begin to tremble. "Marry me. Please. It's you I want." And she would set to weeping softly. . . .

It was, so far at least, the scene that seemed to be the most satisfactory. He would bend toward her with just the right mix of the rough and the smooth. He would reach for her face. He would brush her eyes with his lips, and at last, his mouth would find hers. . . .

The scene might have worked to perfection, but it was here that Ana Magdalena's other heel became wedged between two cobblestones and snapped off in the road. But it hardly mattered. She knew she was nearly there. Already she could smell the river. She could feel the air currents that told her she didn't have far to go.

"Wait! Señora, I think I hear something!" Berta strained to hear.

The raging torrent of Andreina's tears dried up at once. She sat bolt upright in her rumpled bed. And indeed, they *did* hear something. Unmistakably. Someone was moving about in the house. They could hear the distinct sound of an armoire door being yanked open.

"It's her," exclaimed Berta.

"It's she!" wailed Andreina vaulting out of bed in her *déshabillé* and scurrying to open her bedroom door. Hercules Figueroa da Cunha slammed the armoire shut. Face livid, he approached Andreina.

"Don't I have a stack of boiled shirts somewhere? Where are they? I thought I left them in the drawer. Could you have sold them to some peddler in the street?"

"Shirts!" shrilled Andreina, throwing her hands high in outrage. "Boiled shirts is all you can think of when your daughter's virtue is at stake! Even now, it may be too late! She's run off with that Ballado fellow, and she's contracted to marry someone else!"

At once her absentee husband became all attention.

"Ballado? Did I hear *Ballado?*" In a frenzy, Hercules hurled himself across the courtyard. He yanked the porter's door clear off its hinges.

One after the other, he wrenched the arms of the two women who sat outside sunk in the plushy, tufted backseat of his borrowed Victoria and hurled them, squawking like chickens, into the street.

"Dolt!" he raged at the coachman as he pushed him off the seat, "give me that whip. And see to these ladies if you've nothing better to do."

Andreina and her servant kept enough presence of mind to follow him at a safe distance. They stood in the doorway staring at the scene being played out in the street.

The Victoria lurched forward. The horse, galvanized by the sharp sting of the whip, leapt ahead, sending up a swirling cloud of dust. Almost at once, the carriage swerved and, tipping dangerously on two wheels, sideswiped the corner house before careening out of sight.

The coachman pulled himself up and dusted off his injured grandeur. He turned to the women in their picture hats.

"Whores," he spat. "*Putas, y hijas de putas!*" and he made a great show of stalking off, dignity intact.

But the two ladies were not to be outdone. Ceremoniously, in a dreamy minuet, they helped each other up, lending one another a helpful arm or hand, as the need might be. Solemnly, they dusted each other off, readjusted each other's clothes, redraped their boas with great and patrician majesty, and revised the rakish tilt of their frilly picture hats.

" 'Dolt, see to these *ladies* if you've nothing better to do!' " One of them mimicked Hercules Figueroa da Cunha.

" '*Puta,* '" mocked the other in a campy falsetto, "*puta! Y hija de puta!*"

"*Chocha de plata!*" sneered the first.

"*Coño de oro!*" crowed the second, and with that master stroke both ladies doubled over, howling with laughter until the tears streamed down their heavily rouged cheeks.

Mistress and servant watched them stagger down the street arm in arm, whinnying and neighing. Berta shook her head disapprovingly. "Such disrespect to the master," she whispered. But before she could gauge her mistress's reaction, Andreina was seized with an alarming sensation, one she had never before experienced. Her head arched backward. Something dark and alien hemorrhaged from her mouth. She knew she must be laughing. She heard the echoes smash like waves on the harsh and sterile walls of room after room, crescendoing and eddying and crescendoing again, until the whole house rang with it.

She leaned, spent, against the doorpost. Recovered at last, she propped the door shut on its broken hinges. "*Putamadre,*" she said, "we'll have to see to this tomorrow for certain. *Mañana por seguro.*"

Hercules reined in the Victoria outside the Barco de Oro.

"Where's Ballado?" he shouted.

"Ballado?" Slapping his trouser leg with his serviette, the waiter disappeared inside the dark recesses of the waterfront bar. At last the bartender emerged.

"Ballado's gone. Downriver. I think he sold his boat."

"Downriver? Where?"

The bartender shrugged. "Ask on the docks. Maybe someone there can tell you."

Hercules whipped the horse, although its coat was already flecked with lather. But when he arrived at the dock, he decided he didn't want to ask anyone anything because sitting on the pier, wearing a clinging wine-dark silk velvet dress, dangling her heel-less shoes over the water, he beheld a woman more captivating, more enticing than any on whom he might ever have laid a passing stare. Carelessly, he hitched the reins on a convenient bollard. He swaggered slowly and deliberately to where he could stand and look directly up into her exquisite face. He saw that she was crying. Ceremoniously he removed his hat.

"*Buenas tardes!*" he greeted her in a freshly acquired baritone. "The coach is waiting. Can I coax the luscious lady for a ride?"

He was unprepared for her reply.

"Father!" she exclaimed, aghast, as she leapt to her feet.

But he was quicker than she was. He blocked her path as she ran toward the end of the pier. He caught her in midair as she jumped. Then he carried her, kicking and screaming and pummeling him all the length of the pier and onto the street until at last he thrust her into the carriage.

"Get in" was all he had breath left in him to say.

Then very methodically, he shut the carriage door behind them.

Berta applied the pumice stone to Andreina's knees and elbows until they glowed.

"Enough. Get me the towel." Andreina stood up in the water. "We'll see. If she isn't here by eight, I'll leave without her. I'll say she had a headache."

Berta busied herself laying out fresh underwear.

"Not that!" snapped Andreina. "I'll wear black. It's only proper, and tonight propriety is our strongest suit."

She seemed positively carefree as Berta rubbed her back dry.

"Señora thinks she'll turn up?"

"Of course she'll turn up. Hercules never had any trouble finding a woman. I don't expect things will change now. But where he finds her is another matter."

And at that very moment, true to her prediction, the porter's door crashed as someone kicked it open. Not ten seconds later Hercules stood in the doorway of his wife's bedroom, holding Ana Magdalena trussed up like a chicken in his arms.

"Madam," he said to her, "did you by any chance misplace a daughter?" He dropped Ana Magdalena onto his wife's canopied bed. "Try not to be so careless next time," he growled as he strode out the door.

Andreina threw herself on her daughter. "Oh, my darling child, you're just in time! The bathwater's still warm. Berta will lay out your clothes."

She couldn't understand why all Ana Magdalena wanted to do was sob and sob.

"Berta, help me untie her." But already Berta's capable fingers were busily at work struggling with one knot after another.

"He left," sobbed Ana Magdalena.

"There, there," her mother murmured in a commiserating tone.

"He left without telling me!" Ana Magdalena yielded to choking paroxysms of grief. "He left without telling me a thing!"

Even before Andreina saw the carriage arrive punctually at a quarter past eight, she had already guessed the identity of Ana Magdalena's mysteriously retiring suitor. But if there was any doubt left, the sight of the carriage with its gilded lanterns and its garlands of cherubs bearing the benevolent grains and benign fruits of the season dispelled it altogether. It was none other than the excursion vehicle of the great family Orgaz.

"Child," she urged her weeping daughter, "come and see." She persuaded Ana Magdalena to dry her tears and blow her nose before leading her to the window fronting the street.

"Look, isn't it magnificent?"

But Ana Magdalena had no mind just yet for magnificence. She could only marvel that her velvet dress had sustained no permanent damage from the flow of her tears. She was just beginning to reflect that from an ill wind there may blow some good and that, had her father not caught her in midair, swimming would most certainly have ruined the dress altogether.

"It will be a brilliant soirée, one we can neither of us afford to miss. Berta has even reheated the bath water for you. Let's not disappoint her."

Passively, Ana Magdalena allowed her mother to remove her clothes. She kicked her ankles free of her silken drawers.

"My, my," her mother mused, half to herself, "you are really becoming quite the young lady. Quick, the carriage is waiting. Into the bath!"

Andreina wouldn't hear of letting Berta soap Ana Magdalena. Instead, she gave her whispered instructions about laying out Ana Magdalena's clothes.

"It's useless," lamented Ana Magdalena. "I can't go with eyes like these. They're all red and swollen. Everyone will see."

"I've thought of everything, my dear," Andreina reassured her. "We're wearing mourning: formal dresses, tocques. I even found those adorable little crepe veils we wore when your dear Aunt Josefa died. There's no problem at all. And if anyone asks, we'll say there's been a death in the family."

IV

Already in those days, particularly in Malyerba, time had begun to show a remarkable plasticity. Like putty, it could expand or contract. It could ball itself into a knot or, equally, stretch out in long, elastic strings, metaphorically speaking. It was perhaps in the knowledge of the havoc these ladies would make of punctuality that Ana Magdalena's suitor had insisted on lending them the service of his own footman, and on placing his very imposing carriage at their disposition.

All the same, no one was particularly surprised when two mysterious, heavily veiled ladies, dressed solemnly in black, entered the salon in which their host's literary soirée was already coming to a close. Heads turned briefly to satisfy fleeting curiosities, but the matter under discussion was far too riveting to allow a more significant flight of attention. Ana Magdalena and her mother (for it was they) tiptoed past the bombé ormolu chest on which the gentlemen had deposited the formal silk top hats that were still then de rigueur at serious literary gatherings of this kind, and, as inconspicuously as possible, took their seats.

The substance of the discussion escaped them at first, but as their eyes became accustomed to the dim light of the parlor, so their comprehension quickened.

"Lacunae? *Lacunae?*" a red-faced gentleman with muttonchop whiskers was ferociously repeating. "What kind of esoteric drivel is *that?* Lacunae!"

"Ignorance, my friend, favors the unprepared mind," observed a thin, lacrimose, sallow-complected Jose Asunción Silva, who turned out to be a poet. "The serious man of letters has a solemn obligation to leave lacunae to permit his reader to penetrate —"

"Penetrate! *Penetrate!*" crowed the muttonchopped gentleman. "We should all like to penetrate!"

"Gentlemen, gentlemen, there are ladies present!" remonstrated their host, who was none other than the illustrious Federico Orgaz y Orgaz himself.

Heads turned. The room was stifling. Ana Magdalena and her mother took advantage of the momentary lapse of literary decorum to crane their necks.

"There seem to be nothing but men," remarked Andreina, agitating her fan.

"No," replied Ana Magdalena. "I see two women —"

"Where?"

"In the last row. In mourning."

"Perhaps they, too, sustained a death in the family!" Andreina slyly whispered from behind her fan. But the ladies couldn't help observing that the male literateurs were also, all of them, in black formal dress, prompting them to speculate that mourning must be the attire appropriate to such elevated gatherings.

The discussion resumed. "Indeed, our great Machado de Assis, Twain, even the magnificent Laurence Sterne himself, believed in unorthodox digressions. Sterne even leaves us a marbled page, a *blank* page —"

"Nonsense," growled the celebrated Federico Orgaz y Orgaz, "all of you are missing the point. Twain, Sterne — gringos! Children of dust! What can anglos know of our great literary tradition handed down from generation to generation by our great and illustrious Hispanic forebears? I say to hell with white spaces! Fabulation! Fabulation is what is needed, the endless and obsessive elaboration of the narrative line to form labyrinthine arabesques, polyhedrons, dodecahedrons of astonishing and dizzying complexity. In my narrative —"

"In your narrative, no one can follow anything," grumbled the muttonchopped gentlemen (in whom, had the ladies had more than a passing knowledge of literature, they would have recognized the famous Brazilian journalist, Euclides da Cunha, the first [after John of Patmos] to author *The End of the World*). "You practice one prevarication after another. It's a wonder there's anyone left patient enough to turn the pages."

"Evidently, my friend, you must have turned at least a few of them yourself," remarked Federico Orgaz with considerable hauteur. "My narrative returns literature to its ancient source in the great oral tradition, to the brilliant and mesmerizing fabulation of the Arabs."

"Arabs? *Arabs?*" piped up the matinee idol novelist and perennial presidential also-ran, Vacio-Llares, "if not for the great edict of 1492, our great Catholic monarchs would have been forced to harbor in their breasts the cultural nemesis, the scourge of Spain, Jews and Arabs. Arabs and Jews! Our culture would have succumbed like the great Spanish peninsula to a devastating and irreversible desertification, to be reduced to the very decadence of a putrid Iberian Constantinople, a cesspool of verbal corruption and linguistic dissipation such as the world has never seen —"

"Wait!"

"Nonsense!"

"No, no. Don't interrupt!"

The gentlemen were on the verge, it seemed, of coming to literary blows. The heat was so unbearable Ana Magdalena wanted to tear off her clothes.

"If the critics are able to develop a following for the new literature, then *I* say —"   .

"The critics be damned!"

"*Critics?* Did I hear you say *critics?* My friend," proclaimed Federico Orgaz y Orgaz, "critics don't matter. I crunch critics for breakfast," he shouted. "*They* haven't survived. *I* have!" He jabbed at his chest with a stubby thumb.

Above the thunderous applause, Andreina almost had to shout. "Isn't he *magnificent?*"

"Which one?"

"Your suitor, dear child, Federico Orgaz y Orgaz, the illustrious and *sole surviving descendant* of the famous elongated and moribund Conde Orgaz, the one who had the great and singular honor of sitting on his deathbed for our incomparable El Greco himself."

Ana Magdalena was beginning to have trouble breathing. Even her mother, chameleonlike, began to take on the rarefied color of their literary surroundings. "Could we have some fresh air?" she gasped.

"Be patient, child. I think it's coming to an end."

And indeed, Federico Orgaz y Orgaz was elbowing his way toward the row in which they sat. He bowed formally. "A pleasure you ladies could attend." He bent over Ana Magdalena's hand. "And what a delight!"

"The honor is ours. May I present my daughter?"

"Ana Magdalena Arzate de Figueroa," murmured Ana Magdalena, curtsying sweetly. She noticed he had hair growing in his ears.

"Charming! Charming! Is it permissible to see what lovely face hides behind such a tantalizing veil?" and he lifted the heavy black crepe that shielded her eyes. The signs of grief he saw there momentarily threw him into some confusion. But Andreina was quick to interpose.

"We've had a death in the family. Our dear cousin Clotilda . . ."

"I'm terribly sorry."

"It was not unexpected, poor thing. She died in childbed giving birth to stillborn twins after a pregnancy so interminable they had become petrified inside her womb, imagine!"

"I seem to remember hearing something of the sort." He contemplated Ana Magdalena solemnly. He cupped her chin in an enormous, fleshy hand. "I'm sure such a lovely young lady doesn't always look so glum."

"Smile, child," her mother prompted. "Show Don Federico your marvelous teeth."

"You ought to be a lion tamer." Ana Magdalena smiled at him. She could actually picture him stuffed to bursting in the white silk trousers and black shako of a hussar, brandishing a chair.

"You wouldn't even need to snap the whip!"

The moment they were alone, Andreina clamped her daughter's wrist in a grip of iron.

"Don't you think you were a little forward, talking to a great man like that? You want to watch your step. Remember, a contract is no better than the parchment it's written on. I can't understand what you're thinking of. And while we're on the subject, who gave you permission to wear my dress?"

"What dress?"

"The wine-red velvet dress."

"I wore it to La Paz."

"Yes, but this isn't La Paz."

"I thought we were past that."

"You thought, you thought, did you? I like that! You thought of nothing but yourself, of your precious Ballado. Thank goodness he's gone. At least now we can see to the wedding in peace."

But there was to be little peace, as it turned out. Early the following morning, the Orgaz coach returned choked nearly to bursting with a profusion of floral decorations. Federico Orgaz y Orgaz had outdone himself. It required five extravagantly liveried Chinese footmen to carry them inside. Already the patio was filled to overflowing.

"My God," moaned Andreina, tearing at her hair, "where will we put them all?" But her question was mainly rhetorical. The only room left was the parlor. Cachepots and planters occupied every available shelf, every surface, and the parlor rug was cluttered with them. Once the footmen had finished discharging their load, they somersaulted backward all the way to where the coach was waiting and, still bowing, they drove off.

Andreina was on the verge of shutting the porter's door, when she remembered the hinges had snapped. "*Putamadre,*" she said, bemused, "we'll have to see to this. Tomorrow ... *mañana por seguro.*"

Ana Magdalena was witness to none of this early-morning pageantry. In her narrow virgin's bed, she slept the sleep of young girls whose hearts are in a state of total if temporary collapse. It was nearly noon when she awoke. She stretched her lovely white arms in honor of the morning.

The entire house smelled of flowers.

"What's that I smell?" she exclaimed as she leapt out of bed. She stood barefoot, shivering in the parlor doorway.

"Good heavens," she called to Andreina, "what's this? Some new scheme you're dreaming up?"

Andreina came running. "Child, you're awake. Don't stand there barefoot. You'll catch cold."

"Are we opening a botanical garden? Where did all this come from?"

"From your suitor, my dear, from the great man himself. It appears he's quite taken with you and your cheeky remarks."

Indeed, reflected Ana Magdalena, they were the kind of flowers a lion tamer might favor: huge protea, suggestively phallic anthuria, enormous, fleshy succulents, a menacing Venus Flytrap Gigantea that filled an entire corner of the parlor, threatening to consume all who came near it. Goodness knew to what prodigious lengths he must have gone to bring such a jungle within their four walls.

Orgaz y Orgaz lost no time presenting himself on the heels of his triumph. The very next morning he sent a footman with his card on a silver salver requesting the pleasure of Ana Magdalena's company if he were to be granted permission to call.

In those days it was customary for an affianced couple to meet, but only in the presence of a *dueña,* a role normally undertaken by the matchmaker herself. Doña Eduviges was eager to assume her responsibility at once. Already at the appointed hour she had taken up her position in a cramped corner of the parlor, under an enormous stag's horn fern. From where she crouched, she could hardly observe the fiancés, concealed as they were behind three potted palms, but the click of her knitting needles was enough. She knew they could hear her, they knew she was there.

Federico raised Ana Magdalena's hand to his lips. "Such tiny little hands and feet," he exclaimed admiringly. "How did you like our soirée?"

"It was . . . it was . . ." Ana Magdalena seemed at a loss for words. ". . . rather boring."

"Then you are not a devotee of literature. What a shame!"

"Oh, literature is fine as long as you don't have to read it."

"That's exactly why I write!" he confided with great solemnity.

"Because you don't like reading?"

"Because I find I prefer reading whatever I write to anything written by anyone else! Now take your mother, for example. Your mother, like me, is something of a fabulist."

"She is?"

"Certainly! That story about the stone twins — she got that from me, from my prize-winning oeuvre, *A Retroactive Death.*"

"Maybe you got the idea because somewhere you heard the story of my Aunt Clotilda."

Federico displayed some signs of annoyance. He patted her hand. "On the other hand, you, my dear, are a metaphorist."

"I am?"

"Yes. You like metaphor."

"I do?"

"Yes."

Ana Magdalena studied him uncertainly. "What is metaphor?"

"It's a comparison: one thing is like another."

"That's certainly true."

"No. A *specific* thing is like another *specific* thing."

"Such as?"

"Well, for example, I am like a lion tamer."

Ana Magdalena began to laugh. Federico immediately joined in. "But it's you. It's you, my dear, you're the lion tamer. And I'm just an old literary lion ready to give you a nice friendly paw." Federico growled and made a droll show of extending a fleshy hand before laying his grizzled head in her lap.

Doña Eduviges sensed things had gone quite far enough for a first encounter. She rapped on a wooden chair rail with her needles.

"Time's up, my doves! It's nine o'clock."

Shortly following the floral deliveries the bees began arriving. They arrived in twos and threes, inconspicuously at first, because the first were pilot bees, but within a day swarms of them had taken over the entire parlor. Ana Magdalena stood in the doorway, watching them in dismay as they feasted on the sticky pistils of the anthuria and the Venus Flytrap Gigantea. They were building their hives in the sagging springs of the upholstery, elaborating honeycombs in the festooned drapery valances and in the recesses of the ceiling joists, until there was no other solution — the entire room had to be closed off.

The invasion presented what could have been a serious impediment to the progress of the courtship. There was no other apartment suitable for a lovers' meeting, not in the Figueroa establishment, certainly, and no young lady in good standing ever entered the home of her husband-to-be. It was Doña Eduviges who hit upon the ingenious notion of placing Don Federico's magnificent excursion vehicle in the service of her client's courtship.

At first he required some encouragement. The idea was apparently not to his liking. Ana Magdalena speculated that perhaps he suffered from the considerable unease occasioned by motion sickness. But when she entered the carriage the next day, she found Federico sitting in the depths of the velvet cushions, a manuscript in hand. Strung about his neck on black elastic bands was a dowager's pair of reading glasses.

Ana Magdalena took her place. Doña Eduviges sat in the opposite plush velvet seat, this time knitting what appeared to be a scarf of interminable length that coiled and writhed about her like a snake. She affected not to stare at the lovers.

Federico raised his reading glasses to his nose. "The manuscript on which I am presently at work is titled — of course, you understand, this is completely confidential, you are not to breathe a word of it to anyone, especially not your mother — the manuscript is titled *The Seamstress Saved from Shipwreck*. It's about an unfortunate lass who has no means but her needle and her wits. Her climb to fortune and success finally lands her in the lap of the minister of the Bolivian navy!" He began reading in a very loud voice at an astonishing rate of speed. Doña Eduviges' needles clicked furiously. Prodded by their vehemence, the snake undulated alarmingly before coiling at her feet.

The heat in the carriage was unbearable. Ana Magdalena thought she would suffocate. She felt the nausea rising. "Please, could we have a little air?"

Federico glared at her. He rapped smartly on the coachman's window. "A little air for the lady," he commanded, almost without interrupting his reading.

The coachman lowered a window. Ana Magdalena couldn't help observing how good-looking he was, and she shifted her position so that from where she sat she could happily observe his calves. The streets were filled with people: peasants; footmen; servants; Indians struggling under their towering loads, dogtrotting through the thoroughfares, scurrying to the side of the road as their carriage passed to avoid its dusty onslaught.

"You're not listening," Federico Orgaz y Orgaz observed testily. He removed his reading glasses and rolled up the manuscript. It lay reproachful as a truncheon in his fist. They returned in a stony and sepulchral silence to deposit Ana Magdalena at her mother's house.

Doña Eduviges relaxed her professional aloofness to address herself in confidence to her client. "If, in the discharge of my duty, my presence in the coach in any way inhibits the gentleman in his pursuit of the lady, I shall be quite happy to join the coachman on the box." She did not find it necessary to add that from the driver's seat, she could observe the lovers perfectly.

The invasion of the bees had long since made the parlor uninhabitable. Mother and daughter sat at the kitchen table, where late into the night they labored to monogram all one hundred and four essential linens for Ana Magdalena's trousseau.

Ana Magdalena expressed some astonishment at her suitor's single-minded literary mood. Never at a loss to miss her opportunity, Andreina was quick to reply.

"Nonsense, my dear! He reads to you because he wants to impress you with his considerable achievements. He wants to reassure you that he is after all a man of substance and not some flibbertigibbet fly-by-night."

But privately, Andreina was sure that Federico was resorting to reading his manuscript out loud to cover his discomfiture at their having to meet in such close quarters with Doña Eduviges. And the more she thought about it, the more the explanation gave her satisfaction.

"You'll see," Ana Magdalena warned her. "Tomorrow Doña Eduviges won't even be there, and he'll be reading just the same."

And sure enough, the following day, she was not surprised to find Doña Eduviges costumed in a motoring cap and goggles — although later Andreina would remark that they were entirely inappropriate — sharing the driver's seat with the well-favored coachman. Her anxiety momentarily revived that her meeting with Federico might be less impersonal this time; but to her great reassurance, almost before she sat down, he was already placing his dowager's glasses on his olympian nose, about to resume reading to her. "Where we left off yesterday, the heroine, you remember, was . . ."

But as he read, her satisfaction gradually gave way to an incapacitating migraine.

"Federico," she said at last, "you don't mind if I call you Federico? I have a splitting headache. All morning I've been shelling peas!"

"Shelling peas!" he cried, dumbfounded. "Why, that's remarkable! That's exactly what my heroine is doing! On the very next page! I can't believe it! She's shelling peas!"

"Does she have a headache, too?" Ana Magdalena wanted to know.

He put down the manuscript. As he took hold of her hand, he affected a pout. "It's hard to imagine such pretty little hands shelling peas. You ought to be smoothing your ruffled lion's mane." He was about to touch her hand to his brow.

Just in time, there came a staccato drumming on the window pane. Doña Eduviges was staring down at them through her goggles. Again she gave the window a smart rap. In her estimation, things had gone far enough. They could hear her saying something horrible to the coachman. At once, to the growing dismay of her illustrious client, the coach made a sharp one hundred and eighty–degree turn in the middle of a teeming thoroughfare. Doña Eduviges leaned down. "Time for you lovebirds to go home," she shouted through the coachman's window.

At last it became apparent to Andreina that Federico intended to extend the sacred obligations of literature to include courtship itself. But Ana Magdalena's happy discovery — in that moment when Federico had raised her hand to his temple — that an equivocal gesture was almost sure to trigger Doña Eduviges' immediate disapproval, provided her with what she hoped might prove an effective discouragement.

The following day, she put her intuition to the test. She stepped into the coach and took her place at Federico's side. He raised her hand to his lips somewhat perfunctorily. She sat perfectly straight, hands folded in her lap waiting for him to begin. He busied himself rearranging and sorting out the pages he intended to read to her, while he adjusted his frumpy dowager's glasses and cleared his throat of an imposing amount of literary phlegm. At last he was ready.

Ana Magdalena waited for what she considered a decent interval, during which time she amused herself stealing a glance now and then at the coachman's shapely calves, and at the welter of life in the streets they passed. Then, slowly, she began to incline from her strictly vertical position until it seemed her forehead was about to come to rest on Federico's arm. Slowly, she raised a tiny hand just suggestively enough to trigger the obligatory tapping of Doña Eduviges on the handsome coachman's window before she ordered the carriage to reverse direction and head for home at once.

"What the devil!" exclaimed Federico, temporarily thrown off balance by the vehicle's gyrations. But if he was disconcerted, it was only momentary. He resumed his reading almost at once.

"Good God," moaned Andreina, clutching at her fob watch, "there's so much to do. If it weren't for the bees you could meet in the parlor, and put your hands to some kind of use while he insists on reading to you. I don't see how we can possibly have everything ready in time."

And indeed, fulfilling the linen clause was presenting serious difficulty. For her own trousseau, Andreina herself had received a chest full of Holland sheets expressly loomed for her in Brussels, where until recently it was still customary to make a respectable bed with lace-edged sheets the size and spread of a clipper ship's sails. She was now engaged in trimming them to more modern size, carefully removing the lace, which then had to be replaced and refitted with the kind of devilishly invisible stitches that cause blindness in dedicated seamstresses half her age. And there was little more than a month to go.

"These daily readings are eating us alive!" exclaimed Andreina. "There must be *some* way you could return from these interminable outings of yours a little bit sooner." She took a seam ripper to the lace.

"We mustn't forget to invite your friend Aurora Constancia to the wedding, and her dear husband what's his name —"

"Alejandro."

"Yes. But dear God! Where will we put them? The parlor is out of the question! We'll have to give them my bed, they'll love the canopy! I'll just sleep on the floor."

"But, Mother, Alejandro won't be coming."

"How do you know, dear child?"

"I know. Alejandro isn't coming." She refused to say more, but after a certain interval, time enough for mail to be exchanged, there came a teasing reply from Aurora Constancia, all dotted with her global little "i's." "Alejandro says he has pressing matters to attend to. Who she is, he refuses to say. So be sure you line me up a promising escort!"

"I told you, he won't be coming."

"What a pity. But it certainly makes the sleeping arrangements less complicated. We'll let Aurora have your room, and you can sleep with me."

"But I thought you liked to sleep till noon." Ana Magdalena's expression was full of daughterly concern.

"Very well, *I'll* take your bed. She'll have to bunk with you."

It was because of Andreina's thoughtless impatience that Ana Magdalena began reducing the time preceding her threatened familiarities to a barely decent interval. The day came when no sooner had Federico Orgaz y Orgaz begun to read than the coach came to an abrupt and wrenching halt, dislodging his reading glasses from their position on his nose.

Federico was not happy. He opened the coach door. "Stop!" he said. He got down into the street. From where Ana Magdalena sat, she could observe what happened next.

"Get down," he ordered Doña Eduviges.

But Doña Eduviges was apparently not displaying any intention of giving up her seat.

"Get down," he repeated.

"It is my sacred duty —"

"I don't care how sacred is your duty. Get down at once. You are a meddlesome, interfering, miserable old harpy, and the sooner you get down, the better for you. Now will you step down or do I have to commit the grave public indignity of fetching you down myself?"

Doña Eduviges's face turned to stone.

"I'm warning you," said Federico. His expression was grim.

"One, two —" At the count of three, he mounted the coachman's ladder, and unceremoniously taking hold of Doña Eduviges' person, he hauled her to the ground.

"You'll pay for this, *pendejo!*" she hissed. "No one, no matter how exalted, ever manhandles Doña Eduviges!"

Sustaining the courtship without the aid of a dueña was out of the question. Necessity offered up the person of none other than Andreina herself. The day she first assumed her new responsibities she brought along one of the monstrous clipper-ship sheets. She sat in the carriage reducing it to size while Federico attempted to read.

"Hold it here," she ordered her daughter. "Excuse us, won't you?" she interrupted Don Federico. "Move over. Just a little bit." And with a noise that was wrenchingly unpleasant to the ear, she applied sharply honed scissors to the fold.

Federico continued to read. But almost immediately it became apparent that while there was room in the coach for three persons, or for two persons and a clipper-ship sheet, for *three* persons and a clipper-ship sheet the room was insufficient.

Almost at once a solution presented itself. No one could remember exactly who suggested it at first. But it proved to be entirely satisfactory. Federico sat in the coach and continued to read without interruption, while Andreina sat with him and continued to sew. Ana Magdalena was left to occupy the driver's seat with Hortensio Medina, the remarkably well-favored coachman.

It was because of this arrangement that Andreina began to notice certain coincidences that could not naturally be explained. During nearly every passing séance there appeared in what Federico read certain elements that seemed to relate to her life of the previous day. For example, on Wednesday she had worried her fob watch so much she had dislodged the winding button, and there on page 67 of Don Federico's manuscript the very same timepiece appeared. Or earlier in the week, Ana Magdalena had found her gold ring where Andreina had misplaced it months ago in the parrot's cage, and on page 33, although there was no mention of a parrot, there appeared a similar gold ring. There were other more startling and discomfiting revelations, but Andreina was too busy fitting the last lace to the wedding sheets to allow them much weight.

The day of the wedding was almost upon them. Federico lent Ana Magdalena his carriage and a footman to meet Aurora Constancia and her five pieces of luggage at the railroad station. Ana Magdalena could hardly wait till the footman had shut the door behind them.

"Did you get a look at the adorable coachman?"

Aurora Constancia shot a knowing glance through the coachman's window. "Quite impressive calves," she remarked.

"It isn't just his calves."

"So you've forgotten poor Sergio Ballado!"

"Oh, Sergio! That was just a schoolgirl whim."

"What about those fevered kisses?"

"That's not anywhere *near* what I'd do with *him* . . ."

". . . if you could just peel his tight silk stockings off! And you'd have to make sure Federico was busy reading!"

Ana Magdalena laughed. "Unfortunately, I could almost count on it."

"*Pobrecita,*" sympathized her friend. "Just remember what I keep telling you. Once you are married, it's the grasshopper's summer. You can do anything you want!"

And true to her friend's prognostications, nearly everything turned out for the best. By the day of the wedding, the linen requirement had been met, Andreina had conceived an unholy devotion to literature (especially literature that is read aloud), and Sergio Ballado had been almost entirely supplanted in Ana Magdalena's affections by the handsome Hortensio himself.

V

When Hercules Figueroa da Cunha's aunt Ofelia arrived from Salvador to settle in Malyerba, the event went unmarked by fireworks. But a year later to the day, thanks to her generous contributions to our various civil authorities, Ofelia had opened an establishment in an old abandoned convent. She had rooms to let by the day and by the hour, and the pleasures to go with them. Hercules had more or less made it a convenient pied-à-terre. Shrewd in business and in love, Ofelia had sized up her nephew from the start.

"Don't mess with my chickens, dear heart, or you'll spoil them for laying," and she let loose a belly laugh that scared the pigeons off the roof.

For nearly ten years, Hercules had managed to comply with the house rules, which is why, the morning of his daughter's wedding, Ofelia had to drag him from the gaming table where he had played out another of his losing streaks — not that he was especially troubled by it, as he had been losing other people's money already for some time.

"Get on with you. We're closing up. I thought we all agreed, we're going to the wedding."

It dawned on him that Ofelia was splendidly turned out in hat and boa, ready to face the world at an hour when ordinarily she could be found between her satin sheets. He rose with some difficulty.

"*Dios mio,*" he groused, "you women are all the same, always looking for a priest. My wedding to that accursed woman was the last time I ever had truck with the clergy. But the least little pretext, you women go running!"

"Get dressed," was Ofelia's only comment.

In those days, it was still customary to announce prospective marriages by a quaint system referred to as "publishing the banns," although in fact there were no publishers in the accepted sense, and almost no one remembered what "banns" meant. Normally the banns were announced at certain recognized intervals preceding the glorious day when the affianced couple proceeded in separate carriages from their respective homes to the Cathedral of the Holy Faith, which occupies the central square in which the effigy of Simón Bolívar sits mounted on a rearing stallion in the noticeable heat of its own equestrian priapism — a testimony to the unimpeachable patriotism of both horse and rider.

As a little girl, Ana Magdalena used to stare in wonderment at the curious appendage, although Andreina always stemmed her questions with a "Shhh." Now, circling the square in an open Victoria lent by the groom expressly for the purpose, her borrowed Alençon lace wedding veil spread out behind her like a peacock's train, and accompanied on either side by Aurora Constancia and Andreina in severe but elegant black, she could not fail to notice — as did the many wedding guests — that attached to the rearing horse's private member was a collection of what she took to be balloons.

Ana Magdalena nudged Aurora Constancia. She leaned toward her mother as far as the spread of her train would permit.

"Mother —"

Andreina shushed her. "Act as if you hadn't noticed. What crude prankster could have dreamed up such a thing?"

Ana Magdalena lowered her eyes. But the sight was an unfortunate one, the sort of lapse that inspires giggles in bridesmaids and already-nervous brides.

"*Please!*" Andreina whispered. "Try to control yourselves!"

The carriage came to a halt where the coachman parked it in the imposing horseshoe created by the many other carriages of the guests. The great cathedral doors stood open. From the rear, Ana Magdalena watched the crowd. Led by Federico in a splendid suit of morning clothes, his silken ascot fastened by a diamond stickpin and his top hat in hand, the procession wound at a stately pace across the square and up the cathedral steps.

"They're wasting their time," Ana Magdalena remarked to no one in particular.

Andreina was appalled. "What are you talking about?"

"We might as well wait here."

"We'll do nothing of the sort. There is to be a ceremony, and I'm here to see that it takes place!" She hooked a firm arm through Ana Magdalena's. Aurora Constancia carried Ana Magdalena's train aloft to keep it from snagging on the cobblestones.

At first Andreina did not understand the confusion she began to detect among the guests, who no sooner had they entered the dark and cavernous recesses of the cathedral could be heard murmuring among themselves. She attributed Ana Magdalena's misgivings to a bad case of nerves, but when they reached the doors, she could see for herself: the candles were unlit, there was a notable absence of flowers, and the altar had been stripped bare. A gaggle of elderly ladies were kneeling on rags, scrubbing the marble floors of the sanctuary with brushes and steaming hot water. There was evidence of not a single priest. Ana Magdalena and Aurora Constancia succumbed to a new paroxysm of the giggles.

"My God," moaned Andreina, "there has been a terrible mixup!" She headed in the full flush of her determination toward where Federico stood.

"I demand an explanation," she announced to all who would hear. "Where is Doña Eduviges?"

It was only then that everyone assembled noticed that the influential matchmaker was not in attendance, as would normally have been the case.

"Doña Eduviges has been fired," growled Federico.

"Fired! Oh great God, he fired Doña Eduviges!" Andreina was on the verge of hysteria.

Beside himself, Federico turned to his best man. "Go flush me out a priest, any priest. Even an acolyte will do."

At last a harried-looking young cleric appeared in a shabby, ill-fitting soutane.

"What is the meaning of this? Can you tell me?" stormed Federico. "There was to have been a wedding here this morning."

"Wedding? Señor must be mistaken. Have you checked the banns?"

The whole assembled company followed Federico to the vestibule, where the banns were posted. And there he read with horror:

"In holy matrimony: Federico Olympio Orgaz y Orgaz and Ana Magdalena Arzate de Figueroa." Both their names had been crossed out.

"I could have told you so," moaned the devastated Andreina, "no one in his right mind ever dismisses Doña Eduviges."

Federico grabbed the priest by the scruff of the neck.

"Listen, you miserable, craven little scarecrow, tell that puffed-up bishop of yours that from now on if he looks to the family Orgaz y Orgaz for any kind of emolument whatsoever, he can go scratch." He released the poor priest with such force that he went staggering backward, arms flailing, down the cathedral steps. He maintained his balance, however, by sliding on his heels, a trick he had perfected in the seminary. It was just the touch needed to restore a certain lightheartedness to the proceedings. The guests burst into giddy applause and the young priest bowed. Ana Magdalena and Aurora Constancia succumbed to a fresh spasm of the giggles.

Federico lost none of his aplomb. "Onward," he commanded, "to city hall. Let's see if the civil authorities won't prove a little more reasonable."

Reassured, the guests made their way across the square and climbed into their carriages.

When Hercules emerged from his leisurely toilet in starched collar and spats, the entire receiving line of Ofelia's young ladies was ready and waiting to greet him, decked out in their frilly hats and parasols and their contrasting pastel dresses. Ofelia busied herself at the last frantic minute pinning frangipani blossoms to their hats.

"There's nothing like a little frangipani," she murmured, "to lend the occasion a nice smell of sanctity! And now, my chickens, into the carriages! We've kept them waiting long enough."

It was impossible to tell whether by "them" Ofelia meant the drivers or the wedding party, but when the two carriages arrived at the foot of the cathedral steps to let off their pastel passengers, the square seemed unusually quiet, and the carriage stands were all but deserted.

They couldn't help noticing the curious addition to the statue of Simón Bolívar.

"It's a healthy horse that uses condoms," remarked an observant Victoria, elbowing Mercedes in her mint-green ribs.

"Aiee! *Madre de Dios!*" Mercedes gasped, cupping her hand to her mouth. Several of the other girls began to titter.

But a vigilant Ofelia silenced them at once. "*Que barbaridad,*" she observed, restoring dignity to the proceedings.

The little flock, escorted by Ofelia, trotted up the cathedral stairs with a wheezing Hercules bringing up the rear. To their unhappy consternation, a remarkable sight greeted their eyes. A flock of elderly ladies were polishing the marble floors of the sanctuary, sliding over the pavings with rags tied to their feet.

"I expected to enter the holy of holies," quipped Hercules, "not a geriatric skating rink."

The young ladies laughed obligingly.

"There must be some mistake," Ofelia temporized.

Trapped in the moment of their uncertainty, they stood captive in the church vestibule. In the deserted square, they could see a black-clad figure advancing toward them at a purposeful clip. At last, Hercules recognized the matchmaker.

"It's Doña Eduviges!" he cried. "How can she be here and not with the wedding party?"

"Because," purred the matchmaker who had overheard, "the church had to be fumigated. Poor things, they wound up at city hall. But they left me behind to make *sure* to tell you where to find them. If you hurry, you may still be able to catch them!"

"How sweet," murmured Ofelia.

It was anything but sweet. Doña Eduviges had already exhausted her every shameless trick to scuttle the occasion, and she was counting on this one last touch to sweeten her revenge. She already relished the horrified looks as Ofelia — mistress of Malyerba's night — mingled with the wedding guests, strutting the pastel plumage of her little flock of night birds. But she had not counted on the added embellishment of the refulgent Hercules himself.

It was a happy wedding caravan that approached the city hall. Originally a viceroy's palace, the building, which still houses our civil authority, rivals anything ever designed by Palladio — a jumble of pillars, pediments and imposing cornices which for the past two centuries have been considerably embellished by revolutions and pigeon droppings. Already Andreina was heartsick. She dreaded the imminent vulgarity that was about to sweep them all in its plebeian grip. Her worst fears were about to be amply confirmed.

As the guests made their way up the severe granite stairway, an usher met them, white gloves flailing.

"To the rear. Everyone to the rear."

"But," sputtered Federico, mopping his brow with a silken handkerchief, "this happens to be a wedding party."

The usher nodded. "On Thursdays the judge's chambers are in the rear."

The assembly made its way around the wing of the viceroy's palace to the sunken courtyard, where a glass-paned revolving door marked the more modest service entrance. Because of the length of her veil, Ana Magdalena had to double up with Aurora Constancia in order to pass through. Once inside, they found themselves in an endless basement corridor lined on either side by hard oak benches. Every seat was already crammed with day laborers on their luncheon break, women of the sort who haunt the street corners selling pencils or Chiclets, many of them with children. There were ruffians who had never done an honest day's work in their lives; there were barefooted Indians from the provinces with mud between their toes, and some of the women were visibly pregnant, even sitting down.

"God save us," moaned Andreina, crossing herself. Ana Magdalena and Aurora Constancia hugged each other in a state of near-collapse, while Federico's guests stared at the crowd in shocked disbelief. At that moment, an usher appeared.

"Are you all here to be married?" The hall became silent. People bent forward to hear.

"Yes, by all means," Federico joked, his amiability restored, "but not all at once." The crowd showed faint signs of amusement.

"Please ask your guests to wait outside."

"Outside!" protested Federico. Some of the crowd began to titter.

"We only perform group weddings on Thursdays. We reserve the corridor for the eleven A.M. shift."

"But what about my witnesses?"

"Ordinary people don't require a flock of witnesses. Two at the most will do."

Federico's patience was wearing thin. He tapped Vacio-Llares, his best man, on the shoulder.

"No," said the usher. "The state supplies your witnesses."

"And what if I prefer to supply my own?"

"If everyone supplied his own, there would be twice the number of people the capacity laws allow."

"But you don't expect my daughter to manage her lovely Alençon train all by herself," interjected Andreina in her haughtiest style. Federico glared at her. He turned to the usher.

"My dear man, I'm translated into forty-four different languages. If you imagine . . ."

"Sir —" The usher had Federico by the elbows.

". . . You can't simply push a man of my stature around . . ."

"Sir —"

". . . like any other low-born riffraff —"

"Sir, you are in the precincts of a democratic state!" To everyone's amazement, Federico began shaking hands with the usher with whom only moments before he had been about to engage in an unseemly *mano à mano*.

"Aha! It looks like he's greasing the skids," whispered a worldly-wise Aurora Constancia.

And indeed, the usher swung open the ornately carved doors of the judge's chambers. His Honor, Judge Esteban Gutierrez, sat on the dais, rocking back and forth on his judicial bench beneath an official portrait of El Magnífico, our then great Señor Presidente.

"*Hola!*" Judge Gutierrez waved. "Federico Orgaz y Orgaz, my most beloved author! What's up?"

But before Federico could enter, a bailiff barred his way. Federico shook hands with him as well, and he immediately became all obsequiousness. "Do come in," beamed Señor Esteban Gutierrez, "do come in."

"Don Esteban! What a pleasure finding my old compatriot here." Federico clasped His Honor in a fraternal embrace.

"What's the happy occasion, my friend?"

"I'm getting married."

"Today? Thursdays it's groups only. All day. One shift after another. What a shame!"

Federico took his hand.

"Oh, there's no need of that between friends," said Esteban Gutierrez as he nonchalantly transferred Federico's contribution into a side pocket, "but why don't you take your lovely bride outside — on the lawn out in the courtyard. I'll see what I can do!"

At a sign from Federico the guests began to file out through the revolving doors.

"What's going on? What's going on?" Andreina demanded.

"Federico wants us in the courtyard," whispered a knowing guest.

But evidently there was some confusion, owing to the size of the wedding party. A few of the guests had already made their way out to the courtyard, but when they noticed hesitation on the part of those remaining within, they began to clog the revolving doors, trying to reenter. While some guests pushed trying to get out, other guests were struggling to come back inside.

Ana Magdalena surveyed the confusion. When she eyed Aurora Constancia, she could no longer contain herself, and she had to stifle an unbecoming snort in her Alençon lace train.

"Control yourself. That's heirloom lace, not a handkerchief," hissed Andreina.

Eventually the hubbub subsided. The remaining guests made their way outside just as His Honor appeared, attired in formal judge's robes. But before the formalities could begin, there was a violent commotion as the entire crowd of Indians and day laborers piled through the revolving doors, straining for a closer look.

Unperturbed, the judge cleared his throat. "Welcome to the seat of the state. Let the betrothed couple come forward."

The Thursday crowd immediately pressed forward as well, forcing the guests to close ranks about the bride and groom.

"We are gathered here today . . ." His Honor intoned with appropriate solemnity.

The ceremony had barely gotten under way when Ofelia came running up, agitated and all out of breath. "Yoohoo!" She waved her eight girls forward. "It's over here! Hurry," she implored her little flock, "they're going to start without us."

Heads turned, and everyone craned their necks to see.

"Oh *look,* how lovely," Ofelia exclaimed rapturously, "I just *adore* garden party weddings!"

"Shhh," admonished some of the guests, exasperated at her lack of decorum. "There's a wedding going on."

"Oh, I know, I know," Ofelia assured them in happy tones. "It's my grandniece. I'm so happy for her." And she pushed all eight of her beauties right up front, where they could view the ceremony close up and people could view them.

To Ana Magdalena's amazement, a row of gorgeous attendants suddenly materialized to either side of her, dressed identically in frocks of contrasting pastel. "You didn't tell me there were brides-maids!" she exclaimed to Federico.

Federico tightened his grip on her arm. "My dear, please try to control yourself."

But quite suddenly Ana Magdalena became all seriousness. His Honor was intoning the vows.

"Do you take this man as your lawful, wedded . . ."

". . . husband. I do," she swallowed. She tried hard not to think of Sergio Ballado. But her chin began to tremble and before she could stop herself, she had begun to cry.

"And do you, Federico Orgaz y Orgaz . . ."

Ana Magdalena was sobbing so loudly she was afraid her heart would break before she — or anyone else — could do a thing about it. Consternation spread among the guests. One of the peasant women boldly stepped forward to offer the bride a soiled hand-kerchief, and Andreina, entirely overcome at the sight of her daughter weeping uncontrollably — and weeping, moreover, into her priceless heirloom Alençon lace veil — collapsed in a dead faint into the arms of a conveniently near and most attractive man. That man, as it happened, was Hercules Figueroa da Cunha.

"My, my, my," breathed Ofelia, "what a beautiful bride! Let me be the first to congratulate you." Ofelia swept the weeping Ana Mag-dalena to her generous, heavily perfumed bosom. "There, there, my sweet, don't weep. This is just the beginning. There's more to come!" She opened her jeweled bag to extract the tiniest of lace hand-kerchiefs, this one saturated with smelling salts. It was just what Ana Magdalena needed to restore her to her senses.

"Who are you?" she inquired, staring straight into Ofelia's heavily rouged face.

"Darling, don't you know? I'm your great-aunt Ofelia from Salvador. I'm so touched you remembered me."

"I never knew I had an aunt."

"Probably because I'm on your father's side."

But bloodlines notwithstanding, Ana Magdalena found she rather liked Ofelia. An aunt like that might just lend the family a sadly absent sense of zest.

"Ofelia, let me present my husband, Federico —"

But before she could complete the introduction, Ofelia interrupted.

"Oh, yes, I'm delighted! And I insist you meet my dear little chickens. This is Marta — in powder blue; Alicia — in becoming lavender; Trinidad — in stunning magenta; Victoria — in sentimental rose; Eugenia — in glowing peach; Maria — in daffodil yellow; Mercedes — in mint-green; and last of all Cecilia — in breathtaking turquoise."

One by one, each of the rainbow beauties shook hands with the bride and groom.

By now the guests had lined up to offer their congratulations, too. Some of them assumed, like Ana Magdalena, that the rainbow girls were some sort of bridesmaids. But a number of them knew otherwise.

Meanwhile Hercules was having a terrible time. In the midst of such a public and festive event, his dilemma was putting him through his own private hell. When some fool woman first fell swooning in his arms, catching her had been purely a test of his reflexes. Much to his distress, however, he discovered that his prize was none other than Andreina herself. Circumstances prevented him from uttering the first words that came to mind, but he congratulated himself that, for the moment at least, his wife was far from conscious.

His immediate reaction was to try to pass her off into a more willing set of arms. But willing arms failed to present themselves. Relieved that the civil ceremonies were over, and able to breathe once more with the departure of the hangers-on, the guests were in a celebratory mood. They crowded the receiving line, eager to congratulate the bride and groom. Hercules caught sight of Ofelia and sought to attract her attention, but she was busy passing out business cards, extolling the gracious amenities of her establishment — "What! You haven't heard of La Nymphaea?" — and had no eyes for Hercules nor sympathy for his unusual predicament.

From time to time he anxiously scanned Andreina's face watching for signs of returning consciousness. Increasingly he found his glance lingering on the microscopic down that lent her cheek a luminescent glow, and the smoky and troubling luster of her eyelids; but more than anything, it was her expression of rapture that he found seriously incapacitating. When the guests finally became aware of him (after the bride and groom disappeared in a last frenzy of waving and blowing kisses), they found him sitting spellbound on the grass, cradling Andreina — still unconscious — in his arms.

VI

Nowadays in Malyerba, rapport between the sexes has undergone something of a change, but in those days any intercourse between unmarried couples was subject to a strict protocol. Following a wedding ceremony, however, no matter how improvised, all inhibition was supposedly thrown to the wind, and the enamored couple, freed of all restraint, melted into each other's arms in a fever of pent-up emotion that varied in direct proportion to the length and ardor of the courtship, and the implacable determination of their dueña.

Now, having been properly married — if not by our ecclesiastical authorities, at least, and at considerable expense, through the good offices of the state — Ana Magdalena found herself alone for the very first time in the company of Federico Orgaz y Orgaz. She sank into the soft velvet upholstery of his magnificent carriage, barely able to contain her feeling of shock. The wheels began to roll. In a fever to record their moment, Federico raised his camera to his eye. He located Ana Magdalena in the viewfinder. He lowered the camera again.

"What's this stuff you have here?" He fingered her cheek.

"What is it?"

"Probably that dreadful woman's lipstick." He handed her his silk pocket handkerchief. "Spit on this." Again he tapped her cheek. "There."

"What 'dreadful woman'?"

"The mother vulture with all her little night chicks."

"Oh, you mean my aunt Ofelia!"

"Good heavens! She's your *aunt?*"

"Great-aunt, actually. Anyway, I thought you knew her."

"Knew her? Whatever gave you that idea?"

Federico busied himself returning the handkerchief to his pocket. "Do you think you can give me a nice smile? Turn your head — like this. That's it! Hold it!" He pressed the shutter release. Satisfied, he set the camera down.

Ana Magdalena sat stiffly, her hands demurely folded in her lap. It was clear Federico didn't want to hear about Ofelia. He was groping for something in the folds of the upholstery. At first she imagined it might be some kind of gift, some jewel perhaps, a ring. But she was quickly set straight. Federico got hold of his frumpy old lady's glasses. He raised them to his nose. Even before he reached under the seat to extract his manuscript, she recognized the familiar signs. He cleared his throat. "Just listen to this," he said.

Doña Elvira made her way, still in her driving cap and goggles, to the presbytery. She demanded to see the bishop ("that miserable wimp," she called him), although it was in the middle of the dinner hour. She knew His Eminence must still be at meat, and the thought of disturbing the secretion of his digestive juices perked up the sagging ventricles of her shriveled old heart. At last he appeared in the dimly lit vestibule of the cathedral residence. Before he could so much as say "My child," she was at him.

"Your Eminence, bless this poor luckless matchmaker. Never in all the years of my exemplary service have I ever experienced such a cruel setback! The engagement of my clients has proved an unqualified disaster. You might as well strike the wedding banns at once."

"But —" Ana Magdalena tried to interrupt.
Federico ignored her.

She was weeping great poisonous tears, which missed staining the carpet for the very reason that she was still wearing her goggles. But, in order to see, she had to shake them out at last when she was preparing to leave. They discharged a green, pestilential fluid.

"My child," said the bishop, "console yourself. I will see to the matter at once. Pray for me," he whispered piously as he gave her his ring to kiss. (He had no idea how much he would come to need her prayers! But that is getting ahead of the story.)

Federico swelled with authorial satisfaction. He glanced at Ana Magdalena.

"But how do you know that's what happened?" Ana Magdalena innocently asked.

"What do you mean, 'what happened'? Of course, it happened. I wrote it, didn't I?"

"Yes, but how can you be sure?"

"Dear, just listen, will you? Try not to interrupt. As it is, there's hardly any time." He looked out the carriage window. "Good God, we're nearly there!"

"Where?"

He gave her a quizzical look. " 'Where? Where?' " he mimicked. "How do I know till we get there?"

He returned to his manuscript.

With difficulty, Doña Elvira knelt on her arthritic old knees. She brushed his ring with lips dry as shinbones.

"The old geezer," she thought to herself. "That ring of his alone is worth three of my hard-earned commissions."

Mercifully the carriage came to a halt in the gravel driveway fronting Casa Orgaz. Hortensio held the door for her. As she gathered up her train, she gave him a long and lingering look. She was a married woman now. She could look him straight in the eyes. But, and she found this very strange, the directness of her gaze seemed to confuse him and he looked away.

She turned to Federico to see if he had noticed. But he was already directing the guests who had arrived ahead of them, positioning them on the imposing double marble staircase, with the rosy façade of the great house of Orgaz as a backdrop.

"Move in tight! Tighter! I want to get it all!" He squinted through the eyepiece, but the light was too bright. Impatiently he gestured to his best man for the black photographer's drape. "Smile, everyone. Hold it!"

A great discharge of flash powder went off.

"Hurray," the guests shouted, clapping furiously. Ana Magdalena could see that their eyes were already fastened on the champagne. She caught sight of Aurora Constancia in the crowd. But before she could make her way in her friend's direction, she felt a restraining arm on her shoulder. It was Ofelia.

"Don Federico," Ofelia called in a voice loud enough for everyone to hear, "can't we have at least one picture of you with my precious little niece?"

Federico looked annoyed.

"Everyone behind the lovely couple," Vacio-Llares obligingly called out.

"Make sure everyone is evenly positioned," Federico warned as he handed the camera to his best man.

The guests happily rearranged themselves. Federico took Ana Magdalena's arm.

"Smile," commanded Vacio-Llares.

"Your hands are cold," Federico remarked to her. "You ought to get some rest."

"Did my trunk arrive?"

"You'll have to ask Severina."

But before she could ask who Severina was, Vacio-Llares had released the shutter.

"Let's have everybody drinking champagne," shouted Federico, repossessing the camera. "Everyone raise a glass."

Ana Magdalena scanned the crowd. At last she spotted Aurora Constancia in a remote corner of the ballroom. She made her way toward her.

"Have you seen Andreina?" she wanted to know.

"My God! Don't you know? Your mother passed out, right into the arms of some perfectly delectable man. An absolute Adonis."

"No, I can't believe it. What did he look like?"

Before Aurora Constancia could begin to describe him, a flock of liveried waiters began distributing canapés. Although she tugged insistently at Ana Magdalena's arm, the guests hurled themselves on the trays with such ferocity that, by the time they were able to get near, there wasn't a single morsel left.

Aurora caught sight of Ofelia surrounded by her eight beauties. "Holy Mother! What's that relic doing here with her gang of oil pastels?"

"What gang?"

"Those floozies all turned out in their Sunday best?"

"*Floozies!* I thought they were bridesmaids!"

"You poor thing. Don't you know?" Aurora whispered something in Ana Magdalena's ear.

"You mean a real *establishment?*"

"She was even handing out *business cards.* In the middle of the wedding! Her place is called 'La Nymphaea'; can you beat it?"

Ana Magdalena broke into a smile. "But that's what I like about Ofelia."

"What?"

"She's so direct. She's my aunt. Great-aunt, actually."

"Oh, look. Here comes Andreina now."

Ana Magdalena turned to follow the direction of her friend's gaze. She paled visibly. "My God!"

"What's the matter?"

"That's Hercules."

"You *know* him?"

"Of course, dummy. He's my father."

But she barely recognized him, so remarkable was the transformation that had taken place. He was holding Andreina, one hand on her shoulder. He gazed tenderly into her eyes.

"You never told me your father was a hunk. Why don't you introduce me, darling?"

"You want to *meet* him?" asked Ana Magdalena, incredulous.

"Why not?"

Ana Magdalena felt strange, as if all at once Aurora Constancia had become someone else. She looked at her with new eyes. She saw the deeply arched eyebrows, carefully plucked and penciled. And her lips had been etched with a dark liner, and glowed a carmine red. "My God," she said to her friend, "you can't imagine what he's like —"

Before she could elaborate, Aurora interrupted her. "What did you think, darling? I'm not going to devour him. I just want to shake his hand."

Even before a formal meeting could take place, Hercules' gaze had become riveted on Aurora Constancia. His eyes grew wider as they followed the play of her glorious cheeks beneath her tight red satin dress. Never in his life, he decided, had he ever laid eyes on such an undulating creature.

A serving woman tapped Ana Magdalena on the arm.

"Don Federico has been looking for you everywhere. The matriarch wants to meet you."

"What's that?"

"That's what he calls his mother, Doña Clemencia. Come along."

"Are you Severina, by any chance?"

"Not by chance. Why?"

"Has my trunk arrived?"

"Your *trunk?*" she huffed. "I should think you'd have your head full at a time like this without bothering with trunks."

Señora Orgaz was a very old woman. Even free of her party finery she would have struck Ana Magdalena as a frightening old mummy, but ghostly in her white powder, her cheeks heavily rouged, with false eyelashes and midnight blue eyeshadow generously applied, her presence was terrifying.

Federico stood at her side. He bowed formally. *"Mamacita,"* he said, "it's never too late to meet the bride."

Ana Magdalena curtsied.

"Isn't she lovely," croaked Clemencia Orgaz. "I want her all to myself." She fastened a skeletal claw on Ana Magdalena's lace-covered arm. "Why don't you leave us, dear?" She dismissed Federico. "Now, let's see you, child." Her iron grip forced Ana Magdalena onto the burgundy velvet poof at her feet. "Sit down next to me. I'm blind as a bat, you know." She smiled confidentially. "Sometimes I can't even see to put on my shoes. The older you grow, the farther away your feet get. I'm afraid they'll disappear altogether. Severina thinks someday I'll need a telescope." She cackled at her own pleasantry.

"And what does Federico think?"

"Oh, that boy! He never has any time for mama. He's too busy winning prizes. Between us, I could never stand his writing. That's why he gave up reading to me long ago."

"He did? What a pity," sympathized Ana Magdalena.

"Oh, I was just as glad to cure him of the habit."

"You cured him? How?"

"I'll show you." She began fumbling for something under her chair.

"Why didn't I see you at the wedding?"

"Oh, they *never* let me out. They're frightened of what might happen. The last time I went out, they didn't like the stir I caused one bit."

"Oh, did you do something naughty?"

At last the old lady extracted an enormous black ear trumpet from under her chair. She leaned close to Ana Magdalena's face. Ana Magdalena caught scent of her crocodile breath.

"You bet I did. I went through the entire alphabet. Every letter, from A to Z. Everyone thought I was completely demented, but my memory's clear as a bell, you know! Of course, Federico took it personally. He thought it was a reflection on his work. I don't know how he ever got such an idea. It may have been because it happened in the middle of his reading." She leaned back in her chair. She raised the trumpet to her shriveled old lips. "Ba, be, bee, bo, boo, ka, ke, kee, ko, koo," she crowed at the top of her lungs. "Da, de, dee, do, doo." She was cackling, rollicking about in her chair and enjoying herself immensely.

At once Federico was at her side. "Stop that nonsense. Everyone will think you're gaga. Stop it at once!"

"Fa, fe, fee, fo, foo!" She was beginning to gather momentum. "Ga, ge, gee, go, goo!"

"If you don't stop, I'll call Severina."

Clemencia began to plead. "Oh, no, no, not Severina. You don't know what she'll do to me. Please not Severina."

"Then you'd better control yourself."

The old woman nodded. She was weeping.

"And put that unspeakable object away."

Ana Magdalena almost felt sorry for her.

"Don't pay any attention to her." He took Ana Magdalena by the arm. "There's something in the pantry I want to show you."

He propelled her swiftly across the ballroom through the dense clusters of celebrating guests. They reached a pair of swinging doors. Federico pushed them open.

The sight that greeted her eyes was nothing short of chaotic. Cook's boys were everywhere, slicing onions, peppers, goodness knows what. Others were dismembering artichokes. In a corner a legless man sat peeling potatoes in a great mound of skins, tossing them, white in their sudden nakedness, into a gigantic cattle trough. Other people sat on the floor, beheading guinea hens and plucking geese in a blizzard of feathers. Food trays were laid out everywhere. At the far side of the room, under a massive ventilating hood, an extraordinarily corpulent man in a chef's hat presided over a roaring wood stove. He worked stripped to the waist except for an apron. "*Putamadre!*" he roared at his assistants, "what's holding you bastards up?"

Ana Magdalena had never seen so many servants, so many assistants, all chopping and plucking and shouting at once.

"Why didn't you cater it?" was the first thing that came to her head.

Federico laughed. "Oh, but I did. All these fellows come straight from La Merced, every one of them — on loan from the warden."

"From La Merced *Prison?*"

"Shhh. They'll hear you. And I'll tell you something else: they were so happy to get a day's furlough, I didn't even have to pay them."

"But what makes you think they won't escape?"

He shrugged. "With the armed guards outside? It's highly unlikely. And there's a few like that fellow over there peeling potatoes. He can't get very far. But that's not why I brought you here."

He led her to a passageway that evidently served as a pantry. In it was a table mounted on casters. It had been covered with a pale pink linen tablecloth decorated with white and rose carnations and draped with garlands of green leaves.

"My dear, you see before you a lavishly decorated cake stand, but I'll bet you can't even see the cake."

"It must be because you didn't write it yet," teased Ana Magdalena. But there was not the slightest hint of levity in Federico's eyes.

"The bakery pretends someone canceled the order."

"Oh my God! Doña Eduviges," gasped Ana Magdalena.

Federico nodded. "And now, of course, they say it's too late. After all, Rome wasn't built in a day. A wedding cake takes at least two days — for the regulation three tiers, anyway."

"But the guests don't really need a wedding cake, do they?"

Federico shrugged. "If we stuff them tight enough, they won't be able to eat one. But they expect to see one at the very least."

Ana Magdalena thought for a moment. "That top hat you were wearing earlier, what did it come in?"

Federico's eyes narrowed. "What does my top hat have to do with it?"

"Hatboxes!"

"I don't see what you're getting at."

"How *many* hatboxes do you have?"

"How should I know how many hatboxes I have!"

"Why can't you ask your valet?"

"There is no valet. Severina is the valet, the cook, the parlor maid. Severina does everything."

"Then tell her to bring them down at once."

"Then what?"

"Then maybe she can ice them."

"Holy Mother of God."

"Of *course*," she urged him, "it's only just for show. . . ."

Federico looked doubtful.

"In shop windows they display fakes all the time."

"Yes, but —"

". . . and lots of times it looks *even better than the real thing!*"

Improvising had always struck Federico as rather shabby, but this was shamming. He swept her in his arms. "What a genius!" The resounding kiss he gave her struck her squarely in the eye.

In the ballroom the guests were being plied with more champagne and more canapés. It would probably be hours before the kitchen was ready to serve up dinner. Federico paced rapidly, alternating his attention from the kitchen to his guests. He was entirely unaware that, out behind the kitchen, the armed guards had mysteriously come into possession of several cases of champagne. All he imagined was that the guests were going through it like water.

"At this rate," he said to Ana Magdalena, "it probably won't last till dinner."

"Why don't you see if the chef has made any headway," suggested Ana Magdalena.

But when Federico returned to the kitchen, he found Severina cowering behind a stack of hatboxes. The chef was threatening her with a soup ladle.

"You expect *me* to ice a bunch of boxes? The cheese must have fallen off your cracker a long time ago! Just because your namby-pamby guests want a wedding cake, you expect me to prostitute my profession? I may be a jailbird, but I am a man of principle, a chef, raised and trained in the gastronomic arts, not a window dresser. I'll have nothing to do with it. And that's final." He hurled the soup ladle into his stockpot with a homicidal splash.

Federico intervened. He took the collection of boxes from Severina's shaken grip. "Go at once and bring me Ana Magdalena!"

"What does she know about it?"

"Do as I say."

By the time Severina returned with Ana Magdalena in tow, still in her Alençon lace veil, the kitchen had taken on an air of bedlam. Cook's boys rushed about amidst a clatter of sauce pots. Serving men tripped over the trays of canapés piling up on the floors. Everyone was shouting at once. She found Federico in the pantry, arranging the hatboxes in an attractive pyramid.

"What took you so long?" he asked. "Don't you think this looks elegant?"

"Very," Ana Magdalena nodded.

"Do you know how to ice a cake?"

With hardly a moment's hesitation, Ana Magdalena turned to Severina. "Get some lard. And sugar. You'll need lots of sugar. And while you're at it, get a pastry tube!"

"They say there is no sugar," Severina said when she returned at last.

"Then substitute."

"Substitute what?"

"Flour. Anything powdery will do."

"But —"

"No buts," said Federico. "How it tastes doesn't matter. Just make sure we have lots of pretty roses." Exhilarated by his newfound sense of adventure, he took Ana Magdalena's arm. "Come on, my darling! Let's show the young bride off and titillate the guests."

But long before the time came to serve the cake, an event occurred that was to make the Orgaz household the topic of conversation for some decades at least. While the guests happily devoured one tray of canapés after another and the bartenders popped cork after cork, the armed guards, encouraged by their first round of champagne, began a resounding chorus of the national anthem, which they sang with all the boozy sentiment at their command. More corks popped as another case of champagne mysteriously slid out toward them from the kitchen door. Swept up in a tide of patriotic sentiment, they clasped their arms about each other. Swampy tears coursed down their cheeks.

"Home of freedom, seat of liberty." They repeated all the unfortunate lyrics everyone has come to expect from musical offerings of this type.

But by then the words were immaterial. They slurred most of them anyway, but they slurred them at full tilt.

"Why can't those bulls pipe down out there," remarked the chef. "You can't expect me to cook with all that racket going on. When I compose a sauce I need the concentration of a god if I'm to get the balance right."

In the salon, Federico made the rounds, Ana Magdalena on his arm, nodding here, smiling there.

At last he pulled her aside. "Sweetheart, I can't get away just now," he murmured. "I still have to butter up Contreras y Gasset about next year's literary prize. I think I've got an excellent chance of snagging it. Go in the kitchen will you, dear, and see how Severina's coming along?"

Back in the garden, the patriotic fervor had ground fully to a halt.

"Praised be Saint Lawrence," crowed the chef, "sounds like the bulls have cooled it at last! I think it's time to serve the soup."

"Soup's on." The signal passed from mouth to mouth. Instantaneously all work ceased. Saucepans were thrown clattering to the floor. Cook's boys, serving men, and scullions seized whatever food they could carry. Canapés slid to the floor, immediately to be swept up by another flurry of hands.

It was at precisely this moment that Ana Magdalena pushed open the swinging doors. Instantly she was subdued from behind by a meat cutter's assistant who had done time for aggravated assault. He had her in a choke hold with one hand over her mouth.

"I got the main course under wraps, chief. What'll I do with her?"

"Take her along," yelled the chef. "There isn't time to truss her up. Come on, you sons of bitches, it's now or never!" He kicked open the kitchen door.

"Wait," pleaded the legless potato peeler. "Wait for me! Someone please wait. I'm coming, too! Help! Someone, please help!"

But by then his moans fell on absent ears. The kitchen had been swept clean of everything, including Ana Magdalena and the cake stand with its fabulous newly iced wedding cake.

It was Vacio-Llares who responded to the potato peeler's pleas for help. Wedged between two guests backed up against the kitchen doors, he was puzzled at first by what he heard. But eventually he recognized that the cries for help continued unabated. He pushed open the swinging doors. What he saw made him gasp.

"Amigo, come quick," he called to Federico. "They've disappeared!"

Federico shot across the ballroom, creating instant panic among the guests.

"Stop them!" he shouted, pointing an angry finger at the luckless serving men, who had the misfortune still to be passing canapés to the guests, unaware of what had transpired in the kitchen. "Stop them at once!"

A number of the gentlemen threw themselves on the waiters, happily after the ladies relieved the latter of their serving trays. Women screamed, others passed out canapés. Some of the guests forced one of the waiters to the ground. The bravest among them stomped him where he lay, staining the beautifully inlaid parquet floor.

"This is scandalous," Federico roared. "Where are the guards?"

Eventually it became all too plain. The back garden was strewn with empty bottles, testimony to the champagne that had given rise to so much patriotic dissonance. The patriots lay like the apostles in Gethsemane, sound asleep.

Ana Magdalena was not there to hear Federico address the guests, or to hear him tell them that unfortunately, owing to circumstances beyond anyone's control (he somehow omitted mentioning the guards), all traces of dinner had vanished from the kitchen; or that the magnificent wedding cake, which he himself had designed and which was to have been the pièce de résistance, had disappeared altogether, leaving not a trace.

Andreina was not amused. "You *know* I have no stomach for violence, no matter how unruly servants get. That sort of thing would never have happened if I'd been in charge. Only an idiot would dismiss Doña Eduviges. My, she must positively be marinating in her own vindictive juices. First the church, then city hall, and now this travesty. And of course the statue of poor Bolívar."

But Hercules was only half listening. He had caught sight again of Aurora Constancia.

"What poor Bolívar?"

"You're not listening," remarked Andreina frostily.

Hercules found himself wishing his wife would faint again. Abruptly Andreina snatched the champagne glass out of her husband's hand. "Please, take me home," she snapped, exasperated. "I've had enough!"

But her restive mate had other fish to fry.

"Wait here, I'll be right back," he promised.

When Hercules sidled up to her, Aurora Constancia gave him her most beguiling smile. "I would just *love* a ride to the station, but my train leaves at eleven" — she gave him a long look — "and I have to pack my things."

He took her arm. "Where are you staying?"

"With Andreina."

"Andreina! She won't be back."

"What happened?"

"She fainted, poor thing. The commotion must have been too much. They're waiting for the doctor now."

"Where is she?" Aurora Constancia's eyes darkened with concern.

Hercules ignored her question. "This way." He herded her into the street. His eyes scanned the curb. "Follow me. Do you have much luggage?" He had spotted one of Ofelia's carriages. As they approached, he was relieved to see the coachman was not in attendance. "Hop in." He held the door for her.

When they pulled up before the darkened Figueroa establishment, the porter's door was still off its hinges. Hercules pushed it ajar. He lit the entrance light. "My, my, how things have changed!"

"Then you haven't lived here for a while?"

"Hardly. My poor wife could never understand me." He pushed

open the parlor door. Instantly he became aware of an odor like the ripe and moist decay of the jungle.

"Oh, not in there, not in the parlor. Why don't you come inside and help me pack," said Aurora Constancia.

Hercules followed her into the bedroom. It amused him to let his eyes roam over all the familiar reminders of his past: the dresser, the bed with its trumpeting angels, the canopy.

"Why don't I stretch out here while you get your things together," he said.

"Perfect," she smiled. She began to undo her straps. Lazily, she pulled them off her shoulders one by one. She let her dress slide to the floor. He was stunned to discover that she was virtually naked. She had on a black net brassiere, and a matching garter belt held up her stockings.

"I can never reach these nasty little hooks," she said. Slowly, she moved toward where he was lying on the bed.

He raised a lazy hand to help her. Her breasts bounced toward him like twin dolphins in happy abandon. He let the brassiere fall to the ground. She began undoing his buttons and reaching for his sex. But Hercules' sex was in detumescent retreat. He was having trouble catching his breath.

"Get off!" he gasped. "Get off! My collar's too tight!"

He sat upright in bed, breathing heavily. He watched the swing of her alarmingly full breasts as she undid his tie. She removed his shirt and stroked his chest. Slowly she took off his spats, his shoes, and his trousers. At last he lay there, panting like a beached whale. His garters still held up his socks.

She laid a manicured hand on his crotch. Hercules sat up once more. He looked her squarely in the eye.

"Lie down," he said.

She did as she was told.

"Like this," he said. He squeezed her knees tightly together. He sat looking down at her, doubt written all over his face.

"Do you think you could close your eyes."

She obliged. "Like this?" she murmured.

"Yes. Like that."

Satisfied, he removed his shorts. He lay down next to her. She began to stir against the pressure of his fingers busying her sex. "No!" His vehemence startled her. "Try not to move."

"Like this?" she said.

His voice was hoarse. "Lie still, dear, can you?"

But Aurora Constancia had been poorly stayed with much too long. Low moans began to take leave of her elbows, and her knees. They flew out of her ears and her eyes. And one tiny angelic sigh escaped from the dark tangle of swampy jungle weeds that lay between her legs.

"Stop!" he said to her. "Why can't you just lie still?" Again he tried to oblige her, but his heart was not in it because she could not stop the orchestra that her body had become.

"Dear," he said, exasperated, "I need you to lie very still." Then he had an inspiration. "Couldn't you pretend something terrible has happened? Why don't you pretend to faint?"

Andreina made her way through the thinning crowd of guests. She came upon Federico in the vestibule. He had had no time to be concerned for Ana Magdalena or anything else. He was trying to reach the warden on the crank-up telephone.

"Do you know where I can find my daughter?" she asked.

"*Putamadre!*" He slammed the receiver down on its hook. "He's probably out drinking again. I know that rascal." He smiled disarmingly at Andreina. "Señora, I haven't had a moment. I'm sure you understand. I haven't the slightest idea where your daughter went. Ask Severina. Severina knows everything." And he raised the receiver once more trying to reach the jail.

All Andreina knew was that she was about to be parted from her only affection, from the daughter who was all she held dear in this world, and probably in the next. She had rehearsed over and over again the things she would tell her at this, the most poignant juncture in all the years of their attachment, the moment of their separation. She would sit with her on the edge of the bridal bed. At last she would tell her the things she had always wanted to say, but had always thought better of saying — all the disappointments of her marriage, the stored grievances, the sleazy betrayals, the unutterable sadnesses of her blighted life. She would hold a small, delicately edged handkerchief in one hand, but she would not raise it to her eyes. She would draw her spine up straight, straighter than she had ever held it, and the tears would not come. She, Andreina, would be brave as she had always been brave, faithful to the tradition of the stoic Arzates, she, linked in name only to the feckless Figueroas. She would tell her daughter to be brave, that it wouldn't hurt because it would be quickly over. She would assure her that her home was always waiting for her, and should things become difficult, she, Andreina, would always be there for her, ready to open her maternal arms to her every need and whim, ready even to share the last mite of her grass widowhood. If only she could hang on to the reward money. Ah, but it was a dark voice, a demonic voice that had made her stoop to such a thought, she knew, and she repeatedly brushed it aside, lest temptation stand in the way of everything she was preparing to say to her daughter.

She entered the great salon in search of Severina. She wandered into the dining room where the walls were hung with a collection of imposing mirrors. The lights were only dimly lit and as she passed each one of them, she was startled to see a middle-aged woman, her face severe, haggard, ridged with wrinkles, a reflection that she only belatedly recognized as her own.

She came to the library with its animal skins mounted like trophies on the leather-covered walls, and the fireplace overhung with the skulls of jaguars and an ancient blunderbuss; she entered the morning room, the *sala de tertulias,* in which that fateful literary gathering had been held; but search as she might, she encountered no one. The rooms were deserted. She reached the great circular staircase, and when she came to the second-story landing, she found endless carpeted corridors stretching out in all directions. She was at a loss to know which way to go. She passed room after room. They all appeared to be empty. Here and there she saw a headboard or naked bedsprings leaning against a peeling wall. She knew each corridor must parallel the central courtyard, but whenever she turned a corner, she found the same carpeted vestibule, furnished with an antique coromandel screen. At last she found a room in which there was a birdcage of Arabic design with a bird in it. But when she approached, she saw that the bird had evidently been mounted by a taxidermist, whose apparent ineptitude had allowed the stuffing to leak out.

She wanted to bolt. She walked faster and faster, almost ran, through door after door, until at last she found herself in a corridor facing the back stairs, but although the runner had been removed and the treads were bare, they seemed familiar somehow, as if someone was intent on playing her a trick.

The ceilings of the servants' quarters were of a dark and musty wood, slung low over a stale and mournful atmosphere.

"*Hola!* Anyone here?" she called out.

A gray-haired woman appeared in a doorway. The overhanging ceiling bulb was naked and etched her face in skeletal relief.

"Yes?"

Andreina had a way with her own servant, but she could tell this woman was different. For one thing, she was not from the country.

"I'm looking for my daughter." She smiled her most engaging smile.

"I don't know why she would be here," said the woman.

"I didn't think she was here," explained Andreina. After all, what would her daughter be doing in the servants' quarters, although it was a thought she was careful not to voice aloud. "I came looking for Severina."

"I *am* Severina," the woman assured her, "and I don't know anything about your daughter." She turned away.

"Then you haven't seen the bride?"

"The *bride?* My goodness, I thought I recognized you! I'll get my uniform at once."

They searched all the apartments, but look where they would, they found no trace of Ana Magdalena. At last, Severina found Federico in the vestibule, but he was now busy talking with the police chief. There was no one else to ask because by then all the guests had left. Including Hercules, as Andreina discovered to her great chagrin.

The kitchen staff was already out of breath with running, stumbling over backways and ditches in their haste to reach the river. It was a moonless night, and the annihilating darkness favored their escape.

"Son of a bitch," cursed the cook's boy, "these fucking wheels keep getting stuck!"

"What are you, some kind of schmuck? Take the cake and leave the stand behind!" In the darkness his cellmate grabbed at the cake. "*Mierda!*" he squawked, "what's this? Some kind of hatbox! Come on! Just throw that shit away!"

Cramped in his arm lock, Ana Magdalena was trying to break free of the meat cutter's assistant.

"Mmmm," she said into the dishrag they had used to gag her mouth.

"Chief, I think the main course is trying to squawk!"

"Let her blab over dinner — all she wants."

"But chief —"

The chef stopped in his tracks. "What now," he shouted, infuriated.

"What if she's trying to tell us something?"

In the momentary distraction, Ana Magdalena's right arm escaped. She tore away the gag. "The river is *that* way."

"Where?"

"That way," she pointed. "The way you're headed now, you'll be right in time for lock-up."

"She's right."

"Bullshit! You can't trust someone like her. She's nothing but a parasite!"

But the lifers would have none of it. "Why should we listen to that proletarian shit? What did you ever do but pass out a bunch of lousy leaflets?"

"Maybe, but in the war of the classes, she's on the wrong side."

"Listen, *hijo de puta,* I'd knock your teeth in — if you had any left!"

"But can't you see she's part of the problem?"

Some of the crew were already exchanging blows. Others began to join in. The cook's boy began to squeal. "Let go! Let go! He's right. You can't trust snobs like her. Look what passes for cake if you need any proof!"

"*Cáyate,*" yelled the chef, trying to quell the disturbance. "You can argue dialectics over dinner."

Roundhouse punches flew left and right. Ana Magdalena felt the meat cutter's assistant loosen his grip. She started to run. She shed her shoes. She shed her precious Alençon veil. She was sprinting so fast her feet pedaled air. She already knew where she was headed. She had seen the red neon sign of her aunt Ofelia's establishment blinking in the distance, close enough so she could make the letters out, and although her lungs were ready to shatter like glass, she knew that if she could last another few yards she would reach La Nymphaea and safety.

VII

The carriage door swung open before the entrance to La Nymphaea. Already a gathering of gentlemen stood waiting in the street outside. As she stepped off the running board, Ofelia was happy to recognize several of them from the wedding party. She congratulated herself that outings like this were certainly good for business.

One by one the carriage disgorged eight rumpled beauties, their dresses badly crushed in the close confines of the single vehicle left to them by the straying Hercules.

"Chop, chop, every one upstairs." Ofelia clapped her hands. "I want every one undressed and ready for business!"

No one budged. All eight beauties stood frozen, watching in disbelief as Ana Magdalena, flushed and breathless from her sprint, fell into Ofelia's arms.

"*Hola, niña,* what brings you here?" Ofelia exclaimed. "*Pobrecita,* come inside. What happened to your shoes?"

But before anyone could swing the imposing monastic doors of La Nymphaea wide, the heavens apparently intervened. A pair of white silk slippers alighted on the threshold, and when they all looked up awestruck expecting further divine manifestations, they saw that the cloud floating indolently in the starry night sky bore an uncanny resemblance to Ana Magdalena's former wedding veil.

Ofelia crossed herself. "*Santa Virgen!* We've no time right now for miracles. There's just time to open for the evening."

All eight beauties scrambled up the lushly carpeted central staircase as fast as their cramped limbs would allow.

"And leave those gowns out for pressing. We're going to stage another outing before long," Ofelia called after them.

She turned to Ana Magdalena. "Come with me to the kitchen, niña. We'll ask Sidonia if she will just make us a nice little cup of something sweet. I want you to tell me everything."

But Ana Magdalena had caught sight of the "convent" parlor. She was instantly enraptured. "My God, how lovely! It's just like Ali Baba and the Forty Thieves, all gold and red velvet."

Ofelia threw her head back and laughed till the roof joists rattled. "It's not gold, child, only brass. Go in, go on in and see if you like."

Ana Magdalena tiptoed into the vast ground-floor room. There were Art Nouveau sconces here and there, and divans and mirrors everywhere. And most curious, there was a circular settee in the middle, where people could lounge while admiring the surrounding splendor from various angles. Ana Magdalena had never seen anything quite like it.

"It's awfully stylish!" she exclaimed, impressed.

"Well, of course. With a decor by Toulouse-Lautrec? You couldn't go wrong!"

But Ana Magdalena had never heard of Toulouse-Lautrec. Her attention was caught by the tinkling notes of a piano. She hadn't noticed him when she first entered the parlor but now a slight, pale-skinned negro was adjusting a tiny turned-leg piano stool. He launched into a sizzling keyboard warm-up. She had never heard such riveting music before.

Ofelia smiled. "You like it?"

Ana Magdalena nodded.

"That's jazz," explained Ofelia. "The only worthwhile thing ever to come from the *norteamericanos,* that and money, of course."

"*Norteamericanos?* I didn't know they were black."

"Oh, *norteamericanos* are white. It's the musicians who are black. Descended from Africans. Like me."

Ana Magdalena examined Ofelia carefully. She saw a woman of uncertain age and indeterminate skin color, with very curly, reddish hair. "Black?"

"Umhumm." Ofelia nodded, lighting a strange-looking little pipe. "There's a little color in your family, too."

"God! He's stupendous. What's his name?"

"He won't say." She lowered her voice. "I call him Ropes, but he doesn't seem to mind."

102

"Why would he mind?"

"You'd know if he ever let you see his neck!" Ofelia let out a clap of laughter so loud the mirrors rattled. "Come on, let's go find Sidonia. My sweet tooth needs a little soothing."

But Ana Magdalena couldn't stop herself. Ropes's music was driving her crazy. She raised her voluminous wedding skirts and broke into a cakewalk. Happily, Ofelia joined her. Clapping and strutting, they took a couple of turns around the room.

"Oh, darling," she exclaimed, "isn't this fun! And you're a lovely dancer! Come on, let's have something in the kitchen! There's just time for a little gossip before I send you home!"

Ofelia pushed the swinging doors open. "Sidonia," she announced, "Meet my little grandniece! We're just back from her wedding!"

Sidonia brushed her hands on her apron. "Ah," she smiled, "*la novia!*"

"We need a little something hot to warm her up before Julio drives her back home in the carriage."

They huddled over the kitchen table, blowing the steam off Sidonia's hot chocolate.

"Now, tell me everything," gushed Ofelia. "Start from the very beginning. How did you wind up here on your wedding night? And how did you *ever* manage to marry such a dolt?"

Ana Magdalena told Ofelia about the hatboxes and the wedding cake, and how just as she reentered the kitchen, the crew had kidnapped her. She told Ofelia a lot more besides, and the more she talked, the more she found things to confide. It was a long story, and as she told it, she remembered with a certain nostalgia her plain brown dresses and her high button shoes and the birdsong, and the promise of the sunlight on the road as the convent gate swung shut behind her that morning long ago.

"My God, Ofelia, none of this would ever have happened if I hadn't found out I know how to swim!"

Ofelia laughed. "Listen, girl, swimming is the very least of your worries. What are you going to do locked up in a big house like that one? You need to have some fun. You'll have to come to visit me."

"Oh, why couldn't I have gotten to know you sooner?"

"Because, child, it wouldn't do. After all, I'm a professional."

"Just because you run an establishment?" Ana Magdalena was wide-eyed.

"Of course, *niña*. It's the oldest and the proudest profession in the world. Come on quick, before we let the customers in, I'm going to show you everything."

The former convent of the Capuchins had been confiscated together with all other lands and property belonging to the church by the dictatorship of 1910. Originally it had sheltered a small flock of young ladies who aspired to join the order. There was a vast chapel, which had not yet been demolished by the earthquake of 1992, and the adjacent building housed the kitchens, a refectory, a visitors' salon, and a library. Above were two dormitories large enough to accommodate up to sixty young postulants eager to incarcerate themselves for a lifetime of penance and prayer, while they scratched under their hairshirts to quell the itching of their tender, uninitiated skins.

But Ofelia's great pride was the upstairs rooms, where each of the eight beauties had her own special place to receive guests, all coded by color, so that if a customer happened to forget the lady's name, he could remember her by hue. All of the rooms displayed magnificent burnished antique furniture of various periods, but what Ana Magdalena noticed most of all were the old-fashioned washstands and water pitchers. And the mirrors.

In addition to the main building, there was a curious adjacent structure that could be reached either from below through the cloister garden, or from above by a connecting corridor. It had the appearance of a well, with an enclosed spiral ramp, so that, except at certain intervals, people could come and go unseen. Along the way, cells belonging to the nuns who had been cloistered for life lay behind iron grilles, each one with its small window facing out. This structure, which Ofelia referred to as The Screw, stood empty of any furnishings except for the original plank beds, which still lay gathering dust.

"All kinds of things could be done with it, *niña,* if I only had time. But there's so much to do. It's such a shame. I could handle double, triple the traffic. As it is, some nights we have to turn people away. It's word of mouth, *niña*. A satisfied client is the best advertisement.

104

There's so much demand now, I hardly know what to do with it, unless I open The Screw!"

"But what happens when all your customers marry?"

"Marry? But that's when they become regular lifetime subscribers. Married men are the backbone of any house. It's the respectable family men, the bankers, the lawyers, the doctors, especially the politicians — anyone in public office, it makes them feel big. Important. They come here, party, meet their friends, watch each other go upstairs. Some of them have their repeat favorites, others like to play the field. They can smoke their vile cigars, tell off-color jokes, drink as much as they can hold. They can play a hand of cards while they paw an ass or two. They can even get ashes on the rug. They feel at home. It's the way the world was supposed to be before some spoilsport invented matrimony!

"And the girls like it, too. If they have to lie under some clumsy fellow, or someone with bad habits, for example, they know it's only for ten minutes, or an hour at the most, not for a lifetime. They just change the sheets! And if it's a man they like, a man who really gives them pleasure, maybe he'll ask for them next time around. And meanwhile they can pretend it's him anytime they're back with the other guy!"

They returned to the great vestibule. Sidonia was letting in the customers.

"*Dios mio,* here come the troops. Let me try to find Julio quick so he can take you home. Why don't you wait in here?" Ofelia ushered her back into the now deserted kitchen.

Federico ordered Hortensio Medina to drive Andreina home in the modern motorcar he had only recently purchased from Henriod & Schweitzer, the famous Swiss manufacturers. She arrived at a darkened house, hair in complete disarray from the fifteen-kilometer-an-hour rush through the night-deserted streets. But she had no mind for her coiffure just then. She was filled with concern for her only daughter and her unexplained disappearance. A terrible anxiety welled up inside her.

Even before she could light the vestibule lamp, she knew at once: a savage air had escaped into the house. It had the smell of ripe and decaying jungle rot. When she saw to her horror that the parlor doors had been left ajar, she knew with certainty that someone had intended to do her a great wrong, and when she lit the gas light she discovered the bees. They were everywhere. They had burst like an explosion of fireflies on a summer night. She could hear them gnawing at the wood of the support posts, at the ceiling joists. They had infested the rush seats of the chairs, they had suspended their combs from the dowels of tables, and when she looked under her bed, she discovered that a cluster of nests already hung like cows' udders from the bedsprings.

Because of her deep distress, she only discovered Aurora Constancia's note when, at last, she prepared to bed down for the night on a mat in the kitchen, the only area left undisturbed by the bees.

My dear Andreina,

We looked everywhere for you. i would have liked to say good-bye, but it got so late and Hercules (!) had to take me to the station so i wouldn't miss my train. Please tell dear Ana Magdalena how i wish the best for her every happiness. And yours.

At last she understood: the open parlor door, Aurora Constancia's "lateness." It was Hercules — Hercules, her dark and tireless nemesis, with his raffish spats and his rampant appetites, who had been the ruin of her life, her house, and her serenity. And now she had lost the one comfort he had ever given her. She resolved that, no matter what happened to her daughter, she would make sure to keep the reward money to console her for her loss.

"Señora!" gasped Berta, as she tripped over the sleeping form of her mistress when on the morrow she entered the kitchen at five A.M. to set the breakfast fire. "What's the matter?"

But Andreina had lapsed into a state of severe catatonia, which deprived her of speech. She lay paralyzed on her mat eyeing the ceiling.

Ana Magdalena sat in La Nymphaea's now deserted kitchen, idly sipping the remains of the hot chocolate in her cup, waiting, as her aunt had told her to, for Julio, Ofelia's coachman. She could hear the captivating sounds of the piano. She inched open the swinging doors and peered through. In the great parlor she could see the girls sitting on the settee or reclining on the divans in the most languid of poses. Some wore gorgeous evening gowns. Others were attired in exactly the same kind of lingerie Aurora Constancia had sported that distant day in the river. She saw them through a film of something she could not quite identify. They were talking in quiet tones, and under it all, the haunting notes of the piano player filled the room. As she watched, now and then a gentleman came into view. After appraising the rainbow girls from a distance, he would approach one or another of them, take off his hat, and begin to make conversation. It was exactly like any other party or reception, except for the skimpy attire of some of the ladies.

Half of her wondered why the coachman was taking so long, but the other half let the swinging door swing wider. As she watched, Ana Magdalena felt her throat constrict with sadness. She wanted to dance the cakewalk like the rainbow girls. She began to think she did not exactly want to be married, at least not to Federico Orgaz y Orgaz, and maybe not even to Sergio Ballado or Hortensio Medina. But she knew she didn't want to be a spinster either. She wished she could lie under a good strong man now and again who could make her heart leap.

She allowed the door to open wider still. At that very moment she caught sight of him. Even in profile his look was unmistakable. It had to be him. No. Could it be? Yes! It was Sergio Ballado.

Ana Magdalena had always kept a cool head about her, but now, for the first time in her life, she felt a herd of wild horses galloping in the narrow white corral of her bridal bodice. She watched Sergio Ballado enter the parlor as the others had done. She saw him hesitate. She imagined she was soaping herself again in the river — a churning smock waved and called for help. Now, without a moment's hesitation, she unfastened her wedding dress and let it slip to the floor. She kicked off her miraculous shoes. She ran through the swinging doors just in time to see him approach Alicia, evidently the girl of his choice.

"No!" she said to Alicia. "This one's mine!" She threaded her arm through his. "This moment has been waiting for me. For a very long time."

*   *   *

Federico had done what he could. After he had seen Andreina safely off, he had himself driven the ornate Orgaz excursion vehicle to the jail. Sure enough, just as he supposed, the warden had closed up shop for the night. He went to look for him in the local watering hole.

"My God," moaned the warden, already sunk deeply in his cups, "every one of them? Escaped? And they took your wife along?"

"All except the guards and waiters."

"Where are they now?"

"Locked up. In my pantry."

"Your *pantry! Chingada!* I'll have to call up reinforcements."

"I wish you would. I nearly stripped the telephone crank bare trying to call you! I'd like to get to bed. And if any of those scum so much as touch my wife, I'm warning you, there'll be the devil to pay, and I'm not speaking lightly!"

At last, after seeing to the final disposition of the occupants of his pantry, Federico was able to lock the doors. Because Severina had long ago retired, he had to extinguish all the lights himself. There was no point in waiting any longer for Ana Magdalena. God alone knew what would happen to her. Preoccupied, he stood before the mirror applying wax to his mustache. He teased and twirled it into the perfect parabola. Holding his black satin mustache sling in place, he let the elastic snap against his scalp. He was ready for bed.

When Ofelia returned to the kitchen with her coachman in tow, she nearly tripped on the obstacle that lay in her path. "Well, well," she said to herself as she bent down to see what it might be. She was surprised to discover that Ana Magdalena had disappeared clear out of her wedding dress, but she didn't overly trouble herself because it was clear to her that, whatever she said, Ana Magdalena could look after herself and that, as soon as she needed to, she would return. Her main concern was for Hercules. If he came home to find his daughter's wedding gown in La Nymphaea's kitchen, he might express some curiosity about how it came to be there. Quickly she picked up the shoes and dress and stuffed them in a bread bin.

"Wait for her here," she ordered the coachman. "And, Julio, when she comes, be sure to tell her where I put her things." And pushing open the swinging doors, she reentered the parlor. There were customers to greet, introductions to be made, wine to be poured, but above all, she loved to keep an eye on the proceedings.

To her great satisfaction, there were even more gentlemen present whom she recognized from the wedding party.

"Good evening, Your Honor," she greeted Judge Gutierrez with all the expansive style at her command, "how does the evening find you, and wasn't it a perfectly lovely wedding and wasn't she the sweetest bride?" She took him in tow. "Let me introduce you to Alicia. You probably recognize her from earlier today. She simply adores dignitaries, don't you, dear, and she knows exactly how to please them! Why don't you take His Honor upstairs?"

Ana Magdalena tried the first door she came to. It was locked. She led Sergio Ballado down the corridor. She tried the next. It opened. She led him into a room that was entirely furnished in lavender. She locked the door.

She turned to face him. "Aren't you going to undress me?"

She could feel his rough, capable hands begin to tug at the straps of her chemise.

"No, not like that," she whispered. She placed his hands on the hem of her chemise.

Years later she would still remember Sergio Ballado's first words to her: "How come you look so much like a bride?"

"Because I am!"

He let the chemise drop. "Then where's your husband?"

"Right here," she said.

"*Here?* Oh no, lady! You got it wrong."

Before he could make for the door, someone outside in the corridor tried to turn the knob. Ana Magdalena raised a finger to her lips. "It's just a manner of speaking," she whispered. "Don't be concerned."

Someone began to knock very loudly. Ana Magdalena raised her chemise above her head.

"My God!" Sergio Ballado whispered, utterly awestruck. "Who could have imagined such a treasure!" He cupped the soft white orbs of her breasts in his hands and his mouth found her nipples. Her head began to swim. Never, never had she been transported like this, not even on Aurora Constancia's bed in La Paz. Her body excused itself and went to hover in the corner of the room, just below the ceiling. A voice came out of it she didn't recognize. It howled like a caged animal.

"Look!" he was urging her. "I want you to look at me!"

She opened her eyes. He had her facing a mirror. His head bent over her shoulder. He slid his hand toward the dark and liquid tuft between her legs. She closed her eyes. She felt as though she were sick, miraculously sick, as if something were happening to her, as if he were easing the insides out of her, sliding them out thicker than blood; she felt as if she were going to die. But it was an ecstatic death, full of swirling color.

"Open your eyes," he said to her. "I want you to see what a bride looks like."

A wail came from just below the rafters. It was the sound of a woman in pain. She recognized the voice. It was the voice of Andreina. She wanted it to stop. But it wouldn't stop. She left her body where it fell. Her legs remembered what to do. He bowed his head between them. He was receiving her host, he was drinking her wine. Somewhere a voice was screaming. He had something up inside her. He was twisting in some kind of agony. His mouth was opening and closing. A fish was swimming inside her.

"*Madre!*" he was screaming, "*madre!*"

Someone tried the doorknob. There was knocking on the door. He had his hand over her mouth. They were breathing together, two salmon swimming up a river gone dry, two snails lathered in foam.

Someone was trying the door.

"Go away!" she was crying. "Go away!"

After a time it was darker, and much later it got quieter. She couldn't remember sleeping. When she awoke, the man lay beside her breathing the thick air of sleep. She shook him.

"I can't stay here," she said. "I have to go."

"But I'm paying for the night," he mumbled.

"But it's not my room. I told you, I'm a bride. I have to go home."

He sat bolt upright in bed. "You're not going anywhere. You're a whore, the most magnificent whore. With the soul of a whore! And the cunt of a whore! And the tits of a whore! And don't let anyone tell you anything different." And to remind her of what he knew, he began to trouble her ears, and her neck, and her breasts all over again until the ceiling joists wailed and whined, and the walls gasped and thundered.

Nothing like it had ever happened before. Ofelia knew something was wrong. Her girls were in the wrong rooms. There was a terrible mix-up somewhere, and how could she even begin to sort it out on one of their busiest nights? Eleven of the wedding guests had shown up, vying with the regular clientele. Twenty-eight customers were still waiting in the bar, busy playing cards on the green baize gaming tables. She knew she couldn't keep them there forever.

Even before Hercules came home, she was feeling close to overwhelmed, but she could see at once that something terrible had happened to him. She had seen him drunk, yes, but never, never with the stuffing quite gone out of him.

"What's the matter, you hardly look yourself at all! Sit down, my friend, and tell your auntie everything!"

He placed a grizzled head on her shoulder. "She rode me like a broomstick!" He began to sob in short, choking little gasps. "She was like a hellcat," he whispered. "A valkyrie."

"My God," she said, "you need a drink. Pepe!" She called the bartender. "Give us two whiskeys. Neat. Make them doubles."

All of a sudden a thought occurred to her. She eyed him full of suspicion. "It wasn't one of my girls, you old satyr, was it?"

"No," he said mournfully.

"Where?"

"Where what?"

"Where was it?"

"Andreina's."

"My God!" she breathed. "And after all these years!"

But Hercules was much too drained to set her straight.

Barefoot, clad only in her chemise, Ana Magdalena crept downstairs. It was perhaps a mistake to leave Sergio Ballado upstairs covered only in the heavy sleep of his exhaustion, but there was no turning back. A wedding night of a tamer sort still awaited her, but first she would have to find her clothes, and she would need a coach to get her there.

As she reached the midfloor landing, she peered through the

balusters. A rude shock awaited her. Hercules sat not fifteen feet away, swirling the dregs of his drink with a swizzle stick. Ana Magdalena gasped. There was no way to retreat, she knew. Only one choice was left to her. She tiptoed down the great staircase, and still unobserved, made a dash for the kitchen. She flung open the swinging doors. Instantly she heard the howl of someone in pain. The coachman stood stunned and bloodied where the door had struck him across the nose. As she darted inside, Hercules stood up. To her horror, she saw him advance toward the kitchen.

"Quick!" She pulled the coachman toward the outside door. "There's no time to waste!"

"But your clothes! Your shoes!" protested Julio through the handkerchief he held to his bleeding nose.

"This is no time for modesty. You'll have to bring them to me later." She pushed him through the door.

The carriage came to a halt at the foot of the double marble staircase of Federico's house. Ana Magdalena got out and waved Ofelia's coachman on. The house was dark. As she climbed the endless flight of stairs, a feeling of anxiety began to take hold of her. She could hear the hoofbeats of the horses disappearing in the night. She reached the doors. They were locked, as she already knew they would be. Her hands searched the doorjamb until she found the porter's bell. She pulled the rope. It gave off a feeble, broken little clank, but nothing happened. The night was turning chill. She sat on the doorstep waiting. Her thin chemise gave her little warmth. She hoped Julio would be returning soon with her things. But when the coachman searched Ofelia's kitchen he found that Ana Magdalena's clothes had vanished.

It was time to do something. It was long after midnight. Judge Gutierrez had decided to stay the night but Alicia had nowhere to take him. Her room was still locked. For an all-night stint, the wooden plank beds of The Screw hardly appealed to her.

"I've already used another room twice. Would you mind letting me have my own room back?" she appealed to Ofelia. "His Honor wants to spend the night."

But when Ofelia tried the knob to Alicia's room, she found

it locked from inside. No wonder there'd been such confusion! Things were beginning to make sense. But when she went upstairs with the passkey, a violent phenomenon leapt at her naked from the bed.

"That's enough, now! For Christ's sake, can't you leave a man in peace? This room is occupied. I'm paying for the night. As it is, we barely got started." He turned to where his partner lay. "Hey, hey, where's the bride?"

"What bride?" gasped Ofelia, her back to the wall.

"Where'd she go?"

"You had someone with you?"

"Quit ragging me," he raged. "Where is she? What's going on?"

But long before Ofelia summoned Alicia, she had a pretty good idea what her story would confirm.

Chilled to the bone, Ana Magdalena rang again. She waited. She could see the windows were dark. The night wind stirred the dead leaves. Somewhere a cricket chirped. Why hadn't it occurred to her before that by climbing onto the marble railing she could edge her way along a shallow molding until she managed to reach a casement? She made her way carefully, holding onto the vines that grew in dark abundance along the wall. Happily, the window was unlocked. She could just reach the handle. She pushed it open and lowered herself inside.

"Halt! Who's there?" A guard appeared from the shadows.

"The bride," she responded without a moment's hesitation.

"Dressed like that? What do you take me for?" He tightened his grip on her arm.

"Don't play tin soldiers with me." She brushed him off. "I've had a hellish night. Take me to Don Federico at once if you don't want any trouble. He must be worried silly."

But the sentry was standing guard on orders of the warden. He had no idea who Don Federico was, or where he might be found. "Wait here," he said.

As soon as he was gone, she found a corner in the parlor that seemed not to be too drafty. She curled up in the angle of a sofa and soon was fast asleep.

When she opened her eyes, Federico was bending over her, his silhouette outlined in the early-morning light. She could see he was taking in her appearance and her scant attire.

"Ana Magdalena! Good heavens. We looked everywhere for you! What happened to you?"

She sat up and rubbed her eyes. "I was kidnapped," she said matter-of-factly.

"Yes, but how did you get here?"

"I escaped. I ran —"

"From where?"

"All the way from the river."

"The *river* —"

"Well, you didn't think to send a coach. They were dragging me along. They had me in a choke hold. They wouldn't let me go. They gagged me so I wouldn't scream, and they tied me to a tree."

Ana Magdalena was beginning to like her own story. She knew she could go on like this forever if Federico didn't interrupt.

"I had to watch them —"

"You *watched* them —"

"I had to watch them eat. They were swilling caviar and drinking champagne. They stuffed themselves with canapés, the brutes, and they wouldn't let me have a thing. I was so hungry I thought I would die. Then they untied me. They wanted me to do a dance for them. Miserable brutes, I showed them absolute contempt. So they took away my dress and shoes. They forced me to watch while some ugly lout teetered about in my gorgeous satin slippers. It made me sick. They took everything — my dress, my shoes. Holy Mother, what a night I've had. I didn't know if I'd make it home alive." And she began to sob very convincingly.

"My darling! You escaped, and you were very nearly naked. Severina, get her something to wear. Poor darling, you must be chilled to your precious little bones!"

Severina muttered something under her breath.

"And get her some breakfast."

Ana Magdalena noticed Severina staring at her, pursing her accountant's lips.

"My precious ran nearly naked all the way from the river." Federico was nearly choked with emotion. "You're a heroine, twice over." He took her hand, and before she knew it, he was addressing her in

114

honeyed tones. "I'm so proud of you, my sweetheart!" He leaned even closer. "I'll tell you what I'm going to do: I'm going to lock myself upstairs. And night and day, day and night, I'm going to write. I'm going to write something extraordinary. I can't be disturbed on any account. You are going to see to everything: bills, the running of the house. I want three meals a day and a change of clothes. I'm going to give the world a major work, a stunning romance; it will overrun the entire Amazon Basin, and before it's done, it will spill over both the southern and northern hemispheres! I'm going to call it *The Love Queen of the Amazon*. And you, my darling, will provide just the right touch of inspiration!"

VIII

Ofelia awoke completely ravaged from the previous night's misadventures. Barely had she settled the appalling brouhaha upstairs and sent Sergio Ballado packing, when she'd had to contend again with Hercules. "What," he had wanted to know, "was that good-for-nothing Ballado doing upstairs?"

"He paid the night," muttered Ofelia, clearly out of sorts.

"He paid the night, did he? Then how is it you're booting him out now?"

Ofelia had been in no condition to withstand a full-scale inquisition. "Why don't you ask him? But it's time for bed," she remarked. "And you, especially, could use a beauty sleep!"

It was, therefore, particularly irksome, on her arrival in the kitchen for a noontime breakfast, to find Hercules expostulating vigorously in loud and outraged tones with the already overtaxed cook.

"I want to know how these things turned up!" he was shouting.

"Señor has only to ask *la patrona*."

Hercules turned to Ofelia. "Ah. Finally. I've been waiting for you all morning. What does this mean?" He held up a severely crumpled white dress. But it was not so crumpled as to be unrecognizable. Ofelia was caught off guard, and for a moment, untypically, she was entirely speechless. "And these?" He shook the white satin slippers at her accusingly.

It was what Ofelia needed. "If it's Cinderella you want, don't look at me."

"What do you mean? Isn't this your establishment? Well? How did they get here? By what miracle, I should like to know."

"I haven't the vaguest idea," sniffed Ofelia. "Sidonia, I'm in with-drawal this morning. Quick. Get me some coffee before I begin sucking blood."

"Sidonia refuses to tell me where she found them."

"Good for her."

"I insist on an answer."

Ofelia was at her wit's end. Not only was Hercules insufferably demanding the minute he got a bee in his bonnet, but for the past several months he had overlooked paying any rent at all. She was actually toying with the idea of moving him out.

"First, why don't you settle your account before we go any fur-ther?"

Hercules' eyes narrowed. He shook a menacing finger at her. "Very well," he shouted, "if you won't cooperate, and Sidonia won't tell, I'll have to appeal to the higher authorities. Just remember, there are plenty of people who would be *very* interested to know exactly how these relics got here, not the least of them the chief of police!" And, dress and shoes in hand, he strode out the kitchen door, slamming it hard behind him.

"Sacred eyeballs of Jesus!" exclaimed Ofelia, finally surrendering to her migraine. "That man thinks his backside weighs a ton!"

"*Don't worry,*" counseled Sidonia. "All we have to do is keep our stories straight. We never saw *la novia*. She never sat here with you drinking chocolate. We don't know how the dress got in my bread bin. Nothing! Señora can count on me. Anyway, mark my words, he'll wind up paying Don Federico a visit. I already know what he's after."

When Severina showed Ana Magdalena to her bridal "apartments," she was astonished to discover that the room was bare except for a bedspring, leaning against the wall. Her trunk had been deposited, unopened, in a corner.

"I'll have Hortensio fetch up a mattress from the stables," Sever-ina declared.

Ana Magdalena wrinkled her nose. "Isn't there a chiffonier of some kind, or an armoire, so I can unpack my things?"

"Perhaps one can be found."

"And the bathroom?"

"Down the hall," rasped Severina.

Despite the minimal amenities, Ana Magdalena managed to refresh herself adequately. She refrained, however, from washing her face because, although she knew it was childish, she wished to keep Sergio Ballado's kisses there as long as she possibly could. She emerged from her ablutions ready to face whatever the day might bring.

At that very moment the porter's bell began a vigorous clanking, and there seemed to be nobody but herself willing to answer it.

"*Sí?*" she said, craning her neck as much as possible to try to see through the porter's window.

"*Mierda!*" someone growled. "Don't give *me* that '*sí*' shit! Open up at once!"

It was Hercules. She recognized what he was carrying.

"What is the meaning of this, missy?"

This time she was too quick for him. "Thank God! You found them!" She clasped her hands together fervently, "Andreina was *sick* when I told her!"

"Told her?"

"The cooks took them — when I was kidnapped!"

"You're babbling."

"No! The cooks from La Merced! They took away my clothes so I wouldn't run away."

"You're telling me Don Federico hired the crooks from La Merced to *cater?* Oh, my God. You married a buffoon, my girl. Wait till the chief of police hears about this!" Hercules held up her wardrobe for inspection. "Do you know where these were found?"

She was all innocence. "Where?"

"La Nymphaea!"

"Good heavens!" she exclaimed sweetly. "Then how did *you* happen to get them?"

But Hercules ignored her question. He turned on his heel.

"Wait!" she stopped him. "You can't take my things away."

"They're state's evidence now, my girl."

"But they belong to me."

"You wouldn't be trying to tamper with the exhibits?" He shook her off. "Don't you know kidnapping is a serious crime?"

118

The day's vexations had only just begun. No sooner had Ana Magdalena stretched out after lunch, than Severina came knocking at her door.

"There's a gentleman."

"Then show him in the parlor."

"I did. He wants to see Don Federico."

"Tell him Don Federico is writing. He doesn't want to be disturbed."

"You tell him. He doesn't want to budge. He says he's prepared to stay the night."

When Ana Magdalena entered the visitors' parlor in her hastily belted dress, she found a funny tub-shaped little troll deferentially clutching his bowler hat. He was sweating.

"Can I be of help?"

"I take it you're the señora? I want a word with Don Federico."

Ana Magdalena eyed his bulging leather suitcase with some suspicion. "Don Federico has left me with strict instructions he is not to be disturbed." She punctuated her words with little emphatic chops of the hand. "Under any circumstances. You know how temperamental writers are. But you can talk to me about anything you like," she purred, crossing her legs.

"I'm afraid I am not at liberty to discuss the matter with anyone but him."

"Oh, señor!" She threw her tiny hands up despairingly. "I'm afraid you don't understand." She leaned toward him confidentially. "Why, tomorrow morning at ten, there's another gentleman coming to see Don Federico who has been waiting since October, and July is nearly over!"

The troll remained unmoved either by her predicament or by her generous display of cleavage. "I'm afraid I have nothing to communicate except to Don Federico. Would you allow me to try knocking at his door?"

"Oh my goodness, no." she gasped, crossing herself. "It's out of the question. Nobody *ever* bothers him when he's writing in the mirador!"

"Very well, then, I'm quite content to wait."

Her eyes narrowed. "Señor, please be candid." She pointed to his suitcase. "Are you here by any chance about my wedding dress?"

"My dear madam." He blanched visibly. "I hope you don't take me for a tailor!"

"Then who?"

"Onofrio Sebastián y Colón, at your service." He gave her a little troll's bob.

Within the mirador, Ana Magdalena could hear Federico clacking away at the typewriter, firmly impervious to interruptions of any sort. Try as she might, she could not get him to respond to her knocking.

Señor Sebastián y Colón was likewise not to be swayed from his purpose. By the time Ana Magdalena returned, he had spread out an enormous ledger on the mahogany parlor table, over which he was bent, making entries. Folders were scattered everywhere.

"I'm utterly crushed, señor. Don Federico refuses to come down," Ana Magdalena told him. "Perhaps you'd better think of coming back tomorrow."

"I'm under strict orders to see Don Federico alone, and to wait as long as necessary — if need be — for the privilege."

"It's getting late. Can I offer you some supper?"

"Oh my, yes! And a little port wine. And a blanket and pillow would be nice."

Ana Magdalena went upstairs to collect Federico's dinner tray. It was piled high with his soiled and sweaty underclothes.

"Federico?" She knocked at the door. "He intends to spend the night! He says he'll stay as long as he needs to. He looks very much as though he means it."

Although it was nearly midnight, all she could hear was the furious clacking of Federico's typewriter.

On the morrow, Señor Sebastián y Colón sent back the breakfast Severina served him to the kitchen. "I never eat greasy foods for breakfast," he declared firmly. "It's bad for the health. The body is like a sleeping animal. It has to be wakened gently." He suggested a puree of mangoes and papaya, and a café au lait laced with rum. "That's *much* better," he declared amiably. "And could you please give these a little shine," he said, handing Severina his cordovan leather shoes when she came to fetch his breakfast tray. "I'm afraid they've gotten rather scruffy."

By midday, Señor Sebastián y Colón had run out of room. His sets of folders had spilled into the corridor, and as Severina was bringing him his lunch, she slipped on them and nearly fell.

"What's *this?*" Señor Sebastián y Colón raised the plate warmer to inspect the food.

"A little tripe."

He wrinkled his nose. "Oh, I couldn't eat *menudo!*"

"Then eat the rice. You just have to scrape it off."

"That's for the kitchen staff to do. But there's hardly any rush. Just bring it back when it's ready. Meantime, I'll take a little sip at the wine!"

Severina stomped up three flights of stairs to the mirador. She knocked. "Señor? Señor?" The clacking came to a halt. "Señor, this has gone far enough! I quit."

From where she stood listening on the lower landing, Ana Magdalena could hear Federico's voice shouting from within.

"You *can't* quit."

"And why not?"

"Because we owe you too much money."

"I quit anyway," shouted Severina, and she began stomping back down the stairs. The door to the mirador flew open. "All right, I capitulate," he grumbled. "Where is he?"

Ana Magdalena scurried down the stairs well ahead of them so as not to be discovered. She watched Federico enter the visitors' parlor. She could hear perfunctory greetings being exchanged. Severina pulled the parlor doors shut before returning to the kitchen.

Ana Magdalena crept to where she could see through the gap in the sliding doors.

"Onofrio Sebastián y Colón," she could hear the troll announce as he fished out a business card, "assistant to the assistant manager of the Colonial National Bank."

Federico tossed the card aside.

"It pains me terribly to have to pay you this visit."

"The pain is all mine, I assure you," Federico replied.

Señor Sebastián y Colón panted about the room collecting his folders. "Due to a little oversight, if I may say, my assistant neglected to inform me he had no reply from you to our letters."

"Your letters?"

"You never received any letters?"

"Probably, but I never open any."

"Well. Where was I? Oh, yes. Well. Quite simply, the bank can no longer honor your overdrafts."

"My dear sir, *what* overdrafts?"

"We have here" — he riffled through one of the folders — "a draft made out over your signature for fifty thousand."

"Fifty thousand!"

"My manager thought it was rather unusual."

"Made out to whom?"

The troll raised a pince-nez to his watery eyes. "Andreina Arzate de Figueroa."

From her listening post behind the door, Ana Magdalena gasped.

"Oh, I'd quite forgotten, yes, of course!" cried Federico, striking his forehead.

"The books show you are already over seventy thousand overdrawn, seventy thousand eight hundred sixty-three, to be exact."

"Including the fifty thousand."

"Unfortunately, excluding the fifty thousand. If señor would care to take a look . . . " He opened the ledger lying on the table.

Ana Magdalena watched them poring over it. A sharp tap on her shoulder made her start with surprise. Severina was eyeing her with a look of extreme disapproval. "You're wanted in the kitchen. There's someone out there who wants to see you."

"*Niña!*" exclaimed Berta as soon as Ana Magdalena appeared. She wrapped her arms around her mistress. "The señora, your mother, is dying! I can't get her to move. She won't say anything, for two whole days now, she doesn't speak!" She held a handkerchief to her eyes.

"Severina, tell Hortensio to fetch the motorcar. We need to go at once!"

But when they were finally set to leave, Hortensio insisted that Berta ride up front with him. He stuck Ana Magdalena back in the rumble seat. "Señora is the señora now," he explained. "It wouldn't do to ride with servants!"

When they pulled up in front of Andreina's house, Berta exclaimed, "Holy Virgin! I almost forgot — we can't go in there. The bees have taken over the house. We have to enter from the kitchen."

Without knowing it, they were about to witness another in a long and tiresome string of miracles. Ana Magdalena entered the kitchen to find her mother stretched out on a kitchen mat. She knelt at her side. "Mother? Mother?" she called softly. Andreina showed no response. Indeed, it was difficult to tell whether she had heard anything at all. Ana Magdalena held her wrist to see if she could feel a pulse. She touched her forehead. "Berta, see if you can find me a mirror — even a feather would do."

Ana Magdalena held Berta's little pocket mirror up to Andreina's nose. A very faint cloud of moisture collected on its surface. "She's still breathing. Quick! Go with Hortensio to fetch the doctor!" Again she looked at Andreina. It seemed to her that her mother had stirred slightly. "Mother," she whispered, "I've come to talk to you. It's urgent."

Andreina lay without moving.

"It's about money!"

Andreina sat bolt upright. "*Hija! Hijita!* My own precious daughter, you're back! What happened to my little girl? I looked for you everywhere!"

"I was kidnapped by the kitchen staff," explained Ana Magdalena, "but I managed to escape."

"Without harm?" Andreina asked her pointedly.

"Oh, they just roughed me up a bit, but they were perfect gentlemen."

"And Federico?"

"He's locked up."

"*Locked up?*"

"Writing."

"Oh, writing. Of course."

Berta helped Ana Magdalena get Andreina to her feet. She tottered to the kitchen table, where she sat down with a sigh. Ana Magdalena knew how much her mother was counting on Federico's settlement. She couldn't imagine how she would bring herself to tell her what she knew. But all at once she jumped up from the table. "The bees! Of course! Why didn't I think of it sooner!"

"What bees?" Andreina wanted to know.

"*Your* bees. You wouldn't have to lift a finger. Your fortune is already at your fingertips."

Andreina was baffled. "Talk sense, child. I can barely breathe as it is. I can't see what you're getting at."

"You can sell honey. The bees are already working for you. They feed themselves. They don't need to be paid. They won't join a union, and they'll never, never quit. It's free enterprise at its very best — right here at home."

Ana Magdalena had to explain to Andreina about free enterprise. "It's when you get more and more by spending less and less."

"But dear child, that's the devil's work. Why didn't we think of it sooner? But now, thanks to Don Federico's settlement, it won't be necessary."

"Fifty thousand escudos, is that right?"

Andreina tried to hide her discomfort. "Fifty thousand. Yes."

"Mother, it might be better if you stuck to bees."

Long after Ana Magdalena's visit, Andreina still had not resigned herself to her true life's work. But once she managed to swallow her disappointment, she began the difficult process of extracting honey from the pelmets, the upholstery, the bedsprings, and wherever else the bees had hived. Because she knew chance favors the prepared mind, she protected herself against bee stings with a singular costume she confected out of opera gloves, Alençon lace netting, and a garden party picture hat that Berta had unearthed for her. When she smoked out her bees it was with the best Havana cigars, and unlike the majority of apiarists, she always worked indoors, away from her neighbors' scrutiny.

"*Kidnapped!*" The chief of police stared hard at Hercules. "No one reported a kidnapping. All the warden described was a breakout. You're sure?"

"It's what the young lady said."

The chief of police gave a baffled tug at his mustache. "Of course, we can't press charges or file a suit of any kind without a complaint, or some sort of evidence. You say you found the señora's wardrobe somewhere in La Nymphaea. What, if I may inquire, were you doing there?"

"I live there."

"Very well, but how did these things get there?"

124

"Exactly."

The captain drummed his fingers on his desk.

Something had been staring Hercules in the face. Ofelia and Ana Magdalena must have had nothing to hide, or they would surely have offered him money. But Federico! What would he say if he knew where his wife's wardrobe had been found, let alone her wedding dress? Of course! He had been barking up the wrong tree all the time! Hercules stood up to leave.

"Just a minute." The police chief reached for Ana Magdalena's clothing. "Where do you think you're going with those?"

"I beg your pardon?" Hercules swept his daughter's dress back out of range.

"I can't let you leave here with the evidence."

"But you said there isn't any charge."

"There wasn't till you came."

Soon Ana Magdalena discovered that Severina showed a tendency to disappear. Once, for example, she searched for her everywhere, only to find her in Clemencia's room.

"When are you planning to serve lunch?"

"There is no lunch. No one sent me shopping."

"But you go to market every day."

"Not without money, I don't."

"Then take some money quick and go at once. Choose something that doesn't need much preparation."

"And where do I 'take some money quick'?"

"Wherever you normally get it from."

"I don't normally get it anywhere. Don Federico gives it to me."

"Then go to him at once!"

"I thought he didn't want to be disturbed."

The woman was getting on her nerves.

"Go this minute, and tell him I sent you. You can't prepare lunch without money."

Clemencia was chuckling. "Federico never has any money, poor boy. Sometimes he even tries to borrow from me."

"From his own mother?"

"Oh, you don't know the half of it." She sat on the bed, struggling to reach her feet. "Could you help me on with my shoes, dear? That

Federico! He must have gone and pawned my shoehorn. It wouldn't surprise me a bit."

If her lunches were disappointing, Severina's dinners beggared description. Ana Magdalena stared at the roasted yam, the boiled chayote, and the fried jicama lying inert on her handpainted Havilland plate. She rang for Severina.

"What now?"

"Can't you dress these poor defenseless tubers up a bit? Maybe with some kind of sauce?"

"I can't turn loaves into fishes. You want sauce? Get me money for sauce."

Seated opposite her, Clemencia picked at her supper. "It's exactly like baby food," she enthused. "*So* good for my teeth." She leaned confidentially toward Ana Magdalena. "I only have seven."

"Doña Clemencia, what happened to the footmen?"

"What, child?"

"The footmen? What happened to them?"

"Oh, once upon a time the house was crawling with footmen and we had all sorts of maids."

"What happened to them?"

"Federico had to let them go."

"Then who were those men somersaulting backward — the ones who brought the jungle flora?"

"Oh, that must have been those Chinese acrobats he borrowed from the circus once."

"Doña Clemencia, I must talk to you. Federico has made some very tricky investments. He needs seventy thousand right away."

"That boy, that boy, with his harebrained schemes. Investing in jungle flora, I ask you! No wonder he's always broke. Don't pay him any mind."

"Señora, I need your help. There isn't even grocery money. Look at this. You call this dinner?"

"But it's awfully good for people who have trouble chewing."

"Maybe, señora, but I have all my teeth!"

The tines of Clemencia's fork rang against her plate as she methodically reduced everything on it to mush.

"Doña Clemencia, I hate to ask you, but don't you have —"

Clemencia raised a restraining hand. "Oh, don't bring up my jewels. Listen, child. My jewels are a source of endless speculation. I have three fabulous sets, you know, from my dear departed husband — who was my second cousin. We were the last of two lines. We inherited everything. One set of emeralds, one of rubies, and one of sapphires. The emeralds were the most astonishing. They were set in solid gold with lots of diamonds. Oh, my dear, they could take your breath away."

"Then you still have them?"

"Oh, yes. I still have them, in a manner of speaking."

"And has Federico ever asked you to sell them?"

"Federico would never dare ask me such a thing. He knows how much they mean to me. They're all I have, dear girl. Besides, they're worthless."

"Worthless?"

"Listen, child. Federico thinks I don't know. He thinks I'm too old to notice things like that." She lowered her voice. "I might as well tell you: they disappear."

"Disappear?"

"Yes. For weeks at a time. Then, of course, they reappear. First the emeralds, then the rubies. And just three months ago the sapphires disappeared. Oh, they come back, but it takes some time. First they remove the precious stones, then they match them with glass of some sort. It looks like the real thing. Almost. But my dear departed husband, the lover of my heart, he knew. He had mines. He showed me how to tell. You put them on black velvet. You hold them to the light. You examine every facet very carefully, and you look for the colors as the gemstone bends the light. It's the colors, my dear. The colors tell you everything. They sing."

"And these colors are different?"

"Well! My dear, these colors are tone-deaf!"

They were interrupted by Federico's voice bellowing from the mirador. "You call this dinner? What kind of miserable shit is this? Pig fodder, that's what. Fit for brutes."

"He's calling." Ana Magdalena excused herself from table, "I'm coming!" she trilled.

He was standing in the embrasure of the door. Against the light streaming from the windows of the mirador, his frame appeared enormous. The stairs were littered with fragments of mashed jicama and Havilland.

The floor of the mirador was covered with little piles of paper, and stacks of volumes filled the shelves. The overflow hugged the walls. On a rickety hairpin table, an enormous typewriter of the Black Maria variety wobbled.

"Federico, dear, I'm so glad you called. I need to ask if I can see the books."

"You have all the books you need right here!"

"Not that kind of books."

"Don't trouble your head about any accounts. Just ask me for any money you need, dear, that's all you have to do."

"What you're saying is you don't keep books."

"Listen, I can't be bothered with trivial, neurotic details. I'm a man entirely bowed at the service of my art! You're married to a great writer, sweetheart. A man of genius! It's your poor little imagination that won't let you see how rich we'll be! I'm composing *The Love Queen of the Amazon*! Wait till my oeuvre is translated into forty-nine different and separate languages. Minimum. Not counting dialects. Publishers will be tearing at each other's testicles vying for the rights. They'll be begging for my toilet paper. And you're worried about a mere bagatelle."

"But meanwhile could you let me have a little bagatelle now so we can eat something tomorrow or maybe Doña Clemencia —"

"And you're not to bother *mamacita!* Don't talk to her about money, and above all, don't bring up her jewels. They're hers, to do with as she pleases. I would never ask her to part with a single one of them. They mean everything to her. She bathes with them, she wears them to bed."

Suddenly, he changed the subject. "You're such a precious, adorable *niñita!* Why don't you come here?" She could hear his breath coming in short rasps. "Those bad men kidnapped my poor starving little sweetheart! Oh, the nasties! Come! Give your big, literary lion a kiss!"

He pushed her toward the truckle bed, on which more manuscripts lay. He swept them majestically to the floor in a great flutter of pages. She struggled beneath his considerable weight as he set about removing her clothing, pulling here, tugging there, covering her squirming body with his hot, carnivorous kisses. "My passionate *niñita,* you like it, don't tell me you don't like it, making real love for the very first time. Now you'll see what a real man is like! I'm going to pierce you like a sword. I'm going to come out the other side of you. I'm going to pin you like a butterfly!"

But almost immediately it became apparent to Federico that his wife was not quite the virgin Doña Eduviges had made out. She lacked the precious bit of qualifying tissue and the more he wondered what had become of it, the more it let the hot winds out of his sails.

IX

As she pulled on the former convent bellrope, Ana Magdalena shivered in the early-morning chill. She waited, hidden in the deeply recessed doorway. At last Sidonia appeared.

"Oh look, it's the bride!" she greeted her. "Come in, come in."

Ana Magdalena slipped inside. "Is la Señora Ofelia awake? I have to talk to her."

Sidonia ushered her into La Nymphaea's parlor. It was cold and empty at that hour, but Ana Magdalena did not have long to wait. Ofelia swept in, still cocooned in her peignoir. She threw her arms around Ana Magdalena.

"*Niña,* I hoped you'd show up. Why don't we join Sidonia in the kitchen; it's sad and depressing in here so early in the morning. Let's have a little resurrection by coffee, don't you think?" She was all giggles and laughter. How could Ana Magdalena begin apologizing, or even explaining to her what had happened that night after she allowed the kitchen door to swing open wide? Holy Virgin, she prayed to herself, help me in my hour of need.

"Apologize? Oh, *niña,* don't even think of it. My house is your house." She put a maternal arm around Ana Magdalena's girlish shoulders. "Listen." Ofelia dropped her voice. "You should have heard that man go on about you. What did you do to him? He didn't want to leave. What a time we had throwing him out."

"But it's my fault. It was me. I took him upstairs. I used the first room I could find."

"Listen, *niña.* Stop blaming yourself. It could happen to anyone. You just had a little impulse."

"He's been giving me impulses nearly all my life."

130

"Then it's an obsession. How lucky for you. Most people wait all their lives for an obsession, and all they seem to catch is colds. Does your obsession have a name?"

"A name, yes. But no address. Oh, Ofelia, I wish I knew how to find him."

"What's his name?"

"Sergio Ballado."

"Hercules might know."

"*Hercules?*"

"Oh, my poor child, I shouldn't have to tell you this after all the things you told me. Your father rooms here in the house."

"*Caramba!*" Ana Magdalena leapt to her feet. "Is he here now?"

"Sit down, sit down. He's out catting, very likely. Don't get so worked up. What can he do to you? You're a married woman now."

"You know he has my wedding dress —"

"I know! I tried to hide it in the bread bin."

"And now he won't let me have it back."

"What do you suppose he wants with it?"

"He went to the chief of police!"

"With your gown? The scum! That settles it." Ofelia rose from the table. "Come on, *niña*. We have lots to talk about. Let's go upstairs, where we won't be interrupted. And Sidonia, please prepare Señor Hercules' closing statement. We're going to straighten that boy out."

No sooner had they entered Ofelia's sitting room, Ana Magdalena began to cry.

"Oh, my dear little child, did I say something tasteless? Hercules can't help it. It runs in the family, darling. All our men are midnight gauchos."

"Oh, Ofelia."

"It's a hereditary trait."

"It's not that." Ana Magdalena was now weeping in earnest. "I don't know what to do," she wailed. "Federico hardly has enough to send the servant out for bread. And every time I ask for money, he tells me he's writing something important and doesn't want to be disturbed." Briny rivulets began coursing down her cheeks.

"That's ridiculous."

"My mother was sure he was the perfect match, and the worst part of it is, I don't even like him."

"You mean, you don't feel *anything?*"

Ana Magdalena shook her head.

"What's he like in bed?"

"Like a conquistador with a butterfly net!" Ana Magdalena broke down completely.

"Oh, *pobrecita!* Conquistadors are the very worst." Ofelia found a tiny lace handkerchief. "Here. Blow that miserable little nose."

"In *this?*"

"Go ahead, be reckless. I've dozens others like it." Ofelia clucked sympathetically. "My word, *niña,* I had no idea. What are you going to do?"

"That's just it. I don't know."

"Because you see, *niña,* I've been thinking." Ofelia studied her thoughtfully. "You seem to have such unusual abilities. . . ."

"I do?"

"That Ballado fellow is just the beginning. I don't see why you should waste all your talents on one man, even if he *is* a literary giant."

"But what am I going to do for money?"

"That's just it, *niña.* That's what I'm trying to tell you. You may have lost a wedding dress, but I think we've found you a profession."

At first Ofelia's suggestion made her dizzy. What if she were free to come and go? To desert Clemencia's claustrophobic company, turn her back on Severina's dour and sullen disposition, ignore Federico and his stuffy literary obsessions? And amuse herself at the glittering soirées in La Nymphaea's parlor! Even if she felt a nagging aversion to the clientele — 'the troops,' Ofelia called them — at least she would be able to dance to Ropes's giddy music! She could kick up her frisky young heels to the cakewalk, and glide sinuously to the captivating strains of the tango!

Dear God, how she missed Aurora Constancia's lively company. The wedding was the last time anything had made her laugh. And Sergio Ballado, with his glistening teeth and his magnificent eyes, could be her regular visitor. They could sport every night before the mirror, ablaze with longing, drunk on love, raising up the agonizing lament of the roof joists, liberating the beatific voices of the rafters.

"Oh, Ofelia, what a great idea," Ana Magdalena sighed.

"It's settled then. That's wonderful. We'll have a little celebration three Sundays from tomorrow, a secret initiating ceremony — just for you!"

But her initiation was not like anything Ana Magdalena could have imagined. For one thing, by the time she pulled the bellrope of La Nymphaea for Sidonia to admit her, she had seen so little of Federico she had come to feel almost anything but married.

The parlor was silent. All the downstairs rooms appeared to be deserted.

"They're upstairs," murmured Sidonia. "This way."

As they climbed the stairs, Ana Magdalena began to hear sounds of laughter. Sidonia opened the door. If Ana Magdalena was surprised to find Ofelia enthroned in her great canopied bed, resting on an enormous mound of pillows, imagine her astonishment to discover all eight beauties, dressed in identical color-coded pastel nightgowns, piled in beside her, and to her utter amazement, two children as well. True, it was an enormous bed, as Ana Magdalena discovered while circling it to meet Ofelia's embrace.

"*Niña,* you're just in time. Do you like pancakes?"

"I *adore* pancakes."

"Make another ten for her," she ordered Sidonia, who hurried back downstairs. She patted a place left vacant in the overcrowded bed. "Don't be shy. Jump in. This is our regular Sunday morning blowout. Well, I think everyone's met before, but it never hurt a body to go by some kind of name." Ofelia pointed. "Cecilia, Marta, Alicia, Trinidad, Victoria, Eugenia, Maria, Mercedes — we'll quiz you later — and this tiny one here is Eugenita, named after her godmother over there, and the young man is our Eduardo, but here at home we call him Pardito because he's brown and funny like a little bear. You know, when people come out funny sometimes we call them assbackward people. And that's why we call him Pardito, right, *chiquito?*" She tickled his belly.

"*Sí,*" he lisped. He turned his face shyly into his mother's breast. Occasionally, he sneaked a peek at Ana Magdalena.

"Well, here you are!" Ofelia considered Ana Magdalena for a moment. "Everyone, what do you think? We're full up with colors. Why don't we call her Blanca?" She eyed Ana Magdalena quizzically. "Because, you know, *niña,* we all of us here have house names. It's not who we really are. We're fantasies. Men keep us dreams. We don't exist for them except by name, or color, but that's not what we are. Trinidad, here, spent three years in jail in Trinidad before she became a breakout artist. And Marta organized the shirtwaist factories in Lima, and Victoria is a virtuoso pianist . . . but enough! You'll get to know us all. Because, everybody, Blanca's coming in. She's going to be our Virgin Bride."

Everyone cheered. Victoria hopped out of bed in her lace-edged satin nightgown to fetch a magnum of champagne.

"Come on, everyone, who's going to get the glasses?"

Ofelia struggled to open the bottle.

"Here, give it here." Marta twisted and eased the cork clear across the room.

Mercedes caught the first blush of bubbles in her glass. She passed it to Ofelia.

"No, no, *querida,* Blanca is our special guest today!"

Pardito began to wail. "Aw, give him a little taste." Eugenia nudged Maria.

His mother let him dip a grubby finger in her glass. She watched him lick it off his finger. "That's all, *chiquito!* There isn't anymore!"

Everyone raised a glass. "To Blanca, the Virgin Bride!"

"And what a bashful bride she is," teased Alicia. "She comes up to this poor unsuspecting fellow. 'This one's mine!' she says. Before you know it she has him in a half nelson."

"And we weren't even married," observed Ana Magdalena gravely.

"Just remember, young lady, you owe me one good john!"

"If he's that good, you might have to wait till I'm through with him myself," cracked Mercedes. They laughed so hard, Ofelia's bed shimmied and groaned.

"Just a minute, let's put frivolity aside," interrupted Ofelia, "it's time to give away 'the bride.' "

At Ofelia's signal, they all splashed Ana Magdalena with their dregs, in the time-honored custom of houses everywhere.

"To Blanca!" they cheered.

"Is that lady living here?" Eduardito whispered to his mother.

"No, *chiquito.* This lady's going to come in afternoons, at least at first," Ofelia explained to everyone. "And now, because today is special, there's a little something for everybody."

Ofelia reached under her mound of pillows and pulled out eight envelopes of different colors. "And there's even a white one here. For Blanca."

"Let's have a little music," crowed Trinidad.

Instantly they all jumped out of bed. The phonograph needle scratched out the throbbing rhythm of a tango. Everyone grabbed a partner. In their silk satin nightgowns they slid across Ofelia's bedroom floor, dipping, swooping, returning for yet another pass. Everybody grew silent watching Ana Magdalena dance. There was something about the way her body moved, the sharp blades of her pelvis arcing, sweeping, bending under and now over her partner, until at last, each one of the beauties stopped and stood watching in amazement, some standing on tiptoe, craning their necks, others perching high on Ofelia's bed.

Because whenever she danced, Ana Magdalena knew she could make everything in the world come to her — even Sergio Ballado, and later, when she tore open Ofelia's letter, she was sure of it because it read:

Favorite hangout of this particular species is a riverfront bar. It's called the Barco de Oro. I heard it from a horse's ass! Good luck and kisses.

Your "auntie,"
Ofelia

Ana Magdalena had never been in a bar before. She entered the Barco de Oro with some trepidation. She chose a dark alcove, where she could bury herself in a corner seat. "Give me a cognac," she whispered to the waiter. Sooner or later, she knew, Sergio Ballado would probably show up. She could wait all night, if need be. She sat alone, and although she could hear voices all around her, and here and there she could even make out flashes of conversation, the darkness walled her inside her own thoughts. Her entire life passed before her. It had taken some curious turns. Goodness knew where it would take her now, but whatever happened, she was a married woman. She would have to stay with Federico, and if it meant taking the bitter with the sweet, there was nothing she could do about it.

She sat on the crude wooden seat staring at the amber liquid in her glass. She took her first sip. She had begun to walk the tightrope of her future; her past lay like a net of green innocence below, and if she fell, it would do nothing to catch her. She took another sip. Her eyes became accustomed to the darkness, and one by one the voices she heard began to claim their masters. It was then she recognized him. He must have been sitting there from the beginning, at a table with four or five others, drinking and playing dice.

The room was a small one, but as she crossed it, every one of her footfalls seemed to her like a casting of the dice. She waited a moment before tapping him lightly on the shoulder. He looked annoyed at being interrupted, but then his eyes stared wide. "It's the bride! It's *la novia!*"

Even from outside he could hear his cronies calling to him.

"You won! You won it all!" He didn't care. He had her by the waist. They were running down a pier. They came to a boat lying at anchor. Her feet couldn't remember how they got there. He leapt aboard and stretched out a hand to help her. "Jump," he said. He caught her in midair.

Many years later Ana Magdalena could remember only the hold of that ship where destiny had led her. She could still picture the hull made of carefully fitted, tarred planks of wood. But there her memory stopped altogether, because all she could imagine was that the floor of the hold had been covered with flowers, a solid bed of them, and that she must have rolled on petals fragile as the wings of night moths, and that their bodies, hers and Sergio's, had been coated with the powdery, moon-colored dust of the wings of cecropias, and that the linens were of the massed and funereal petals of faded chrysanthemums; and that when he pressed his mouth to hers she felt the ephemeral beating of a hummingbird's wings, and that when he entered her at last her body raised its bone spoon to another of his lips and that she became the exquisite tube of the moist, night-blooming cereus, and that she held him in the sticky sap of her embrace like the wriggling and pathetic tarantula that squirms helplessly before dawn when the enzymes began their slow process of liquefaction and returned their bodies to their ancient roots at the fountains of the oceans, in the blankets of the fog. All this she imagined in the twinkling of an eye, or perhaps an eon. And of the myriad moments of her life that she reviewed throughout her time thereafter, and even at the moment of her death, it was always this one that stood out from all the others as the most satisfying.

But for Sergio Ballado, satisfaction was quite another matter. He had plans. He was going to be rich. "Listen, woman," he said to her, "there's no room for us in this pissant town. Why don't we both get out of here?"

"I can't," she breathed. "I'm married."

"But it's me you're in love with, not some poor *pendejo* you got yourself mixed up with. It's me you love!"

He lay on his side, head propped on his hand. He let his gaze meander over the wavering contours of her body as the ship's lantern bathed her in its honeyed light.

"But I'm married to Federico Orgaz y Orgaz."

"Then you're quite the lady, but for a lady, you're still the queen of whores. No woman knows how to make a man feel more like a man than you do! Never, never, in all my life, I never bumped into something like you, I swear it. Listen. Tomorrow I'm leaving for Belém. I'm going to work the excursion boats for the rich *yanquis* who go upriver to shoot game. And when I get back, I want you to be waiting because I'm going to come back rich!"

But it would be some time before Sergio Ballado could begin to deliver on his promise, and that, long after Ana Magdalena had begun making her way alone every afternoon through the siesta-deserted streets to that convent doorway, where she no longer had to pull the bellrope because Ofelia had given her a key. And if she had to invent ingenious stratagems to make sure no one in the Orgaz household knew where she went, at least she had encouraged Severina to serve a more satisfying spread.

Because Federico never sat at table, preferring to eke out the last rays of daylight working in the mirador and typing late into the night, Clemencia was left to entertain her at dinner with endless stories from her past. In those first years Ana Magdalena used to listen quietly, and often she remained absorbed in her own thoughts. When more wine was needed, or a fresh helping of meat, she would press the recently electrified button on the table to her right, and a grudging Severina would emerge muttering from the kitchen.

After dinner, before Severina began clearing the table, Ana Magdalena laid out the money for the next day's menus. She methodically noted these sums in a little book she always carried in her purse, but she was careful never to show it to anyone. She asked Severina for the current day's receipts, which she would add up quickly in her head.

"You're three centavos short, I think?"

Severina always feigned outrage. "Three centavos!"

"It must be here." Ana Magdalena tapped the receipts with her pencil. She knew Severina had a passion for licorice sticks, although, dour as she was, she would be the last to admit to anything so frivolous. "I'll deduct it from your pay."

Try as she might, Severina found it hard to grumble, because for the first time in almost as long as she could remember, she was getting a regular salary from her masters instead of being the one always to extend them credit.

After dinner Ana Magdalena would wait for Severina to help the doddering Clemencia up the stairs to bed before returning to the mirador with a freshly folded change of linen. Often, Federico would open the door just wide enough to exchange his dirty dinner service for a clean set of underwear.

"No! Don't say a word!" he would whisper on those happy occasions before he shut the door. "*Ella me tiene por el culo.* The muse has me by the collar," he would explain. "I don't want to be disturbed."

At other times he would want her to come in. He would clear his throat, and adjust the frumpy old lady's glasses she had come to know so well. She would have to sit on the truckle bed, which was the only place to sit — other than his composing chair — in the sparsely furnished room.

"My heroine is a beautiful young girl. She's born to a good family that has come upon hard times," he prefaced his reading, and cleared his throat.

Many years later, when she appeared before the town fathers, Ostencia Candelaria remembered when her mother had first showed her her lace maker's bobbins. It was a time when the world was first conceived, and nothing, not even vice, had been invented. There were no words for things like overhead, or commissions, or money, and people went about trading things for other things, or sometimes favors for other favors, and they worked only when they needed something or when they felt like it. . . .

Although the activities of the day had thoroughly exhausted her, Ana Magdalena took great pains not to stretch out on the bed as he droned on. Gradually she perfected a way of falling asleep sitting up. It was in this manner that Federico continued to read to her late into the night. At last, hoarse and exhausted himself, he would remove his glasses. Instantly, she was awake, because she knew that once he had removed his glasses, he could see every detail, even in the far distance, and that he would not fail to notice her drooping eyelids or the unnatural stillness of her hands.

"Lovely," she would murmur.

"You have nothing else to say?"

"I have to sleep on it." And she would excuse herself and hurry off to bed.

As time went on, though, she developed an incapacitating re-sistance to hearing Federico read. Ultimately it prompted her to approach Ofelia about a change of schedule.

"It's not for the money, it's the way he reads. And those granny glasses drive me crazy."

Ofelia was overjoyed. Already, working part time afternoons, her Virgin Bride had become the star turn of her establishment. Just wait and see what it does for business, she said to herself as she embraced her niece.

"My house is always your house," she assured her. "Anyway, I was wondering when you'd ask."

To explain her evening absences, Ana Magdalena had to dream up a revised schedule of alibis. She brought Federico his change of linen just before the dinner hour.

"Severina will bring you supper tonight," she warned him. "I have to go help my mother with the bees."

Federico was not happy. "The bees be damned! I want to read you Chapter Three."

"But she has no one to help her harvest the honey."

"Why can't she milk her damn bees — or whatever nasty thing it is she does to them — at a more convenient hour?"

"That's just it," she explained. "You can't extract honey except at night — when it's dark. The bees become irritable at any other time."

Federico found her story suspiciously exotic. He wished he knew something more about the culture of bees. It was like the matter of her virginity. Ever since their first encounter he had meant to bring it up, and the more he thought about it, the more it rankled him. Grudgingly he gave her his consent.

"Remember, *ars longa, vita brevis.* And make sure you remember to turn out the lights."

Some few weeks following her change of schedule, Ana Magdalena entered La Nymphaea's parlor to discover a tall black gentleman who was apparently assembling a curious contraption on the alcove table.

"What's that for?" she wanted to know.

He shot her a playful look. "Whoowhee, sister, they been tryin' figure out this sucker 'bout a hundred years!"

"What is it?"

"Clockworks, little lady."

"But it's made of wood."

"Yessir. It be ironwood. Only it don't need no winding. No button, no winder, none of them wasteful motions. This here be pure motion, elegant motion, nothing but. Now watch this fulcrum."

"Fulcrum?"

"Yes, sister. 'Give me a fulcrum, and I'll move the world.' You know who said that?"

"No."

"It been 'bout a hundred years."

"Since someone said it?"

He threw his head back and hooted with laughter. "That I heard it from my tutor. Now I starts this wheel in motion, and after I starts it, it just go on and on. And *on!* It don't stop till someone stop it. I kept telling them all the *possibilities.* Why, it my Emancipation Proclamation! But nosiree! They wasn't having none of it."

"Why not?"

"Because emancipation awful bad for business." He shook his head. "With this contraption, no one have to work."

There was something not quite right about this gentleman. Ana Magdalena couldn't understand what he was doing in La Nymphaea's downstairs parlor. She went upstairs to change. When she returned, she heard him talking to Ropes in a melodious patois, but she couldn't make out a word of what it was they said. Occasionally she could hear them slap their knees and hoot with laughter.

That evening two Indians came to La Nymphaea. They both wore white homespun nightshirts, and their dark, coarse hair hung loose past their shoulders. Each carried a bow and a quiver full of arrows. Ana Magdalena rose from the settee to greet them. They came toward her unblinkingly, and touched her hands and her arms as if they were looking for something. When she took them upstairs, they spoke to her in a soft language with curious clicking sounds, a language she had never heard. Then, happy as children, they lifted her arms, and at the sight of so much hair, they fell laughing to the floor. One of them took her hand and made her feel along his arms and legs. She had never felt such soft, hairless, honeyed skin. They both took to laughing once again. She was surprised that they only seemed to want to touch her. They did not remove their clothes. When it was time to go, they each tapped her forehead and her eyes. One left a poison arrow for her, and the other gave her a fur bag studded with the toenail clippings of an animal. They left, walking on the balls of their feet so soundlessly they might as well have disappeared.

Before receiving her next caller, Ana Magdalena sat quietly, contemplating the evening's curious events. But it was not until much later that the inspiration came to her to ask Ropes about his curious friend.

Ropes flashed her his diamond-studded grin. "Yes, sugar, I know who you mean. That's old Benji. He come by to fix my metronome. I send for him when the spring gets broke."

"But I saw the clockworks! They were wood."

"I don't know nothing 'bout no wood workmanship. He fix my *metronome*." He clamped his mouth shut tight and began to hum, swaying to the music.

* * *

Often in those days Ana Magdalena dreamt of Sergio Ballado. Sometimes she would stir and awake from them howling like an animal,
and sometimes in the morning or at lunch, Severina would pointedly
remark that after a very long absence the wolves must be back,
roaming the night gardens while the household slept.

Clemencia would take it as a cue to lapse into a deep and passionate nostalgia. "I remember our honeymoon. Enrique, the husband of
my heart, thought we should visit the Alps. Well! I never had much
use for Alps. They're just very high hills in those awful middle-
European countries. In Peru, we get hills like that all the time, but to
call them Alps! We wouldn't dream of it. I told him, if you're so set on
putting on airs, the best thing to do is go to a spa. Take the waters.
Wallow in mud baths up to your chin. But our very first night in
Marienbad, my dear dead mother appeared to me, just imagine. She
was barefoot. I could see her bunions were red and frightfully
swollen. Of course I took it to be a very bad sign.

" 'Take everything you can and leave at once,' she told me. 'You
only have an hour.'

" 'But Enrique won't leave till he's taken the waters!'

" 'He was always so stubborn,' she said. 'Well, suit yourselves, but
by tomorrow this place will have burnt to the ground!'

" 'Already then I could hear voices, people half crazed with fear
running in circles all over the courtyard. 'Wake up! Wake up!' I
shook Enrique, but of course he was such an extraordinary sleeper,
he refused to budge. That man! One time he slept through a
devastating earthquake. When he woke up, he couldn't imagine
what he was doing on the floor. It never occurred to him that he
hadn't simply fallen out of bed until he realized that where the
ceiling should have been, he was looking at the sky. 'Clemencia, my
little cockroach,' he said to me, 'that's extraordinary! You know, I
didn't feel a thing!'

"Anyway, I had to pack our trunks myself, but they were so heavy!
How was I to move them outside? 'Get up,' I shouted, 'can't you see
it's burning?' And in fact, when he finally sat up in bed, we could
actually see the flickering red of the flames through the lace curtains.

"He leapt out of bed and threw open the terrace windows. He
groaned and sweated, pushing one heavy trunk after another to
safety. But there was something very strange, because outside there

wasn't any sign of fire! I knew my mother never made mistakes. Not till we had managed to save everything and the very last trunk was piled with the others on the beautifully manicured lawn, did we hear an explosion, a kind of popping sound. It was the entire kitchen going up in flames! We could hear bin after bin of potatoes exploding as they baked. We listened spellbound. Only when the embers died out did I discover he was still dressed in his nightshirt, poor darling, he was frozen through and through! I had to put him in a trunk to thaw him out." Clemencia rolled her hooded old owl's eyes. "You can't imagine what we were doing when they found us in there!"

Eventually, thanks to Sergio Ballado, a string of gentlemen began arriving from Brazil. Although none were *yanquis* exactly, each of them requested Ana Magdalena by name. First came a pair of Shipibos. They were followed by an anxious ethnographer who was evidently hot on their trail. He was followed some days later by an explorer of the Amazon who had lost his way, and who was reported to be the son of an American millionaire, although he had an abnormally small head, which he claimed was not so much the result of inherited wealth, as of an unfortunate encounter with some hostile head-shrinking Jivaros. He carried a letter addressed to "Ana Magdalena, Novia."

"I'd like to read the letter first," she explained, barely able to contain herself. "It's a matter of pressing importance which cannot wait. Would you mind stepping outside?"

Hastily she shut the door. She tore the letter open.

"My dearest," she read, "my very own Salvation!"

I am counting the months till destiny brings us back together again! The jungle is waiting for us, holding its breath. Toucans, birds of paradise, every tree will burst with music.

The *yanquis* are terrific bosses. They have "bucks" to burn. They'll be great customers. They think nothing of spending 100 *dólares* for a glass of whiskey. They love whiskey. Tomorrow, we are going up the river for game.

Wait for me, sweetheart! We will cruise the Amazon. I'm going to set you up in the most gorgeous riverboat, all white, white veils, white frangipani everywhere. We'll call it *La Novia*. I'll be at the oars day and night rowing all the customers out to meet you. My adored one, we are going to make a fortune!

Anytime now, my darling!

Yrs. fondly,
Sergio Ballado, esq.

P.S. I am sending you four more customers. This time would 15% be OK?

It was about that time that Clemencia first began to float. Nobody seemed to notice, or perhaps no one wished to draw attention to the embarrassing abnormality of her behavior.

Ana Magdalena fidgeted all evening over dinner, barely able to contain her anxiety, as the time wore on and Clemencia launched into one nostalgic reminiscence after another.

"In my day, we had to ride sidesaddle because that was the fashion for well-brought-up young ladies. It was thought that dressage played fast and loose with one's virginity." She chuckled. "What did they know!"

"One day I was coming back from goodness knows where. There was a terrible thunderstorm, hail the size of Fabergé eggs. My dear, my mount refused to move. I had to cover his eyes with my riding habit. But even then, the thunder spooked the poor beast so! Lightning struck the trees, and sent them whirling like matchsticks every which way. I rode and rode through the downpour. Of course, when I got home, I wasn't wearing a stitch. I never heard the end of it. And my hands were frozen to the reins. They had to pry my fingers loose. But I never lost my seat, which is more than I can say for my virginity!"

At last, dinner was over. It was time for Ana Magdalena to leave, but she had to wait in unbearable suspense while Severina conducted Clemencia, snail-like, up to bed. But tonight Clemencia showed no signs of wanting to keep step with Severina's halting progress. Instead, she floated serenely up the stairs. Ana Magdalena saw to her amazement that her feet were gliding a full inch above the floor. Severina seemed not to be aware of anything unusual. She continued coaxing Clemencia up one riser to the next, entirely oblivious of the miracle that had taken place. Once she reached the first landing, Clemencia turned around. She winked at Ana Magdalena.

By the time Ana Magdalena was able to leave, the streets pulsed with eerie bursts of lightning. As she ran toward La Nymphaea, the wind began to swell. Barely had she reached the threshold when the sky unleashed a torrential downpour. With every clap of thunder La Nymphaea's parlor shook. Merriment fizzled. People exchanged terrified glances. Only Ropes seemed unperturbed. He was playing a simpering little minuet.

Ofelia succumbed to a suffocating panic. "For the love of God, play something more lively."

Ropes seemed to pay her no attention. Instead, he swung into an insipid sarabande. Ana Magdalena saw a rotund, bespectacled gentleman in a powdered wig seat himself close to the piano. In his hand he held a large, gold key. It was attached by a string to an enormous kite, which rasped against the parlor ceiling like a trapped and panicked nightmoth.

"Quaking balls of fire, it's 'bout time!" cried Ropes. "You got your rod all propped outside?"

The gentleman nodded.

"The folks here like to have died of fright! What took you so long?"

"Boy, you know how it is: us old boys still like to diddle with our toys. It just takes us a little longer."

Ropes broke into wheezy laughter. At once, the rain and thunder ceased. Everyone could hear the water streaming off the eaves.

Ofelia clapped her hands. "Pepe," she shouted to the bartender, "drinks all around!"

Still laughing, Ropes swung into a cakewalk.

"Would this charming lady like to take an old unregenerate sansculotte upstairs?" the bewigged gentleman whispered to Ana Magdalena. When he stood up, however, she saw he had apparently made such unseemly haste to get there he was not wearing any breeches.

Ana Magdalena leaned over toward Ropes. "Just who is this outlandish fellow?" she whispered.

"I got tricks of my own, girl," he purred under his breath. "That Benji."

"I thought you said Benji fixed metronomes."

"*That* Benji Banneker. *This* be Doctah Frankling!"

X

Federico had already managed to amass an impressive collection of threatening letters from his publisher. Although the first several had been mild in tone, with time they became more and more acerbic.

> Your contract clearly stipulated completion in twelve months. As of this week, *The Love Queen of the Amazon* is already four years overdue. If the lady refuses to arrive within another thirty days . . .

Thirty days! Thirty years, more likely, for an oeuvre of such magnitude, and especially the way things were going. From the first he had encountered certain difficulties. Because he had never done any manual labor (he was happy to say) in his life, and, God willing, never would, he had only sketchy ideas to draw on as to what kinds of survival schemes a young heroine like his Ostencia Candelaria might resort. He was aware, naturally, that women made lace and things of that sort. And he was also aware that everywhere the world over, convents prepared their young charges for lives of watercoloring and impassioned pianism as well, although he had trouble imagining how a woman could manage to wrest a living from either pursuit (and indeed, very few women can imagine it, either). Of course, almost anytime he cared to he could observe peasants and Indians of either sex carrying loads or digging with sticks; but if he considered people like that at all, it was certainly not as persons who might in any way engage his authorial attention. He preferred fictionalized heroines like his Ostencia Candelaria, who was of the purest Spanish stock.

He began to consider that he might be out of his depth somewhat, until it occurred to him that he had, under his own roof, the very informant he required. But if he were to interview Ana Magdalena with any measure of success, he knew he would have to help her overcome her tendency to fidget. Because already for some time she had shown an unexplained reluctance to respond to his advances, he was determined not to give her the wrong impression as to what he had in mind. He decided therefore that the best, most neutral terrain in which to initiate his research might not be in the mirador, and to this end, he instructed Severina to arrange for a meeting with Ana Magdalena in the library, and to summon him at once when she was ready. She was to take pains not to interrupt them, but at a discreet moment, she was to knock softly and enter with a tray of tea and biscuits.

When he appeared at the appointed hour, Ana Magdalena was already waiting for him. She sat curled up in an enormous leather armchair, close to the fire. He chose to seat himself where he could more keenly observe her every reaction, but at a sufficient distance from her not to stir up any disquieting sentiments. She noticed at once that although he seemed not to have his dowager's glasses, he was armed with a notebook and a variety of writing implements. As if he read her hesitation, he flashed her a reassuring smile.

"*Chica,* dear girl, let me set your doubts at rest. I'm not going to read to you this time."

"Oh, what a pity," she diplomatically replied.

"And now that that's settled, my dear, how are you? I hope you're not too bored rattling all around this great big house alone. Are you finding things to do? And is Severina giving you everything you want? If she gets out of line, just tell her you'll have to talk to me. She'll shape up in no time."

At that very juncture the subject of his conversation kicked open the door. She entered with a tea tray laden with cups, sugar, and milk, and a generous arrangement of sweet biscuits. With an exaggerated clatter she placed them on the low table fronting the fire.

"Will that be all?" Severina grumped.

"Señor . . . ," added Ana Magdalena pointedly.

Severina would have preferred to ignore her prompting, but she could no longer claim to be an unpaid volunteer. "Señor," she grunted as she slammed the door.

No sooner had she departed than Federico fervently clasped Ana Magdalena's hand. "My dear, how splendid you are!"

"Oooh!" she exclaimed, completely ignoring him, "jelly biscuits! They're my favorite." She broke out of his grasp to help herself.

"I could never get her to say 'señor' in all the years she's been waiting on me — except the day she threatened to quit. How on earth did you manage it? And with such tiny little hands and feet!" Federico passed her a linen napkin, which she placed over her lap. "Tea?"

As he poured for her, he began. "You may wonder why I didn't ask you to the mirador, but it seemed to me that the library was just the place where two old allies like us could talk freely about what's on my mind." He glanced at her to see how she was reacting. She had her mouth full of jelly biscuit, which she was devouring with apparent relish.

"What's that thing up there?" She pointed to the chimney.

"What thing?"

"The thing that looks like the claxon on a motor car."

"Oh, that's the family blunderbuss."

"Blunder-what?"

"Buss. It's an antique gun — been in the family at least two hundred years. But what I *really* want to talk about this morning has to do with my heroine."

"Your heroine?"

"Yes. My principal character, Ostencia Candelaria."

"Oh," she said.

"The protagonist of *The Love Queen of the Amazon*."

"Oh, I thought the protagonist *was* the love queen of the Amazon."

Federico let out a little chuckle. What a bright, intelligent young thing she was, he thought. There would be many things to teach her when he had the time. "You're right. Of course she is."

"Go on," said Ana Magdalena, helping herself to another jelly biscuit.

"My Ostencia is a girl of good family that has fallen on hard times. She has to scramble to make a living for herself and her invalid mother. But of course, they're almost always destitute. She doesn't know what to do next. Of course, every girl knows needlework. . . ."

"God's little booties! You told me all this stuff before." Ana Magdalena rolled her eyes.

Instantly on the alert, he took up his clipboard and pen. "Where did you get that rather quaint expression?" His pen was poised for her response.

"Oh, please! You know I can't stand needlework!"

Federico scribbled something. "My dear, although I think like a genius and write like a distinguished author, you would never guess what trouble I sometimes have expressing myself. I hope you'll make certain allowances for my deplorable clumsiness." He took up his notebook once more. "When you were living at home, did your mother —"

"Oh, Andreina, yes. She just loves needlework. She used to do it all the time."

"What kind of needlework?"

"Oh, monograms. Trousseau work. For rich people." Federico continued to scribble. "There wasn't any money in it."

"What else did she do?"

"Oh, all kinds of things. I don't want to get into it just now. She was really counting on that reward money you promised, but —" Ana Magdalena reached for her fur bag.

"Why can't she be content to wait? Next time you see her tell her you're married to an internationally recognized man of letters; my publisher is going to owe me millions."

Ana Magdalena rummaged about for her pencil and her little black book. "When?" She held the pencil poised awaiting his response.

"As soon as *The Love Queen* is completed."

"When is that?"

Federico paused. "My dear —"

"Don't they pay you something in advance?"

"They already did."

"They did? How much?"

"One hundred fifty thousand." Ana Magdalena made a note in the little black book.

"What happened to it?"

"Well, my dear, first there was a wedding, you may remember, quite an expensive affair as it turned out. There was the judge to pay . . . "

Ana Magdalena made a concluding note before closing her little black book. "Federico, why couldn't your heroine —"

"— Ostencia Candelaria —"

"Yes, Ostencia Candelaria." She replaced book and pencil in her bag. "Why couldn't she arrange to sell herself?"

Federico was taken aback. What was she doing coming up with a thing like that? "You're not suggesting — ?"

"Oh, but I am. Not on the street, of course, nothing sordid like that. But supposing for a minute she worked in a house, not just an ordinary house, but a tony sort of establishment with fancy amenities. A decor by Toulouse-Lautrec and a black piano-playing professor from New Orleans, things like that, and what's more, the house has an illustrious clientele: inventors, famous exhibitionists — you know, people like that Benjamin Frankling —"

"Historical personages. What a quaint idea."

"And all she has to do is be nice to the troops."

"The *troops?*"

Ana Magdalena couldn't very well explain that Ofelia liked to refer to her clients with a certain irony. "You know, the clientele." She lowered her eyes modestly.

Suddenly, spread out before him, Federico beheld the magnificent sweep of the novel which was sure to bring him fame, and considerable fortune, which might even place him in line for international acclaim and the coveted Gunpowder Prize. He would chronicle the history of a house of pleasure. His readers couldn't fail to see from the cast of characters who came to call exactly what he had in mind: conquerors who would kill the natives, missionaries who would convert them. What a grandiose scheme! A parade of the great men of history: La Perouse, Diderot, Voltaire, the firebrands of revolution: Morelos, Hidalgo, O'Higgins, Lords of Xibalba like Somoza or Ubico, or even the magnificent Trujillo. The march of progress led by the great stockmen of Argentina, the great husbandmen of Guatemala, of Cuba, the *señoritos* of the single crop: indigo, cotton, coffee, rubber, sugar, bananas. It would all be there, a splendid tapestry of hemispheric history.

"My darling," he said, clasping Ana Magdalena's hands, "I've just had a magnificent, a phenomenal idea!"

But Ana Magdalena was no longer paying much attention. She was finishing another jelly biscuit. "If you'll excuse me now, I really have to go." She dabbed a wet finger at the crumbs. "The morning's already running away with the spoon in its mouth." Before she ducked out, she swiped the last jelly biscuit from the dish.

She could hardly believe her good luck: she had escaped total suffocation in the library! She ran laughing and skipping to the carriage house in search of Hortensio Medina, who had begun teaching her the intricacies of operating the Henriod & Schweitzer. She had grown so used to walking back and forth from La Nymphaea that she had never given it a second thought until it occurred to her what a clever idea it would be to learn to drive a motorcar. Of course, the obvious thing was to have Hortensio chauffeur her, but she was inclined toward a certain discretion. If he drove her, sooner or later he might understand exactly where she went in the early evening hours, and what she did once she arrived there.

Repeatedly he showed her how to turn the crank. Try as she might, her arm was not strong enough to start the motor.

"Bear down harder. Careful. Don't let it break your arm!"

A wild impulse seized her. It flung her magnificent dark hair in a violent arc. The motor sputtered to life.

"Let go! Quick," shouted Hortensio, "jump in." She bolted toward the driver's side, but Hortensio, evidently forgetting that it was she who was going to drive, took the full smack of her body against his. They both went down sprawling. As the car lurched forward, Hortensio protectively covered her body with his, and happily the vehicle passed over their cowering forms without serious mishap.

Hortensio leapt to his feet. He began to chase after it. "Stop!" he shouted, "stop!"

But the vehicle turned a deaf ear to his entreaties. It continued at the lively pace of three miles an hour across the gravel driveway and onto the gracefully sloping lawn, where, as they watched horrified, it lost contact with the ground, and, as if in a dream, slowly pitched over on its side, its motor still running.

It was the first of many harmless mishaps. There were no injuries, either to the vehicle or to its passengers. But Hortensio Medina's indifferent arms began to take a beating. In bed at night, they remembered the protective barrier they had formed around Ana Magdalena's person. They refused to stay empty, and the more

Hortensio tried to silence them, the more they clamored for respite.

It was for this reason, perhaps, and perhaps because of a similar impulse on Ana Magdalena's part, that learning to drive became for them a pastime, rather than the means to an end. Every afternoon, just after lunch, when the streets became haunted by the dust of the siesta, Ana Magdalena in the company of Hortensio took to the roads. Spurred by the intoxication of the empty streets, Ana Magdalena discovered speed. Their excursions took on the mad edge of recklessness. They traveled long distances at astonishing velocities sometimes exceeding thirty miles an hour.

It was on one such excursion that on a stretch of deserted road, the Henriod & Schweitzer sputtered to a halt. "My God, what *can* be the matter? The machine is running down." Ana Magdalena was the picture of distress.

Hortensio swung his well-shod legs onto the pavement. He lifted the hood. "It's probably the crankcase. You seem to be leaking oil," he said. He headed back to where he kept his tools.

She placed a delicate gloved hand on his arm. "Wait," she said. "Why don't you teach me how!"

She lifted out a tarpaulin from the rumble seat, and spread it on the ground.

"What are you doing that for?" he said. "We're not taking anything apart."

"You can't be sure." She smiled at him.

He raised the hood to show her how to open the crankcase and where to add the oil. He explained to her the subtle and mysterious action of the lubricant, but when he demonstrated the movement of the pistons, it was all too much for Ana Magdalena.

"I feel faint," she announced.

Hortensio felt the weight of her person as she slumped against his chest. His lungs began giving him trouble.

"Hold me. I think I'm going to fall," she said.

"Señora, people might —"

"People be damned. Just hold me. Like this."

"But señora, it's not good to mix with servants."

"What makes you think I'm mixing?"

"But señora, the crankcase —"

152

Ana Magdalena had to muffle his objections with her lips. After a remarkably short time, he gave up the struggle. He allowed her to lead him to the tarpaulin with hardly a whimper — perhaps because she had made sure to wear the flimsiest of blouses, through which he could discern the tortured heaving of her breasts.

"Could you unbutton my bodice," she whispered. "I think I need a little air."

Shortly thereafter, they abandoned speed altogether in favor of tinkering with the engine. They parked as much as possible in cool, shaded places, well away from the prying eyes of inconvenient passersby. There were, however, times when Ana Magdalena preferred to take the wheel alone.

It was on one such rare occasion that as she sped past Ofelia's establishment in midafternoon, she saw an enormous wooden van parked in the street outside. Workmen were sweating and struggling to move vast objects down an improvised ramp and onto the street. Imposing canvas screens were stacked against the walls. La Nymphaea's doors were open wide, but there seemed to be no one in view from the establishment. She parked the car and went inside. She found Ofelia directing the crew as they unloaded the last items from the van. "In there! Cretins," she mumbled under her breath to Ana Magdalena, "every one of them cretins and sons of cretins, big hulking dummies with sawdust for brains. Their mothers must have tried to pry them loose with knitting needles and sadly botched the job!"

"Ofelia, *que pasa?*"

"Oh, *niña,* it looks like I'm finally going to do it. We're going to open the Screw. I'm calling it La Tuerca! Isn't that the perfect name? I'm so proud! Imagine the luck! The Manaus opera house auctioned off all their old sets. I even bid for a swan boat, and just in time to beat out Gulbenkian, too! And look: every one of them is marked."

Indeed, Ana Magdalena could read for herself: "Alcestes, Act III"; "Orlando Furioso, Act II"; "La Clemenza di Tito, Act II"; "Fledermaus."

"My God, Ofelia, I've never even been to the opera," sighed Ana Magdalena.

"You're still young, my dear. There's plenty of time. Meanwhile we're going to have our own gala blastout like Malyerba has never seen. But there's so much to do! I can't imagine how it'll all be done in time."

"In time?"

"For the inauguration. Haven't you heard? Everyone will be here, all our old customers. The councilmen, the lawyers, the municipal judges, even the parole officers. And the chief of police is lending us a contingent of armed guards. The mayor has even invited El Magnífico himself!"

"El Señor Presidente?"

Ofelia nodded. "I'm not supposed to know about it, but I have my private sources." Ofelia's laugh rattled the roof beams. "God's little kneecaps, I can't wait!"

From where they were standing, they could observe workmen carrying flats and positioning them against the individual cell walls of La Tuerca.

"Good gracious, no," wailed Ofelia above the din of hammering, "I want it to look more like a jungle. The waterfall goes over there, against the wall of the central courtyard."

On the roof, a crew of men was installing a mechanism from which was suspended a flock of colored lanterns shaped like little clouds.

"The clouds are my idea," enthused Ofelia, clasping her hands. "All we need now is some fluffy little cupids — for the ambience. Don't you think they'd be scrumptious?"

She led Ana Magdalena down the ramp. Already some of the cells were finished. One was furnished like the boiler room of an ocean-going steamer. Another resembled a place of execution. There were racks and pillories, and in the corner stood an iron maiden.

"For the 'special tastes,'" explained Ofelia coyly.

But almost every other cell was decorated like the jungle. Painted backdrops dripped with lianas, orchids bloomed against the ceilings, and here and there monkeys swung half hidden by giant philodendron leaves. "And La Tuerca itself will be transformed into a giant, enclosed bird cage," Ofelia announced. Everywhere Ana Magdalena looked, there were bars, little swings, and perches already dangling from the ceiling.

"My dear!" exclaimed Ofelia, "you can't begin to imagine the scope of it. There'll be singing and dancing. And fireworks! It will be the grandest thing this town has ever seen. It'll be news for years to come. And good for business? You can't imagine. The inauguration is only weeks away and already the tickets are nearly all sold out. People were scalping them on the street for positively astronomical prices! They were getting so much money, when I heard about it, I immediately arranged to print another batch."

Early that evening, as the maids were still bustling about replacing the cuspidors, Ana Magdalena was greeted by a client the likes of which she had not yet observed in those remote reaches of Peru. He was an enormously burly Scotsman, as it turned out, with great tufts of red, frizzy hair. He entered the parlor clutching a writing tablet; a pen was wedged behind one ear. He was, moreover, armed with a phrenologist's calipers, which hung from a string about his waist. Ana Magdalena took him upstairs, but when he caught sight of her fur bag and the arrow she had mounted on the wall of her room, he forgot to undress. He snapped his tablet open. He asked to know her name.

"Blanca."

"And the name of this establishment?"

"La Nymphaea."

"Ah, yes, of cour-r-rse." He scrawled rapidly in his notebook. "And now, little madam, where did you come by these intr-r-riguing ar-r-rtifacts?"

"They were gifts," she replied, "from two gentlemen who dropped by recently."

"People who tr-r-rade in ar-r-rtifacts?"

"No, as a matter of fact, men of the jungle."

"I didn't know you serviced indigenes."

"We admit anyone who pays."

He seemed particularly interested in the size and the shape of her visitors' heads.

"Would you say they were roughly the size of my head?"

"I would say they were much smaller."

"Yes, but was the shape of the head like mine, longer than it was deep? Or was it squat and round — like a cannonball?"

He insisted she apply the calipers to his head. Ana Magdalena began to wish he would leave.

"I'm afraid your time is nearly up," she remarked in her best professional tone.

He chose to ignore the hint.

"Because, you see, there is good reason to believe that if their heads were small, and r-r-round, as I str-r-rongly suspect they were, they have a ser-r-riously impair-r-red capacity for r-r-ratiocination. And now, little madam, I want you to descr-r-ribe exactly what they did in here."

"I'm very sorry, Mr. . . ."

"Dar-r-rwin. Just call me Carlos."

"Carlos, those are the confidences of the house. I am not at liberty to say, just as I would *never* mention that you had confined your own activities to asking me the most ridiculous, not to say offensive, questions."

And without any palliating niceties, she ushered him downstairs.

Severina could ignore matters no longer. She trotted upstairs to the mirador and knocked vigorously on the door.

"Don Federico?"

Federico admitted her. She had to remain standing at the door, however, because manuscripts were scattered everywhere. There was no place left in the mirador to stand, let alone sit down.

"Don Federico, I'm afraid your mother, Doña Clemencia, is getting ready to leave us."

"You're joking!"

"Not at all, señor. Your mother is slowly rising to heaven!"

Federico was counting on Severina to see him through his current literary endeavor. But clearly she had begun to take leave of her senses. He regarded her with a sense of deepening dismay.

"Señor doesn't believe me. Heaven is calling her. Every day she ascends a little closer to God, señor. Mark my words, one day soon, Doña Clemencia will take her place among the blessed. If señor doesn't believe me, he should see for himself."

Concealed behind the balusters of the grand staircase, Federico watched as Severina led the floating Clemencia down the flight of stairs to the dining room. In this manner Federico first learned of his mother's saintliness.

"*Carajo!*" he exclaimed that evening when Severina brought him his dinner tray. "I never thought I'd live to see the day. And what a terrific embarrassment. Isn't there some way you could keep her down?"

"I'm afraid she's irrepressible, señor. She'll join the blessed any time," warned Severina. "We'll just make sure she's not wearing her jewels when she does."

"Just leave the jewelry to me," growled Federico.

The evening was perfect. The sky was golden in a sunset streaked with clouds of the deepest red and orange. The massive, wrought-iron street gates that led to the convent garden and to La Tuerca stood wide open; to either side stood the ticket takers. Already the street was animated with crowds of spectators, all wearing the regulation costume of the day: snap-brim fedoras and Chesterfields, regardless of the weather. Here and there a particularly short person was to be observed, hinting at the presence of a woman in disguise. Everyone pressed and pushed forward, eager to have a look at Ofelia's legendary establishment, and to be among the first ever to be admitted to La Tuerca in its rehabilitated form. The ticket takers were mobbed. At the gate, people began to shove each other violently, pushing one another to the side.

"Easy, easy, now, gentlemen," urged the ticket takers, "there's plenty of room."

But when the public pressed past the gates, ticket stubs in hand, and toward the grandstand that had been erected in the courtyard, they saw that nearly every seat was already occupied. As the general altercation swelled, fisticuffs broke out. Ticket holders began to discover that for every reserved place, two and sometimes even three numbered tickets had been issued.

Ofelia was beside herself. If a riot broke out, which seemed imminently in the cards, it would provoke a scandal. Her furnishings would be ruined, and her plans and schemes would come to nothing. The crisis called for something bold, something so audacious she knew she was incapable of imagining what it might be. Surrounded by her girls, she was in a fever of anxiety.

At this fateful juncture, El Magnífico and President-for-Life Ochoa-Vicente arrived at the head of a motorized delegation of local and federal officials. Seeing the enormous multitude milling outside, His

Excellency was unable to pass up an oratorical opportunity. He stepped from his highly polished DeSoto. Because he was of an uncommonly short stature, he motioned to an aide-de-camp, who made a stepping stone out of his locked arms. Supporting himself on his aide's shoulder, El Magnífico hoisted himself up onto the hood of the vehicle. He raised his arms for silence. Immediately the crowd fell into a reverential trance.

It was at this moment that Ofelia threw open the street door of La Nymphaea. Draped in her black turkey-feather boa, she stood surveying the crowd and the motorcade, arrested in its progress by the crushing throng. She listened spellbound as His Excellency began to speak.

"Gentlemen," he addressed the crowd, "and ladies."

A titter rippled through the throng. To everyone's knowledge, there were no ladies present of whatsoever kind.

"It is a great privilege to be called upon to preside at the rededication of one of our country's foremost institutions . . . "

His aide-de-camp tried to attract El Magnífico's attention, but El Magnífico was launched, and, short of a thunderbolt, nothing could stop him. "Seldom in the course of our office-for-life have we had such a singular honor. We are about to cut a ribbon today on an edifice that symbolizes over two centuries of selfless service." The aide-de-camp yanked at El Magnífico's pants leg.

"Never-r-r, never-r-r," he thundered, kicking his aide-de-camp in the teeth, "have so many owed so much to those few who sacrifice their comforts that the thirst of multitudes may be quenched."

El Magnífico was just beginning to warm up. He was entirely oblivious of the growing chorus of snickers and snorts that greeted his almost every word. His aide-de-camp, however, was hellbent on saving His Excellency from persisting in a disastrous political gaffe. He activated the DeSoto's ignition. The vehicle lurched forward, hurtling El Magnífico into the crowd, where he fell, to the cheering shouts of the multitude, into the convenient arms of a team of ironsmiths. The ironsmiths bore him in triumph to the threshold of La Nymphaea, where they deposited him at Señora Ofelia's feet.

All smiles and affability, Ofelia ushered His Excellency inside. His complement of dignitaries was quick to follow. Julio, Ofelia's coachman, closed the great street doors. Within, His Excellency beheld the splendor of Ofelia's rainbow girls, all turned out in their pastel best. Sidonia, assisted by the upstairs maids, all stiff and starched in their uniforms, served champagne. Ofelia proposed a toast. "To His Excellency, President Plenipotentiary, Caudillo-for-Life, El Señor Magnífico, Ochoa-Vicente y Ruiz." Glasses were raised. In the hushed silence, the mob could be heard. Outside in the street they were cheering El Presidente. Inside The Screw, they were rioting.

EL MAGNÍFICO DEDICATES BORDELLO

were not the words that headlined the morrow's newspapers, for the simple reason that, except for a few presses owned by his friends, El Magnífico owned them all. Nor was the event buried on page 46, where assassinations and coups d'état are normally assigned, because El Presidente never missed a rotogravure opportunity. The national press of the following morning greeted breakfast readers with the announcement that El Caudillo had reopened a famous national monument, the penitential cells of the Capuchins. His photograph, statesmanly mustaches bristling, occupied the entire front page.

A brief reportage described the fireworks display but made no mention of any riots. It omitted saying that, with the onslaught of a tremendous pyrotechnic display, the crowds fell to gaping in wonderment at the heavily armed detachment of lawkeepers who, with the cooperation of the chief of police, stood lined up on the roof, rifles at the ready; or that the explosions came at fast and furious intervals, reminding everyone that, inside and out, they were within firing range. But it did describe at length the rain of fire that ended the event, and the lancework set piece in which thousands of individual colored salts simultaneously exploded, displaying El Magnífico's official portrait to thunderous applause.

When Ofelia saw the photograph of El Magnífico, she gave way to feelings of acute distress because even her arm, hooked around El Presidente's in welcome, had been cropped.

"When the arm is cut like that, it's very bad. Anything cut off is sure to bring bad luck."

Exhausted by the events of the previous evening, she took to her bed, completely forgetting that the police chief was due for his monthly visit at a quarter to ten. Try as she might to head him off, Sidonia was unable to prevent his determined progress up the stairs. He marched into Ofelia's bedroom.

"I think you're expecting me," was his ill-mannered greeting.

Ofelia moaned. She rolled over in bed.

"If you need time, I'll be happy to wait." He thoughtfully sat down at the side of the bed, where she could observe him through one half-open eye as he stroked his mustaches and gave them a jauntier twirl.

"Sainted Mother!" she exclaimed at last, swinging her varicosed legs out of the bedclothes. "There's never *ever* a moment's peace."

She made her way to her wall safe, which lay concealed behind the portrait of her late and sainted mother. Muttering the numbers to herself, she aligned the tumblers in the familiar combination. The door swung open. She lifted out a canvas bag. She shut the door and spun the dial once or twice.

"It's all there," she said to the chief. Unceremoniously, she dropped the bag in his lap. She hoped the weight would hit him where it hurt.

"And the receipts?"

"All written out in longhand, and tallied up. And now, *puta-madre,* let me *sleep.*"

She swung her tired old legs back under the covers. But her day had only just started, and it showed no signs of wanting to be done, because at that very moment, El Señor Presidente was presenting his credentials to Sidonia, from whom he demanded an immediate audience with her mistress, whom he referred to as La Incomparable. But before he was able to reach the incomparable presence, he had the good fortune to intercept the chief of police on the richly carpeted grand staircase.

"Good morning, Your Honor." The chief of police tried to pass El Señor Presidente self-effacingly. But he was a big man, and El Señor Presidente was of very minimal stature, and there was no way he could manage to avoid him.

El Señor Presidente reached out his hand. "And a fine morning to you," he offered.

The Police Chief transferred what he held in his concealed right hand to his now concealed left hand to meet the presidential hand-shake.

"And what, if I may ask, are you hiding there, an incendiary device — or is it just another slop pot?" He wrenched the police chief's arm nearly out of its socket. A cascade of coins showered the grand stairway of La Nymphaea.

"Arrest this fellow right away!" El Presidente barked to his re-placement aide-de-camp. He motioned to a uniformed soldier who stood at attention. "Pick up every one of these babies, son, and do it on the double. And you." He motioned to Sidonia. "Watch to see he doesn't take a shine to any of it. I'm going to need every escudo!" And he bustled up the stairs to La Incomparable's bedchamber.

"Mmm," said El Magnífico, as he buried his bristling mustaches in the vast cleavage of Ofelia's somnolescent breasts. "You smell so *good!* My incomparable one is like a rose of Sharon, like the lily of the valley," and he rapturously began quoting the Song of Solomon in all its smarmy detail.

"Oh, for God's sake," moaned Ofelia, unable to rivet her eyes shut any longer. When she recognized her visitor, however, she sat bolt upright in bed. "Your Excellency, Señor Presidente, Caudillo-for-Life, is it you, Señor Ochoa-Vicente y Ruiz?"

"It is!" El Caudillo smiled rapturously. "My little *Bouboulita!*" And he buried the presidential nose once more in her opulent cleavage before making her the generous gift of his entire person, all four feet, six inches of it.

When Ofelia at last made her appearance known to the world at large, her eyes shone with a dangerous glow, and her cheeks, which normally took an abundant layer of rouge, were flushed without benefit of any help at all.

El Señor Presidente emerged shortly thereafter, looking fit — and ready for business. The soldier handed him the canvas sack.

"Is it all there, boy?"

Sidonia, who had observed the entire proceedings, assured him that it was.

"Good! And now, Bouboulita, your Caudillo would like a word with you."

He ushered her into her parlor and shut the doors. There are no reports of what was said there, neither the text of El Caudillo's official words, nor the substance and tone of Ofelia's off-the-cuff remarks. But it is safe enough to say that when the two of them emerged, Ofelia's face was ashen. El Caudillo, however, appeared to be brimming over with good health and sufficient vigor to heft the considerable weight of the canvas bag. "Here, boy." He winked at the young soldier. "And make sure it doesn't get away."

XI

When his publisher's final demand arrived, Federico paid it no more heed than he had any of the others. He was swept up in an obsession so intense he hardly saw Ana Magdalena at all.

From time to time, when she brought his clean linen at day's end and removed his dinner service, she found another page of material that he had balled up, evidently in frustration, and cast aside. This she would pry open and, sitting on the mirador landing, smooth out the creases and begin to read.

... a redhead whose hair was half-hidden under a governess's snood. She rocked an enormous perambulator, on which a heraldic crest appeared.

"Shhh." She raised a finger to lips thin as shilling slots. "For Christ's sake, don't wake him. He's been a holy terror all afternoon."

Ostencia Candelaria could not see the governess's charge, veiled as the baby was behind mosquito netting.

"Boy or girl?' she asked sweetly.

"Neither," snapped Miss Teasdale. "He's not your ordinary baby."

"And this is not an ordinary house," Ostencia Candelaria felt it only fair to warn her. "Of course, you are welcome to stay as long as you like," she whispered so as not to wake the baby, "but normally, we don't take children."

"I should think not," replied Miss Teasdale. "I'm just waiting for the old boy to wake up." She swept the mosquito netting aside. Inside was a fully grown man.

"Good heavens!" exclaimed Ostencia Candelaria.

"Heaven has very little to do with it," sniffed Miss Teasdale. "Meet Don Pedro, First Emperor of Brazil."

Ostencia Candelaria was flabbergasted. "Brazil? I never knew Brazil had an emperor."

"It has two. This one's the first, all right, but the second isn't far behind."

"But doesn't the first one have to be dead?"

"*He* doesn't seem to think so," observed Miss Teasdale.

As if to prove the point, Don Pedro awoke at that very instant with a shattering howl. He bawled and screamed, and held his breath until the imperial face turned blue.

"Oh, shut up," snapped Miss Teasdale, unperturbed. "He's always like that after napping, little bugger. You can't dissolve parliament until you've had your supper." And she bopped him on the noggin.

Quite unexpectedly, the undercarriage, which was constructed something like a rumble seat, flew open, discharging a fat, pink, diapered infant who fell hard onto the marble tiles of the passageway. It, too, began an earsplitting yowl. "Aw, for Chrissake," snarled Miss Teasdale, "he always threatens to procreate the second Don Pedro just so he can have his way."

"You mean the second one's Don Pedro, too?' asked Ostencia Candelaria.

"Of course, although just now he's only seven months old. But he'll be emperor in no time at all."

Miss Teasdale stooped to pick the squalling infant up. Almost immediately . . .

Fragments such as this one she would add — along with Sergio Ballado's love letters — to the growing collection of literary curiosities she kept hidden under her pillow because she superstitiously believed that sleeping on them would help to swell her clientele.

Clemencia's was the first Orgaz body not to lie in state. And it was a good thing, too, reflected Federico, because it spared the family's strained expense accounts.

Severina came knocking at the door of the mirador at seven one morning. "Don Federico?"

Groggily, for he had been working through the night, he opened the door.

"She's gone!"

For one alarming moment Federico feared she meant Ana Magdalena. "Who?"

"The Señora Clemencia."

"Oh, the matriarch," breathed Federico with a sigh of relief.

"But, señor — " Federico couldn't understand Severina's agitation. "The jewels, señor — they're gone!"

"How can you concern yourself with trifles in the face of such a tragic loss? My precious *mamacita* is gone." And he collapsed on the stairs, weeping uncontrollably.

But Clemencia was not quite gone in the normal sense. In the days preceding her disappearance, she had hovered just below the ornate medallions adorning the mansion ceilings. Severina had had to feed her by extending a pole to which she had affixed a fork. Putting Clemencia's shoes on required her to reach up almost to the limits of her arm span.

The previous evening, she had helped Clemencia improvise a bed in the branches of the chandelier. But after Severina departed, and long into the night, Clemencia had trouble breathing. The room was far too stuffy. She propelled herself with great difficulty to the window, where she tried to kick open the casement, and when it flew open at last, the night air sucked Clemencia out. After a shaky start, the wind caught her and lifted her up over the rooftops. Ana Magdalena returned from La Nymphaea just in time to see her sail majestically out of sight.

At the very moment Severina was breaking the sad news to Federico, Clemencia was entering the outer reaches of the Van Allen Belt. From where she floated, she could see deserts and craters, and endless canals. She could observe cities and farmland, and the thick jungles that used to ring the equator. And because her eyes had become accustomed to celestial vision, she could see the huts and the houses that sheltered all the human beings on earth. And she could see the people living inside in embarrassing detail.

"How amusing they are," she chuckled to herself, "fighting and struggling, and pulling and snatching, and arguing and killing, and

throttling the life out of one another. They don't need natural ene-
mies like the rest of creation. They have each other, poor dears."

But her last thought was for Severina — for the years of intimida-
tions, indignities, and grudging abuse she had suffered at her servant's hands. She watched to see what she would do. Severina picked
up the jewels that Clemencia had carelessly left clogging the bathtub
drain and pocketed them. But by the time she repaired to the Monte
de Piedad to pawn them, Clemencia had entered the realm of the
blessed, and she could no longer see if the final revenge she had
planned for Severina would succeed.

Ofelia was not herself. Ever since El Presidente's visit, she had taken
to her room entire days at a time, and only Sidonia saw her to serve
her tea, and to take her temperature, to smooth out her bedclothes,
and give her her daily enema.

Once a month, a man from the Bureau of Mines arrived in
Malyerba to collect El Magnífico's cut. His visit replaced that of the
chief of police, who lingered in jail still fighting a graft-taking charge.
But whereas the police chief, recognizing Ofelia's boost to the local
economy, had taken only twenty percent, El Magnífico helped himself to fifty, with ten percent of the net going to the collection
division of the Bureau of Mines. During these visits, in particular,
Ofelia took a turn for the worse, and it required nearly the entire
month for her to recover somewhat, only to be visited again almost
immediately thereafter.

Her girls had to come to her one by one, because she insisted she
was sensitive to noise, and preferred to be whispered to. Ana Magdalena made certain to pass by Ofelia's room whenever opportunity
offered, but each time she found her increasingly weak and ill
disposed.

"*Niña,* why is it that when a woman finally learns to relish life, her
salad days are gone? Damn infirmity, damn decline, damn decay, and
damn corruption! When I think of all my lovers, all the men who
were crazy to marry me, and how I threw it all to the winds because I
wanted a profession."

"Would you think of doing differently?" Ana Magdalena asked her
sympathetically.

"Only if the money was good." And Ofelia gave the kind of

feeble, pathetic little laugh that barely raised the dust on her satin coverlet.

The time came when Ofelia sent for Ana Magdalena. "*Niña.*" She could barely make herself heard. "There's just enough money in the safe to give my girls one last fling, one final blast-off to end all blast-offs, because when it's over, I won't be here. And La Nymphaea will be a thing of the past. You're the one I want to liquidate everything. Pay Sidonia and the others from what's left, and when everyone and everything has been moved out of here, leave the doors open. Let the dead leaves and the dust pile up. I want the old walls to lie down and give their bones up to the ground the way the elephants do when they shuffle back to their ancestral burial grounds in Africa. Give my body to the purifying fires. Scatter my ashes over the Amazon, the river of my birth. It's where I came from, and where I want to end up. Promise me, *niña,* promise me you'll do as I ask."

Ana Magdalena nodded solemnly, but she couldn't say anything because her voice was choked with crying.

Severina had never entered a Monte de Piedad before. She tripped on the worn granite stairs and nearly fell, which ought to have struck her as sufficiently inauspicious a beginning to warn her away altogether. But she was not to be deterred. With unflinching determination she hobbled up to the jewelry section and emptied her apron pockets onto the glass counter with a clatter.

"*Momentito!*" said the clerk.

He took all three sets to the faded booth in which the appraiser sat, black jeweler's magnifying lens wedged deep into one eye socket.

At last he looked up from the sapphire set he had just examined.

"Ask her how much she wants for the lot."

"All three?"

The jeweler nodded. The clerk turned to Severina. But she did not wait for him to repeat the question.

"One million escudos. Not one centavo less."

The appraiser, who could hear everything from inside his glass-paned console, gave a whoop.

"Tell granny we'll give her fifty for the settings."

"How's about fifty?" the clerk said.

"I'll take one million for the lot. The settings are free."

The appraiser raised himself on enormous muscular arms. When he propelled himself into the aisle behind the jewelry counter she saw he was without the use of his legs.

"Listen, granny, young thugs who come in here like you get hauled away for a lot less. Where did you get these anyway? They're fakes."

Severina heard a ringing in her ears.

"*Fakes?*" she whispered hoarsely. The young clerk rushed to put a chair behind her.

"Why don't you sit down," he offered solicitously.

"Never mind that," grumped Severina, her true colors suddenly flaring up. "What do you mean, they're fakes?"

"The settings are good. White gold and platinum. But the stones are paste."

Severina broke down entirely; that is, she consented to sit.

"Paste," she repeated numbly. "You're sure?"

"Yes. The settings probably held the real thing — once — but now the stones might as well be gumdrops."

"My God," she breathed almost inaudibly.

"I can lend you fifty on the settings."

Briefly she considered. "No," she snapped, her disposition suddenly restored. "I think I know where they'll bring more."

The clerk slid them toward her across the counter. She pocketed them in her apron.

By the time she reached the Orgaz entrance stairway, her moral indignation was thoroughly aroused. She made her way directly to the mirador. She knocked. "Señor? Señor?"

Although the hour was by no means early, Federico was just turning over after a brief night's sleep. He opened the door.

"*Sí?*"

"I found the jewels," she announced. She watched him carefully to see how he would react.

"I thought you said they were gone."

"I thought so, yes, but I found them clogging the drain. Poor thing, she must have forgotten them after her last bath."

Federico reached a hand for them.

"Not so fast, señor. We have a little something to discuss."

"Don't you want to sit down?" Federico coolly motioned her inside.

She eyed all the boxes piled high with books and manuscripts. There was no place anywhere for her to sit. "This will do very well," she said sternly, standing her ground.

"Well?"

"Well, nothing. If these jewels are fakes, how is it that they used to be the real thing? And I know because when I first came to work here, the matriarch sent me to have them appraised."

"And what makes you think they're fakes?" Federico eyed her sarcastically.

"I can tell by looking at them." She stood glinting at him with her basilisk eyes.

Federico wasted no time. "What are you trying to insinuate? Give me the jewels."

Severina backed away.

"I said, give me the jewels." He seized Severina by the shoulders. She dug into her pockets.

"All of them," he demanded.

She dug farther.

"You're fired," he said. "You have ten minutes to pack. You'll be on the eleven A.M. *rápido* to Tierra del Fuego. And don't try anything funny because I'm driving you to the station myself."

"But I haven't got the trainfare, señor," lied Severina.

"I'll front you," Federico cooed. "We'll just pawn these little baubles on our way to the station."

Prematurely, in the midst of her girls' party deliberations, two weeks short of the visit from the Bureau of Mines, Ofelia breathed her last. The neon sign that had livened the street for the past ten years with its garish call to arms was extinguished. Ana Magdalena, anticipating the event, had Sidonia hang a sign on the bolted street doors of La Nymphaea:

CLOSED DUE TO ALMOST CERTAIN DEATH

Ofelia died surrounded by her family of sorts. Her girls took turns relieving each other around the great canopied bed with its sweat-stained satin sheets. Sidonia and the other maids suspended all their other duties to bathe her, and change her nightgowns, and empty her slops. They dressed her hair and kept her makeup fresh, because she didn't want her moribund appearance to distress her girls.

With her last breath, she asked for Eduardito. When he saw his "auntie," his knowing child's eyes detected the frightful green complexion beneath her elaborate makeup and coiffure. He set to screaming hysterically and had to be taken from the room. Instead, Maria put Eugenita in bed beside her. No sooner did Ofelia's trembling hands recognize the little girl's pudgy arms and legs than she took a deep and satisfying breath and, with a smile of contentment on her face, expired.

No priest could be persuaded to bury her, and it was just as well. Her girls had to respect her savage wishes after all. They found some roustabouts willing to carry her body to the river's edge. Late at night they laid her out on a pile of firewood, and stayed to watch her burn.

Ana Magdalena had all she could do in the next few days attending to the closing of the house, helping the girls pack up, seeing to the servants' severance pay. Barely able to see by dawn, she rushed home in the early-morning hours to snatch a fitful sleep. And it was fortunate she did because the day Federico marched Severina downstairs to the stables, he found the Henriod & Schweitzer parked in its customary place.

That day Ana Magdalena awoke toward noon with a feeling of not knowing exactly where she was or who she was. Then she remembered: Ofelia was gone. She rubbed her eyes. Grieved as she was, she was not so bereft she could entertain no thought of eating.

She went downstairs. The kitchen was deserted. In search of Severina, she wandered about the bare servants' rooms with their straw pallets, each with three austere pegs for the occupants to hang their uniforms and what few clothes they might possess.

On Severina's bed she found a hastily scribbled note. "To the señora" it read.

"Your Federico thinks he's God's gift to literature, but he's nothing but a common thief. I hope you keep mounting thickets of moose horns on that mighty brow. I wet myself laughing every time I think of it."

Ana Magdalena absently folded the note and stuffed it in her pocket. In Severina's absence, she would have to start the fire. She packed the stove with paper. She remembered the note. Much as she derived a certain satisfaction, at least from parts of it, she thought it best to burn it with the rest. She struck a match.

She was just using her last crust of bread to sop up her omelette, when Federico came stomping in from his trip to the station. Although she had no way of knowing where he might have been, she could see the thunderclouds gathered on his brow. Innocently she asked, "Where's Severina?"

He looked ready to strike her.

"She's fired!"

"Fired! Oh, my goodness! Who will do the cooking and the cleaning and the marketing and the washing? Hortensio?"

He gave her a withering look. "That's what you're here for. And don't bother me. My publisher pretends I'm now five years overdue. I'm certainly not coming down again till the manuscript is done." He stormed up the stairs. When he slammed the door the whole house shook.

There was no sign of dishrags or soap. Ana Magdalena wondered dispiritedly where such things were kept. She swished cold water over the plate and stood it on its rim to drip. The plate, however, had a mind of its own. It wobbled unsteadily for a moment before sliding off the ceramic drainboard, and shattered into a hundred tiny fragments on the kitchen flags. She began to look for a dustpan and a broom, but the cleaning implements had allied themselves with the departed Severina. They remained hidden and obstinate in the mysterious closets and corners to which their former mistress had consigned them. *I hope you go on planting thickets of horns on that mighty brow.* Whatever she thought of Severina, she had been, in some ways at least, something of an ally after all.

But now La Nymphaea was a thing of the past — if not quite yet an archaeological curiosity — and Ofelia, her protecting angel, was gone. How she ached to see the sweep of her ringed hands as she told a story, or expressed elation at a sudden find. How she missed her "*niña,*" or "my dear little girl." Here she was nearly twenty-two and Ofelia had still cosseted her like a child. There was no one else like her; not Andreina, absorbed as she was with her never-ending bees, mouthing eternal platitudes of motherly concern; not Clemencia, an exotic talking mummy from another world. Ofelia and La Nymphaea and the rainbow girls — each one of them — had become a familiar flower in her own personal garden, nourished by tears and laughter and companionship. What was she going to do now that it was over?

She would have to wear the uniform of servitude, practice intimacy with the mops and rags, polish the silver, set the barrels out before the rains, measure her life in rounds of baking, cleaning, and preparing sad little suppers — living by the clock of the everyday, while Federico sat in his mirador like some king spider, drawing her and everyone around him into the spinning of his web.

Age would find white hair for her, wrinkles, a hesitating step; she would fall by Malyerba's wayside, shiver in the company of ghosts.

And Sergio Ballado, what was keeping him? Where was he with his once pressing urgency, his *gallo de oro*, that golden rooster of his, rumbling through her dreams like a carriage over rough cobblestones, rattling her certainties like peas on a hot stove? She was nowhere. The door had opened and shut behind her. Everything was coming to a standstill. She imagined the slow winding down of people trotting in the street, the broken ring of the angelus, like a clock going dead.

They were all going — Victoria, Mercedes, Alicia, Marta, Cecilia, and the faithful Sidonia — and all the maids, and the children! It was too overwhelming even to think about. It weighed on her like a stone. She sat in the kitchen unable to move. She thought of Aurora Constancia. She would know what to do. If only she could visit her, now that she had the time. Or she might visit Andreina and help her with the bees, or clarify the honey in the long afternoons, while the shadows stretched and yawned and went to sleep.

She let herself into the ballroom. It smelled musty as if it hadn't been aired out since the wedding. The parquet floors groaned and complained under her feet. She trudged up the grand staircase. Her feet sank into the deep red plush of the runners. She passed one empty room after another, room after room, dust-laden and forlorn. She reached her room at last. She slumped down exhausted on the bed, remembering how the house had shuddered when Federico slammed the door.

There'll be a servant here by dinnertime, I promise you. That was what she should have said. But there was no servant and no way to pay for any servant. She thought of Sidonia and the younger maids: Honora, and Rosa, and Matilda. And there was Julio, too. Casa Orgaz was certainly big enough with all the rooms to tidy, all the gardens to be seen to. Hortensio could always use some help.

She smacked her palm to her forehead. It was staring her in the face. Why hadn't she thought of it? My God, what if they had already left? She could almost see the street doors of La Nymphaea gaping wide, dust settling on everything, owls roosting in the rafters.

She flew out of bed. She tore off her dressing gown so vehemently she ripped it at the seam. Pulling on stockings was such a stupid waste of time. Her arms flailed helplessly as she struggled into her linen jacket. She ran to the stable. She cranked up the Henriod & Schweitzer. She raised a huge blossom of camouflaging dust as she backed out of the stall. She spun the car around and thundered out the gate.

The curb outside La Nymphaea was already crowded with vehicles — vans of all kinds, and wooden lorries filled with bulging objects secured beneath enormous brown tarpaulins.

"Wait!" she cried, leaping out of the car. But not one face was familiar — all were drivers, roustabouts, and moving men. She pushed through the carriage entrance and threw open the kitchen doors.

"Sidonia!" she cried breathlessly. "My mind's made up. I'm taking you along." But before Sidonia could emerge from behind a cluster of china barrels, Ana Magdalena was out in the vestibule again, shouting up the grand staircase: "Everybody, everybody, come down quick! Come hear the latest bulletin!"

Twelve pairs of heels clattered down the stairs. Everyone pressed into the kitchen. Servants and girls sat wherever they could, perching on counters and china barrels.

Ana Magdalena raised her hands for silence. At that moment a moving man pushed his way in. "Off the crates, little ladies, we're moving them right out."

"You'll have to hold on for a minute." Ana Magdalena smiled at him sweetly. "Federico just fired Severina," she announced. "He won't come down again until he's done with *The Love Queen of the Amazon*. There's only Hortensio left to worry about, and I know all about taking care of him," she smiled.

Everyone listened expectantly.

"We can leave here today, and scatter, everyone to the four winds, or" — she paused for dramatic effect — "we can set up house at Casa Orgaz because my house is your house and it has rooms by the hotelful! And, best of all, we can have the party Ofelia wanted us to have, we can have it right away in our big new headquarters and invite all our old clientele. That way there'll be almost no letup in business."

"Let's drink to it!" shouted Mercedes. Everyone was clapping and hugging everyone else. Sidonia broke open an already sealed case of champagne. Ana Magdalena uncorked the first bottle, spattering foam everywhere.

"To Casa Orgaz!"

"Let's have a little music," yelled Victoria. Everyone pushed through the swinging doors into La Nymphaea's parlor. Ofelia's enormous settee was upended on its side ready for hauling out, but the piano was still where it had always stood against the alcove wall. Victoria reached for a piano roll.

"Wait!" cried Ana Magdalena. "We have to get Ropes!"

Everyone looked at her.

"Ropes?" Victoria asked, mystified.

"Yes! The piano player. Where does he live?"

The girls began to shift uneasily, to whisper among themselves.

"What piano player? What are you talking about?" asked Victoria. "There's never been a piano player!" She beckoned Ana Magdalena close to the player piano so she could watch the mechanism. The roll was already turning. The piano began to play a melancholy tango.

Ana Magdalena stood alone in the alcove. Everyone else was dancing. A terrible sadness came over her, the kind of sadness people have when they know it's time to go. She watched the keys depress. All at once she saw Ropes's fingers fluttering over the keyboard. He gave her his rueful, diamond-studded grin. "Aw, sugar, I can't be tickling these ivories forever. I'se tired. I got noplace for me now Ofelia's gone."

"You'll come with us!" she whispered.

"Naw, sister. Let me go."

"But the house won't be the same without you."

"Sure it will, sugar, long's you got my piano rolls."

She could see his eyes were troubled. She wanted to embrace him.

"Easy, sister, watch my neck. Them rope burns never let me rest." He gave her a dark look. "Don't never trust no white man — ever — and if he ain't white, he *still* better be dead!" He threw his head back and hooted with laughter before he disappeared.

Long after La Nymphaea reverted to the state in which Ofelia first came upon it when she arrived from Salvador, sometimes in the chill of our deep Andean nights, the mournful tinkle of a distant piano can still be heard playing a long-forgotten cakewalk. When he paid his last, astonished visit, the collector from the Bureau of Mines was the first — but not the last — to hear it.

XII

The grand opening was only a week away. The rainbow girls lounged on Ana Magdalena's bed, nibbling chocolates with their Sunday-morning champagne. The pancakes had long ago been cleared away.

"Come on, everyone. We've been at this all morning. Someone come up with a name."

"Why not La Casa Blanca —"

"Except Washington already holds the copyright," a blasé Mercedes pointed out.

"You mean we could be sued?" asked Maria, wide-eyed.

"Either that or liberated," cracked Mercedes.

"Don't be silly. Come on, everybody, let's think of *something*. It's very nearly noon," pleaded Ana Magdalena.

"Why can't we just call it Casa Orgaz?" proposed Marta.

"But that's so common," sniffed Eugenia.

"It's perfect," exclaimed Ana Magdalena happily. "It's simple and it comes right to the point."

Peeling walls had to be spackled and painted, sagging doors and shutters rehung, and rotted casements replaced. Ana Magdalena directed the work crews in a final frenzied flurry of preparation. While glaziers, painters, and carpenters hammered and sawed, the first Hoover miraculously appeared east of the Andes and was immediately put to use vacuuming the dust.

Moving men delivered truckloads of antique furniture, washbasins, and mirrors from Ofelia's house, and Julio brought the rainbow girls, depositing them at the foot of the double marble stairway, where Ana Magdalena had strung garlands of frangipani blossoms to welcome them.

To their great delight, each found her own bed-sitting room decorated in her personalized color scheme. Sidonia was appointed housekeeper; she occupied the newly painted and furnished servants' quarters along with the other maids, while Ana Magdalena took over Clemencia's old suite, with its enormous bathtub, temperamental antique safe, and the mahogany secretary, where she could spread out Ofelia's desk set and keep the books and the money handy.

She couldn't think where to place all the flats Ofelia had inherited from the Manaus opera house. As she lingered one last time in La Tuerca examining the waterfall, the lianas with their flying monkeys, the giant bird cage with its swings and little perches, the boiler room of the ocean liner, and the place of execution, a deep and suffocating sadness came over her. She even discovered a little room furnished in the style of Velazquez and, obscured by its position underneath the stairs, a giant gilded swan that looked as though it could have been purloined from a children's carousel — except that it seemed to be a boat!

"How curious," Cecilia said to her, wiping away a tear, "I wonder what she had in mind, putting all this stuff together?"

"Ofelia? She wanted to cater to the 'special tastes.' La Tuerca was going to be her *confitería,* her little candy shop."

"What a terrific idea."

Ana Magdalena nodded. "Hold it!" she called out to the foreman of the moving crew. "Pack all this stuff up, too, because we're taking it along."

At last it was over. La Nymphaea was empty. Ana Magdalena did as Ofelia had asked. She opened the doors and the windows wide. But she kept the key, enormous and rusted — not for any sentimental reason, but because she forgot it where it hung on the chain close to her heart.

"Don't pay any attention to the noise," she mollified a nervous Federico, "it's only the servants moving in. They'll settle down in a day or so."

"You mean there's more than one?" Federico grumbled. "Just how do you expect to pay them, I'd like to know?"

"Oh, the honey's bringing in enormous profits," Ana Magdalena reassured him. But she was more at a loss to explain the blast-off they were planning.

"Why not tell him it's the maids," suggested Sidonia. "We're having a little jollification just for us. That way, he won't think of coming down."

"And by the way," Ana Magdalena added, "they're planning a little housewarming for their relatives. Things may get a little rowdy, but it's really just for them. I knew you wouldn't mind."

For some days, Ana Magdalena paced the great public rooms of Casa Orgaz. She stood in the entryway, entirely immobilized by the grand staircase under its soaring cupola, all stone and glass, pinned to the vault by its massive chandelier. How could she manage to soften the uncompromising granite columns of the courtyard? she wondered.

She began by cordoning off the library and the literary salon in deference to Federico and his literary tastes. Next, she converted the visitors' parlor into a cloakroom.

With the help of Hortensio and Julio, she inventoried all the props and backdrops for the boiler room and the other bits and exotic pieces inherited from La Tuerca. But Casa Orgaz was still and cold. It had no room for fantasy. "*Dios mio,*" she groaned, "even if we had the time, there's no place to put any of it. Better store it all in the basement."

She had them fill the courtyard with enormous tubs of potted flowers, hibiscus, bougainvillea, and trumpet vines. The columns began to bend a little at the hip. But there was no room for any of Ofelia's whimsical theatrical effects, her cheap celluloid clouds, her frilly little cupids. When Hortensio and Julio installed Ofelia's settee in the center of the ballroom, overpowering as it had seemed in La Nymphaea's parlor, the ballroom swallowed it at a single gulp.

"It won't do at all," wailed Ana Magdalena. "No one will ever even see it. We need something bigger, grander, something nearly spectacular." Her hand shot to her mouth. "I have it. Julio, Hortensio, quick! Get the swan boat! We'll stuff it full of gorgeous pillows for our rainbow odalisques!"

*   *   *

The inauguration may not have conformed exactly to the farewell Ofelia had originally intended, but the crush of clientele in the ballroom was elbow to elbow. Cigar and cigarette smoke hovered like hazy camouflage over the crème de la crème of Malyerba's notability. There was His Honor, Judge Esteban Gutierrez; the deputy mayor, Don Horacio de León, representing His Honor the mayor, who was recovering from the chicken pox. There were lawyers and advocates, and doctors, and two archrival plastic surgeons from Brazil who nearly came to scalpel thrusts over their sudden passion for magenta (in the person of Trinidad), until Ana Magdalena insisted they draw lots.

There was a stunning gastronomic spread served up by Pepe in the dining room. Some of Malyerba's most dedicated eaters vied with one another to determine how many oysters Florentine they could down at a single sitting. The bar was well stocked, and although the prices were exorbitant, the supply threatened to run out. As midnight approached, Pepe resorted to popping the corks of jeroboam after jeroboam of premium champagne, but by then most of the guests of Casa Orgaz had entered another dimension altogether. The ballroom began to sway, slowly at first, gathering momentum, tilting dangerously, until it passed into a celestial realm, spinning in mad and frenzied orbit in a universe altogether free of gravity.

Federico was beside himself. These weren't servants! He knew better. Noise! Music! Laughter! Screaming at all hours of the day and night. Children crying. And once the fire department actually arrived, horns blaring, in the middle of the night. Did Ana Magdalena think she had him fooled?

Unable to sleep, he ran a superstitious hand over his forehead; he felt no bumps, no telltale signs. But there was no ignoring the evidence. And there was her collection of extravagant excuses, mostly having to do with bees. Already on their wedding night her virtue had appeared to be in a shocking state of disrepair. She might, of course, be the kind of medical rarity Krafft-Ebing wrote about. And then there was the matter of her editorial advice. Hadn't she been the one to suggest that his Ostencia Candelaria sell herself? Hadn't she used those very words? And after all, why not? It made for a titillating narrative. But as the years wore on, her frequent absences tipped the balance in his mind. Except that now, after nearly six years, all of a sudden she was home.

He had the urgent desire to wrench open the door, to storm downstairs and over the furniture, to throw the assembled revelers outside and bolt the doors of Casa Orgaz. But what would he do with all that silence, all that quiet? Would it put food on the table? Would it keep things running as smoothly? He wanted to tell Ana Magdalena what he knew. His legs wanted to run away with his head. Be still, he said to them; he knew he was trapped. And he couldn't go snooping, gathering evidence. There were too many maids, too much activity. If he let himself be caught, he would have to go through the tiresome motions of defending his honor. He would have to make an awful scene, probably even brandish something. And what would become of the golden goose, so to speak, the backbone of his livelihood? Literature, he reflected, had always been a most exacting mistress. Dear God, what a complicated but richly ironic situation. It could be the subject of a novel!

He wondered for a moment if in the course of her career any of his literary coterie had come to patronize his wife; but after all, he reflected, he was their dean, and if any of them ever happened to ring the bell, in the long view, they were lending support to his literary habit. He rubbed his hands together. It was not a bad tradeoff, he smiled to himself. It was an arrangement many writers might envy. And if he wished, he could even make use of local research material.

It was way past nine, and still there was no sign of Ana Magdalena. When he heard the sound of footsteps on the stair, he threw open the door. But what he saw there made him abandon all thought of his night demons. Here was a heavenly vision with a breakfast tray. He rubbed his stomach in anticipation, though not so much of the scones, or the boiled egg, or the steaming pot of tea.

He heard his voice drop to a baritone. "Come here. What's your name, sweetheart?"

"Matilda, señor."

"Matilda, what a lovely name, and that's a lovely breakfast tray."

He found his hand on her white organdy apron string. With one tug he had it unfastened. He noticed her hair had a dizzying smell.

"Can you call me Federico?" he crooned.

"Your egg's getting cold, señor."

"Let me see you try: Fe-der-i-co," he coaxed.

But Matilda had no intention of becoming a breakfast sensation. "I'll call you a son of a bitch if you don't get your paws off me at once."

He found himself lunging toward her, pressing his lips against her teeth. But Matilda had lost her patience for kisses. Before he knew it, Federico had crumpled to the floor.

"*Puta!*" he howled, clutching at his manhood. "Get me the señora at once!"

"I'm on my way," Matilda assured him cheerily.

Even before Ana Magdalena reached the landing, Federico had miraculously recovered. He waved at her furiously.

"You can't keep that woman here. Fire her. Fire her at once!"

Ana Magdalena bent to pick up the crumpled organdy apron from the floor.

"Did you hear me? I want her out of here."

Coolly she lifted the teapot lid. "What's the matter, darling? You haven't *touched* your breakfast. Was your tea too cold?" She gave him a sympathetic look. "Or did you try to read to her?"

That was the year it rained almost without letup. With the rising waters, Malyerba began to be swept with a pestilential tide of prophets. They gathered like starlings, clustering everywhere: at the corners of streets, clinging to doorways, clogging the flooded thoroughfares, shouting and expostulating, hawking rosaries, holy pictures, and miracle water from Lourdes — guaranteed to cure every illness but a broken heart. Good prophets quoted Paul at the top of their lungs: "Let every soul be subject to the higher powers, for the powers that be are ordained by God"; bad prophets anathemized tax collectors, invoked fire and brimstone against the established order, and condemned civil authority of any kind. They quoted Matthew at full throttle: "Provoke not thy children to anger."

Because the river tides rose so alarmingly, even an establishment as secure as Casa Orgaz was no longer immune. Hoping to trade virtue for shelter, preachers clamored at the door at all hours of the day and night. Ana Magdalena gave strict instructions that none of them must be allowed inside. For that reason Honora was prepared, although it was an inappropriately early hour, to make fast work of her first caller.

"How are you, ma'am?" He flashed her a perfect set of teeth. Honora knew immediately he must not be from Malyerba.

"It's awfully wet outside. Won't you let me in?"

"I'm very sorry."

"My name's Horatio Alger, and here's my card." He slipped it in between the bars.

Honora was about to slam the porter's window shut.

"Just a minute, ma'am. I have something here for your señora!"

"Here we have many señoras," Honora replied testily.

"In my father's house, there are many mansions," Horatio Alger piously replied. From his breast pocket he extracted a soggy letter. "It's addressed to Ana Magdalena, Novia."

But before Honora could reach for it, Horatio Alger had already returned it to his pocket.

"Tell your señora to come down. After all the trouble I've been through, I'm making sure I deliver it in person." He smiled widely at Honora.

Ana Magdalena had just awakened from a troubled sleep when Honora entered her room. She rubbed her eyes. "Honora," she groaned, "you're just in time. Get me a steaming cup of tea."

"There's a letter for señora from a man who says he has to give it to you personally."

"What kind of man?"

Honora read from his business card, "Horatio Alger, 'Rags to Riches with a Smile.'" "I *never* saw such perfect teeth," she remarked wistfully.

"Did he say what kind of letter?"

"I don't know, something about a bride."

The effect was volcanic. "About a *bride?* Aiee, Honora." Ana Magdalena leapt out of bed. "Run, run. Tell him I'll be down almost at once!"

But by the time she had had her tea, dressed her hair, applied her rouge, wondered what to wear, and opened the porter's window of Casa Orgaz, she discovered that Horatio Alger had disappeared, along with the letter and the perfection of his teeth.

In her panic to find him, she threw open the doors. Too late, she saw that the street was choked with prophets of every persuasion, many of them perched atop soap boxes, the better to hurl imprecations at one another — and keep their feet dry. But the instant they noticed the open doors of Casa Orgaz, they pushed and knocked one another over in their haste to reach the entrance first.

Before she could slam the doors shut, however, Ana Magdalena was intercepted.

"Good morning, little lady." She knew at once from his stunning set of teeth that it was none other than Horatio Alger.

"Quick, get inside! There isn't any time to lose!" She bolted the doors fast before ushering him into the visitors' parlor, which already then was cluttered with the coatracks and hat stands required by her steadily growing clientele.

"Señor?"

"Call me Horatio, or Holy for short. It's what my daddy used to call me, God rest his preacher's soul."

"Won't you sit down?"

His smile vanished. "In *here?*"

"They tell me you have a letter for me."

"That's right, little lady, but first I have something here I want to show you." He snapped open his avocado plastic Bible suitcase.

Ana Magdalena groaned. "I'd like to have the letter, please."

"All things come in their season — as the Good Book says. I've got Bibles here of every persuasion," he continued. "I have a *dee*luxe edition of the King James Version; the Douay, for your more Catholic tastes; or, if you prefer, I have your one-size-fits-all edited by the Southern Synod of our very own American Baptist Bible Council that's a *real* seller!"

"But we already have all the Bibles we need," Ana Magdalena assured him rather impatiently.

"And let me tell you, you need every single one of the Bibles you have, little lady. I don't want to pry, but I *heard* you were set up in business —"

"A tricky business, Mr. Alger."

"Hard work, service with a smile — long as business is good, it means you're in the Lord's grace, sister."

Ana Magdalena was beside herself. "Not if there's the devil to pay."

"Oh, the devil's nothing to worry about, so long as you pay him with a smile."

"Could I see the letter now?"

"By jiminy, I nearly forgot." Although the letter had very nearly dissolved, when she saw the handwriting, she knew. She nearly immolated what was left of its contents in her eagerness to tear the envelope apart.

"It's him, dear God, it's him!" She hustled 'Holy' Alger out with unbecoming haste.

"My Adored One, my Salvation," she read.

This is a letter from your River Rat. We are penetrating deep into the interior. The *yanquis* are spreading out their hunting operations. They are taking out the backwaters. They have already cleaned out over 60! tributaries! They don't let up for a minute! Night and day they drink whiskey. It's their blood, their medicine. They brush their teeth with it. They even use it for snakebite. We'll be in Malyerba very soon.

She clasped the letter to her breast. She read the rest with difficulty because her eyes were brimming over with tears.

> Any day now, my beloved.
> Yrs. ever,
> Sergio Ballado, esq.

P.S. I'm sending you more customers. How about 20% this time? My expenses are getting out of hand.

The rains ceased. A blinding sunlight shone on Malyerba's streets, now miraculously swept clean of prophets. But everywhere the floods had left their mark. Mud and silt had seeped into the cellar.

Shod in Wellingtons, and with her faith in free enterprise happily restored, Ana Magdalena pushed open the massive basement doors. The smell of mold nearly choked her.

Accompanied by Cecilia and the uncertain beams of her flashlight, she made her way through the ooze.

"Ooof, it's damp in here!" Cecilia exclaimed.

They found themselves in a vault of brickwork, much like the vaults of factories designed for the production of sugar that she had seen illustrated in her convent geography book. It seemed to stretch the entire length of the house, interrupted at regular intervals by piers.

"Oh, look, there are the Manaus opera flats!" Ana Magdalena exclaimed, shining her flashlight so Cecilia could see them.

But many of them were soaked beyond redemption. They found four immense terracotta amphoras embedded in the mud, and when they reached the opposite end, they came upon a collection of musty trunks and wardrobes, all of them covered with a generous heaping of mouse droppings.

"Euuuu!" exclaimed Cecilia.

"Yes, but just think, if we could clean it up, wouldn't it make the perfect *confitería?*"

Andreina always said she was waiting to visit Casa Orgaz until she knew her daughter was settled. Months, even years, went by. True, Ana Magdalena always paid her the kind of duty visits people pay to mothers everywhere. But lately Andreina had become so obsessed with the nurture of bees she had begun talking to them in baby talk. She kept elaborate, color-coded charts on the kitchen wall, on which she documented the come and go of her bee colonies. Talking to her through her Alençon lace shield was like talking through a speaking tube.

But immediately following the calming of the waters, Ana Magdalena was amazed to receive a first, breathless visit from her mother.

"*Niña,* she's gone!"

"Who?"

"Berta."

It was as much of a shock to Ana Magdalena as it was to Andreina. Neither of them could imagine an existence unassisted by Berta. Mother and daughter sipped tea in the library, the only room left free of the various appurtenances pertaining to Ana Magdalena's enterprise.

"She left her hammock."

"In the storeroom?"

"Strung on the hooks. And her clothes. They're still there, hanging on the pegs. My God, *hija,* it's as if she stepped over the threshold into another world."

"She took nothing?"

"Only the shirt on her back, as far as I can tell."

Andreina poured herself another cup of tea. "And why anyone would want to go anywhere in the pouring rain — unless they absolutely had to —"

"In the pouring rain? Then it's only recently —"

"Two days ago. I was busy smoking the bees. My Havana must have gone soggy. I went to the kitchen for matches. She was gone! I didn't think anything at first, but by suppertime . . ."

Andreina decided to give her two or three more days, but when Berta failed to reappear, she set about making inquiries for another servant girl. But try as she might, she was unable to find anyone willing to work in a house where the human beings had become almost entirely legendary.

Hardly past the Fiesta de los Reyes, Ana Magdalena received yet another family visit.

"Who is it?" she asked Honora.

"It's not the Three Kings," was Honora's rueful reply. "I think it's Señor Hercules."

Ana Magdalena groaned. "*Dios mio.*" She slid out of her cool pink satin sheets. "Tell him I'll be down in just a little minute."

After making sure to spend the maximum time at her toilette, she entered the cloakroom. Hercules stood up to greet her. She noticed his hair had turned a steely shade of gray, and there was something unsettling about his appearance. She wondered if he hadn't shrunk.

He arched an ironic eyebrow. "I hope I'm not disturbing the great lady. So. The *casa de putas* lets you live like a queen. Very good! From what they tell me, you've become the mistress to the world. But poor Federico thinks you're still the little mistress of his house, is that right? You've learned to play both sides of the fence, haven't you?"

Ana Magdalena had never liked the way Hercules put things.

"Look," she said, "If you're here to stir up unpleasantness, at least leave married women out of it."

"That's just the point," he remarked. He slipped a large package from the cloakroom rack.

"What are you doing?"

"I'm about to show you." He undid the plain brown wrappings. Although by now it was terribly crumpled, Ana Magdalena recognized her wedding dress. She watched, horrified, as her miraculous shoes tumbled to the floor and lay capsized on their sides. For one disturbing moment she slipped through a gaping crack in time. His smirk brought her back to earth.

"I got them back from the police chief in exchange for a little favor."

"You can't be serious! What would I want with those old things?"

But Hercules was not to be diverted. "Don't turn your nose up quite so high, missy. They're worth money."

"Money doesn't interest me —"

"Maybe, but it interests me very much." His voice took on a snide, insinuating tone. "I'll tell you what. I'm going to do you a little favor. Don't you want to know what it is?"

She waited.

"I'm going to make sure these little items don't fall into unfriendly hands, and every month, you'll give me a salary."

"You're planning to work here?"

"What do you take me for, some kind of pimp? No. I'm going to store these articles in a safe place — as a kind of collateral — and every month I'll come visit you with the chief of police for my little five percent?"

"Don't be ridiculous. The chief of police is still in jail."

"It may interest you to know that just before he went into hiding, El Magnifico declared a general amnesty. The chief — your late aunt's favorite — was cleared of every charge. He's innocent."

He knew from her expression that he had her. He stood up. Ceremoniously, taking his time, he carefully rewrapped the articles and moved toward the door. "And by the way." He stopped. "I know how happy you'll be on the first to receive our little visit."

*   *   *

That morning Ana Magdalena's steps on the mirador stairs were heavy. She carried Federico's breakfast tray with its solitary egg boiled a precise three and one-half minutes and its sterling silver egg scissors in place. As she approached, she could hear the typewriter already clacking at a furious pace, although it was barely noon. At the top of the stairs lay his dirty dinner service from the previous night piled high with soiled underwear and crumpled balls of paper.

She knocked. "Federico?"

At last the clacking came to a stop, and the door opened just wide enough for her to pass him the tray.

He placed a finger to his lips. "Shhh," he whispered. "She's here now. She's got me cooking. I'm nearly boiling over!" He took the tray and shut the door.

On the landing her eye was caught by a piece of crumpled paper. ". . . magnificent gold braid," she read.

She picked it up. She smoothed it out as was her habit.

. . . ushered him inside. He wore a military uniform adorned with magnificent gold braid, but already it seemed too heavy for his reduced frame.

"Don Simón," the maid stammered, barely able to breathe, "Ostencia Candelaria is waiting for you."

The salon, however, was crowded with all manner of *yanquis* who had only just that day debarked from the carrier *Enterprise*. They occupied every sofa, every banquette. Simón Bolívar had to stand. But the strain was too much for him. He began to cough.

At once he was surrounded by a flock of ship's doctors and paramedical personnel, all uniformed in their dress whites.

"Sir," they said to him in perfect English, "that's a terrible condition you have there. Open wide. Let's see that rasping throat."

But Simón Bolívar was beyond the military might of the *norteamericanos,* past the ministrations of their trained medicos, their pills and bronchoscopes of stainless steel.

"Alas," he coughed, "I think it may be a little late." He extracted a handkerchief of the finest linen, which was soaked through with blood.

"How unsanitary," observed the military medicos, turning their backs on the unsightliness. "These people lack the most elementary hygiene."

"*Buenas tardes,*" Ostencia Candelaria greeted him.

"It's already very late. I have to catch a barge down the Magdalena at dawn," remarked Simón Bolívar.

She took him upstairs. She lay him on the bed and sponged his burning brow.

"I never told you about Manuela," he said, "the woman who means more to me than all the world. . . ."

But Ostencia Candelaria knew there was something important he still had left to say. "Don Simón," she whispered, "wouldn't you prefer to make a closing statement?"

"I thought I'd keep it for my dying breath."

"As you wish," she said, "but I have pen and paper handy."

"Very well. Say this. 'Remember, patriots, as a matter of course, the North Americans —"

"*Yanquis —*"

"No!" he exploded. "This is to be a closing statement! Let's show some dignity!" After a paroxysm of coughing, he continued in a more modulated tone. "The North Americans, under the guise of helping us, will justify repeated invasions of our soil, subjecting our peoples to endless exploitation and suffering.'

"Is that all, señor?"

"It's quite enough. And date that 1830. The sixteenth of December. Now let me tell you about Manuela, soul of my soul, spirit of my s—"

"I hope I'm not disturbing you," said the chief of police as he sat down with Hercules in the visitors' parlor. It was the first of the month. Ana Magdalena handed him a canvas sack.

"It's all in there, twenty percent, all with the receipts."

"All tallied up?"

"All written out in longhand."

Hercules was puzzled. "Just a minute —"

"Oh, don't worry, your five percent is in there, too," she assured him with exaggerated sweetness.

Hercules was annoyed, as she knew he would be because he

knew the police chief would be unable to resist taking his cut before passing it along. But there was nothing Hercules could do about it. He had her, but she had him, too. She was his daughter, after all. When they left, Ana Magdalena felt a great sense of relief wash over her. Later, if she thought of them at all, it was to reflect that they were like a monthly period — unpleasant, but inevitable. And very bad for business.

Even reduced to net proceeds, money always cheered Hercules up. It made him feel the need for more. With Ana Magdalena's not quite four percent stashed away in his jacket pocket, a new spring of confidence animated his normally somewhat leaden gait. He made his way across town towards Andreina's house, smiling, tipping his hat, trading greetings with the passersby. His wife's business seemed to be thriving. If he played his cards right, he might just be able to tap her for a loan.

But at the porter's door, something made him hesitate. He had been absent for some time. He disremembered the door being off its hinges, or the origins of the disrepair. He went instead to the kitchen door. He turned the knob. At once he became aware of a sound he had never heard before. It was the hum of a thousand thousand tiny wings, fluttering and beating, thousands of minuscule pollen sacks rattling and rubbing against one another; it was the sound of a honeyed universe, and at the heart of it lay Andreina.

Hercules stared. He was not horrified. He was transfixed — not by the languor of her expression, which long ago when she had fainted at Ana Magdalena's wedding had put him in such a discombobulated state, but at the insects moving in purposeful columns over her body, swarming into the dark heart of that cavity from which her spirit had long ago departed. Her body had become a hive. Its every member, its every tissue, had become crystallized, sanctified by the sweet celestial sap of their secretions.

"*Hola!*" he shouted to anyone who might be there to hear. Instantly the bees were upon him, squadron after squadron, swarming, stinging, beating their ferocious wings. Hercules began to run, screaming as they stung him; he made for the river, and when he got there at last, he was happy to plunge in. He remained underwater till his lungs were ready to give out. When he finally came up, the last of the bees had disappeared, and his jacket, weighed down by Ana Magdalena's not-quite-four-percent, lay at the bottom of the river.

Because Hercules had been away from the company of priests so long, he stood (because he could not sit) in the cathedral rectory, stiff, ill at ease, every part of his body grotesquely swollen.

"My poor man." Monsignor exuded pity and concern.

"Don't trouble yourself on my account. I've come to see if you can bury my wife."

Monsignor was certain he could bury any wife, whether or not she acquiesced. But he sensed something different here.

"Is there a problem?" he asked. "I assume she's not alive."

"No," replied Hercules, "it's worse than that. She's candied."

Monsignor was taken aback; but when he learned that she had died the rare and blessed death of one sanctified by bees he became ecstatic, because he knew that at last we in Malyerba would have our local saint. But although Andreina's spirit was uncontestably among the blessed, the problem remained of disposing of her mortal body here on earth.

After some reflection, monsignor, together with Hercules, formulated a course of action. They searched the length and breadth of the parish, but nowhere could they find six pallbearing apiarists. At last, for safety's sake, they decided that the house itself would have to become the sainted Andreina's mausoleum. It was boarded up. Doors and windows were sealed shut in the course of an otherwise perfectly normal funeral ceremony. Turned out in fashionable black, Ana Magdalena, accompanied by Federico, shed every tear she could muster. The entire crowd joined in the responses while monsignor sprinkled the house with holy water.

But neither the bees nor the rainbow girls were listening. To forestall any embarrassment to Federico, Ana Magdalena had given her employees the day off, and the bees were planning their exodus, now that their queen was dead.

XIII

Federico swiveled slowly in his composition chair. There was no doubt about it: the walls of the mirador had begun to move. At first he had not been aware of it, but as the months passed he could no longer ignore the horrifying phenomenon, and he knew that if he didn't complete *The Love Queen* soon, they would come to entomb him and choke him at last.

He sat watching them in a state of ironic fascination: the books, the bookshelves, gradually everything had become obscured by the mounting piles of manuscripts, which with every passing day reached closer to the ceiling.

He had, however, kept the avenue to his encyclopedias fairly clear; from where he now sat, he could see plainly that the "B" volume was still accessible if he approached it very cautiously.

For years he had been promising himself that, sooner or later, he would look "bees" up, but following a long period of existential doubt, he had decided that information was useful only if you could do something with it or about it. He had absolutely no intention whatsoever of raising bees himself, and although he would have liked to know if what Ana Magdalena had told him about "milking" them was true, he was afraid to discover that her information was more than peripherally inaccurate. He didn't want to confront her, particularly not if it stirred up any unpleasantness.

But now the situation was no longer the same. God rest her industrious soul, poor Andreina was crystallized. The information was no longer of any relevance to him or to anyone else because the bees were a thing of the past, and Ana Magdalena was home at all hours of the night, and most hours otherwise, as the level of noise could amply attest.

He made his way on hands and knees — because he knew from bitter experience any careless movement might dislodge priceless material from its place — to the volume whose location had burned itself into the suspicion centers of his overactive brain. He reached for the "B" volume and found the place. Still on his knees, he read: "Correct bee management requires that the hive be opened whenever it is necessary to determine conditions or to manipulate the frames and hive bodies. As far as possible," he read with growing apprehension, "as far as possible it should be done under proper conditions of weather, namely on a warm, sunny day, one without wind."

Federico closed the book. The pages fell together with a slap, but he couldn't have felt it any more keenly had it been a slap in his own face. He knelt on the floor of the mirador, measuring the racing of his heart.

Following Andreina's exemplary demise, Ana Magdalena spent endless afternoons with the shutters drawn, nursing her migraines. She was hardly able to keep Casa Orgaz afloat. For this reason the police chief's monthly visit took her entirely by surprise. Accompanied by Hercules, and ignoring Sidonia's vigorous protests, he barged into Ana Magdalena's darkened bedroom.

"I assume everything's in order?" he barked by way of introduction.

Ana Magdalena rolled over in the darkness. "Can't you show a glimmer of respect if not for the living at least for the dead?" she whispered.

Hercules cleared his throat. "I don't see why you're making such a fuss. After all, I'm the one who found her, and you don't see me carrying on."

"Very well." Ana Magdalena sat up. If that's how you want it." She vaulted out of bed, dislodging the mound of embroidered lace-edged pillows at her side. She flung herself toward the door of Clemencia's antique safe, which in the considerable heat of her sentiments she wrenched completely off its hinges. She extracted the canvas sack.

193

"It's all in there." She glared at the chief of police.

"Including the receipts?"

"If you want receipts, you'll have to dream them up yourself!"

By the time they left, she was so infuriated that her migraine had begun to shrill and whine inside her head. She tried piling a mountain of embroidered pillows over her ears.

"*Madre de Dios,*" she muttered between clenched teeth.

At once something struck her pillow fortress with a thump. Puzzled, she sat up. On the floor, she noticed an antique satin jewel-encrusted slipper that lay on its side where it had fallen. She picked it up. Inside it bore a label, now almost completely obliterated. Never in her life had she laid eyes on such exquisite footwear. Suddenly a cold wind shook her to the bone. She knew that shoe. Hadn't she struggled once to shoe Clemencia — in this very room, in this very selfsame shoe?

"*Madrina de Dios,*" she mumbled, thunderstruck.

In response, the second shoe dropped. It landed squarely on her head. Instantly her migraine disappeared.

"Ouch!" she protested to the ceiling. But what she saw there made her gasp. Clemencia sat with her legs entangled in the crystal chandelier, shaking in silent mirth.

"Clemencia, my darling. It's you!"

Clemencia placed a bony finger to her bloodless lips. "Shhh," she whispered, "don't make so much noise. Can you help me down off this dreadful thing?"

Ana Magdalena looked helplessly about, thinking to improvise a ladder of some sort.

"Oh, don't bother with that," said Clemencia, reading her thoughts. "By now, I'm nearly weightless. Any mound of pillows will do. Just make sure you stack them right."

Ana Magdalena piled pillow on embroidered pillow. Mesmerized, she watched Clemencia untangle her spindly legs from the arms of the chandelier and, easing herself onto the pillows, slide gracefully to earth.

Even without her habitual clairvoyance, she would have known at once that Clemencia's visit was meant to be a warning. Even through her stockings, she could see that Clemencia's bunions were swollen and extremely red.

194

"Clemencia, *pobrecita,* you must be footsore, poor thing."

"Oh, you don't know the half of it," she lamented as Ana Magdalena helped her slip off the stockings bunched about her ancient and emaciated legs. She made her sit at the edge of her bed, where she could soak her feet in a warm mustard bath.

"Listen carefully, *niña.*" She took hold of Ana Magdalena's hands. "You are about to have the visit of a lifetime."

"Another one? I very nearly succumbed to the last."

"Yes, but this is going to be different. Don't be deceived. It may seem fortunate at first, but will end up bringing very little good."

"Who is it?"

Clemencia looked about to make sure they were still alone. She bent down to whisper in Ana Magdalena's ear. Her breath smelled of the open fields, of sage and marjoram and thyme.

"It will be someone pale; he's going to want to shower you with money."

When she had unburdened herself of all she had to say, she sat placidly swishing her old afflicted feet in the basin. Suddenly, she remembered something.

"What became of the old sourpuss? I almost forgot to ask."

"You mean Severina? Federico fired her. He put her on the eleven A.M. *rápido* to Tierra del Fuego. And without a centavo of severance pay!"

Clemencia let out a whoop of triumph, but it was a reckless thing to do, because the sudden intake of air into her collapsed old lungs sent her ricocheting like a punctured balloon. She careened madly, blubbering and farting about the room, before sputtering out the casement into the late afternoon rain. When Ana Magdalena ran to the window to see where she had disappeared, she was amazed to discover the arc of a double rainbow spanning a glorious night sky.

Sergio Ballado stood as far from the mirror as his cramped skipper's cabin would permit. He studied his pompadour. Intent on achieving the perfect blend of elevation and sheen, he applied more brilliantine. He caressed each strand with as much attention as his comb, which had become increasingly toothless from almost constant use, would allow. Already he detected the slightest of stains on his otherwise impeccable whites, but despite vigorous rubbing, the stains showed no signs of wanting to retreat.

"*Puta,*" he mumbled under his breath. Hard times were stalking Sergio Ballado. From the moment the crew dropped anchor, things had gone badly. Although they pumped out the bilge, the water level remained at its own obstinate level, a clear sign there was a new leak. And as they were battening it down, sure enough, one of the hatches had sprung another hinge.

"*Puta,*" he muttered again. He surveyed his appearance. Hair slicked back, form-fitting cotton shirt left open at the neck to reveal a generous display of hair, and sailor pants, buttoned at either side of an abdomen sleek as a panther's, rooted in a promising bulge. The effect was, for the most part, entirely to his satisfaction — but for his beard. If only he had had the presence of mind to shave, if not daily, at least from time to time as he skippered the *Amazon Queen* with its load of determined *yanqui* hunters up the sun-drenched tributaries of the river. But no, *putamadre,* he had taken the easy way, grown a beard, and now, arrived at last in Malyerba, he had had to resist the impulse to shave it because any fool could foresee the disastrous effect. With his brow and temples already tanned an irresistible copper, his chin and jawline would emerge from their perpetual night the appalling color of a week-old corpse. And what would Ana Magdalena think? She might not even recognize him. At the very thought of her, he felt his trousers tighten. "Calm down," he said to the beast who was causing all the tension. "Especially in hard times, the animals have to wait their turn!" He threw his handsome head back in exuberant tribute to his rather vulgar sense of humor. *She* wouldn't mind it, he knew. And the pants were of a sturdy manufacture. They could withstand the most rigorous of tests.

He felt the beast prick up its horns.

"*Ándale!*" he said. "Get a move on. Let's see what juicy tidbits La Nymphaea has to toss you!" He vaulted up the corrugated steel stairs onto the deck, and lowered the dinghy. It hit the water with a splash.

When he reached shore, he shipped the oars and tied the dinghy to the same wooden pier where, as a younger and more innocent man, he had tied up after a day on the river. After all this time he was going to find *la novia* again.

He began to walk along the dirt paths that led to the Calle del

Grito, the street where he remembered La Nymphaea stood, but as he passed the Barco de Oro, something told him he should stop inside. "Hold your horses," he said to the beast, "we're taking a little detour first, a very tiny one." Evidently the beast disapproved of this capricious change of plan. He felt it turn sullen and peckish. "And don't you get cranky on me. You know what happens when you act nasty."

Although it was little past noon, some of his sporting friends were rolling the dice, exactly where he had left them nearly seven years ago.

"*Hola!* It's Ballado! *Saludos, hombre!* What happened to your chin? It looks like the place where two legs meet!" They all guffawed heartily. Sergio Ballado's romantic escapades had become a thing of legend, and he was barely twenty-nine.

Despite their unfeeling remarks, they were genuinely happy to see him back from Brazil, because they knew he would have money to burn. They pumped him for stories about the *yanquis* and the hunting expedition; he ordered drinks all around; and especially for Malyerba, the time began to fly.

When he heard four o'clock strike, he stood up, aghast.

"Easy, easy, pal, where are you going?"

"To La Nymphaea. To see the girls."

"At four o'clock? Come on, there's time for a few more rounds till supper. You can see the girls at dinnertime."

"I'm meeting someone."

"At La Nymphaea? Boy, haven't you heard?"

"Heard what?"

"It's empty. No one's left. The only girls there now are the cats and screech owls."

Sergio Ballado looked stricken. "Then she never got my letters."

"Letters? Now you're sending letters? Before you didn't know how to write!" Sergio Ballado's friends were looking at him strangely.

"Well, I wrote letters to *la novia*."

"Ah," they sighed indulgently, "*La novia*. Do you know what's become of her? Listen, *muchacho*, it's quite a story."

Sergio Ballado sat back down. His cronies began telling him about Ofelia, and the inauguration of La Tuerca, and El Magnífico's visit to Malyerba. And by the time their recital ended, Sergio Ballado knew without a doubt that he was still in love with a very enterprising woman and he knew he could find her at Casa Orgaz. What they had neglected to tell him, however, was the name by which she had acquired her professional renown. He rolled out of the Barco de Oro. Although it was raining hard, he was ready to believe the streets were golden with the sun's last setting rays. No sooner had he reached Casa Orgaz than the sudden shower stopped, and a double rainbow brightened the sky directly above the entryway. He pulled the porter's bell.

"Let me see Ana Magdalena," Sergio said to the lovely Matilda, when she opened the door.

"Who?" Matilda looked at him vacantly.

Although Sergio Ballado's knees were ordinarily very down to earth, now he felt them turn to jelly. He thought quickly.

"Madam Ofelia," he said.

"Madam Ofelia is deceased, rest her soul. You want the lady of the house. You want Madam Blanca." And she threw open wide the door.

As he waited for Ana Magdalena, he heard the loud talking and laughter of the customers, but his mind was elsewhere — on the evening to come, on the candlelight dinner he had prepared, on the sound of the river as it lapped gently against the bow. And all the while, he felt the beast stir restlessly, evidently entertaining secret projects of its own. "Don't try anything funny on me, you rascal, or you'll get us in a fix," he whispered. At last he heard rustling in the vestibule.

"My darling, I thought you had disappeared forever!" She threw herself in his arms. But the cloakroom did not lend itself very well to impassioned embraces.

"Come away, *querida,* there's a candlelight dinner waiting for you on board."

She stood back to take in his altered appearance. "*Dios mio,*" she exclaimed dismayed. "With that beard you look just like a litterateur! And where are all the *yanquis* you promised to bring me?"

He looked at her impatiently. "You must be joking! *Yanquis* would never be caught dead here — or anywhere else."

"Why? What's wrong with Casa Orgaz?"

"Casa Orgaz is off-limits to *yanquis*. They have their own city with their own houses, and their own cyclone fence. When a hill is in the way, they just flatten it and build a swimming pool."

"But in the end aren't they just like other men? Don't they like love like everyone else?"

She could sense his mounting exasperation. "Can we go now?" he grumped.

"*Querido,* please! I have to feed Federico first."

"Federico?"

"Sweetheart, I know it's been a long time," she remarked pointedly, "but don't forget I'm married."

"Still hitched to that poor donkey with his ears in the clouds?"

"Don't complain. Better in the clouds than here in the cloakroom. Wait for me, *querido,*" she coaxed. "I'll be just a little minute."

At last, she was back. She had shoehorned herself into a cherry red satin dress, all peplums and swags. "We're off, my darling. I've left Sidonia in charge. She can take in the customers and collect the cash."

The rainbow had disappeared. They sped into the last fading light of evening. When they reached the pier, it was nearly dark.

"There she is," Sergio Ballado announced, waving proudly, "the *Amazon Queen.*"

Her heart sank with something of a thud. Even in the twilight she could see it was a rusty old tub that had seen much better days.

He must have sensed her disappointment. "Wait till you see, *querida,* what a surprise I have in store."

She shivered as he rowed her across the dark waters. Unexpectedly, a sudden squall sent two-foot waves tearing toward the dinghy, and although it ended almost as soon as it began, the spray soaked Ana Magdalena to the bone. Her gorgeous dress was a bedraggled mess of soggy dark red satin, and the evening hadn't even started.

"I wore it new for our reunion and already it's a wreck."

"Don't worry, *chica,* I'll get you fifteen others just like it in Belém."

Once he had helped her up the wobbly rope ladder, he took her in his arms. He held her body pressed close against his. His mouth found her mouth.

"You're shivering, *querida,*" he whispered. He lit a storm lantern. "Come below," he said. He raised a hatch cover and helped her over the raised threshold and down the corrugated metal stairs.

The place they entered was only dimly lit. Sergio yanked a lever. Deep in the bowels of the hull the engine leapt to life.

He pulled her toward him. She stood trembling like a filly at the starting gate, while slowly he unzipped her dress and peeled it from her icy skin. He began to plant little kisses on her mouth and hair. He gave his hands time to reacquaint themselves with her body after their very long exile, to explore the rediscovered continent that was her skin, skirting the promontories, grazing the valleys, letting the tide of his desire swell on her shores.

Ah, Sergio Ballado, she sighed to herself, *even if I had no eyes or ears to nose you out, my skin would know you, and my tongue would taste you, and my hands and my fingers and my arms would tell me it was you, because it's you I picked from the very beginning. You, and only you.*

She felt herself dissolve, the mouths of her being opening, preparing to accept the whim of the tides as they lapped and pulled at the thousands of tiny translucent fingers her body had become.

He lowered her onto some kind of blanket he had hastily spread out on the floor.

"In *here?*" she asked, distressed.

"But *chica,* it's the warmest place. We're in the boiler room."

Ana Magdalena had never been made love to in a boiler room before. She could feel the thumping of the pistons, humming, plunging, throbbing. She let the colossus lull her in its shuddering embrace.

So much time had gone by, so many things had happened since she had last been with Sergio Ballado. She remembered his spectacular lovemaking through a kind of haze. And here he was, back from the jungles of the Amazon, writhing and rocking like a snake, taking her breath away with his fevered kisses. She felt the beast prowling the moist and savage night air of the jungle. It was more than she could bear. She had the mad desire to tame it, to feed it guavas from her lips. Her body began to shudder, prey to the fit of its own divine and very secret epilepsy. The horned god had her quaking in its grasp. She couldn't stop the snapping of its phosphorescent jaws. She wasn't sure if the cries she heard came from a very great distance, or whether they welled up from her own terrible, dark blood. Again. And again. She couldn't stop. She couldn't breathe. Sergio held her down. All around her the waves were rushing, under and over her. She was being swept along by the fierceness of the rapids, brimming, spilling over the edge. "Aiee, aiee!" Her scream disappeared in the torrent of white water.

"*Querido.*" She shook him awake. "We have to get an engine."

"But we have an engine," he said with the patience people use when they talk to little children. "We're on the *Amazon Queen.*"

"You don't understand. Not here. In Casa Orgaz. A real live engine, exactly like this one."

She began telling him all about Hercules and about the police chief, and their tasteless depredations. All through dinner, she laid out her plans for Casa Orgaz.

"I'll be bankrupt in no time. There's nothing I can do about it — unless I open La Confitería and *querido,* darling, you're going to help."

"Confitería? I don't think I follow you."

"Yes. La Confitería. We'll dish up all kinds of bonbons for the 'special tastes': we'll have carousels, and classrooms, and birdcages — just like Ofelia wanted. Only we'll do it on a grander scale. And that's where you come in. We need a real live engine for the boiler room, one that hums and throbs and shudders. An engine just like this one."

She was galvanized by yet another inspiration. "Oh, I know what we'll do."

"What?"

"Dismantle the *Amazon Queen!*"

"*What* about the *Amazon Queen?*"

"So we can extract her engine."

"You must be joking!"

"Not at all. Here's what we do. You get your crew to dismantle her. It shouldn't be hard. Then we lift out the engine."

"But, *querida,*" he objected, "how am I going to get back to

Belém? Anyway, there's not a metal saw in Peru that can do the job unless we send away to Lima."

"Or Manaus," she cleverly pointed out. But Sergio Ballado remained noticeably unmoved. "Why are you being so difficult? If you loved me, you'd make a little effort."

"Please, *chica,*" he begged, "be reasonable."

"But —"

"But nothing. It takes a long time. For one thing, the Belém & Amazonas Excursion Company would never agree."

"This old tub? They will if I buy her for better than salvage."

"And how do I and the crew get back to Belém?"

"But you'd stay here, don't you see. Let the crew shift for themselves. Oh, come on! Those are just petty and insignificant details. If you loved me you wouldn't be so obstinate."

But Sergio Ballado had other ideas. He sidled very close to her.

"*Chica,* tell me something, how do you do it?"

"Do what?"

"That thing you do."

"What thing?"

"The thing you do when it goes like this."

She squirmed voluptuously. "Oh," she purred, "the snapping? But that's you, *querido*. You do it to me every time."

"You're sure there's no one else?"

"Only you!" She cast down her eyes with becoming modesty. After all, she didn't exactly want to lie to Sergio Ballado. She changed the subject. "More sausage, please. And rice. Mmmm, this *feijoada* is sublime. I never tasted anything so good!"

By now Sergio Ballado had come to appreciate so many beauties at first hand that he had fairly lost count, but he knew that in Ana Magdalena he had at last found a unique and extremely rare form of erotic virtuosity, and he began to elaborate to himself the many ingenious schemes by which it might bring comfort to a sad and needy world.

"Come on," he said to her. "I keep telling you. This is no place to launch your career. Malyerba is a pissant town. I can't see for the life of me what keeps you here."

"I keep telling you, I'm married."

"Married? You don't need Casa Orgaz. You could have your very own pleasure palace right in Belém. Listen, once in Rio a friend took me to visit a place where they had a rainbow of skin — colors you wouldn't believe — that would put those simpy pastel girls of yours to shame. There was even a 'panther' — with skin as shiny and blue as the night."

"Blue skin!" Ana Magdalena shivered. "Anyway, it doesn't change a thing. I'm still married," she stubbornly insisted, "and there's nothing I can do about it."

"You could get an annulment."

"What's that?"

"You get it from the Pope. When you want to marry someone else. But it costs a lot of money."

"How much?"

"Oh . . . maybe a hundred thousand escudos."

"A hundred thousand escudos!" Ana Magdalena laughed derisively.

"Of course. What do you think? The Pope has to eat. You don't expect him to live like the blessed angels on nothing but air."

"My God!" Ana Magdalena was deeply impressed. But the idea of an annulment failed to appeal to her. The more she thought about it, the clearer it seemed. She was already married. She didn't see the need to go through all of it again.

"No. It's too expensive."

"And where's my cut for all the customers I sent you?"

"The ten percent?"

"I think it was twenty."

"I have to check." She smiled. "It's all written down."

"I've got to head back to Belém tomorrow, before noon. Why don't you bring it when you come to see me off?"

Ana Magdalena affected a pout. "*Querido,*" she said, "it's getting awfully chilly. Let's have dessert in the boiler room."

In the predawn light Sergio Ballado helped Ana Magdalena negotiate the treacherous rungs of the rope ladder in her stiletto high heels. He carefully committed to memory the delicious grooves of her ankles, the vulnerable and indecent nakedness behind her provocative patellae, and the tantalizing promise of her thighs, because he knew he would not see her again for a very long time. But already then, even as he rowed her to shore, he had begun to formulate the scheme that would free *la novia* at last.

"*Chica,*" he whispered between impassioned farewell kisses, "remember, I'm coming back for you. And when I do, it'll be on a special boat, a walking-beam paddlewheel steamer. It will ride the river smooth as Jesus tiptoeing over the water, all new paint and veils. And you'll be waiting. No more passengers, no *yanqui* hunters, just you. And me rowing. Promise you'll be waiting?"

Ana Magdalena was tired. Her dress was soaked. It had shrunk so much she couldn't even zip it closed no matter how hard she held her breath.

"*Querido.*" She teased a pomaded strand of his straying hair back into place. "Next time, bring me an engine. And please, make sure it works."

It was close to noon when at last Federico gave signs of stirring. Ana Magdalena brought him his breakfast tray, set as usual with three scones, one egg boiled a perfectly precise three and one-half minutes, and the sterling egg scissors he liked so much. She found him in a state of creative exaltation.

"*Chica,* quick! Come in here and shut the door. Sit down, sit down." He swept the trundle bed free of manuscript pages. "All this is trash. I've had an absolutely *stunning* breakthrough."

Ana Magdalena had her mind on other things. "Couldn't it wait till this afternoon?"

"It won't take a minute." Federico's volubility was beyond containment. "I'm plotting my dénouement." He fumbled with excitement as he tried to adjust his frumpy old lady's glasses to his nose.

"The way I've written it, Ostencia Candelaria's reputation as a succubus has spread over all the Amazon, attracting scores of enthusiasts who trample down the jungle in a fever to reach her. Ecologists are deeply concerned, but not surprisingly, the world powers are impotent. At last it becomes obvious to everyone, the sole agent powerful enough to shut her down is the Holy See —"

"But you're not going to shut her down." Ana Magdalena spoke with something more than normal concern. "She's barely gotten started."

But Federico had begun to read. He impersonated all the voices, lounging decadently in his austere composition chair, flicking imaginary cigarette ash with a nonchalance verging on degeneracy. He drawled, he sneered, he affected an insinuating nasality. He read as she had never heard him read before.

It was a troubled Roman Curia that met in plenary session, determined to stem the tide of Ostencia Candelaria's spreading depredations in the Amazon. All Brazil and all Peru had been sucked into her irresistible sphere of shamelessness. Venezuela and Bolivia were teetering on the brink. It was a curia that cringed before the demoniac vision of a possessed Southern Hemisphere panting, bouncing, heaving dangerously out of line, uniting in an enthusiasm even Simón Bolívar himself could not have foreseen.

"Remember," warned Cardinal Parmigiano, "divine intervention is no longer possible at the succubus level. Entropy sets in. The entire sorry system trembles on the edge of total chaos, beyond any rational control." He paused for effect. "I suggest we immediately dispatch an agent."

"An agent?" sneered Cardinal Provolone. "What agent among you could possibly *hope* to resist the wiles of a succubus? Only St. Anthony, as far as I'm concerned, and unfortunately, he's not back from the desert yet."

Cardinal Gorgonzola spoke. "It's entirely possible that through my very close Renaissance connections, I might be able —"

"Your connections are so stuffy, *cara,*" drawled Cardinal Mozzarella, "they all but choke on their own spit."

"But they owe, *cara,* they owe — after all those favors I did them. Now, I grant you, John's a perfectly respectable little assassin, but what we really need is someone who's seen it all, done it all, someone so sated, so immured to lubricity — even in its most virulent forms — as to be completely impervious."

"You're looking for a sin-snob, *cara.*" Mozzarella's voice dripped with sarcasm. "And I can't think of a single soul in our little circle who might remotely qualify, can you?"

"*Cara,*" purred Cardinal Gorgonzola, "how about Alexander the Sixth? Wouldn't *he* be delicious?"

"The Borgia? Oh, sublime. Oh, *cara,* I'm positively *dying.*" Entirely won over, Mozzarella smacked his lips. "Call him up at once. Ask him if he's willing to be drafted."

"I'm afraid he's slightly incommunicado, at least just now. The poor sod's been underground about five hundred years!"

"All the more reason, *cara,*" Mozzarella drawled. "He won't be able to rise to an occasion of sin — no matter how compelling."

After suitably Byzantine deliberations, they narrowed the field to all but two candidates: John the Twenty-second, antipope of Avignon, and Alexander the Sixth, sire of Lucretia Borgia, Cesare Borgia, and numerous other proliferating little Borgias. They put the matter to the vote. Alexander won over John by a narrow margin because, although John was more adept at the arts of poison, Alexander had laid public claim to a more exciting private life.

Swept up by his narrative, Ana Magdalena realized she had become nearly oblivious of time and of the *Amazon Queen,* which was about to weigh anchor for the return run to Belém. Federico took a breath.

Exhumation proceedings were immediately instituted, although they thought it prudent to borrow liberally from the rites of exorcism as well. But evidently they must have laid on the formulae too thick, because although posthumously Alexander the Sixth remained seventy-two years of age, and would remain so till the resurrection of the flesh, they were surprised to raise a pale and simpering adolescent.

"What luck," remarked a captivated Cardinal Parmigiano, "he's as pretty as a putto."

Ana Magdalena gave a gasp. She leapt to her feet.

"What's the matter, *chica?*"

"I just remembered. I think I left the kettle boiling."

But before she could scoot past the piles of manuscripts and make it to the door, a distant whistle sounded. It came from the direction of the river.

"Oh, my God! It's already boiling over!" she exclaimed as she bolted toward the stairs.

Ana Magdalena ran to the safe. She grabbed the sack containing

Sergio Ballado's twenty percent. She knew if she could just manage to get the Henriod & Schweitzer started, she could reach the river in time, but the car had grown temperamental with time. It stalled repeatedly, and by the time she reached the riverbank it was nearly one. The *Amazon Queen* had become a minuscule dot about to vanish round the bend of the river, and Sergio Ballado, certain that he had been stiffed, sat brooding below decks. He could no longer see the desperate flutter of Ana Magdalena's huge white handkerchief or appreciate the weight of her heavy canvas sack.

XIV

Federico sat frozen in his composition chair. Why was it there was always some excuse? If it wasn't the bees, it was the kettle, or the time of day or night. This time Ana Magdalena had cut him off practically in midsentence.

He reviewed his situation. It was all too clear: he was wedged between the Scylla of his publisher's wrath and the Charybdis of not being able to finish — of not *wanting* to finish because, because, *putamadre,* he had to admit it to himself at last: if he forced Ostencia Candelaria to close up shop, there would be very little left to write, and writing, well, dear God, it was the very air he breathed.

His was a three-dimensional dilemma as well. On the one hand, more than ever he itched to let Ana Magdalena know exactly how he felt, but on the other, once he told her, what would become of Casa Orgaz and his daily change of clothes?

There must be a solution, but every time he searched for it, he found himself beached on the rocks of his own ontological end-game.

He had it! He would *not* finish the manuscript; he would defer the moment of truth. He would busy himself arranging all his material into some kind of coherent sequence, and after he had retyped it carefully, he would return at last to Cardinal Parmigiano's "How fortunate! He's really as pretty as a *putto.*"

By then he would have a notion as to how to proceed.

There is no point speculating what might have happened had Ana Magdalena and Sergio Ballado never made love on the *Amazon Queen* — or, for that matter, whether or not they actually made use of the boiler room, had not the sudden squall resulted in chilling Ana Magdalena's person to the bone. But even though Sergio Ballado had been sadly incapable of providing Casa Orgaz with its long-awaited Yankee clientele, he had watered the already burgeoning shoot of Ana Magdalena's entrepreneurial imagination.

In the weeks following his visit, no matter how heavily burdened she was by her business affairs, she scrupulously set aside fifteen minutes a day to visualize her ideal. Her imagination — already inhibited by certain economic restraints — was further limited by considerations of discretion, which dictated that, because of Federico, the only suitable location for her pleasure parlors would have to be the cellar. After sweeping it clean of alluvial silt, she would partition it into any number of fun-loving little cubicles, much as those she remembered from the carnival she had visited as a child, and which she still remembered with something of a shudder.

Of course she didn't cast La Confitería in anything but a rosy kind of light, and she was already certain that her building schemes, no matter how modest they might have to be, could be dressed up later to astonishing effect. She began by interviewing a bizarre collection of persons who styled themselves architects before settling on a strange-looking apparition, one Arturs Patagonia, whose mother hailed from some obscure Baltic republic or other, and whose father had run with the pampas gauchos.

When Patagonia saw the cellar, however, he flashed her a troubled look from eyes green as a lemur's. "Good heavens, Señora, you have quite a problem here." He scratched his head. "Do you have the faintest idea what's involved?"

"Let's not look for any problems. Just build me ten or twelve little cubbyholes."

"My dear young lady, before you can even dream of sinking piers, you have to suck up all this mud and pump the water out. And you'll have to pour a subfloor to prevent the ferocious incursion of the termites who at this very moment are chewing away so much of Peru. And a suspended plank floor will have to be laid before we can even begin to imagine cubicles of any description. I'm afraid it's going to cost you a fortune." He beamed at her with the unconcern of a gurgling newborn. "If I were you, I'd forget the whole thing."

But Ana Magdalena was not to be dissuaded. "How much will it cost?"

"Two million escudos, at the very least."

Ana Magdalena was appalled. "*Dios mio!*"

"My dear little lady, perhaps you want to reconsider."

Ana Magdalena knew that the very next day she would have to endure yet another monthly visit from the chief of police accompanied by Hercules. "Señor Patagonia," she said, "let me speak very plainly. I can't afford to reconsider."

Arturs Patagonia took on his habitually troubled air. "But how can you afford a project of such magnitude?"

"I can afford it perfectly well. I'll have to borrow money."

"And just who will be stupid enough to lend it to you?"

"Any bank — if I supply collateral."

"And if you can't pay? They repossess your business," warned Arturs Patagonia.

"Perhaps they're not so stupid after all."

But Ana Magdalena soon discovered there was no way to offer Casa Orgaz as collateral without involving Federico; and although she explained to every banker who cared to listen that Federico was entirely too busy to become involved in even the slightest of formalities, she found no one willing to so much as hand her an application.

On the verge of admitting defeat, she found herself once more in the trollish presence of Señor Onofrio Sebastián y Colón, who sat dwarfed behind an enormous mahogany desk, where he now worked in the offices of the IFF. Ana Magdalena had never heard of the IFF. It was to be some time before she learned that its conditional acronym stood for the International Fiduciary Fund, with world headquarters in New York.

"It's no problem at all." He fixed her with a calculating stare. "There's no need to involve Don Federico if, for example, you have a business to put up."

"Then you take a business as collateral?"

"Absolutely. In fact that's all the IFF ever takes. The IFF is a forward-looking group of financiers dedicated to development, to assisting certain kinds of businesses in improving their profit margins," Señor Onofrio Sebastián y Colón explained, "and your business fits our guidelines perfectly. Let me introduce you to our loan coordinator for the Southern Region."

Ana Magdalena shook hands with Mr. Perkins, who in real life was a whiskey distiller. "How long have you been keeping the hotel?" he asked her. Señor Onofrio Sebastián y Colón translated.

Ana Magdalena had never claimed Casa Orgaz was a hotel, but she did not bother to deny it, either.

"And you keep a registration book?" Ana Magdalena, knowing the wisdom of honoring her clients' discretion, had never kept a registration book. "Because it will be one of the conditions of our agreement that you keep a registry at all times for our inspection at the desk."

Mr. Perkins examined her ledger sheets. "Now you say there's nineteen rooms. All on the second floor?"

Ana Magdalena nodded.

"And on the third floor?"

"That's just the bookkeeper's office," she said, carefully avoiding Señor Onofrio Sebastián y Colón's eyes. She gave Mr. Perkins her most guileless look. Mr. Perkin's thin lips curled in the intimation of a smile.

"And you charge how much a night?"

"One hundred escudos."

"Isn't that a little steep?"

"Not if it includes room service," Señor Sebastián y Colón hastily explained.

"Very well. Judging from your documentation, you seem to conform in every respect to the IFF's guidelines. We'll have your loan ready to sign, seal, and deliver just as soon as our appraiser can complete his on-site visit. You'll like Mr. Effingham, I know. He's an awfully nice guy. Just let him have his head, and when he's through, he may want to ask you a question or two, but it's only a formality."

Mr. Bob Effingham's visit to Casa Orgaz occurred, not at nine A.M. as might have been expected, but during the peak of business hours. Customers on their way upstairs had to step around his considerable frame as he methodically set about measuring and cataloguing every step with the thoroughness and dedication of a bloodhound.

"Where are your bathrooms, little lady?"

Ana Magdalena affected not to understand. She made as if to usher him back downstairs. Mr. Effingham glared down at her from his impressive height. His face was as overripe as an autumn pumpkin, but now his expression took on a wintery cast.

"Don't try to interfere with my inspection, ma'am. I need to see those upstairs toilets flush."

Before she could stop him, he was measuring the distance between each bedroom threshold to the nearest water closet. Ana Magdalena reflected that it was only by Ofelia's grace that he had not yet noticed the comings and goings of the clientele, when at that very moment a door opened.

Mr. Effingham took out a stopwatch. To Ana Magdalena's horror he positioned himself in the corridor. When the occupants emerged, he made a notation, and immediately following the same occupant's return, this time accompanied by another client, Mr. Effingham made a summarizing comment in his book. "I think I've covered everything," was his terse remark.

"Is this your lobby?" He indicated the ballroom with some displeasure. Ana Magdalena nodded. He pointed to the player piano.

"That's the first thing that's gotta go. That kind of background is strictly passé."

Seated behind his executive desk, Mr. Perkins explained to Ana Magdalena the terms of the loan contract she was about to sign. He gave her a little crescent smile.

"Our loan is contingent on your fulfilling certain rules." Señor Onofrio Sebastián y Colón translated. "You are to permit an on-site inspection semiannually by Mr. Effingham and members of his staff. You are to keep a registration book at the front desk at all times, which must be available for their examination. But the main issue is efficiency. That's what we need to talk about. Have you ever considered that there are ways you could do more to maximize your profits?"

"Tell him," she said to Señor Onofrio Sebastián y Colón, "that we're efficient as it is, as efficient as we care to get."

"That player piano has to go. Mr. Effingham made a special point: Time-motion studies show that music is key. Hens lay better, production lines move smoother, all depending what music you give 'em.

And the IFF is prepared to lease you, as one of the terms of your loan, a complete replacement sound system at reasonable rates."

It began to dawn on Ana Magdalena that the IFF must have known all along that Casa Orgaz was not exactly a lace-curtain bed-and-breakfast.

Señor Sebastián y Colón translated. "He says that the IFF has a sound system that works miracles. They use it everywhere — in airports, department stores, wherever they want to loosen people in the purse strings. And through the IFF you can subscribe to it at cost. You subscribe by the year. For priority clients — such as yourself — it's only one hundred and twenty escudos for twenty-four hours."

Ana Magdalena gave Mr. Perkins her best smile. "Twenty-four hours! But we only work for twelve!"

"You can always turn the music down," Mr. Perkins reassured her. Sebastián y Colón neglected to translate his concluding observation: "But you can never turn it off."

Ana Magdalena didn't want to appear ungrateful, especially now that her two million were nearly within grasp. "Very well," she said.

"Terms of the loan are a principal of two million escudos at nine and a half, that is to say nineteen actualized, with five points origination fees. Up front."

Mr. Perkins handed Ana Magdalena the pen. She signed with a trembling hand.

"And now." Mr. Perkins turned to Señor Onofrio Sebastián y Colón. "Give the little lady her check."

Ana Magdalena sat stunned. The face amount read 1,900,000 escudos.

"What happened to the other hundred thousand?"

"Oh." Señor Sebastián y Colón waved a dismissive hand. "That's just the origination fee. It comes off the top."

Readying La Confitería occupied all of Ana Magdalena's daytime energies. With Patagonia's help, she hired engineers and carpenters. She hoped that the incessant clacking of the Black Maria would prevent Federico's noticing so much as the ring of a hammer or the buzzing of a drill. Because of the sudden flood of his discarded manuscript pages, she surmised that he must be happily immersed in retyping the manuscript, which had grown to an uncontrollably dense, convoluted one thousand pages with no end in sight. In fact, unknown to her, the more he typed, the more the manuscript seemed to acquire a mysterious life all of its own. He discovered that the same episodes had a nasty habit of reappearing in later chapters, although often in a flimsy new disguise, but sometimes — and this was the most troubling — without any change at all. Whenever he stumbled on another such duplication, he had to begin typing all over again. Absorbed in a task more Herculean than sweeping out the Augean stables, he labored nonstop day and night, snatching an exhausted catnap here and there a dreamless sleep. His breakfast trays overflowed with the limp spaghettis of typewriter ribbon that the Black Maria had pounded into terminal submission. Whenever Ana Magdalena was able to snatch a moment away from overseeing the construction crew, she found that he spared her hardly a moment more than opening the door to admit his breakfast, lunch, or dinner would allow.

Every day Arturs Patagonia appeared with more obscure drawings for her approval. He would further embellish them with arcane remarks or rambling diagrams. But in the course of their volatile association, it became clear to Ana Magdalena that architecture was one of the very last things on Arturs Patagonia's mind.

"You don't happen to have a T square handy?" he would ask as an absentminded afterthought. Or he would interrupt himself in mid-thought:

"Listen, listen," he would whisper ecstatically, placing a long, aristocratically tapered finger to his lips, "can you hear them? Oh, the resolution is exquisite! I've *never* heard them knock so clearly!" He was referring to a column of warrior termites who were at that very instant declaring hostilities against her freshly laid floor, although she didn't know it, and Arturs didn't care.

"Oh, it's *beautiful*," he rhapsodized. "If you happened to have a stethoscope handy, you could hear them quite distinctly."

"Just make sure the walls are soundproof," she cautioned with her habitual insouciance.

"In life there are no guarantees, dear lady. Guarantees are merely Expectation," he gestured dismissively. He admitted to being a devotee of an obscure Eastern cult. "We must Clear the Mind of Thought," he would explain. "The Mind is our Single Greatest Impediment."

Only after the double soundproof walls had been installed did they discover that, once the doors were closed, none of the little cubbyholes had any light in them at all. But Arturs Patagonia was unperturbed. "We can run a series of lights off the main circuit, a lamp here, a lamp there. Do you happen to have a voltmeter handy?"

After weeks of delay because a special conduit had to be ordered all the way from Manaus, holes were drilled, pipe was run along the ceilings down both rows of enclosed rooms, and sockets were mounted. Everything was finally in place. There was great excitement among the rainbow girls. As Arturs Patagonia prepared to trip the master switch, he raised his fine-boned hands for quiet. His dedication was as brief as it was cosmic.

"Let there be one thousand oms."

As the ten fantasy rooms neared completion, Ana Magdalena realized she needed people to staff them. She wished Ofelia were there to give advice. But that very morning she received a letter postmarked La Paz.

"*Querida* Ana," she read,

Life has carried me very far from the calm riverbanks where you knew me as a girl. But I'm still afloat! Alejandro is hiding under an assumed name with the insurgents somewhere in the mountains. I never hear from him. Of course his family disinherited him the minute they found out. I had to move back to my parents' house. It was a little quiet there, so I joined a traveling theater troupe. We are rehearsing *La Casa de Bernarda Alba* because we couldn't find any men to cast. But guess what??? We're touring your way in March!!! There's thirteen of us, including the manager. Can you put us up?

Your friend,
Aurora Constancia

A theater troupe might be the very thing to help her solve her problem. Ana Magdalena was already in a fever of excitement trying to decide what furnishings might best brighten up each of her cubbyholes. She instructed her rainbow girls to poll their customers as casually as possible to discover their principal fantasies, indeed if they had any fantasies at all.

At Sunday morning meetings, her bed was littered with hundreds of little scraps of paper. She and her eight beauties pored over them, sorting out fantasies by popularity and theme. Each of the girls tabulated a particular category: there were fantasies necessitating medical examination rooms and surgical amphitheaters; there were activities peculiar to judges' benches and witness stands; there were oral examinations performed before boards of bored officialdom. Twenty-nine historical fantasies required sixteenth-century cast-iron bodices, chastity belts, and other restraining or corsetting devices. Some proposed simulated tortures of devilish resourcefulness, and several occurred in vehicles of public transport: life rafts, airplanes, racing cars, and first-class railway carriages. The most fanciful one took place in a soaring hot-air balloon, while the most strenuous sustained itself in the aisle of the Manaus opera house during the entire love and death scene of *Tristan und Isolde.*

After much heated discussion, the girls settled on nine settings, with Ana Magdalena holding out for the boiler room, not because they had found anyone who wanted to suggest it yet, but because she had become partial to boiler rooms, and besides, it was one of three sets of furnishings (together with the classroom and the Velazquez room) that had not been entirely ruined by the flood.

Already her project had run well over the 1,900,000 escudos lent her by the IFF, but Ana Magdalena was not overly concerned because happily, she still had Sergio Ballado's twenty percent, and she felt no compunction borrowing from a friend. Painting and decorating began at once. Cabinetmakers were hired to construct pulpits and confessionals; upholsterers duplicated the tufted leather seats of an open Victoria, and the plush seats of a first-class railway carriage, complete with a fold-out thunder mug. Joiners lathed the baroque balusters of the judge's bench and the prisoner's dock. And a basket weaver was hired expressly to fabricate the passenger compartment of an authentic but permanently grounded hot-air balloon.

By the time Aurora Constancia and the Amazon Players arrived in Malyerba, La Confitería was ready for business. Honora and the other maids busied themselves showing the company to their rooms. But kept awake all night by the happy sounds of revelry, come morning the actors concluded Casa Orgaz must be a very special kind of house.

Ana Magdalena was amazed: Aurora Constancia hadn't changed a

216

bit. She waited until the early evening, when Sidonia could be freed to see to the customers, to join her in her room.

They flew into each other's arms.

"My darling, you look absolutely wonderful!" exclaimed Aurora, holding her friend at arm's length.

Ana Magdalena could tell Aurora Constancia had come into her own. She affected a stunning amber cigarette holder, wore her nails lacquered a predatory red, and called everyone "darling" without discrimination.

"There's something I simply have to show you." Ana Magdalena took her by the hand. "Come quick!"

They took the back stairs. From the kitchen, she led her friend into the cellar. She showed her the confessional, the judge's bench, and the prison cell. "We just finished them last week. Aren't they wonderful?"

Aurora Constancia eyed her quizzically. "It looks like a theater. Whatever is it for?"

"For the 'special tastes,' " explained Ana Magdalena in her world-liest tone.

"My God," whistled Aurora Constancia, deeply impressed. "You're not such a dummy after all. What gave you the idea?"

"And wait," Ana Magdalena said, "there's more."

She showed her the hot-air balloon; she activated the cunning mechanism that rotated a floor-mounted scroll on which was painted scenery of the passing countryside. But when Aurora Constancia beheld the Velazquez room with its black-framed mirror, easel, elegant velvet portieres, Catherine de Medici iron corset, and the magnificent costume with its stand-up starched lace ruff, seed-pearl bodice, and enormous panniers, her eyes took on a histrionic glint.

"It's exactly like a painting!" She felt immediately compelled to try the costume on. To her surprise, however, the dress was only a façade; in back it was all but entirely absent.

"What a kick, it fits," breathed Aurora Constancia as she hugged her friend. "It must be made for me!"

The production of *La Casa de Bernarda Alba* was well promoted in Malyerba. It drew tremendous crowds who stayed to lap up Aurora Constancia's performance of the heroine Adela, Bernarda's youngest most voluptuous daughter. They forgave her all the "darling's" she scattered in the text.

Because the run was such a huge success, one by one the actresses came to follow Aurora Constancia's example: they continued to perform in the early hours of the evening, but late into the night they populated La Confitería's player parlors — adding considerably not only to their incomes but to their theatrical experience. In the elegant Victoria the well-upholstered actress who earlier in the evening had played the role of Bernarda Alba cracked the whip over the rumps of a team of horses caparisoned in little more than skin; a shivering defendant cowered in the prisoner's dock awaiting the arrival of an indulgent magistrate; an appealing penitent knelt in the confessional yearning for absolution; and Aurora Constancia held court in the Velazquez room as half an ironclad Infanta.

The Amazon Players were scheduled to tour five other cities before returning to La Paz, but by month's end, *The House of Bernarda Alba* had crumbled to dust. Aurora Constancia's groundbreaking defection led to two more, and then another seven. Even the manager, when he learned that Ana Magdalena might be looking for a bookkeeper full-time, immediately applied. At the close of the run, only the technicians were left to pack up the equipment for the return to La Paz.

Within only a month of its expansion, Casa Orgaz had acquired such a solid and steamy reputation that the new bookkeeper, Hector Maria Jesus Villafane, had to take refuge in the boiler room, the only place left where he could safely keep a second set of books.

But their success owed as much to Arturs Patagonia as it did to the amazing ingenuity of the parlor acts. Installed as a clownish afterthought, his overhead conduit turned out to be the best sound conductor after the telephone. By amplifying every sigh, every moan, and frisson of delight, it encouraged each guest to make La Confitería that much more cozy for the rest.

XV

Ana Magdalena was not in the habit of reading the news, perhaps because her early convent school training had expressly forbidden it. She was entirely unaware of the heroic efforts on the part of all the international experts to midwife a reluctant Malyerba from the womb of our provincial backwardness into the cheery delivery room of development. But she had no trouble noticing when her monthly loan statements began to reflect amounts she did not recognize. She reached Señor Onofrio Sebastián y Colón on Casa Orgaz's new digital telephone. Once the normal greetings and expressions of concern had passed between them, she came directly to the point.

"There seems to be a little mix-up. Your statement this month reflects a surcharge of over one thousand escudos. There must be some mistake."

"The IFF," responded Señor Onofrio Sebastián y Colón, "never makes mistakes. If there's an extra thousand it's because you owe an extra thousand. Remember, we give you ten days' grace before you have to pay. Are you having any problems?"

"I'm having a problem seeing why the premium goes up when the principal remains the same."

"Exactly, dear lady. The principal has gone up, too! Your loan fluctuates with the world price of money. But because the IFF is anxious not to destabilize our clients, we pass some of the increase along to your principal as well."

"How much do I owe you now?" Ana Magdalena's heart beat faster.

"On principal? 2,125,005 escudos."

"But that's illegal and unconscionable!"

"My dear lady, it is neither one nor the other. The terms of your loan make provision for negative amortization. As the interest rises, so does the principal. It's for your own good. Otherwise we'd have to raise the premium a full two thousand escudos. And by the way, the supplies for your installation have finally come in. Mr. Effingham will be bringing his crew out there next week to install your state-of-the-art Entertrainment System."

Ana Magdalena lowered the receiver carefully. She didn't want to hear any more about state-of-the-art anything. She began immediately to reflect how Señor Onofrio Sebastián y Colón's good news could be passed along to her happy clientele.

"Good evening," she said to the first unwitting guest to cross the Casa Orgaz threshold that afternoon. "Our prices have gone up. We're keeping company with our valuable clientele and with inflation, too."

The first of the month passed without a hitch. Hercules and the chief of police each took away their cut, but Ana Magdalena neglected to mention her rate hike. She said nothing of the success of the downstairs player parlors. And when she needed to congratulate herself on the results of her hard work, she had only to consult her new accountant, Hector Maria Jesús Villafane, who was happily buried in the boiler room, keeping double sets of books.

On the third floor, however, matters were not going quite so well. Behind the closed doors of the mirador, an ominous silence spread like fog. It seeped under the doorway and through the cracks, edging its way across the landing and slowly down the stairs.

"Federico?" Ana Magdalena tried to rouse him with her tempting breakfast trays. At first she could hear him mumble something, but as the days wore on, even the mumbling declined, until at last she heard nothing at all.

Gradually she succumbed to a feeling of alarm. She began to wonder what would happen if some horrible fate overtook him before he could complete *The Love Queen of the Amazon*. On every tray, morning, noon, and night, she began to leave little messages, notes of encouragement such as "Don't forget to change your socks!" But no matter how cheery her attempts, all of them met with a stern and literary silence. Evidence seemed to indicate that he had begun eating again, however, because whenever she or Sidonia or any of the other maids went up to collect his food trays, they were always empty.

The flow of discarded manuscript pages ebbed and finally ceased. Although Ana Magdalena had no way of knowing it, Federico was busy editing. Had she pressed her ear to the door for any length of time, she could have heard his gleeful snorts of authorial satisfaction. Equipped with a glue pot and a cruelly efficient pair of clipping shears, which he wielded with all the abandon of a samurai, he spent long hours on all fours, snipping and splicing and gluing page after page, which, for greater convenience, he laid out on the small area of the floor he had managed to clear. He crawled on his hands and knees through the convoluted twists and turns of *The Love Queen of the Amazon,* a happy penitent on the only pilgrimage that counts, the Via Dolorosa of the written word. He was in his element, but his knees were giving out.

One afternoon when Ana Magdalena exchanged his lunch tray for an empty breakfast tray, amid the waste of fractured eggshell, she beheld a note that she immediately recognized as a signal of distress.

Get me some kneepads, for the love of God! Any sporting goods will have them.

He had thoughtfully tucked five mangled bills beneath his empty teacup. It was the first signal she had had from him in nearly three weeks. In her great relief she pressed it to her lips before trotting back down the stairs to the kitchen.

"Sidonia." She waved Federico's note triumphantly. "He wants kneepads!"

"I told you so, señora. When a man is fractious, that's when you have to watch out. *Kneepads?* What the devil does he want with kneepads?"

Ana Magdalena didn't answer. She was already preparing to go out. Sidonia watched her as she skipped through the kitchen smiling. "Poor thing," she sighed to herself, "she's still so young, she can't help making jokes sometimes at his expense. But without literature, where would any of us be?"

Ana Magdalena couldn't ignore Sidonia's nagging question. What did Federico in his Parnassian exaltation want with kneepads? Perhaps, she reflected, he had suffered an attack of religious conversion. She conjured up a perverse vision of him as Saint Michael mounted on the shining charger of authorial determination, attempting to spear the dragon of writer's block with a fountain pen. She crossed herself immediately and the vision vanished. But it was enough to sound her personal alarm, because she looked to the completion of *The Love Queen of the Amazon* for release from the increasingly troubling business entanglements of Casa Orgaz. With the royalties Federico had promised, she would be able to extricate herself from the suffocating grip of the IFF and send her monthly visitors packing.

She stopped short in the doorway of the sporting goods store. *Dios mio,* she gasped, what was she thinking of? The only way she could ever shake Hercules and the police chief loose was if Federico found out! Either that, or she would have to close her enterprise entirely. She stood riveted to the threshold, customers jostling her on either side as they tried to enter.

Her thoughts left her breathless. *Holy Mother,* she prayed to no one in particular, *help me in my hour of need.* But evidently, without realizing it, she must have been addressing Ofelia, because when she finally recovered enough to enter the sporting goods store, the object of her unwitting devotion greeted her matter-of-factly. She had lost a lot of weight, Ana Magalena realized, and her cheeks had formed drooping wattles which trembled at her every word.

"Either I tell Federico everything or I close up shop. What should I do?" whispered Ana Magdalena.

The saleslady smiled at her. "This is a sporting goods, dearie, not a palmistry."

Ana Magdalena stared at the woman. "Excuse me," she blurted, "you reminded me of someone I used to know."

"Someone nice, I hope." The woman smiled, smoothing her dress.

Ana Magdalena didn't want to elaborate. "Actually, someone who kept a sporting goods!"

The woman busied herself unlocking a glass display case, but when she turned around, she held out a pair of diving fins.

Ana Magdalena was confused. "I could have sworn I asked for kneepads." The woman made as if to put them back, but a sudden impulse prompted Ana Magdalena to stop her. "No, wait! I'll take them anyway, but I need the kneepads too!"

Ana Magdalena was sorry to lose Ropes's old player piano. When Hortensio and Julio helped her shove it into a forgotten closet, she couldn't help thinking, *who knows, it may be that this Yankee entertainment system is really heaven sent.* But when Mr. Effingham came with his work crew to supervise its installation, she couldn't bear to watch. She retired to her bedroom and shut the door. She lay stretched out on Clemencia's enormous bed reflecting that more and more, Casa Orgaz was getting to feel like a conveyor belt. She got up to go in search of Aurora Constancia.

"Come on." Her voice was grim. "We're going for a ride."

Aurora Constancia took no notice of her mood. "*Que bueno!*" She clapped her hands. "I'm dying for an outing."

They went looking for Hortensio in the stables, and rounded up Julio, too. Ana Magdalena cranked up the old motorcar. "There's plenty of time before the evening shift. Meantime, let's have a little fun."

She drove fast and flamboyantly, as was her style. Aurora Constancia was very much impressed. "Darling," she enthused, "give your horn another blast. I just *love* to see you make those donkeys bolt."

They sped past the center of town, through the Cathedral Square with its eternally rampant statue of Bolívar, through the market district, and on the outskirts, they followed the road past the shantytowns. In the open country at last, they began to sing. Ana Magdalena breathed deeply. The crisp air brought color to her cheeks. At last they came to a rock outcropping. The car shuddered to a halt.

"Don't you want a tarpaulin?" she asked Aurora Constancia.

"Darling, whatever for?"

"Just for fun." She eyed Hortensio knowingly.

"What a sharpie, you always think of everything," whispered Aurora Constancia.

Ana Magdalena led Hortensio to their favorite hollow between two trees. In less than a minute her mouth was on his. She melted into his capable chauffeur's arms. She had learned to let him tune her like an engine. Limbs entangled, they had no trouble sinking to the ground. His hands fluttered about her as he rid her of her clothes.

In a moment of catching their breath, she saw Aurora Constancia and Julio behind them, watching.

"Please, don't be bashful," Ana Magdalena waved at them. She felt Hortensio stiffen in her arms. "Don't fret, sweetheart," she whispered to him, "they won't bite. They like it just as much as we do!"

But Hortensio, for all his mechanical expertise, was of a private disposition, and his aptitude had a way of vanishing under public scrutiny.

"Come on," teased Ana Magdalena, "don't be a party poop. If you have problems, close your eyes."

Aurora Constancia came to the rescue. She wrapped her lovely Hermès scarf over his eyes. They began vying with each other to see which one of them could lift Hortensio's gloom. They used every ploy at their command, but Hortensio proved a reluctant bridegroom — until, quite suddenly, Aurora Constancia's Hermès scarf came loose. An amazing spectacle met his eyes. For a moment he had difficulty distinguishing between arms and legs, let alone deciding which limbs belonged to whom or where, but something evidently set him straight because he threw himself into its midst with noisy and happy abandon.

"Oh, my goodness," gasped an ecstatic Aurora Constancia, "why didn't we remove your blindfold sooner?"

All day Federico had busied himself cutting here and splicing there. It was already well past three. He was badly in need of something to eat, but there was still no sign of Ana Magdalena. He rose groaning to his feet.

"Brimstone and hellfire!" He threw open the door. "You down there," he bellowed, "where's my lunch?"

His demands met with silence. Unaccustomed to being so flagrantly ignored, Federico made his way downstairs. He threw open the kitchen door. "*Putamadre!* Where the devil are you?" he asked the air at large because the kitchen was deserted. Still in his knee-pads, he trotted through the pantry.

"Why the hell can't a man have anything to eat?" he shouted as he swung wide the doors that gave into the ballroom. But his voice caught in his throat. A gang of workmen lay sprawled in the swan boat, finishing their lunch. Some began tossing a soccer ball back and forth.

Federico took in the forest of ladders.

"*Hola! Que pasa aquí?*" he exclaimed.

Mr. Effingham took in Federico's kneepads. "How about a little football?" He kicked the ball to Federico.

"*Futbol, sí! Pues, vámonos muchachos!*" Federico kicked it back.

The ball flew from crewman to crewman to a growing chorus of enthusiastic cheers. In quick order they upended Ofelia's settee and rolled it to the entrance side of the ballroom. They improvised the far goal by tipping over the swan boat and tossing the odalisque pillows carelessly aside. Federico and Mr. Effingham were appointed captains by popular acclaim.

"*Jefe,*" Federico pointed at Mr. Effingham.

"You bet," nodded Mr. Effingham. The crewmen quickly chose up sides. They tossed for the ball. It fell to Mr. Effingham. "Play ball," he shouted. He gave the ball a kick. Instantly Mr. Effingham's team swept toward Ofelia's settee. A savage kick sent it sailing past the defense.

"Goal!" screamed Mr. Effingham.

Federico passed the ball from the center line. "*Muchachos,*" he yelled, "*aquí!*"

"I got him!" shouted a crewman from Mr. Effingham's team.

"Center!"

"Hey, hey. Off sides."

"*Putamadre!* No off size!" growled Federico.

But still the ball changed teams, reversing the direction of play. Mr. Effingham gave it another savage kick. Again his team scored.

"Goal!" They were hysterical. Nothing could dampen their enthusiasm now, not the downed chandelier, nor the demolished drapery valances. And certainly not the capsized ladders. They merely kicked them aside.

"Goal," shouted Federico triumphantly. It was the first his team had scored and they scored it smack into the heart of Ana Magdalena's pride and joy. At that very moment the ballroom doors swung open. Ana Magdalena watched in horrified fascination as the swan boat capsized with a deafening crash and lay rocking on its side.

Mr. Effingham's team froze in their tracks, trying not to call attention to the general disarray.

Oblivious, Federico gave the ball a kick, but something must have gone amiss because he crumpled moaning to the floor.

Instantly Ana Magdalena was at his side helping him up. "Darling, what's wrong?"

"Aiee," wailed Federico, "my back. You're killing my back."

Ana Magdalena let go. "*O pobrecito!*" she exclaimed, "did you pull something?" She turned to the crew. "Some of you help me carry him upstairs."

But as she climbed the stairs to the mirador, she gave way to a feeling of mounting anxiety. She wondered what Federico might have seen. Had he had a chance to investigate the rainbow rooms, or discover any of their occupants, she wondered. She had no way of being sure, but she was certain that, sooner or later, somehow he would let her know.

Federico was basking, for the time being at least, in the warmth of her attentions. Never before had she showed him such hovering solicitude. She changed his truckle bed, and tucked him in between blankets she had Sidonia warm over the kitchen stove.

"Is my sweetheart feeling better?" She affected an empathetic pout.

But when Federico tried to adjust his position to reply, he managed barely a groan. "Aiee," he winced.

Ana Magdalena shook her head. "We'll have to call the doctor, I'm afraid."

Chastened, Mr. Effingham and his crew set the ballroom to rights. They restored the swan boat to its prominent position in the center of the room and tacked the valances back with a volley of staples strategically applied to mask the tears in the material. They hung and rewired what remained of the chandeliers. By then the guests had begun arriving. Mr. Effingham switched the Entertrainment System on. As his crew folded up their ladders, he adjusted the sound levels. The music crooned and warbled, innocuous as mush. Satisfied, he left his bill for 43,800 escudos at the reception desk with a generous proviso of thirty days to pay.

*   *   *

Far removed from Malyerba, the Capital was reeling in a terrible state of shock. El Magnífico, El Señor Presidente Ochoa y Ruiz, after months in hiding, had surfaced at last — in a Miami jail. Chronically broke, nonetheless Peru prepared for the monthlong inauguration that would usher in his successor, our very own Presidentísimo Ignacio Fuendetodo-Ibañez, who, even before his election, had already shown considerable talent for conspiracy and mayhem. Six and a half living American presidents had been invited to participate in the festivities. Every day, Sergio Ballado haunted the office of the Belém & Amazonas excursion company hoping to be the one chosen to skipper one or another of these dignitaries up the Amazon.

Among them was a populist president, two *gaucho* presidents, and a reading president, an unusual variety which many believed had become extinct following the First World War. There was also a speaking president, but poor fellow, he had to travel by iron lung because his vital signs were showing chronic oxygen depletion. He could be unplugged just long enough for his public appearances where he repeated by rote the speeches worthy housewives wrote for him. There was also a bookkeeping president who showed the trusty kind of acumen at keeping double sets of books that guaranteed him a sinecure for life. The last president was nearly invisible. A super spy, he sent his double to represent him — a man who could impersonate him even better than he could himself.

But sadly, all these dignitaries were already hunkered down in Lima where, for the favor of lending El Presidentísimo's new government a little democratic spin, each expected to take title to a mine. When he found out, Sergio Ballado abandoned hope, which is why he was no longer sitting on the recruitment bench when His Eminence the papal nuncio, Catulo Cardinal Catafalco made his way to the ticket window of the Belém & Amazonas Excursion Company, accompanied by a flock of tender seminarians cassocked in soutanes that exuded little clouds of angel dust whenever they flapped their fledgling wings. Instead, Sergio Ballado was in bed where he was eating a breakfast of beans and rice, which he accidentally spilled on the coverlet and onto the diplomatic letter he was composing to Ana Magdalena Figueroa de Orgaz y Orgaz.

"*Querida,*" he had written her,

Any day now I will be steaming up the great waters on my way back to Malyerba to collect my twenty percent. There is still a way for us to be together if God and the balance sheet allow. But you must prepare yourself to peel off that wretched fellow like a skin. Just remember the snake. "When the hide gets tight, it's time to shed," as the saying goes.

My senses still boil for you, my blood hums and pesters me, and your poor *gallo de oro* is completely out of hand. Nothing I tell him can bring him to reason.

Any day now, my beloved, as soon as they let me ship out. Business, at least in presidents, is far from brisk, but with a little trust in God and his Holy angels, I shall be at your irresistible side, troubling your nature even before you notice it!

Yours,
Sergio Ballado, esq.

He was happy with this letter and its persuasive tone, and just as he was rereading it for the third time, changing a word here, sprucing up a phrase there, wouldn't you know, he managed to spill his entire bowl of rice and beans on the paper and had to begin all over again. It was, he reflected, because he liked to do too many things at once, and do them all in bed.

At the precise moment of his insight, there was a rapping at the door.

"*Senhor? Senhor?*" called the urchin-messenger of the Belém & Amazonas Excursion Company in his lilting Portuguese. "There's a river party of Fathers. The boss wants you to come at once!"

Sergio Ballado leapt out of bed, clumsily scattering rice and beans everywhere. He groped about for his only presentable set of whites and his braided skipper's cap.

"*Momentito,*" he said, "tell him I'm on my way!"

Ana Magdalena had begun experiencing a series of incapacitating nightmares. It was unclear to her, at least at the beginning, exactly what might be causing them. Everyone took for granted Fuendetodo would be sworn in, but when Ana Magdalena heard rumors that the presidential motorcade might stop in Malyerba, she grew almost sick with dismay. She remembered how El Magnifico's debilitating sweep through La Nymphaea had led to the demise of her pro-

tectress and great aunt. Determined to forestall further tragic consequences, she vowed to keep a sharp eye out for any junketing
presidents, and close Casa Orgaz down altogether if any of them so
much as presumed to appear.

But the world is uncertain and full of unpleasant surprises, even in
a place like Malyerba, and although it turned out no presidents ever
again set foot anywhere closer to our city than 900 miles, Ana Magdalena discovered there was no way to prevent them from invading
her sleep. Her dream began innocuously enough. Elected to paradise, Benjamin Franklin was conducting a filibuster before the celestial parliament during which he described the charms of all the
rainbow girls in heavenly hyperbole. Unsuspectingly, Ana Magdalena
allowed herself to attend this particular session of her dream because
she relished hearing the praises of her person, and her staff, and
listening as he extolled the glories of her house. But it should have
come as no surprise that immediately thereafter she dreamt George
Washington paid Casa Orgaz a call. He was accompanied by his not-
yet-born son, George Junior, who was pale and nearly lipless. There
was a rapping at the door. For some reason no one was there to
answer. Ana Magdalena realized that it must be dawn already because
all the servants had gone to bed. But when she opened the door, she
saw it was still night. Waves lapped against the door, but curiously her
feet stayed dry. Not fifty feet away George Washington stood in some
kind of crazy-looking boat, breasting the waves; his son George Junior, however, appeared as transparent as a fetus. No sooner had it
dawned on Ana Magdalena that the child must be suffering from
seasickness inside the womb than Teddy Roosevelt showed up
mounted on horseback. Perched before him on the pommel was his
son Ron, a not-yet-born *gaucho* president like his dad.

Ana Magdalena wanted to let them in, but something made her
hesitate. She began to stammer her apologies. "There's been some
mistake. We don't take children. It's against the rules." She was about
to close the door.

"Please wait!" pleaded George Washington politely.

"These kids are rough," Teddy Roosevelt assured her. "They
may be little tykes, but they're lean and mean and nasty. This one
bagged his first mestizo, and he isn't even born." He gave Ron a
paternal pat.

"But this is Casa Orgaz, not a family hotel," Ana Magdalena managed to blurt out.

"You whores have rules?" Teddy Roosevelt leaned down at her from the great height of his saddle. "Why don't you change them?" He tossed her a $100 bill.

"Couldn't they be allowed to play in the fun house downstairs?" George Washington asked.

"Sure," chimed in Teddy Roosevelt, "they'd get a kick playing with the instruments of torture! Keep 'em out of trouble while the grownups had a go upstairs!"

Ana Magdalena had never considered converting her torture parlor into a childcare facility, but the image of Franklin on the $100 bill held strong persuasive powers. While she hesitated, however, the doors of Casa Orgaz grew to enormous size. They jackknifed, trapping her inside. Suddenly she realized that what she felt pressing against her skin had to be the sharp spikes of the iron maiden. She could hear the not-yet-born presidents playing outside.

"*Basta,*" she wanted to call out. But she knew that the fetus presidents were unable to hear Spanish because they favored a program of English only *in utero.* And anyway they were having too much fun imitating war whoops to pay her any mind. She felt the iron maiden closing tighter and tighter. No one, she realized, ever survives a fetal attack. She decided things had gone far enough.

"Boys," she spoke to them firmly in the language children understand, "your dads are waiting. Time to go upstairs."

His Eminence Cardinal Catafalco was reduced to imprinting the posterior of his august person on the hardwood slats of the passenger bench in the shabby offices of the Belém & Amazonas Excursion Company, breviary open in his lap, his lips faintly sibilating the words of the Divine Office, fortifying his thin and arid soul for the arduous journey up the Amazon because every other plane, train, bus, and limousine had already been commandeered in the service of junketing presidents, foreign economists, IFF officials, gun runners, coca purveyors, CIA heavies, and the few local Mafiosi who had managed to weather the ferocious competition.

As emissary of the Congregation for the Causes of Saints, he was headed on a mission of inquiry into the canonization of one Andreina Arzate de Figueroa, a woman rumored to be so saintly that at her death her body had been crystallized in honey. Although all Malyerba had been alerted to his impending visit by an overzealous Monsignor, no one, not even Monsignor, was aware that Cardinal Catafalco was really coming as the devil's advocate, hellbent, as it were, on impeding the sacred process of beatification in whatever way he could. If he had anything to do with it, Andreina Arzate de Figueroa would never become a saint. On the other hand, he knew that no matter what adverse evidence he might present, the Congregation was eager to raise someone local to sainthood, even someone who had trod the dubious and thorny path of matrimony — even a female — because after its recent spectacular banking debacle, the Holy See had begun to expand its asset portfolio to include more and more of the Southern Hemisphere, and a local saint or two is always good publicity. How could he have begun to imagine that in the person of Sergio Ballado he would meet the happy agent who would show him how to turn contradiction to advantage?

The figure that met Sergio Ballado's eyes as he impulsively threw open the doors of the Belém & Amazonas Excursion Company in his restored exuberance was a pale, transparent man, an ambulatory argument between being and nonbeing. His face showed all the chiseled and uncompromising geometry of an anvil, and although he had taken the trouble to shave, his chin had the necrotic look of an old abandoned boot. Had he cared to remove his traveling biretta in response to Sergio Ballado's familiar greeting, his one concession to vanity might have come to light. Although His Eminence was no more hirsute than an egg, he was unwilling to part with the scraggly hank of dyed red hair that spanned his tonsure like a bridge, the last proud emblem of his vanished youth.

"*Saludos,*" a cocky Sergio Ballado greeted him. "It looks like I'm to be your skipper!"

His Eminence raised a reluctant head. He removed his monocle, which hung from a heavy black silk cord. His tiny eyes squinted at the sudden flood of light.

"*Deo gracias,*" he replied, snapping his breviary shut. "When do we depart?"

It took Sergio Ballado little time to discover the identity of his main passenger, and he immediately recognized in it a sign of divine intervention.

"Come right this way, Your Eminence." He seized his charge in a chummy armlock. "They've already spruced the cabin up for you." He thoughtfully provided his passenger with an ice bucket and a shaker of rum colas. "We'll be on our way in a jiffy. Your seminarians don't mind sleeping on the deck?"

Every evening after supper, Sergio Ballado made it a practice to knock respectfully at the door of His Eminence's cabin. "Father," he would whisper, "this poor sinner needs a little moral counsel," or other sanctimonious words to the same effect.

His Eminence grew to expect this visit. On opening his cabin door, he made the routine sign of the cross. At first Sergio Ballado relied on the promising formula he had committed to his childhood memory. "Bless me, Father, for I have sinned." But as he became more sure of himself, he began casually to mention a very pious woman of Malyerba — a woman of his acquaintance — who, although she had tried to resist the profane state of married life, had been forced into accepting an unsavory match made for her by a mercenary and overly ambitious mother.

It was not until Sergio Ballado had pursued his narrative for the third straight day that he happened to mention Ana Magdalena by name.

"What a curious coincidence," remarked Cardinal Catafalco. "Was her mother's name, by any chance, Andreina Arzate de Figueroa?"

"The very one," nodded Sergio Ballado emphatically. "A more grasping, shrewish sort of woman couldn't issue from the lowest pit of hell."

Cardinal Catafalco was beginning to relish his trip to Malyerba. He essayed a thin, anemic smile. "But when she died, wasn't the good woman found mysteriously crystallized in honey?"

Sergio Ballado shrugged. "Only because the bees swarmed in self-defense."

Ana Magdalena writhed in her sleep. Her fists rained havoc on the bedclothes. The IFF was stripping her enterprise, reducing Casa Orgaz to a shabby storage area, a backstage no-man's-land. Doors gaped, jambs hung with discarded weatherstripping, makeup lights lay broken everywhere. All the valuable amenities lay scattered every which way, begging any passerby to steal them. And when she protested, a cold and haughty Andreina shrugged an indifferent shoulder as if her daughter were of no more importance than a gnat.

"Stop!" she cried out. "Casa Orgaz was never meant to be a warehouse!" But no one seemed to hear her. A demolition crew led by Mr. Perkins continued to sledgehammer partitions of decaying plasterboard, and the dwarfish Señor Onofrio Sebastián y Colón, fortified in a weight lifter's belt, raised the player piano high in the air and sent it crashing to the ground.

"Good God!" Ana Magdalena sat up in bed. "This has got to stop!"

"Señora? Señora?" It was Honora waking her with a calming cup of tea.

"Aiee, Honora, I had the most horrifying dream —"

"Another fetal attack?"

"No." But before she could say anything further, Honora motioned toward the door. "It's nearly nine," she whispered. "Everybody's getting ready to come in."

"*Dios mio!*" Ana Magdalena rubbed her eyes. "It's Sunday, isn't it?"

Honora nodded.

"Give me five minutes to collect myself."

Ana Magdalena wanted to look her best, but one glance at the mirror told her how ravaged her dream had left her. She splashed ice-cold water on her face. She applied skin bracer, dabbed on miracle substances from an assortment of little pots and jars, and applied colored pencils to enhance the natural color of her eyes. Satisfied, she threw open the door.

In twos and threes the girls marched in, and piled into Ana Magdalena's bed. They were still in their nightclothes in the time-honored custom of the house.

She brought the meeting to order. Sidonia and the other maids scurried about serving pancakes and champagne.

"I don't understand what's happening to the customers," Marta complained.

"You *don't?*" Victoria arched a sarcastic eyebrow. "It's that music. It's as dynamic as dishwater. I never before heard anything so vile."

"And it's interfering with our work," remarked Eugenia.

"For instance?" Ana Magdalena inquired. "Can you give me some idea?"

"For instance, it's doing something terrible to the clientele . . . they're so agitated . . ."

"Jittery . . ."

"Jumpy . . ."

"Fumbling," said Aurora Constancia.

"*Fumbling?*" Ana Magdalena was appalled.

"It's not exactly as if they thought of taking time, or anything," drawled Trinidad.

"Why can't we turn it off?" Everyone looked to Ana Magdalena.

"Because it's costing us 43,800 escudos a year. We can't afford not to listen to it." She saw no reason to mention that she had not yet paid Mr. Effingham's bill.

"Listen," Marta was speaking. "I'd know that music anywhere. It's Yankee music. Someone told me once, when I was still in Lima, it has reverse suggestions in it. You can't hear it, but it's there. It makes people do things backward."

"Nonsense!"

"What kinds of things?"

"Crazy things. People break their necks buying all kinds of stuff. Later when they get home none of it makes any sense. Sometimes they can't remember why they chose it, and occasionally they don't remember buying anything at all."

"I have something to say." A formidably endowed Titian blonde spoke up. She was the actress who had played Bernarda Alba.

"Let Hortensia speak."

"We in the basement have formed a simpler vices coalition," she announced. "We want to be rotated with the upstairs girls. Pumping that hot-air balloon leaves me winded every time!"

"Oh my, yes," interjected Aurora Constancia, "specialties can be awfully tiring."

"And we don't make any extra except on tips from time to time," Hortensia resumed. "We need certain privileges just like the rest of you. Time off for 'good behavior' — preferably in quiet, pastel-colored rooms — to get in touch with our spiritual side."

Ana Magdalena's beautiful eyes clouded with dismay. "What happened? I thought everything was going so well."

"That was before the music came," averred Alicia. "Now it's like those Charlie Chaplin silents. In and out, up and down, into your clothes, back downstairs, grab an arm, how d'ya do? In and out . . ."

They all turned to stare at Ana Magdalena. The silence weighed like lead.

Mercedes spoke. "It's not fun anymore."

"It's not supposed to be fun," Ana Magdalena's tone took on a missionary edge. "Love is a dedication. Either you have the calling or you don't."

"Why can't we have the player piano back?" Aurora Constancia appealed to her friend.

All eyes were riveted on Ana Magdalena. "Very well," she sighed at last, "I think I have a plan. . . ."

XVI

$\mathbf{F}$irst thing Monday morning, thirty-six heels clicked their way in perfect unison along the streets and boulevards that led to the regional offices of the IFF. In their spanking-new miniskirts, their undulating hips suggesting all manner of sunny improprieties to the admiring early-morning stares of any of the passersby who might care to crane their necks to have a second look, all eighteen beauties swung purposefully toward their surprise encounter with the totemic guardians of the International Fiduciary Fund.

Mr. Perkins had just had his second cup of coffee brought to him by a fawning Señor Onofrio Sebastián y Colón when the street door burst open. Señor Onofrio Sebastián y Colón raised his pudgy troll's hands in a gesture of astonishment.

"Good Gawd almighty!" exclaimed Mr. Perkins.

His greeting did nothing to stem the advancing tide. It approached without breaking stride until seventeen militant ladies had insinuated themselves, effectively cutting off Mr. Perkins and his assistant from their first line of defense. At a signal from Ana Magdalena, the ladies hoisted themselves onto the edge of the IFF's executive mahogany desks. Thirty-four mercilessly inebriating legs swung back and forth in unison displaying the heady Fibonacci contours of their thighs.

Mr. Perkins took a deep breath. "What brings you ladies here this morning?" He forced a little smile.

Ana Magdalena drew up all of her sixty-three stiletto-heeled inches. "Gentlemen," she began. "Just as *we* would never presume to suggest to you how to run a bank — although if we did, it might be lots more fun — there is almost nothing *anyone* can tell us about the

236

pleasure business. Pleasure, gentlemen, cannot be run, neither by the clock nor any other silly regimental notions. Pleasure bows to no laws but its own, and efficiency is certainly not one of them."

She removed the control panel of the Entertrainment System from the backpack she carried. She tossed it on Mr. Perkins's desk. "Gentlemen," she announced, "this music has to go."

Thirty-four uncompromising legs slid off the IFF's mahogany desks. All eighteen beauties spun on their heels in perfect formation and strode out the doors of the IFF. Ana Magdalena was the last to go.

She winked at them. "Remember, gentlemen, love is the chancy keyhole where mankind stands, trousers sunk about its ankles, squinting at Paradise!" The door shut behind her with a sigh.

Señor Onofrio Sebastián y Colón offered Mr. Perkins another coffee.

"Save it." Perkins waved him aside. "This calls for something stronger." He broke out the bottle of Perkins 90 proof he kept in his bottom drawer against serious emergencies.

"Don't just stand there gawking," he hissed at his assistant. "Get me a glass!"

Señor Onofrio Sebastián y Colón supplied two glasses. But Mr. Perkins was not in a giving frame of mind.

"Smart-ass bunch of broads," he growled. "We'll have to take them down a peg or two."

But neither Mr. Perkins, nor Ana Magdalena herself, nor any of her girls had counted on the arrival in Malyerba of the papal nuncio. As the eighteen victorious ladies swung across the cathedral square, past the rampant effigy of Bolívar, they couldn't help noticing the signs of his imminent arrival. Cardinal-red bunting festooned the splendid facade of the Cathedral of the Holy Faith; it coiled like a consuming dragon along the fence grilles that barred the vestry from curiosity-seekers and peddlers, and snaked its way up the elaborate double turn of the entrance stairway all the way into the bishop's residence.

"*Hola!*" gasped the irrepressible Hortensia. "With all that fanfare, business is sure to boom!"

In the cabin aboard the *Amazon Queen* His Eminence Catulo Catafalco was preparing to make his public appearance. Two rosy-cheeked little seminarians helped him on with his soutane. He stood perfectly still while they fastened all eighty-three buttons from his chin to his insteps. They snapped open the attaché case in which His Eminence kept his traveling cardinal's hat. They fussed over it, untangling the drapery fringes that hung about the brim. They cocked it at a raffish angle on his head.

His Eminence congratulated the mirror on his personal appearance. "How do we look?"

"Like the devil of a fellow!" his assistants gleefully chimed back, clapping their cherubic little hands.

His Eminence wondered briefly if somehow they had discovered the true nature of his errand. He shrugged. After all, what did his suspicions matter? He had them in his pocket, anyhow. He threw open the cabin door. Lined up on the dock, waiting to greet him, the Malyerba municipal brass band, uniforms hastily redeemed from a limbo of mothballs, swung into a solemnly discordant Te Deum.

"Jumping Gesualdo," muttered His Eminence under his breath. At once he assumed his normally sepulchral expression. His twenty-three rosy young seminarians stood at attention in the broiling sunlight, sweltering beneath the black cartwheels of their seminarians' hats.

Sergio Ballado sidled up to him. "How did Your Eminence enjoy the ride?"

"Smooth," winked Catulo Cardinal Catafalco, "smooth as Jesus in silk knickers!"

"Good! And remember that business we talked about?" Sergio Ballado reminded him.

His Eminence nodded. "No problem. Just give me an hour or two to get myself organized," he murmured.

As the Te Deum ended, His Eminence stepped onto the gangplank. The bandleader took this for a cue to launch into the national anthem. His Eminence raised his hand.

"*Silencio,*" he pronounced in authentically sacerdotal Latin. The band came to a jagged rest. His Eminence began to speak.

Federico was famished. He couldn't imagine what was keeping Ana Magdalena. He had just crossed the last *t* and dotted the last *i;* the last period was finally in place. He had completed *The Love Queen of the*

Amazon. He was in a state bordering on delirium, and his stomach was clamoring for a suitably authorial breakfast.

"Enough from the wind section," he muttered aloud, but no sooner had he silenced his digestive juices than he became aware of an unnatural quiet. He opened the door of the mirador a crack. He could hear nothing whatsoever. In his state of giddy exaltation, he succumbed to a dangerous and terrifying impulse. He crept downstairs and peered past the coromandel screen on the second-floor landing. To his great surprise, he discovered that the nearest room was empty. He entered it on tiptoe. Everything except for the mirror and washbasin was decorated turquoise. He raised the turquoise ceramic lid of a powder box that lay on the makeup table, but as he toyed with the soft bristles of the makeup brush, he spattered his dressing gown with an unintentional burst of powder.

"*Putamadre,*" he muttered. He spun around, afraid of being overheard, but his apprehension was groundless. The hallway was deserted.

He tossed the brush aside. As he advanced toward the grand staircase, he discovered that every one of the rooms was unoccupied. He passed a peach-colored room, and a room as yellow and sunny as an egg yolk; but the room that really caught his fancy was the most quirky of them all. The bed was furnished like a mint julep with a giant mint-leaf canopy and pillows like simulated ice cubes; the bedposts resembled gigantic swizzle sticks.

Though he might have liked to indulge his fancy a little further, Federico had something more pressing on his mind. He made his way directly down the stairs to the vestibule. But the new digital telephone had him completely baffled. At last he found the presence of mind to punch 0 for operator.

"Get me Lima," he barked. He recited Vacio-Llares' number by heart, but he found himself one digit short.

"I don't care if there's a number missing. Just get me Vacio-Llares. . . . But everybody knows him. . . . He's a presidential candidate. . . . Yes, that's right."

He waited, leaning against the wainscoting, his fingers drumming furiously. Finally he heard Vacio-Llares on the line.

"Ernesto? Is that you? Orgaz y Orgaz here. . . . Yes! Listen, Ernesto, do you have a moment? . . . Yes. . . . It's very urgent, but first: fantastic

news. It's finished.... No, *The Love Queen of the Amazon*....
What?... Today! Now listen, I want to sound you out about something.... Supposing you are married — ... I *know* you're married.
Hear me out. Suppose you are married to a woman who is everything you ever dreamed of. She's beautiful, she keeps house, pro-
vides you with three meals a day, a daily change of clothes. She's
discreet. She leaves you alone. Morning, noon, and night all you have
to do is write ... No, not checks, *cabrón! She* pays the bills ... Now
listen. One morning it occurs to you she's — well, she's keeping a
house ... No, an establishment, if you get my meaning ... Yes! Yes!
Your wife is a madam ... No, please, Ernesto, I *know* your wife is not
a madam. I'm saying just suppose. Suppose you have the perfect
working conditions for a writer of international repute, and you
discover your wife is a professional. Ernesto, are you listening? What
would you do?... *Shoot* her? Good God! I can't even load a *camera*
... No, no, it's a purely theoretical situation. It has nothing to do with
me, don't you see. It's my denouement ... What? *Erotica?* No, it's a
serious ... What? Oh, *your* latest is erotica? It's an erotic *classic?* ...
Oh, your *publisher* says it's an erotic classic. It doesn't say much for
the reader, does it? It's already an erotic classic and no one's even
read it. Well, good for you. But listen, Ernesto, what would you do?
Pretend you don't know anything, just act naturally?... *Tell* her! Tell
her you know *everything?* Good God! Then where would you be? No
more three-and-a-half-minute eggs, no more underwear. I can't do
that, Ernesto ... No, why would I tell her when it's really her idea? ...
No. Well, the plot ... Yes, it's her idea. Well, not exactly hers —"

But the Lima subsidiary of the IT&T was playing another of its
nasty tricks because just at that very juncture the line went dead.
Federico mopped his brow. He decided that probably it was all for
the best anyway. Good God! He tried to imagine telling her everything, or just strolling by the rooms when things were in full swing,
in a manner of speaking, casually reaming out his pipe as if nothing
were happening. Oh, it was too incredible! And honor was so time-
consuming, anyway. At least it could wait till he had had his morning
cup of tea. He swung open the kitchen doors. He had never entered
the kitchen directly from the ballroom before — except on his fateful nuptial day.

Sidonia started as if she had seen spirits. "Don Federico!" She crossed herself.

"Were you expecting the Holy Ghost?" he quipped. "Brew me some tea at once! And get me some breakfast. I'm absolutely famished!" He perched on a kitchen stool, happily swinging his legs.

Sidonia put the kettle on. "Can I boil an egg for you, señor?"

"Three and a half minutes and not a second more. And I need plenty of butter for my scones."

"Very well, señor." She did not remind him that she had been timing his eggs and buttering his scones for years.

"You haven't seen the mistress lately?"

"They went out."

"*They?*"

Too late, she realized the cat had taken leave of the bag. She tried setting matters straight. "On an important errand, señor."

"More important than my breakfast, in any case," he remarked with some asperity.

Sidonia eyed him with the little round eyes of a trapped animal. "Yes, señor."

"Very well. Send her upstairs as soon as she gets back."

Sidonia waited for Ana Magdalena to return.

"Señora," she whispered, "something's up. I think he's onto something."

"Oh, dear," Ana Magdalena breathed, "what gave you that idea?"

"He came downstairs again this morning. He wants to see you right away."

"What a bother. I'll have to change into something dull."

Ana Magdalena sped through the swinging doors, and through the ballroom to the vestibule. She was about to make her way upstairs when the doorbell sounded. On a giddy impulse, she ran to open the porter's window. She was dumbfounded by what she saw there — but only momentarily. There stood Sergio Ballado. She threw open the door and swept him into her arms.

"*Querido,* I knew you'd come!"

"But you didn't know I'd come with a fabulous proposition! Listen, sweetheart." He grabbed her by the arm. "And listen well. The papal nuncio has just arrived in Malyerba, and it's the *Amazon Queen* that brought him upriver. I told him everything!"

"What everything?"

"I told him that you need an annulment, and you need it right away!"

"Are you joking? What do you take me for? First you promise me *yanquis,* then you're going to bring me a walking-beam paddle-wheel steamer — you can't even come up with a rusty engine!"

"But, *querida,* it's our only hope. Just you and me cruising down the river, remember? Besides, I've already talked to him. He's pre-pared to make a deal."

"What kind of deal?"

"An offer you'd be crazy to refuse. He'll give you the annulment if you sell him Casa Orgaz!"

"You'd better go. I don't have time for your musty old cardinal right now."

"But, *querida,* he'll be coming any minute."

"Any *minute?*"

Sergio Ballado nodded. "He wants to talk to you about your mother."

"You must be crazy."

"He's here to interview all Malyerba. Your mother is about to become a saint."

"That's the limit! Your cardinal will have to wait. I have nothing suitable to wear. Anyway, right now, I'm on my way to Federico."

"There's no time for that. Tell him you'll be just a second. I'm waiting for you here. Five minutes." He consulted his brand-new quartz watch. "Or I'm coming up to get you, understand?"

But Ana Magdalena did not stay long enough to hear his warning. She had already reached the second-floor landing. On the way to the mirador, she threw an apron over her miniskirt. But by the time she arrived at Federico's door and knocked, he had decided that discre-tion was the better part of valor — at least for the time being. He needed money from his publisher before he could risk taking any steps.

"Sit down, *chica.*" He eyed her coolly. "I have something impor-tant to read to you." He seized the packing box in which he kept the manuscript which had grown to monumental size.

Ana Magdalena looked at him aghast. "All *that?*"

"It's finished. *The Love Queen of the Amazon*. And, *chica,* I have a big surprise. I'm dedicating it to you."

"Oh, Federico, what a darling!" She eyed the piles of clutter in mock dismay. "But, sweetheart, there isn't any room to sit. I'd better run and get a chair."

Ana Magdalena bolted back downstairs. She was just recrossing the vestibule when someone set up a frantic ringing at the porter's bell. She was unable to ignore it.

"Ana Magdalena Figueroa de Orgaz?" She nodded. "Sign here."

It was a mailgram from the IFF. She tore open the envelope. She saw at once it was a thirty-day demand to recall their note. "Two million nine hundred escudos — with penalties. They can sit on a saguaro," she muttered as she stuffed the message inside her bra.

Meantime, upstairs in the mirador, Federico nursed the full weight of his resentment. Just when he thought he had her at last, hadn't she wriggled from his grasp again. It was too much for anyone to take, especially someone who had successfully completed *The Love Queen of the Amazon*. Damn the consequences, he was going to have to collar her at once. As he marched down the great entrance stairs, however, the sound of voices stopped him short.

"I told you, I don't have time just now. I'm not seeing anyone," Ana Magdalena was saying.

"But he's ready to make you a fabulous offer. It's all arranged. You don't have to go and queer the deal just because you're feeling stubborn."

"Tell him to come see me tomorrow, if he likes. By then maybe I'll find something more conservative to wear."

"But *chica,* you have enough clothes for a year if you change three times a day!"

"Dear God, you don't expect me to wear *work* clothes!" she exclaimed, at her wit's end. "Not if he's going to talk to me about my mother!"

Quickly Federico tiptoed past the first floor landing and concealed himself by the basement entrance. But no sooner had he positioned himself behind the staircase than there was a hurried sound of footsteps interrupted by the slamming of a door.

The minx! She had eluded him again! He was about to follow her outside when something highly unusual caught his attention.

LA CONFITERÍA, *Inventive Specialties for Discriminating Tastes*

the sign read. It was posted on the basement door. Ordinarily, Federico would have taken little interest in the basement. But now curiosity prompted him to ease open the door. La Confitería's hallway was already brightly lit, although Hortensia and the "simpler vice" girls were still in their upstairs rooms restoring their spiritual sides. Federico pushed open a door. He found himself in a miniature courtroom complete with judge's bench and prisoner's dock. He blinked. Back in the corridor, he eased open another door. Good God! It was a torture chamber, furnished with all the essentials: pillory, iron maiden, and an extremely authentic-looking rack. His sense of outrage was now thoroughly aroused. He threw open one door after another; he discovered a confessional, a classroom furnished with the most amazing charts, and at the end of the row, there was a hot-air balloon. In one room there was even an open carriage, and when he examined it closely, he could not help noticing that it had been enhanced with a number of parts cannibalized from his family's excursion vehicle. He opened the last door. He found himself in a boiler room face to face with Hector Maria Jesús Villafane, who bent over a ponderous set of books, slowly making entries, column after column.

"May I ask what it is you think you're doing here?"

Señor Villafane continued laboriously making his entries. "Sometimes I ask myself the very selfsame question," he mused. "Just to think, all this time I could have been stage managing in La Paz." At last he looked up. "And may I ask what you're doing here yourself? We don't open until four."

"My dear sir, you dare ask me what I'm doing in my own basement?"

Señor Hector Maria Jesús Villafane poised his pen, and wiped his ink-stained fingers on his handkerchief. He studied Federico. "Oh, you must be the literary fellow, the prisoner of the Château d'IFF!"

"I was never partial to Dumas," remarked Federico icily. "And my question still stands. What are you doing here?"

244

"I'm the keeper of certain sets of books, that's the long and short of it. Without me, the entire enterprise folds up."

"Aren't you placing the cart before the horse? Without *me*, there'd be no enterprise — as you call it — at all. Are you aware my books are translated into forty-four different and separate languages, not counting dialects?"

"Maybe, señor," Hector Maria Jesús Villafane yawned, "but — in the long run — books with extra zeros in them are the only ones that count."

Federico had heard enough. But before he could manage to box Hector Maria Jesús Villafane's ears, the accountant had snatched up his ledgers and bolted out the door.

Federico was beside himself. He knew he was going to do something. Something drastic. He knew there was no turning back.

He opened the basement door and listened. No one seemed to be about. He crept back upstairs; tiptoeing through the vestibule, he made for the library, still unobserved. As quietly as possible, he slid the enormous leather armchair until it came to rest, its back leaning against the mantelpiece. Once he had assured himself that it was firmly enough braced to hold his considerable weight, he hoisted himself up till he balanced precariously on the headrest. He found he could just reach the family blunderbuss.

No sooner had Ana Magdalena managed to free herself of the troublesome Sergio Ballado, she ran into Honora.

"Honora, there isn't a minute to waste. The cardinal's due to arrive any moment and I don't have a stitch to wear. Send Aurora Constancia to my room. Maybe she'll come up with some ideas."

"Haven't you heard?" Honora whispered. "She got a letter from La Paz. Her husband's 'disappeared.'"

Ana Magdalena ran to her friend's room. She found her sadly distraught. "He's gone," she said simply. "Alejandro's gone. They sent me his last letter."

"Who did?"

"He had a woman with him in the mountains. Her name is Berta. Here." She handed Ana Magdalena the letter. "She can barely write. Maybe you can make out what she says."

But Ana Magdalena had no time just then, and even if she had, she might not have recognized the hand of her mother's servant, Berta.

"Darling, I'm in such a fix. The IFF wants to recall their note. I have thirty days to pay. And His Eminence is about to call, but I don't have anything suitable to wear!"

"Oh, darling," sympathized Aurora Constancia, "just take my Velazquez dress! Anyway, I'm not in the mood for it just now. . . . It's opulent, sophisticated, and demure . . ."

". . . At least in front," observed Ana Magdalena.

"He doesn't have to know! Just don't turn your back, dummy," countered Aurora Constancia, brightening up. "Anyway, it's against protocol!"

There was hardly any time left. Back in Ana Magdalena's bedroom, Aurora Constancia helped her squeeze into the cast-iron Medici corset. Honora lifted the enormous skirt over her head.

"Quick, Honora, bring me a chair!" ordered Ana Magdalena.

"What kind of chair?"

"A warm one! One Hortensio and Julio can carry!"

Aurora Constancia's fingers flew as she laced up the bodice and helped her friend tighten the pannier drawstring about her waist. They were still busy making preparations as Matilda ushered His Eminence into Ana Magdalena's bedroom, the only room where they could visit undisturbed. He was accompanied by a chubby little seminarian with cherubic creases dimpling his finger joints. His Eminence and his assistant had barely made themselves comfortable when the door of Ana Magdalena's dressing room slid open. Hortensio and Julio bore her, seated in Honora's improvised sedan chair, into His Eminence's presence. She waved them away.

"Forgive me, Your Eminence, if my condition prevents me from curtsying."

"You're not suffering from an injury, are you, my daughter?" Cardinal Catafalco's look was dark with concern.

"No, Your Eminence. Just a little back trouble," Ana Magdalena smiled.

His Eminence cleared his throat. "Word has come to me, my dear, that your sainted mother was none other than Andreina Arzate de Figueroa, whose sad demise is still mourned by the faithful of Malyerba."

"Yes, Your Eminence."

"And that you as a child helped her in her many household tasks."

"Yes, Your Eminence."

"After your marriage, my child, did your mother visit often?"

Ana Magdalena shook her head sadly. "Only once, Your Eminence."

"And what was the occasion?"

"Berta, our maid, had disappeared."

"And you say you were on good terms with your dear and sainted mother?"

"Oh, yes, Your Eminence!"

"Then why is it she only came to visit once?"

"Your Eminence, I can't think why."

"Then let me think for you."

Before he continued, however, His Eminence placed protective hands over his young assistant's ears. "Now," he continued, "could it be you were leading the kind of life your sainted mother might have found sadly repugnant?"

"Since Your Eminence asks, surely he must have some idea," murmured Ana Magdalena.

"Are you aware that, with the distressing stain your reputation casts on your mother's life, she can never be elevated to sainthood unless I make a favorable report?"

"No, Your Eminence. I have only your word."

"And do you doubt the word of the church?"

"No more than I would doubt my own," Ana Magdalena diplomatically replied.

His Eminence released the cherub's ears. "I'm told you're seeking an annulment." He paused for effect. "You must know, my dear, an annulment is not a trivial affair. Holy Mother Church is very fussy, very particular about the candidates whose applications she considers. The process is a long and arduous one. It can stretch over considerable time."

"I won't need it when I'm sixty-four!"

"If the matter is as pressing as you claim, you might consider selling out; the Holy See might be prepared to come up with an offer."

Ana Magdalena knew a providential opportunity when it knocked.

"How much?"

"Would you care to let me see your books?"

"My books?"

"Your business is a sound one, is it not, my child?"

Ana Magdalena caught on in a flash. She rang the little dinner bell Honora had thoughtfully provided. At once Hortensio appeared.

"Yes, señora?"

"Tell Señor Villafane to come here at once and bring the master income ledger with him. He'll know the one I mean."

Once they were alone, His Eminence rose and approached Ana Magdalena. He took her hand to raise it to his lips. But before he could kiss it, the door to the hallway flew open. A disheveled Federico burst into the room. He staggered under the enormous weight of the box in which he kept *The Love Queen of the Amazon*. He paused just long enough to take in the tableau.

"Hold it right there," he rasped. "*I* don't have to watch some degenerate in Cardinal's drag fawning all over my wife! Let go her hand this very minute!" His Eminence tried in vain to protect the cherub's ears.

Ana Magdalena forgot herself. She very nearly stood up. "But Federico, darling —"

"Save your *darlings* for your paying guests," Federico snarled. All the rancor, all the resentment he had allowed himself to swallow bit by bit, day by day, year by year, now rose up to choke him. With considerable difficulty he struggled to extract his family's enormous blunderbuss from inside the manuscript box.

Alarmed, Cardinal Catafalco raised his heavily ringed hands. "Wait!"

But Federico was not in a negotiating frame of mind. "Slippery, perfidious, wanton woman, after all I did for you — giving you a home, supporting your destitute and saintly mother, marrying beneath my position, lending you a taste of respectability, how dare you keep me in the dark about what you're up to in the basement? You could at least have told me about the courtroom! And the torture chamber! And the hot-air balloon! And even the confessional! But no, you simpering little viper, you keep the best material to yourself! Now I have to rework the whole thing!"

"What thing?"

"*The Love Queen of the Amazon!*" By now he was so beside himself that when he remembered to raise the blunderbuss to fire, although he hadn't meant to exactly, he aimed it directly at Ana Magdalena's heart.

"Stop!" cried His Eminence, cowering behind the bed. His young assistant disappeared beneath his patron's robes.

But it was too late.

At that very moment Hector Maria Jesús Villafane entered with the ledger. A tremendous explosion rocked the room. But when the bullet intended for Ana Magdalena struck the cast-iron Catherine de Medici corset directly over her heart, it altered its trajectory eighty degrees to lodge with a sickening thud smack in the heart of Hector Maria Jesús Villafane's ledger.

It was the last straw. "Worthless," roared Federico, tossing the blunderbuss aside. He ripped open the manuscript box. "All worthless! Years and years and years of superhuman effort! Wasted, entirely wasted!" He tore open the casement. It was the very same casement through which Clemencia had floated to eternity. Federico dumped out the manuscript box. A fierce tropical wind swept in from the river. One by one the pages of *The Love Queen of the Amazon* flapped their wings and flew into the morning. They wheeled and circled in the upper air, until they resembled a virtually inexhaustible flight of doves stretching clear to the horizon.

Unperturbed, Ana Magdalena rang her bell. "Hortensio, please take Señor Orgaz downstairs for a calming cup of tea."

"Now, Señor Villafane, I think you can safely show His Eminence the accounts," Ana Magdalena calmly directed. "I think you'll find His Eminence has quite an eye for books."

His Eminence positioned his monocle, the better to study Hector Jesús Maria Villafane's books. At last he cleared his throat.

"I'm prepared to offer five times gross."

Ana Magdalena waved an ashen Hector Maria Jesús Villafane away. "His Eminence and I have business to discuss."

She waited until they were alone. "I believe ten is usually customary."

"Eight," His Eminence countered. "Less twenty-five percent for an annulment."

"An annulment takes too long!"

"That was your husband just now, poor fellow?"

Ana Magdalena nodded.

"We have a short form."

"Quicker . . . ?"

His Eminence nodded. "But unfortunately less reasonable. But it might include your mother's sainthood!"

Cardinal Catafalco leaned out of Ana Magdalena's bedroom window. He whistled through his teeth. She was surprised to see the door open to admit a miniprocession of five little seminarians bearing inkwell, quill, parchment, a box of blotting powder, and His Eminence's seal along with a block of sealing wax. The dimpled cherub shut the door.

"Excellent, oh, excellent," His Eminence beamed at them. "And now, dear lady, may I use your desk?"

Ana Magdalena nodded her consent. While they were occupied, she rang her little bell. When Hortensio and Julio appeared, she asked them to fetch Sidonia at once.

Sidonia slipped in. "Yes, señora?"

"Sidonia," she whispered, "I want you to get everyone ready. Tell them we're going on a picnic. They're to wear their outdoor clothes. And I want the staff in their best taffetas with fresh organza aprons. Everyone's to assemble in the kitchen."

"Yes, señora."

Meantime the sound of gunshot had thrown the house into a panic. Terrified, the girls streamed downstairs. Eugenita was crying. Eduardito was manfully trying to calm her down when Hortensio led a distraught Federico into the kitchen. Almost on their heels, Hector Maria Jesús Villafane burst in, arms waving hysterically.

"Arrest him, and take his gun away!" he shouted, pointing an ink-stained finger at Federico Orgaz y Orgaz. "Just now this fellow tried to kill me!"

Everyone gasped.

"I don't see any powder burns," remarked the cool-headed Sidonia when she returned to the kitchen.

"That's because, praise God, and all the saints and everyone of the holy angels, I came within a ledger-width of paradise."

It was enough of an explanation for Sidonia. She ran to the telephone.

When the police chief arrived, she conducted him directly to the kitchen, where Federico still sat hunched over his sixth cup of tea.

"*Hola!*" The chief of police greeted him. "What's this I hear?"

"He tried his best to shoot me, officer," declared an indignant Hector Maria Jesús Villafane.

The police chief turned to Federico.

"Pooh, pooh. His claims are highly exaggerated." Federico became suddenly affable. "Let's go to the basement, where we can discuss matters calmly and reasonably. Like gentlemen."

He led the police chief downstairs. They entered the courtroom. The police chief took in the surroundings.

"Very interesting," he remarked, settling himself onto the judge's bench. "What exactly is the meaning of this?"

But Federico affected not to notice his impertinence. "The fellow's got it all wrong. It was my wife."

"Your wife did it?" The police chief was incredulous.

"No, my wife is the problem. The gun discharged accidentally before I could teach her a lesson."

The police chief crossed himself. He snapped his notebook shut.

"In that case" — he stood up — "congratulations! Just be more careful next time."

He shook hands with Federico. But on his way out, he made sure to include a quick tour of La Confitería; he whistled a snappy little tune, happily congratulating himself that, thanks to Federico's lackluster marksmanship, he would enjoy even happier returns when the next first of the month came around.

Hector Maria Jesús Villafane waved a cautionary finger. "Don't think I'm lying. The señora is selling Casa Orgaz!"

"She can't! Casa Orgaz is us! We won't stand for it," huffed an indignant Hortensia. "Who would buy it anyway?"

"Cardinal Catafalco, that's who. I saw them! They're about to sign the papers now."

In her bedroom, Ana Magdalena watched Cardinal Catafalco as his bustling little clutch of cherubs hovered over him, replenishing his inkwell, sprinkling each document with blotting powder. At last, evidently satisfied, His Eminence called for his seal. He dipped his pen into the inkwell. He was about to sign.

The door blew open unexpectedly. An infuriated Sergio Ballado strode right up to His Eminence. "What's going on here? First this woman tells me she won't have time to see you, now you're already signing papers —"

Ana Magdalena tried to catch Sergio Ballado's eye, but that eye was so inflamed, nothing, not even true love could soften its belligerence.

"I thought we were going to cut a deal!"

His Eminence never bothered to look up. "I don't remember any deal."

"I set things up so you could buy her business. Now I want my ten percent."

His Eminence scratched his hank of dyed red hair. "Unfortunately, I remember nothing of the sort."

"Look here." Sergio Ballado waved a threatening finger at His Eminence. "I'm going to put it to you straight. The *Amazon Queen* weighs anchor at noon exactly and your return ticket is my broker's fee. And there isn't another boat, or plane, or train that can get you out of here because they've all been leased to the IFF. Anyway," he threw Ana Magdalena a contemptuous look, "Malyerba is a pissant town. No one stops here anymore."

"Divine grace is my travel agent," His Eminence remarked piously. "I'll have to get in touch with her."

Sergio Ballado turned pale. As he strode toward the door, he shot Ana Magdalena a withering look.

"Wait!" she cried. She leapt to her feet, ready to run after him, but the sharp sensation of cold on the posterior portion of her person made her change her mind. Anyway, it was too late: Sergio Ballado slammed the door. Unperturbed, Cardinal Catafalco sprinkled powder over his signature. The young cherub held the document for Ana Magdalena to countersign. Catulo Cardinal Catafalco whistled through his teeth. At once two weight-lifting seminarians entered carrying a tooled-leather coffer. They placed it at Ana Magdalena's feet. They flung open the lid.

Ana Magdalena gasped. She had never seen so much gold. She raised a coin to her lips. Unceremoniously she bit down hard.

"Count it," invited Cardinal Catafalco.

When Ana Magdalena had satisfied herself that all was in order, she rang her little bell. Immediately Julio and Hortensio appeared, ready to carry her chair.

"Thank you, my dear." Cardinal Catafalco bent over her hand one last time to kiss it. "My blessings go with you! You have made me a very happy man!"

Ana Magdalena suppressed the impulse to rise to her feet and curtsy. She motioned for her attendants to carry her out. Carrying the coffer, the two weight lifters brought up the rear.

"Quick, get me out of this!" Ana Magdalena wailed. "We have no time to waste! If we don't stop him, he's going to sail at noon!"

Aurora Constancia came to her rescue. She undid the bodice and unfastened the clamps of the cast-iron Catherine de Medici corset. Ana Magdalena slipped into a little stretch-lace tank top. Aurora untied the panniers. The enormous skirt sighed as it sank to the floor. Honora handed Ana Magdalena her black lace panty hose and her miniskirt. She helped her lace up her traveling boots.

In the kitchen all was pandemonium. Ana Magdalena ran in. "Quick, everybody, there's just time to catch the *Amazon Queen* if we hurry."

Everyone was thrilled. "Oooh, we're going for a boat ride!" Sidonia lined all the girls up. They all stood ready in their outdoor clothes, picnic baskets in hand. The maids stood at attention in their black taffeta best, their organza aprons folded neatly over their arms.

"Oh, good heavens, I forgot Federico. Sidonia, quick, fix me a sandwich. He's got to have his lunch."

"But señora —"

"Do as I say!"

As soon as Sidonia managed to put the sandwich together, Ana Magdalena piled it onto Federico's favorite tray. She took the mirador stairs two at a time.

"Federico?" She knocked impatiently. "Federico?" The sound she had come to know and love so well filtered through the door. It was the clacking of the Black Maria.

"The poor dear." Ana Magdalena's eyes filled with temporary tears. "The muse must have him by the short hairs and he doesn't want to be disturbed." She dabbed the moisture from her eyes. She hoped her makeup wouldn't run.

But Clemencia must have been watching over her, because on her way back downstairs, she felt an invisible hand propelling her across the second-floor landing, past the coromandel screen, and down the endless corridor. In her bedroom — Clemencia's old room — an irresistible impulse drove her to open the armoire. There lay the pair of diver's flippers she had absentmindedly brought home from the sporting goods store. She snatched them up. She joined the others in the kitchen.

In the distance she could hear the *Amazon Queen* letting off steam. It was nearly noon.

"Come on, girls!" she shouted. "We're late already! We'll barely catch him as it is!"

Outside on the gravel walk, she had an inspiration.

"Hortensio, I'll take the Henriod & Schweitzer. It's faster. Everyone else can ride the coach!" she shouted. "Quick! Take the coffer! I'm going on ahead!"

She cranked up the motor. She leapt in. She spun around, gravel spraying all over the courtyard. She pressed the accelerator clear down to the floor and shot out the gate. But she had not anticipated that in Malyerba's busiest, most crowded thoroughfare, the engine would cough its last and give up the ghost entirely.

"Somebody help me," she cried. "I have to reach the docks!"

At once a contingent of idlers and loitering Indians separated themselves from various lampposts and walls. They formed ranks and began to push. The Henriod & Schweitzer limped and lurched toward the river.

When they arrived at the docks, Ana Magdalena opened her hip pack and in her excitement tossed each one of them a gold piece. They jostled around her, kissing the hand of their benefactress.

"This isn't the time for sentiment," she pleaded. But their gratitude was bottomless.

"Sergio! My God! Sergio, wait!" she cried, trying to escape. When at last they let her go, she ran out onto the pier — but it was too late. The *Amazon Queen* had already sailed; her wake still lapped noisily against the pilings.

From where she stood, Ana Magdalena could see Federico's lumbering old excursion vehicle inching its way toward the docks. There was no time to wait. She would have to leave her girls behind, at least until she could persuade that temperamental Sergio Ballado to reverse direction. She knew she would need more than an array of stunning beauties to mollify him, but once her lover realized they were escorting Cardinal Catafalco's coffer, she had no doubt she could convince him to take them all on board.

Quickly she unlaced her Doc Martin's. She tore off her leather jacket; she dropped her miniskirt and peeled off her black lace panty hose. She worried her feet into her diving fins.

The *Amazon Queen* let off a final, fretful blast of steam before she passed out of view beyond the river's bend.

"Holy Mother, help me now," Ana Magdalena whispered, but in her haste, it was the image of Ofelia she conjured up, beads of sweat standing out over her thick layers of makeup. *Bury me, niña, in the river of my birth. It's where I came from and where I want to go.*

She shuddered. She knew the water was swift and cold, but it was now or not at all. She knew that there was nothing anymore that could keep her from that rascally Sergio Ballado, not cold, not wet, nor any other obstacle known to woman or beast. And if she caught her death of cold, there was always the boiler room, and his arms to thaw her out.

She was ready. She took a deep breath and plunged in.